Say I Do

OTHER WEDDING STORIES

A YEAR OF WEDDINGS: TWELVE LOVE STORIES

A December Bride by Denise Hunter

A January Bride by Deborah Raney

A February Bride by Betsy St. Amant

A March Bride by Rachel Hauck

An April Bride by Lenora Worth

A May Bride by Meg Moseley

A June Bride by Marybeth Whalen

A July Bride by Beth Wiseman

An August Bride by Debra Clopton

A September Bride by Kathryn Springer

An October Bride by Katie Ganshert

A November Bride by Beth K. Vogt

HOW TO MAKE A WEDDING: TWELVE LOVE STORIES

Love at Mistletoe Inn: A December Wedding Story by Cindy Kirk

A Brush with Love: A January Wedding Story by Rachel Hauck

Serving Up a Sweetheart:
A February Wedding Story by Cheryl Wyatt

All Dressed Up in Love:
A March Wedding Story by Ruth Logan Herne

In Tune With Love: An April Wedding Story by Amy Matayo

Never a Bridesmaid: A May Wedding Story by Janice Thompson

Picture Perfect Love: A June Wedding Story by Melissa McClone

I Hope You Dance: A July Wedding Story by Robin Lee Hatcher

Love on a Deadline: An August Wedding Story by Kathryn Springer

Love Takes the Cake:
A September Wedding Story by Betsy St. Amant

The Perfect Arrangement:
An October Wedding Story by Katie Ganshert

Love in the Details: A November Wedding Story by Becky Wade

Say I Do

THREE WEDDING STORIES

RACHEL HAUCK
BECKY WADE
KATIE GANSHERT

THOMAS NELSON
Since 1798

Published in Nashville, Tennessee, by Thomas Nelson. Thomas Nelson is a registered trademark of HarperCollins Christian Publishing, Inc.

An October Bride is published in association with the Books & Such Literary Agency, 52 Mission Circle, Suite 122, PMB 170, Santa Rosa, CA 95409-5370, www.booksandsuch.biz.

Thomas Nelson titles may be purchased in bulk for educational, business, fundraising, or sales promotional use. For information, please email SpecialMarkets@ThomasNelson.com.

Scripture quotations are taken from the Holy Bible, New International Version®, NIV®. Copyright © 1973, 1978, 1984, 2011 by Biblica, Inc.™ Used by permission of Zondervan. All rights reserved worldwide. www.zondervan.com. The "NIV" and "New International Version" are trademarks registered in the United States Patent and Trademark Office by Biblica, Inc.™

ISBN 978-0-7852-4978-8 (trade paper)
ISBN 978-0-7852-4980-1 (epub)

Library of Congress Cataloging-in-Publication Data

CIP data is available upon request.

Printed in the United States of America

21 22 23 24 25 LSC 10 9 8 7 6 5 4 3 2 1

Contents

♡

Say I Do

A Brush with Love

RACHEL HAUCK

To
Susie Warren
Beth Vogt
Alena Tauriainen
For being there . . .

Chapter 1

♡

THE CRAZY JANUARY DAY IT SNOWED IN ROSEBUD, Alabama, Ginger Winters sensed a shift in her soul.

In the distance, pealing church bells clashed with the moan of the wind cutting down Main Street.

"Have you ever?" Ruby-Jane, Ginger's receptionist, best friend, and all-around girl Friday, opened the front door, letting the warmth out and the cold in. "Snow in Rosebud. Two hours from the Florida coast and we have snow." She breathed deep. "Glorious." Then she frowned. "Are those the church bells?"

"For the wedding . . . this weekend." Ginger joined Ruby-Jane by the door, folding her arms, hugging herself. "If you're Bridgett Maynard, even the wedding bells get rehearsed."

Ruby-Jane glanced at Ginger. "I thought they were getting married at her grandparents' plantation."

"They are, but at four o'clock, when the wedding starts at

the Magnolia House, the bells of Applewood Church will be ringing."

"Disturbing all of us who didn't get an invite." Ruby-Jane made a face. "It's a sad thing when your friend from kindergarten turns on you in junior high and ignores you the rest of your life."

"Look at it this way. Bridgett dropped you and you found me." Ginger gave her a wide-eyed, isn't-that-grand expression, tapping the appointment book tucked under RJ's arm. "What's up with the day's appointments?"

"Mrs. Davenport pitched a fit but I told her we were moving appointments around since you didn't want anyone driving in this mess. And you know Mrs. Carney wanted you to come out to the house but I told her you weren't driving either."

"Sweet Mrs. Carney."

"Demanding Mrs. Carney."

"Come on, RJ, she's been coming to this very shop, with its various owners, since after the Second World War. She's a beauty shop faithful."

"Either way, she can go a day without you blowing out her hair. Maggie never catered to these blue hairs."

"Because Maggie was one of them. I'm still earning their respect."

"You have their respect. Maggie wouldn't have sold you this shop unless she believed in you. So they *have* to believe in you."

The wind rattled the window and skirted tiny snowflakes

across the threshold. "Brrr, it's cold, Rubes. Shut the door."
Ginger crossed the salon. "I think today . . ." She pointed at the
walls. "We paint."

"Paint?" Ruby-Jane walked the appointment book back to
the reservation desk. "How about this? We lock up, go home,
sit in front of the TV, and mourn the fact that *All My Children*
is off the air."

"Or, how about we paint?" Ginger motioned to the back
room and shoved up her sleeves, a rare move, but since the
doors were shut, the shop was closed, and snow was falling,
she didn't mind exposing her puckered, relief-map skin. "We
can use the old smocks to cover our clothes."

Ruby-Jane had been the first person outside of Mama and
Grandpa to ever see the hideous wounds left on her body after
the trailer fire.

At the age of twelve, *everything* changed for Ginger Winters.
But out of the pain, one good thing emerged: her super-power
to see and display the beauty in her friends. Despite her own
ugly marring, she was *the* go-to girl in high school for hair and
makeup.

It was how she survived. How she found purpose. Her
ability took her to amazing places. But now she was back in
Rosebud after twelve years, starting a new season with her
own shop.

She'd left home to become a known stylist, fleeing her
"burn victim" image.

And she'd succeeded, or so she thought, landing top salon
jobs in New York, Atlanta, and finally Nashville, traveling the

world as personal stylist to country music sensation Tracie Blue.

But the truth remained, even among her success. Ginger was *that* girl, ugly and scarred, forever on the outside looking in.

Face it, some things would never change. If she hoped different, all she had to do was look at her role in her old "friend's" wedding. The hired help.

Ginger tugged the paint cans from the storage closet. Six months ago, when she returned to Rosebud and signed the papers for the shop, she ran out to Lowe's and purchased a pinkish-beige paint to roll on the walls, giving the old shop a fresh look and a new smell, adding her touch to the historic downtown storefront.

But Maggie kept a full appointment book and Ginger hit the ground running, with only enough time to paint and decorate her above-shop apartment.

Then the two long-time stylists who had worked for Maggie retired. And ten-hour days turned to fifteen until Ginger hired Michele and Casey, part-time stylists and full-time moms.

Painting had to wait.

"Can we at least order lunch?" Ruby-Jane tugged open the doors of the supply closet, the long-handle roller brushes toppling down on her. With a sigh, she collected them, settling them against the wall.

"Yes, pizza. On me."

"Ah, I love you, Ginger Winters. You're speaking my language."

Kneeling beside the paint can, Ginger pried off the lid and filled the paint trays, then moved to the shop and dragged the styling stations toward the center, covering the old hardwood floor around the perimeter with paper and visqueen.

"Have to admit, I love this old shop," RJ said, pausing between the shop and the back room.

"Me too." Ginger raised her gaze, glancing about the timeworn, much-loved room. "Don't you wish these walls could talk?"

Ruby-Jane laughed. "Yes, because I'd like to hear some of the old stories. No, because talking walls would really freak me out." She eyed Ginger, pointing. "But one day these walls will tell *our* stories."

"Can we go back to talking walls freaking you out?" Ginger laughed with a huff as she pulled the last station away from the wall. "I don't want any stories going around about me."

She'd heard them already. *Freak. Ugly. She gives me the creeps.*

"I think the walls will tell lovely stories: *Ginger Winters made women feel good about themselves.*"

She smiled at Ruby-Jane, the eternal optimist. "Okay, then I can go with the talking walls. Okay . . . painting. Shoo wee, this is a big wall. Let's do the right side first. Then, as time allows, we'll finish the rest. With the right side done, we'll be more motivated to get the rest done."

"You're the boss."

Adjusting the scarf around her neck, Ginger smoothed her hair over her right shoulder, further covering herself. While she had the courage to shove up her sleeve and expose her scarred arm, she wasn't brazen enough to expose her neck and the horrible skin graft debacle.

Two infections and three surgeries later, Mama had given up on doctors and decided to "leave well enough alone."

Ginger had cried herself to sleep at night, her hand pressed over the most hideous wrinkled, puckered skin patch at the base of her neck.

She knew then she'd never be beautiful.

"You can have a social life if you want," RJ said, helping her with the last station.

"Who said I wanted one?" Ginger headed for the storeroom. "Let's get painting."

Five minutes later, their rollers thick with paint, Ginger and Ruby-Jane covered the wall with fresh color, their beloved country tunes filling the air pockets with twang.

"You ready?" RJ said. "For this weekend? One bride, seven bridesmaids, two mothers, three grandmothers—"

"Yep. Just a walk in the park, Kazansky."

"I still can't believe she didn't invite me. We were good friends until high school."

"Maybe because you dated Eric for awhile after they broke up."

"Well, there's that." *Sigh*. After graduation, when Bridgett and Eric went their separate ways, Ruby-Jane was more than eager to be the new future Mrs. Eric James.

"As for dropping you in high school, I don't know, but her loss was my gain." There were no truer words in this moment.

With an exhale, Ginger relaxed into the repeating motion of rolling on paint.

The shop was warm and merry with the occasional ting of crystalline flakes pinging against the glass.

"Well, that's true, but I like to think we'd have become friends anyway."

Ginger glanced over at her tall, lithe friend. "You can come to the wedding as my assistant."

"And flaunt my shame in front of everyone as the help of the help? No thanks."

Ginger laughed. "Good point. You can get Victor Reynolds to take you to a romantic dinner instead."

"Ha! Haven't heard from him in weeks."

Ginger lowered her paint roller. "Really? Why didn't you say something?"

"Oh, I don't know . . . I'm twenty-nine, divorced, living in my hometown with my parents, in my old bedroom, and when all is said and done, I can't keep the interest of Victor Reynolds." Ruby-Jane's expression soured. "Victor Reynolds . . . who couldn't get a date to save his life in high school."

"You and me . . ." Ginger rolled paint against the wall. "The single sisters in solidarity."

"Ugh, so depressing. At least you have a life calling. A skill." Ruby-Jane loaded her roller with paint. "You can take an ordinary woman and make her extraordinarily beautiful."

"I love what I do." Ginger glanced around the shop. "And I want to make this the best place in the county for hair, makeup, and all things beautiful. Next year, I hope to have an esthetician on staff."

She stepped back to admire the beige-pink covering the dull yellow wall. Beautiful. She loved it.

Making things—women—beautiful was her calling, *her* duty in life. She channeled every ounce of her heart and soul into her work because the truth was, she could *never* do it for herself.

And this weekend Ginger would play her role as a behind-the-scenes stylist, or as Tracie Blue called her, "the beauty-maker," for the Alabama society wedding of the year, if not the decade.

Socialite Bridgett Maynard was marrying the governor's son, Eric James. A pair of Rosebud High sweethearts, the beautiful people, united under their umbrellas of success and wealth.

While Ginger was looking forward to working with Bridgett, she did not look forward to the weekend. She'd have to live among *them* at the old plantation.

"Well, if anyone can make this place a success, it's you, Ginger. Last time I saw Mrs. Henderson, she was still smiling over how you styled her hair."

"Grandpa was the first to tell me I could see the beauty in everyone else." She saw it that day Mrs. Henderson sat in her chair, with her wilting, over-dyed, over-permed hair. "I believed him. He'd buy me a new baby doll every month because I'd cut the hair off the old one. Right down to their plastic scalps." Ginger's heart laughed. "Mama would get mad.

'Daddy, stop wasting your money. She's just going to destroy this one.' And he'd say, 'She's becoming who she's meant to be.'" Ginger added paint to her roller and started a slow roll along the wall, the blue sparkle of her grandpa's eyes making her warm and sentimental.

She missed Gramps, a stable force in her trailer park life, always making her feel safe. Especially when Daddy left. And again after the fire.

Then came Tom Wells. Ginger shook his name free from her thoughts. He didn't deserve any part of her memories. Handsome high school boy who disappeared on her and broke her heart.

She'd pushed him out of her mind until she moved back to Rosebud. Until Bridgett walked into the shop three months ago, begging Ginger to be her wedding stylist, and the boxed memories of her youth in Rosebud, of her high school days, busted out.

"Can I ask you something?" Ruby-Jane said, pressing the last bit of paint in her brush against the wall. "Why did you leave Tracie Blue? Really. Not because Maggie called you about this place."

"It was time."

"Did something happen? It wasn't because of your scars—"

"Nope."

"Because that would be crazy, you know. You were on the road with her for three years. Your scars weren't a factor."

Oh, but they were.

Tears blurred Ginger's eyes as she covered the old wall

with a thick swath of paint. Goodbye old. Hello new. She hated lying to RJ, but talking about her departure from Tracie Blue sliced through the wounds no one could really see.

Ugly. That's what one tabloid called her. She'd found an article on the Internet one day last year naming the ugliest stylists to the stars. And Ginger Winters was number one.

Where they found that odd picture of her with her neck exposed, she'd never know.

Ginger swallowed a rise of bitter bile, inhaling, wrestling to shove the accusation out of her mind.

Yet she wasn't sure how to get it out of her heart. The words formed wounds and scars beneath her skin, creating tentacles of shame no long sleeves or colorful scarves could cover.

Ginger stepped back once again to admire her portion of the wall. "What do you think?"

"I like it," Ruby-Jane said. "A lot."

"Me too." The shop was starting to really feel like hers.

The top-of-the-hour news came on the radio. Ginger peeked at the wall clock. Eleven. "Hungry? Let's order lunch from Antony's," she said, cradling the brush handle against her shoulder, tugging her phone from her jeans pocket. "I'm thinking a large cheese pizza."

"You're singing my song. Oh, order some cheese bread too." Ruby-Jane stepped back, inspecting her work. "Love this color, Ginger. The shop is going to look amazing."

"I was searching online for new light fixtures last night and . . . Hey, Antony, this is Ginger down at *Ginger Snips*. Good, good, how are you? Yes, please . . . a large cheese . . .

thin crust, yep . . . and an order of cheese bread. No, for Ruby-Jane . . . I know, she's a carb addict."

"I am not."

"Sure, one of us will come down to get it." Hanging up, Ginger slipped her phone back into her pocket. "Let's just take the money from petty cash."

As the words left her lips, the bells hanging from the front door clattered against the glass as a customer pushed in.

Glancing around, she rested her roller on the paint tray. Ginger sucked in a breath. *Tom Wells Jr.*

Her skin flamed as she adjusted the dark orange scarf tighter around her neck. She'd rather face Tracie Blue's paparazzi than Tom Wells.

"Well, look who it is. My, my, Tom Wells Jr." Ruby-Jane crossed over and gave him a big hug. "What brings you to town? Ginger, look what the cat dragged in." RJ sort of shoved Tom further into the shop.

"I see."

"Ruby-Jane, hey, good to see you. Ginger . . . it-it's been a long time." He ran his hand over his long, wavy hair as his blue gaze flipped from Ruby-Jane to Ginger who wobbled, powerless in his presence. "Are y'all open? Is Maggie around? I was hoping for a quick haircut."

Ruby-Jane smiled, patting him on the shoulder. "Good ole Maggie Boyd retired." She shoved him forward again, indicating behind his back that Ginger should *talk* to him.

"So Maggie finally took that trip to Ireland? I wondered why the sign said Ginger Snips."

"S-she's in Ireland as we speak. I-I own this place now."
Ginger's voice faded, weak under the thunder of her heartbeat.
She reached for her brush handle and faced the wall. *Get a
hold of yourself. Remember what he did to you.* If she had any
gumption at all, she'd roll him with paint.

"Remember we studied calculus together, Ginger?"

"I remember." She cut him a glance, trying so hard to
be cool, but Tom Wells, with those blue eyes and mammoth
shoulders, was standing in *her* shop.

Ruby-Jane stepped around him, still communicating to
Ginger with glances and expressions. "It's been a long time, Tom.
Since you left town our senior year. What brings you back?"

"Yeah it's been awhile. I-I'm back . . . for the wedding.
Bridgett and Eric's." He seemed reserved, almost shy. Definitely
a lot more humble. "I'm the best man."

Ginger pressed the roller brush against the wall. What?
He was one of Eric's groomsmen? She'd be around him all
weekend?

"I hear it's going to be the wedding of the decade." Ruby-
Jane flicked her hand toward Ginger. "She's the stylist for the
whole shebang."

"Really?" Despite his expression, Tom sounded impressed.
"Not surprised. You were always good with hair, if I remember
right." He brushed his hand over his thick hair again, glancing
around. "As you can see, I'm in desperate need of a haircut.
But looks like you're not open."

His smile darn near skewered Ginger to the wall. *Simmer
down, he's just passing through . . . do not feel for him.*

"Sorry but we're painting today. You can go to the new shopping plaza south of town if you need a cut."

"The roads are horrible," Tom said, stepping close enough for his subtle fragrance to slip beneath the paint fumes and settle on her. "Big backup on Highway 21."

"You know how it is in the South," Ruby-Jane said. "We can't drive in a rainstorm, let alone ice or snow."

Tom laughed, shaking his head. "Very true." He raised his gaze to Ginger. "So is it possible to get a cut here? This is the only time I—"

"Absolutely." Ruby-Jane set her paintbrush down and kicked the visqueen aside, leading Tom to a chair across the room. "Ginger, does this station work?" She mouthed some sort of pinched-lipped command, gesturing toward Tom. "You ready?"

It was then Ginger noticed her arm, peeking out from under the cloak, her scars exposed. And he'd been looking right at her. Could the floor just open up and swallow her whole? She lowered her brush to the tray and tugged her sleeve down, stretching it to the tips of her fingers.

Tom Wells . . . in *her* shop. In her chair . . . waiting for her to touch his hair. The very notion made her feel like she might fly apart.

"Listen, if Ginger doesn't want to—" He tried to get up, but Ruby-Jane shoved him back down.

"She does. She'll be right with you. Ginger, can you show me where we keep the petty cash? I'll run and get the pizza." RJ snatched her by the arm and led her to the back room.

"What is wrong with you?" RJ, who knew perfectly well where the petty cash was located, took a painting of a pasture off the wall, revealing the safe, and spun the dial. "Tom Wells . . . hello!" She reached in for the petty cash bag. "If he's not better looking than he was in high school, I'll eat the pizza and the box. And sweet. He seems so sweet. How unfair, you know? Men get better-looking with age and women just *sag*."

"What's wrong with me?" Ginger kept her voice low but intense. "I'll tell you what's wrong with me. He was the only guy I've ever loved, who ever paid one lick of attention to me, and he dumped me before our first date."

Ruby-Jane took out a twenty, then closed up the money bag in the safe. "His family *moooved*, remember?" She slipped from her paint cloak, dropping it over the back of a chair.

"But he didn't tell me he was leaving. How hard is it to pick up the phone. 'Uh, Ging, can't make it. Dad says we're moving.' Then afterward, he never called or emailed."

"So go in there and botch his haircut if you want, get him back for it. But girlie-girl," Ruby-Jane wiggled her eyebrows, "it's Tom Wells. *The* Tom Wells. Besides, that was twelve years ago. Don't tell me you still hold a grudge."

Tom Wells, a two-named brand which meant gorgeous, athletic, smoldering, knee-weakening, kissable—

Ginger grabbed RJ. "Don't leave me alone with him. Stay here. I'll be done in ten minutes."

"Forget it. The pizza will be cold." RJ smirked and walked around Ginger into the shop. "Say Tom, we ordered too much pizza. Want to hang around for a slice?"

Note to self: fire Ruby-Jane.

The front door bells rang out as RJ left, waving at Ginger through the glass. *No worry, RJ. What goes around comes around.*

"Ginger," Tom said, rising from the chair. "I'm not going to force you to cut my hair."

Their eyes locked for a moment and her pulse throbbed in her throat. From the corner of her eye, she could see the small white swirl of snow drifting over them. Even if she turned him out, she'd have to see him at the wedding. Might as well cut his hair, then she could ignore him this weekend.

"It's fine." She motioned toward the wash bowls, removing the cloak she wore for painting and tying on a clean *Ginger Snips* apron. "Take the one on the right."

Tom situated himself in the black chair as Ginger rested his head against the bowl.

"H-how are you?" he said as she sprayed his head with warm water.

"Good." She hesitated, then raked her fingers through his luscious hair. In high school, she'd daydreamed of cutting Tom's dark, heavy locks. Then when Mr. Bickle paired them as calculus study partners, she darn near thought she'd died and gone to heaven.

The fragrance of his cologne subtly floated through her senses and she exhaled, trying to rein in her adrenaline, but one touch of his soft curls and her veins became a highway for her desires.

This is nothing. Just another client . . . just another client.

Ginger peeked at Tom's face, a best-of composite from the Hollywood's Golden Age leading men. Cary Grant's sophistication with Gregory Peck's smolder all tied together with Jimmy Stewart's lovable, everyday man.

Steady . . . She pumped a palmful of shampoo and lathered his hair, catching her reflection in one of the mirrors.

Her scarf had slipped, exposing her frightful scar, which beamed red with her embarrassment. Ginger pinched the scarf back into place before Tom could look up and see her.

She'd never get used to it. Never. The ugliness. The memory of the fire, of the day she realized she was marked for life. Of lying in bed, tears slipping down her cheeks and knowing no one would ever want her. Even at twelve, the truth trumpeted through her mind.

No one . . . *no one* . . . *no one* . . .

Chapter 2

♡

RECLINED AGAINST THE SHAMPOO SINK WITH GINGER'S
hands moving through his hair, massaging his scalp, driving his
pulse, Tom regretted his fine idea to step out on this snowy day
for a quick haircut.

Had he realized Maggie sold the place to Ginger, he'd have
braved the slick roads and traffic boondoggle to try the new salon
on the other side of town.

Yes, he knew he'd have to see her sooner or later—the latter
being optimal—but not his first full day back in Rosebud. Not
lying back in her sink with her hands in his hair.

He'd thought to leave as soon as Ginger said they were closed
but then Ruby-Jane pushed in and, well, here he sat.

"Ginger," he began, clearing his throat. "How long have
you—"

"Sit up, please." She pushed lightly on his shoulder. When he
sat forward, she draped a towel over his head and dried his hair,

stirring his dawning emotions. "Take a seat." She motioned to the station where Ruby-Jane had deposited him.

He peeked at her in the mirror as she removed the towel and snapped a cape around his neck. "How long have you been back in Rosebud? And six months ago I hear you were on the road with Tracie Blue?"

She angled in front of him, taking up her shears and comb. "And yes, I was."

Brrr. He figured it was warmer outside than inside the shop.

Raising the height of the chair, Ginger combed through his hair, her subtle fragrance sinking into him. She smelled romantic, if he could claim romance as a scent, like a melting, sweet Alabama summer evening. The fragrance gathered in the hollow place between his heart and ribs.

"Trim the sides? A little off the top?" she said.

"Yea, sure, buzz the sides a bit. Don't like it creeping down my neck and on my ears . . ." When she stepped to one side, the paint fumes swooshed in, replacing her perfume and bringing him back to reality. He had come in for a haircut, not a rendezvous with an almost romance of his past.

Besides, she didn't even seem to care that he drifted into her shop quite by accident. Maybe she didn't remember the affection between them, how he flirted with her, seeking a sign, a hint, of her interest in him.

He'd just invited her to the movies when Dad announced they were moving. Leaving town in the middle of the night. Tom didn't have a chance to say good-bye to anyone, let alone Ginger Winters.

"Tip your head down, please."

He dropped his chin to his chest, inhaling a long breath for himself, then exhaling one for her.

Should he just open with, "I'm sorry?" Or just let the past be the past?

She must have had boyfriends since high school. After all, she toured with Tracie Blue, seeing the world, meeting all kinds of people. Maybe she had a boyfriend now. Or a fiancé. He watched her left hand in the mirror. No ring.

"So you never said. How long have you owned the shop?" Small talk. Maybe he could get her to open up.

"Six months." She exchanged her shears for the clippers.

"Are you glad to be back in Rosebud?" He relaxed, attempting a smile, trying to catch her gaze.

"Yes." She tilted his head to one side and buzzed around his ears.

"Good . . . good . . . Me, too."

She snapped off the clippers and reached again for her shears, twirling them between her fingers, a trick he'd like to see again.

Either she was having a bad day or she really loathed him. Yes, he stood her up . . . twelve years ago. Surely she understood, considering the circumstances.

"Pretty rare to see snow in Rosebud."

"Very . . ."

"I'm back too. In Rosebud." He shifted in his seat. "For more than the wedding."

She slowed, glancing up, peering at him through the glass.

"G-good." She faced him toward the mirror, checking the sides of his hair for an even cut.

"It's pretty nice about Bridgett and Eric, no?" All of Alabama knew the governor's son, a former Crimson Tide star tailback, was getting married.

"Yes, it is." The conversation stalled as she blasted the blow-dryer over his head, then pumped a drop of gel into the palm of her hand and ran it through his hair, inspiring a race of chills over his skin.

She snapped off the cape, dusting the final hair clippings from his ears and neck. "Do you like it?" Her words came at him but not her gaze as she turned away, draping the cape over another chair.

"I do, thank you." He leaned toward the mirror. "The rumors were right. You're good."

"Thanks." She waited for him at the reception desk and he wished she'd smile or laugh, or kick him in the knee. Then the ice would be broken. "That'll be twenty dollars."

"Twenty?" He opened his wallet. "That's all?"

"It's Rosebud."

He grinned, slipping a ten and a twenty from his wallet, regarding her for a moment. "I'm sorry, Ginger." The confession came without much thought, without an agenda. He was free to flow where the moment took them.

She froze, reaching for his money, glancing up at him with gleaming hazel eyes. "You're sorry?"

The front door pushed open and Ruby-Jane rushed in with the cold breeze, a large pizza box and three sodas in her arms, the aroma of hot tomato sauce and baked dough mingling with the paint fumes.

"I'm home, kids. Lunch in the back room. Tom, dude, awesome cut. Isn't Ging the best?"

"She's the maestro." He smiled at Ginger, willing her to receive his apology.

"I told Antony you were here in town and he said he'd heard you were starting a church. Is that true?" Ruby-Jane disappeared in the back room, emerging a moment later with a soft-looking cheesy bread stick. "Come on, y'all. It's nice and hot. Help yourself, Tom."

"Thank you, but I can't stay." Tom motioned to the front door, taking a step back. Besides, if Ginger's stiff posture was any indication, he was not wanted. "I have a meeting. And yes, I'm back in town and starting a church. First service is a week from Sunday at the old First United Church on Mercy Road, northwest of town. You know the place." He stepped toward the door. "Ginger, thanks for taking the time to cut my hair. I appreciate it. See you this weekend?"

She nodded. Once. "Guess so."

As the door eased closed behind him, Tom stepped down the sidewalk and into the icy breeze. What was it about Ginger that awakened a longing in him? The ache to be her friend, to laugh with her, to share his heart, to listen to hers, to touch her scars and tell her everything would be all right?

To tell her she was beautiful.

But how could he *ever* be in a romantic relationship with her? What would his parents say?

Shake it off. He didn't come back to Rosebud to win Ginger's heart. He came to start work, to follow God's call, and perhaps restore his family's reputation and legacy. Not to remind people of his father's failing. That he'd packed up his family and exited in the dark of night amid possible scandal, abandoning his church, his reputation, and for a brief moment, his faith.

Tom had to be more than aboveboard. In all of his dealings. For his new church plant to bloom.

But heaven help him, Ginger Winters was as beautiful as ever, if not as raw and wounded as when he last saw her. And as crazy as it sounded, somewhere deep inside him, beneath all the layers of propriety, beneath any trepidation, Tom longed to be the man in her life.

Just like he did the first time he laid eyes on her.

Chapter 3

♡

SHE FELT BAD TREATING HIM LIKE TOILET PAPER STUCK to the bottom of her shoe, but Tom Wells? She'd have been more prepared for the Man in the Moon to walk in asking for a close buzz than him.

After Tom left the shop, Ginger sat up to the back room table, sorting out her feelings, eating pizza while Ruby-Jane talked. "Dang, I might have to recommit myself to Jesus and go to Tom's church. I mean, mercy a-might girl, he's gorgeous and a man of God—"

"Ruby-Jane, please, do not be bamboozled. You remember how the whole family snuck out of town, a scandal chasing after them?" Ginger took a small bite of pizza, her appetite a bit frosted by her own attitude toward Tom. "Like father, like son."

"What was that all about, anyway?" Ruby-Jane said.

"Who knows? Who cares?" Ginger didn't. At least she liked to think she didn't. What kind of sane woman still carried pain about a boy standing her up over a decade ago?

"I care. My future husband *might* be Rosebud's next big preacher." Ruby-Jane slapped another slice of pizza on her plate. "Come on, don't tell me you're still mad at him for leaving town without telling you."

"He didn't just leave. He vanished."

"Ging, they didn't vanish. We heard they moved to Atlanta."

"But not from him directly. I thought we were friends, you know? But not a peep out of him until twenty minutes ago when he walked in here." Ginger pushed away from the table, sad she'd lost her appetite for Antony's pizza. "Can we get back to painting?"

"So you *are* still mad." Ruby-Jane wiped the corners of her mouth with a wadded-up napkin. "It was twelve years ago."

"I'm not mad." But she was and it bothered her to her core. "Come on, let's get back to work. I want to get at least one wall painted before I leave on Friday."

"You know he's Eric's best man. He's going to be around *allll* weekend at this Maynard-James wedding extravaganza."

"I heard. I was standing here when he said it. So what's your point?"

"I think you're into him. Still. And you're mad at him. Still."

"You've inhaled too many paint fumes. I'm *not* into him. I'm *not* mad at him." Ginger headed into the shop, removing her apron and reaching for the slightly paint-stained cloak.

Yet, the thumping of her pulse and the anxious flutter in her chest told her otherwise. She was hurt, really. Worse, she *might* still be into him. Seeing him kicked open a door she thought she'd bolted and barred.

"You know what, Ginger?" Ruby-Jane said, entering the shop behind her, carrying a piece of pizza and her painting cloak. "Not everything is about your past, growing up in the trailer park, or your scars."

Ginger took up her roller brush. "I never said it was."

"When I see you cold and stiff with Tom, being brusque, I know you have feelings for him. *Still.* But you see yourself as that trailer park girl with the burn scars, not good enough for anyone."

"I *am* that trailer park girl." Ginger pushed back her sleeve. "And I'm still very scarred. Look, he's a dude who came in for a haircut. End of story."

"A dude who came in for a haircut?" Ruby-Jane laughed, her mouth bulging with pizza, her brown eyes sparkling. "Ginger, you should've seen your face when I said he might be my future husband. You went pale, then pink, then green."

"You are such a storyteller." Ginger aimed her roller toward the ceiling, rising up on her tiptoes to cover as much of the wall as she could without a ladder. She'd have to get the stepladder from the shed out back to cut in at the top. "Did you check with Michele and Casey to make sure they can handle the appointments for this weekend?"

"Talked to them yesterday, boss. And you know I'll be around to help out." Ruby-Jane took up her own paintbrush. "Don't fall back into high school, Ginger, okay? I like the confident salon owner who knows she's a fabulous stylist." RJ tugged on Ginger's scarf. "Even though you still hide behind this kind of getup."

Ginger moved away from RJ's touch, settling the scarf back into place, concealing the rough, puckered texture of her skin. "Some things will never change."

But other things could. Like the interior of this shop. Like her reputation as a swag shop owner in Rosebud's revitalized downtown, the hometown of Alabama's governor.

Like not letting men like Tom Wells Jr., preacher or otherwise, get to her. Men like him married waif-like blondes with God-kissed, sculpted faces, diamondesque smiles, and pristine, *smooth* skin.

"You know, Ginger, since I've known you, you've hidden behind long sleeves and scarves. I get it." Ruby-Jane eased the roller up and down the wall. "You aren't comfortable with your burn wounds. Just be sure you don't cover up too much and keep a man like Tom Wells out of your life. You never know, he might be your passion's flame."

Oh Ruby-Jane. Didn't she understand? Longing for *that* kind of flame, the flame of love and passion, was the most terrifying fire of all.

Wednesday afternoon, Tom swept the rough, wide boards of the old sanctuary floor with a wide straw broom he'd found in the storeroom. Like most of the church's furnishings, the broom was probably from the 1950s. Starting a new church with only enough funds to pay his meager salary meant he was janitor and secretary as well as pastor, preacher, and counselor.

Dust drifted up from the floor and swirled in the dappled sunlight falling through the transom over the stained glass windows.

He hummed a song from last night's worship practice, his chest vibrating with the melody, the lyrics skimming through his spirit.

. . . you fascinate us with your love.

He'd thought he might have to add worship leader to his duties—with his elementary guitar skills—until a talented young woman, Alisha Powell, volunteered for the job.

Last night Tom sat in the back of the sanctuary observing her first band practice and nearly wept with gratitude, sitting in the presence of God, feeling for the tenth time since he arrived in Rosebud that he'd returned home by the inspiration of the Almighty.

"Well, I see you found the most important tool."

Tom glanced toward the back of the sanctuary. Pop. He leaned on the broom, smiling as his grandfather sauntered down the center aisle.

"Did you come to make sure I worked the broom right?" Tom extended his hand toward Pop.

The old man waved him off and drew Tom into his embrace. "I reckon you can handle sweeping up well enough. But glad to know you can sweep as well as you preach." Pop eased down on the front pew, taking in the altar and pulpit, raising his gaze to the ceiling, then fixing his eyes on Tom. "Preached my first sermon here when I was nineteen." He pointed to the pulpit. "I think that old thing was here way back then."

Tom sat next to him, resting the broom against his leg. "What'd you preach on, Pop?"

"Walking worthy of His calling. Fulfilling every desire for goodness and the work of faith with power."

"Second Thessalonians."

"Good," Pop slapped his thighs and pushed to his feet. "Number one job of a preacher. Know the Word. Live it, pray it, sing it. So, Edward Frizz worked a deal for this old place?" He stepped up and moved behind the pulpit.

"He did me a solid. Found this place for sale, cheap, right before we signed a big, expensive lease on . . ." Tom paused, about to stir up painful memories.

"Your dad's old church?" Pop said it for him.

Tom dashed the broom bristles against the floor as he stood. "That building was in good shape. Way more modern than this place, but expensive. And, I don't know, I didn't want to—"

"Be in his shadow?" Pop leaned over the brown, thirsty wood pulpit. "Remind folks of what happened?"

"I just want to walk my own path. You and I both know Rosebud is populated with a lot of people who attended Dad's church. They know he left under suspicious circumstances. I only found out recently what happened and why we left town in the middle of the night. But I can guarantee there's a boatload of folks with their own ideas. I came here because the Lord directed me. Not to drag up the past and its suspicions." Tom pointed the broom handle at the ancient pipe organ behind the baptismal. "I want a fresh start. Even if we have to do it in this old place. With that big, old organ in place."

Pop came down the platform steps. "Your daddy did the right thing leaving the way he did. Cutting ties. Not taking anything but his family and the necessities."

"Didn't seem so at the time."

Pop made a face. "No, but you turned out all right."

"After a wild detour in college and too many drunken fraternity nights."

"Which led you to say, 'Okay God, I'm Yours,' after waking up week after week with your face in the toilet bowl."

Tom laughed, shaking his head, grateful to be in his grandfather's presence, finding comfort in the old man's wisdom and spirit of peace. "Looking back, I can see God's hand in my life, even in the family's sudden departure from Rosebud, but at the time?" Tom ran the broom lightly over the dry hardwood. "I was convinced Dad and God had ruined my life.

"So, you think anyone under the age of fifty will come here next Sunday morning? Walking over from the parsonage this morning, I realized the church looks and feels so old. White clapboard exterior, steeple, narrow foyer, long, rectangular sanctuary, stained-glass windows."

"You just be faithful to your calling and to the Lord. Let Him do the drawing and choosing."

Tom leaned against the side of a pew. The light had shifted and a kaleidoscope of colors moved across the white plaster. "Think I can do this?"

"Does it matter what I think?" Pop took a seat again and

sat back, hands on his knees, his plaid shirt smooth against his lean chest. "It only matters what He thinks, and that you're confident in His love for you and His leadership."

"Guess that's the trick for everyone who wants to follow Jesus."

"Best thing I can tell you is love Him with all your heart, mind, soul, and strength. You do that and you won't have time for any other kind of hanky-panky."

Speaking of hanky-panky . . . "I ran into Ginger Winters this morning."

Pop furrowed his brow. "Not sure I recall—"

"She's the daughter of the woman—"

"Ah," Pop nodded with realization. "I see."

"She owns a salon on Main Street now. Where Maggie's used to be. I went in to get a haircut for Eric's wedding this weekend and found Ginger there instead of ole Maggie."

"I'd heard she'd retired. But news travels slow out to the farm." Pop peered at Tom with a twinkle. "What's with this Ginger gal? Other than being the daughter of—"

"Right . . . Well, we were friends, starting to get close when everything went down. I didn't even know her mom and Dad *knew* each other."

He never got to ask Ginger how she felt about him. School had just started. They had a couple of study sessions together but not much more. But when he was around her, his heart felt things new and wonderful. He wanted to be a better person.

She, on the other hand, was hard to read. She kept her feelings close.

"Did you break her heart?"

"I don't know. We were supposed to go to the movies the night Dad had me packing my stuff." Tom shook his head, staring past Pop at the choir door. "I never called her. I felt too embarrassed. I didn't know what to tell her. 'We're sneaking out of town. My dad's a jerk.' So I just left it. Never wrote to her. Never called."

"Twelve years is a long time, Tom. I hardly think she's holding a grudge because a high school boy didn't pick her up for pizza and a movie. She might know the whole story since her mama was involved." Pop rubbed his chin. "Though Tom Senior did manage to keep it all so very quiet."

"I don't know what she knows except I stood her up." The Thursday afternoon he had asked her out, after school, he'd almost kissed her as they stood by his car. But Eric and Edward dashed onto the scene, out of nowhere, rabble rousing, full of pre-football practice mischief, and spoiled the whole mood.

Then, seeing her today? He felt like some dangling part of his heart had been put back into place. Ginger was all right. Doing well. And still beautiful. "Well, anyway," Tom said, glancing down, sweeping the floor. "She went on to do some pretty great things. She was a stylist to Tracie Blue. She's a major country music—"

"I know Tracie Blue," Pop said, smiling. "Very impressive for Ginger."

Tom laughed. "And how does an old evangelist like you know about Tracie Blue?"

"Facebook."

"Facebook?"

Pop nodded. "Your Aunt Marlee hooked me up."

"I'm not even on Facebook, Pop." Tom laughed and stamped the broom against the floor.

"Well, get Marlee to set up your profile thingy." But Pop sobered. "Tom, best advice? Don't stew on this Ginger business. Make it right if you think something is amiss, but don't stew. Don't assign thoughts and emotions to her based on what you think and feel. That's how the world gets messed up."

Pop, such a well of wisdom and truth. "She'll be at the wedding. Guess I could find a moment to speak to her."

"Just don't try to make her some sort of project." Pop leaned forward, tapping Tom on the arm. "Let God see to her eternal soul. You point her to Him, not to yourself."

"Yeah, yeah, I hear you. Dad's given me the same speech."

"He should. Because that's what messed him up. Taking on people projects. Feeling responsible. Letting others see *him* instead of Jesus. He always struggled with his pride. I busted him many a time on it. But God redeems. God heals," Pop said. "However, you, dear boy, must remember why you returned to Rosebud. It wasn't just because Edward Frizz called asking you to start a new church."

"And *not* just because I want to see Dad's name and reputation restored."

"No." Pop's laugh barreled from his chest. "You best let that part go. You start worrying about reputations and you'll be sunk before you even start." He pointed to the ceiling. "Gaze at Him, not yourself, your family, the name Wells, *or* the past. You know King Saul's downfall? He cared more about what men thought than what God thought."

Tom listened, mulling, thinking, trying to connect the gnawing in his gut over Ginger Winters with his thoughts, with what Pop was saying, with the truth.

"You know," Pop said, pushing to his feet. "If you want to really help this girl, win her to Jesus."

"Isn't that making her a project?"

Pop grunted. "No, it's showing her love. Everything else is lust or pride. Leading her to Truth, at the risk of your own heart and reputation, is love. How about we finish this over lunch? I'm starved."

Tom anchored the broom against the side of the pew and went to his office for his jacket. *Win her to Jesus?* Was she in need of winning? *How do I relate to her? What do I say?* He muttered in prayer as he returned to the sanctuary, meeting Pop in the middle of the aisle.

A simple but sweet answer to his questions rose up and lingered in his heart.

Tell her she's beautiful.

Chapter 4

♡

THE RAIN STARTED THE MOMENT GINGER LEFT ROSEBUD city limits on Friday evening. Blasting the radio, she was exhausted.

She'd painted late into the evening Wednesday—the one wall took forever and still needed another coat—then filled Thursday and Friday with her regular and snow-day appointments.

In between clients, she answered frantic, last-minute texts from Bridgett suggesting "one more thing" or wondering if "there's time to perm Aunt Carol's hair"?

So now as she drove south toward the Maynards' Magnolia plantation on the southwest corner of the county, the winter light masked by rain-weighted clouds, she wanted nothing more than a long, hot bath and her bed.

Bridgett informed her she was sharing a room with one of the bridesmaids, Miranda Shoemaker. Ginger didn't mind as long as she had her own bed.

To be her charming, make-them-beautiful self, all she required was a good night's sleep. The bridal party wouldn't need her tonight, so she hoped to excuse herself after introductions and slip off to her room.

Tracie Blue always knew that about her. *Ginger needs her sleep.* She made sure she had her own space on the touring buses.

Now, driving the twenty miles down a desolate highway through a frigid, icy monsoon, Ginger exhaled the day's tension, and Tom drifted across her mind.

He was back in town.

Ginger gripped the steering wheel a bit tighter, shifted in her seat, and adjusted the seat belt of her '69 VW Bug.

How could that fact make her heart smile after twelve years? Years in which he'd not once contacted her.

Nevertheless, his presence changed everything about this weekend. She'd signed on as the stylist, to be a person behind the scenes, detached from the wedding, the guests, and the celebration. That was fine with her. She'd perfected that persona while working for Tracie.

But now, a small part of her wanted to be a woman, not just a servant, and to be seen by *him*. She had visions of participating in the wedding festivities, and they disturbed her. Rattled her well-built, well-structured emotional barriers.

She'd only felt this way one other time in her life. In high school. When Tom Wells Jr. was her calculus study partner. *Grrr*, this whole thing irritated her, making her feel like an emotionally trapped seventeen-year-old.

Around the next bend, between the skinny pines and live

oaks, Ginger spotted the golden lights of the plantation house, glowing like a low moon rising on the thin, wet, dark horizon.

She pulled around the curved driveway, parked, and dashed to the veranda, the rain easing off as the storm clouds inhaled for a second breath.

She was a professional. Just the stylist. Detached and aloof, a hired hand.

Shivering in the dewy, cold air, Ginger rang the doorbell, fixing on a smile when an older woman in a maid's uniform answered the door.

"Hey, I'm Ginger Winters. The stylist."

The maid stood aside. "They're in the drawing room."

"Thank you." Ginger stepped inside, offering her hand. "And you are?"

"Eleanor."

"Eleanor. Nice to meet you."

The woman's stern expression softened. "Yes, you too. This way." She led Ginger through a small, formal living room and a massive library, then down a short corridor where laughing male and female voices collided.

Eleanor paused at a set of double doors. "Tonight's dinner is buffet, on the sideboard. Help yourself."

"Thank you." Ginger hesitated as she stepped from the marble hallway onto the plush emerald-and-gold carpet, scanning the room. No one noticed her. But that wasn't unusual.

A pale glow from the teardrop chandelier hovered above the room as if too good for the thick, heavier gold light emanating from the wall sconces and table lamps. On the farthest wall, deep-red curtains framed a working white stone fire-place. Despite its size, the drawing room was warm and cozy, inviting.

Come on in. Even you, Ginger Winters.

Several women sat reclined on a matching set of white sofas by the fireplace, wine glasses in hand. The fire crackled and popped, the flames stretching into the flue.

But the sofas by the fire were not for her. The beauty of the fireplace aside, Ginger avoided flames of any kind. From bonfires to matches, lighters, and sparklers, to men who made her heart feel like kindling.

Speaking of men, she'd not spotted Tom yet. To her right, she saw the groom, Eric, with several others watching ESPN on a large flat screen.

To her left was Bridgett and a mix of folks talking at the wet bar. There was Edward Frizz and Brandi Heinly, one of Bridgett's friends from high school. They were all part of the beautiful and bold to which Ginger had no admittance.

Since no one saw her, should she just walk in? *Hey y'all?* The aroma of roast beef and something cheesy whetted her appetite. She'd snatched a slice of cold pizza for breakfast but had eaten nothing since.

But first, she needed to connect with Bridgett, let her know she'd arrived. Then beginning tomorrow morning, she'd start washing and setting hair for the mothers at nine o'clock.

Ginger inched across the room, arms stiff at her sides. "Bridgett, hey, I'm here."

"Ginger!" A beaming and bright Bridgett wrapped her

in a happy hug and walked her to the center of the room. "Girls, this is Ginger Winters, the one I was telling you about, Miss Marvelous. Her straight iron is a magic wand."

Ginger smiled and waved toward the women on the sofa. "Nice to see y'all."

One of the women rose up on her knees, leaning on the back of the sofa. "Did you really tour with Tracie Blue?"

"I did, yes. Three years." One lingering benefit of working for a superstar? A great conversation piece.

"Oh my gosh, I can't believe it. She is my favorite singer." This from Sarah Alvarez, another bridesmaid and Rosebud High alum. "How exciting. What dirt can you give us on her?" Sarah wiggled her eyebrows as she joined the other women on the sofa.

"None I'm afraid. I signed a confidentiality agreement. She could sue me for more money than I'll make in three lifetimes."

Sarah made a face, shrugged and turned away, rejoining the conversation around the fire.

"Never mind her," Bridgett said, slipping her arm through Ginger's. Her burned one, but she didn't pull free. Her sweater was thick enough to hide the scars. And Bridgett wasn't holding on too tight. "Come over here. You remember my handsome groom, Eric."

He glanced around, pulling away from SportsCenter long enough for a, "Nice to see you again."

"You remember Edward and oh, look, there's Tom Wells—"

Ginger pulled away from Bridgett as Tom entered through

a doorway across the room. A low, creeping shiver started in her bones. "H-hello everyone." She tried for a sweeping glance past the men but her gaze clashed with Tom's.

He watched her with those blue fireballs he used for eyes. One look and she felt engulfed, aching to be with him.

He terrified her more than the man-made flames across the room. Those flames she understood and could avoid. But the kind Tom Wells ignited seemed impossible to predict, avert, or extinguish.

"So, that's everyone," Bridgett said. "Help yourself to the buffet. There's wine and beer, but if you don't drink, the fridge is full of water, soda, and tea. We're just hanging out, talking wedding. Can you believe I'm getting married?" Bridgett squeezed Ginger's arm, giggling, effervescing.

"I'm happy for you." Ginger smoothed her hand down her sweater, tugging at the end of the sleeve to make sure her scarred hand was covered. "It's exciting. Rosebud High's prom king and queen and most likely to marry . . ."

"I know, what are the odds? We're actually getting married. After eight years apart I never thought I'd see him again, let alone marry him." Bridgett leaned over the chair where Eric sat, roping him in her arms, and kissed his cheek. "But, well, love's arrow doesn't miss, does it?"

Oh yeah it does. By a county mile.

"So . . ." Bridgett turned around with a clap of her hands. "Fill your plate and join us girls on the sofa. We can talk hair."

Ginger looked back at the cluster of bridesmaids. By the fire. A sliver of panic cut through her delicate confidence.

"It's easier to eat sitting at the counter." Tom's bass declaration offered a welcomed truth, drawing Bridgett's attention.

"Guess you're right, *Reverend* Tom." Bridgett wrinkled her nose at him. "All right, Ginger, grab a bite but don't let this scoundrel keep you too long. Lindy and Kyle want to talk to you about their hair ideas for tomorrow."

"Looking forward to it," Ginger said, turning to the buffet with a backward glance at Tom. How did he know?

She filled her plate and set it on the counter two seats down from Tom, who nursed a frosty root beer. "Are there any more of those?"

"At your service." He hopped up, rounded the bar, and pulled a cold soda bottle from the fridge. He twisted off the top and slid it toward her. "On the house."

She laughed, covering her mouth with her smooth left hand.

"Wow, I got a laugh out of you." Tom came around the bar and took the stool next to her, relaxing with his elbows on the bar.

"Don't act so surprised."

"But I am. I didn't know I possessed the power."

"Very funny." She lifted the soda bottle and took a hearty swig of sweetness. "Sorry about the other day . . ."

"I get it. Caught you off guard."

Making sure her sweater sleeve covered her hand, Ginger split apart a fluffy yeast roll, the kind her Gram used to make when she was a kid. She popped a steaming piece in her mouth.

"What? No butter?"

She smiled, shaking her head, relaxing a bit. Whether she wanted to admit it or not, Tom Wells made her comfortable. He made her want to be a better person. "My grandma made rolls like these for holiday dinners and birthdays when I was growing up. They were so good they didn't need butter. We'd eat them plain or maybe with homemade black raspberry jelly." Her voice faded. Those times ended right after Ginger turned thirteen. A year after the fire. An aneurysm claimed Gram's life when she was only sixty.

"My grandma made dumplings." Tom shook his head, humming. "Best thing you ever put in your mouth." He peered at her. "But the same thing happened to us. She died and so did the tradition."

"I keep telling myself I'll learn how to do it but—"

"Life gets in the way."

Ginger set her roll down and reached for her napkin. "Thank you." She nodded toward the sofa and fireplace. "For that."

"Bridgett can be a little obtuse."

"Apparently you're . . . What's the opposite of obtuse?"

"Bright, smart, intelligent, handsome, sexy."

Ginger choked, wheezing a laugh, pressing the back of her hand against her lips. She finished swallowing her roll, washing it down with a nip of root beer. "Someone doesn't think well of himself."

He grinned. "I like hearing you laugh."

"Yeah, well . . ." Ginger shifted around in her stool

and adjusted her scarf, making sure it was in place, covering her flaw. Under the heat of his gaze, she felt exposed and transparent, as if he could see the things she longed to hide.

"They've been talking about you." Tom gestured to the women on the sofa with his root beer bottle. "Apparently Bridgett hired some world-renowned photographer for the weekend and they are counting on you to work your wonders."

"Women like to feel beautiful. Especially in photos. Double especially for a wedding."

"You say that like you're not one of *them*."

His words and the tenor of his voice confirmed her suspicion. He read her, saw through her. Ginger tore another corner bite from her roll. "I say it like it's true. Don't read anything into it. Women like to be beautiful and men prefer them that way."

"I suppose so." He turned his root beer bottle with his fingers, glancing toward her. "But there's two kinds of beautiful."

"Only two?" She peeked at him and forced a relaxing exhale. *He's just being nice, Ginger.*

"Touché." His soft laugh tapped a buried memory of sitting in the library, trying to get him to study calc problems for a quiz instead of doodling caricatures of Mr. Bickle. "I was thinking of outside beauty and inside beauty."

"What of all the layers and nuances in between?"

"Touché again." He tapped his bottle to hers.

"Either way, I have a big weekend ahead, doing my thing, making women beautiful."

"Do you enjoy it?"

"I do." She nodded with a strange wash of rising, hot tears. She hid them with a dab of her napkin. "Ruby-Jane says it's my superpower."

"It's good to do something you're good at and that you love."

"I think so." But how could she give words to the underlying truth? That she ached to do it for herself. How she envied women with smooth skin who wore sleeveless tops in the summer with low V-necks.

On her days off, when she cleaned her apartment, she wore a tank top and scooped her hair into a ponytail, feeling free.

"I was thinking maybe you could come to church next week. See me off on my inaugural Sunday." He pushed his hand through the air as if sailing.

"Church?" She cut a bite of roast beef. Funny how talking with him encouraged her appetite. But church? "I don't think so."

"Didn't you go for awhile? When we were in high school?"

"Until my mother suddenly *stopped* going and started working Sunday mornings." She shrugged. "Wasn't sure I liked it all that much anyway."

She bought the message about a loving God. She really did. But when she tried to reckon with Him about the night she was trapped in the trailer fire, about the pain and agony of second- and third-degree burns, she couldn't find love in any of it.

If God delivered those young guys out of the fire in the Old Testament, Daniel's friends, why didn't He do it for her? Did He love them more? She'd concluded that He must.

"Why didn't you go on your own?" Tom said as a commotion arose from the sofas.

A shrill, "I can't believe you're here!" shot through the room before Ginger could answer. One of the bridesmaids, Miranda, launched from the couch and into the arms of a man standing just inside the drawing room doors.

"I told you I'd make it, baby." He swept her up, kissing her, wanting her.

Ginger turned back to her plate, feeling every movement, every emotion of the couple at the door through the ugly lens of jealousy.

She would never have that . . . never. Even if some man did want her, one look, one touch at her relief-map skin and he'd turn away. Experience was her truth.

"Cameron, you made it." Eric broke his trance with SportsCenter and football highlights, coming around to greet the most recent guest.

"Cameron Bourcher," Tom whispered toward Ginger. "I met him at the bachelor party. He's a Wall Street dude, comes from money, almost engaged to Miranda. Or at least she thinks so."

Ginger glanced toward the door, at the cuddling couple surrounded by the wedding party. "Looks to me like she might be right."

Cameron bent down, giving Miranda another kiss, holding her close, his arm about her waist. Her smooth-skinned waist.

"Now we're all here." Bridgett beamed, wrapping her arms

around Eric. "What an amazing weekend. Our wedding, darling. So far, so perfect. Except, oh—" Bridgett turned to the bar. To Ginger. "Ginger, I'm sorry. Now there's no room for you. Cam will be sharing with Mandy."

Everyone stared at her. Even the chandelier light seemed to brighten and angle Ginger's way, spotlighting her embarrassment.

"Oh, okay, n-no problem." But yes, a huge problem. *Floor, open up, let me in.* The slight comfort and ease she'd allowed herself, sitting with Tom, vanished under the hot stares of the beautiful people.

"What? No." Tom slipped from his stool. "Don't kick her out. Cameron can bunk with me and Eric."

Cameron laughed. "No offense, Tom, but I didn't fly a thousand miles to *bunk* with you and the groom."

"Of course, of course," Bridgett said, moving between Tom and Cameron, batting down the contention. "I'm sorry, I should've planned better. Oh, bother, we don't have any more rooms in the house. Lindy could share, but she's such a light sleeper and I promised her a private room. The rest of the family arrives in the morning and will need their rooms to rest and get ready. I'd hate for the staff to have to redo them . . . Oh, I know. Ginger," Bridgett crossed over to her, eyes wide with her pending solution. "You can stay out at the homestead tonight." The bride peered at the others, satisfied with her quick solution.

"The homestead?" Tom said. "That place at the end of the property? It's like a mile away."

Ginger snatched Tom's arm. What was he, reverend attorney? She didn't need his defense. "Tom, it's okay. Don't make more out of the situation than necessary."

"Thank you, Ginger. Yes, Tom, it's a bit far but it's very nice. Daddy's been fixing it up. Ginger, you'll love it. It's right on the edge of the woods."

"Is there a road to this homestead?" Tom insisted on defending her. "Last time I was here, the old road had been busted up. You had to cross a field to get there."

"Yes, Tom," Bridgett said with a sigh. "There's a road, sort of, a *path* really."

"Is it safe?"

"Of course." Bridgett laughed, but not in a fun way. More of an aghast way.

"Look," he said, stepping forward, addressing the entire wedding party like a jury. *Tom, please shut up.* But Ginger couldn't release the words. Speaking out would only draw more attention to this humiliating situation. "Let Ginger stay in my room. I'll go out there."

"Kind of need you here, man," Eric said, securing his arm around Bridgett, holding her close. "You're my best man."

Enough. Ginger hopped off her stool. "Bridgett, thank you for dinner." She mined every ounce of cheer and joviality. "I've not unloaded my things yet so I can easily move. Point me in the direction of the old homestead."

"Perfect." Bridgett walked Ginger through the clustered bridal party, and *guest*, Cameron Bourcher, out of the drawing room, down the hall, their footsteps echoing with fading ooohs and ahhhs over Cameron, who apparently arrived via his private jet.

"Really, Ginger, the old homestead is lovely." Bridgett walked with her onto the veranda, into the rain-soaked night. Bridgett's instructions to the homestead billowed in the frosty air.

"Go to the end of this driveway . . ." she circled her hand in the air. "Turn left like you're going back to the main road. About twenty yards down . . ." She leaned toward Eric, who had just joined them. "Wouldn't you say about twenty yards?"

"Roughly. Just look for the sign."

"Right, the sign. It's on your left. It says 'Homestead.' Can't miss it. Turn there and just keep going straight until you run into the old place. A one-story ranch."

"Do I need a key or anything?"

"Nope, Daddy keeps it unlocked."

"Then how can you say it's safe?" Tom's voice boomed over Ginger's left shoulder.

"Because it's a mile out that way . . . because the plantation is gated." Bridgett swatted at Tom. "Stop being a killjoy. The homestead is safe, Ginger."

"The woods aren't gated." Tom moved to the edge of the veranda, staring into the darkness.

"And what's back there?" Bridgett demanded. "Nothing but deer and wildlife."

"Maybe a bear or two."

"Now you're just making stuff up."

Ginger stepped forward, unwilling to be an object in their debate, tugging her keys from her jeans pocket. "Turn left at the sign?"

"You can't miss it." Bridgett smiled. "See you in the morning. Come early for breakfast. Oh, Ginger, tomorrow's my big day."

"I'll be here at eight to set up." Ginger took one step down. "You're going to be beautiful." If she was banished to the outer regions of the Maynard plantation, she was going to do it with grace. "I'm bringing my A-game tomorrow."

"I knew you would. I showed you the look I wanted, right? The one on Tracie's last album. That was your handiwork?"

"It was, and I'm all set to make you even more beautiful than Tracie." *Now, let's forget this mess and move on.* Ginger moved down the steps, through the freezing rain, keys gripped in her hand.

If she was known only for making others beautiful, if that was her life's signature, wouldn't that be enough?

Slipping behind the VW's wheel, Ginger slammed the door and fought a surprise wash of tears. No, it wasn't enough. The heart wants what it wants. And Ginger's heart wanted love and freedom from her scars.

But for now, she was tired, and mulling this over would only make her sad and she didn't want to be sad. It took too much energy.

Ginger started the engine and shifted into first, willing

her thumping heart to settle down. She'd promised Bridgett her A-game. And being tired and sad was not part of her strategy.

Glancing in the rearview mirror, she saw the rest of the guests had come out to the veranda. They huddled together, laughing, being the bold and beautiful.

Easing off the clutch, she cut the wheel to move around a giant truck with mud on the tires and undercarriage when the passenger door jerked open and a wet, shivering Tom Wells dropped in.

"Excuse me? What are you doing?"

"I'm going with you." He reached for the center dash sliders. "Got any heat in this old thing?"

"Tom, no, you don't have to come with me." Ginger moved the silver slider to the right, powering up the heat. *Hear that, heart? You don't need him.*

"It's raining, freezing, dark, with an obscure path. Shoot, I'd want someone to go with me. Besides, I heard Eric ask if the power had been turned on and Bridgett didn't know. There's a power box on the side of the house."

"Tom, you still don't have to come with me. I'll figure it out." Wasn't that the way she lived life? On her own, figuring it out?

He glared at her through the muted light of the dash and their visual exchange did something to her. Something scary and wild. Like making her want to touch him.

But she'd never touched a man other than to wash his hair.

"Really," she said with a wide, forced smile. "I'm fine." Ginger patted his knee, once, oh so lightly, but she felt a plump of muscle beneath her fingertips.

"Too bad." He caught her hand, giving it a tender squeeze. "I'm riding along. Now, let's get moving."

Chapter 5

♡

THE NIGHT RAIN POURED FROM CELESTIAL BUCKETS.
Tom rode silently alongside Ginger, debating with himself why
he'd forced her to accept his help.

So he could apologize for the past? So he could be near her?
All of the above?

Watching the overgrown and rutted road through the VW's
bouncing headlights, it was hard to see exactly where they were
going. Man, it was dark and wet out. For this alone, he was glad
he nudged in.

"Careful, Ginger, there's a big—" Tom braced as the nose of
the VW Bug crashed into a rain-gutted rut. "Rut." Did Bridgett
sincerely mean to send Ginger out in this gully-washer alone?

"Sorry." She jerked the wheel right, then left, down shifting,
trying to maneuver through the pitted path.

"This is crazy. We're a mile from a marble and crystal plantation with three stories. Couldn't you have slept in one of the
many parlors or living rooms?"

"Tom, don't, please."

Fine. He could tell his ranting only wounded her more. But it just burned him that Bridgett had so casually booted Ginger from the house.

"'With slaughterous sons of thunder rolled the flood,'" he said.

She clutched, shifted, jerked the wheel, voice tense when she said, "So you read Tennyson?"

"Just that one line. He claimed to have written that line when he was eight."

"You don't believe him?"

"I suppose I have to." The VW slowed, wheels spinning in mud, then shot forward, and continued down the so-called road. "I can't challenge him on it, can I?"

She laughed softly. "No, you can't. Do you read a lot?"

"As I have time. Some poetry. Novels. Theology books. Memoirs."

"I love books. Novels, poetry, memoirs, no theology though."

"I remember you as the math whiz." He liked the gentle turn of the conversation.

"I like math, but I read a lot when I was recovering from . . ." She hit another deep rut. Muddy water shot in front of the headlights. "Ah, this is no man's land."

"I'm sure Bridgett didn't realize—"

"Don't say a word to her." Ginger released the wheel long enough to scold him with a wagging finger. "It's bad enough she announced there was no room for me in front of everyone. It's another thing if you go to her complaining on my behalf."

"She should know," Tom said, his voice metered with the bumping and swaying of the VW—which was rapidly losing the rutted field versus small car battle.

"Then speak for yourself. Leave my name out of it. I mean it. I'll be gone soon enough."

He cut a glance her way. The dash lights accented the smooth angles of her face and set off the highlights of her sable-colored eyes.

"Can I at least pay for you to drive this little beast through a car wash?"

Ginger laughed, the engine moaning as she gently eased the car through a hungry puddle and nearly stalled. "Where *is* this homestead she spoke of so highly?"

"Keep going." Tom squinted through the rain. "It's so dark out here."

Another rut and the Beetle Bug's engine whined, stuttered, knocked. Ginger patted the dash. "Almost there, Matilda. Come on, baby."

"Yeah, come on Matilda." Tom ran his hand over the metal dash. "Good girl, you can do it."

The VW splashed through a large puddle, then found traction on a patch of solid ground. Ginger gaped at him, shifting into a higher gear. "Seems even Matilda is subject to your charms."

"Even Matilda? I'm not sure my so-called charms work on any of the ladies."

"Ha, right. Weren't you the one who made sure you had a date every Saturday night?"

"Is there anything your elephant brain doesn't remember?"

"Yes, like why I agreed to do this *wedding*." Ginger groaned as the VW nosed into another pothole and ground to a stop, jerking the two of them forward.

She clutched and shifted, urging the car onward. But the Bug moaned and rattled, and the tires spun without traction.

"Reverse," Tom said. "See if we can back out." Nothing doing. More tire spinning and slipping, more engine lamenting. "Cut the wheel left, then hit the gas."

But the ground was too drenched and the revving engine lacked the horsepower to heave the little car out of the mire.

"Ginger?"

"What?" She stared straight ahead, letting out a heavy sigh.

"We're stuck."

"I'm *so* glad you came with me, Tom. Otherwise I'd sit here wondering all night what happened."

He liked being with her one-on-one, liked when she shed her shyness and timidity. "Fine, I'm Captain Obvious. It's the way I roll." Tom peered through the dash to the edge of the headlights. If there was a homestead on the horizon, he couldn't see it through the rain. Rubbing his hands together to warm them, he glanced back to see if the big house was in view. Might be easier to turn around than go forward. But it wasn't. "So what's your plan?"

"Can we call someone? Who owns that big monster truck? Can they get us out?"

"Scott Ellis owns the truck. I don't have his number but I can try Eric or Edward, have them send him out." Tom tugged his phone from his jeans pocket, calling Edward first, then Eric. No answer with either one. "Guess we're on our own."

"Let me try Bridgett." Ginger reached behind her seat, pulled her bag around, and dug out her phone. Her effort netted the same result as Tom. No answer.

Guess there was only one thing to do. He reached for his door handle. "I'll push. Stay in first gear. When I say go, gently, and I do mean gently, let off the clutch and give it a little gas." Tom cracked the door open, letting in the wet and the cold. "Cut the wheel to the left, and try to find the most solid ground you can."

"What do you think I've been doing?" She motioned to the door. "You're seriously going to push?"

"Unless you want the honors."

She hesitated, then unsnapped her seat belt. "Yes, of course, I should push. It *is* my car."

Tom snatched her arm before she could open her door. "Do you want my manly man card too? Please, I'll never live it down with the guys if they hear you pushed. Let me do this. You're the driver of this team." Beneath the wooly knit of her sweater, he could feel the rough, ribbed skin of her arm. He'd always wanted to ask her about how it all happened. He'd only heard bits and pieces of a trailer fire. How painful it must have been. Then to live with the constant reminder . . .

"We're not a team." She slipped her arm from his touch.

"Okay . . . we are for now. Unless you want to sit here all night." He jostled her shoulder, also coarse and jagged beneath her sweater. "Come on, if I can't push us out of this, I'll hand in my man *and* Marine cards."

She reared back. "You were a Marine?"

"Yes, and still am, I guess. *Hoorah.* Just no longer on active duty. Ready?" Popping open his door, Tom's first step sank into a pool of icy water, filling his shoe with ooze. Nice. He sloshed around to the back of the car, the rain soaking his hair and jacket, slipping down his collar, trickling down his neck and back.

At the back of the old Beetle, Tom anchored his backside against the car, hooking his hands under the fender as he tried to find good footing. He'd bet his ruined Nikes that the temperature had dropped a southern, damp, frigid degree or two in the past fifteen minutes.

"Ginger?" he called, glancing around, the rain water draining into his eyes and the crevasses of his face. "Ready?"

The engine whirred, coming to life. Tom ducked into place. "Okay, go!"

He pushed, his feet anchored against nothing but ooze, as Ginger fed the Bug a bit of gas.

But all combined, their efforts produced nothing but spinning tires and spewing mud. Extracting his feet from the sucking mud, Tom sloshed over to Ginger's window and tapped on the glass. She inched it open.

"Hey, Tom, I think we're still stuck."

He laughed. "Now you're Captain Obvious. I'm going to

rock the car a bit. You didn't eat a lot of food at the buffet, did you?"

"Such a funny man you are." She shut the window and faced forward, a slight, happy curve on her lips.

Yeah, she wasn't as hard and defensive as she let on. Tom rounded back to the VW, the rain still thick and heavy. If it took *this* to get to know her, to break down the barriers, he'd do it again. And again.

"Okay, Ginger, give this Beetle Bug some juice!"

The engine rumbled as she let off the clutch. Tom rocked the car, straining to dislodge it, adding his Marine muscles to the German horsepower.

Come on . . . He'd dealt with worse in Afghanistan. *Lord, can You get us out of this?*

The car lurched free, dropping a shivering, soaked-to-the-bone Tom into the mud. The red taillights beamed five feet ahead. Ginger tooted the horn in celebration.

Thanks, Lord.

Pushing out of the mud, Tom scrambled for the passenger door. But Ginger stuck out her hand as he started to sit.

"I just had the car detailed."

"W-what?"

"And these are leather seats."

"Y-you're joking." Meanwhile, rain slithered down his face, into his ears, and pooled at the base of his neck.

"Yeah, I'm joking. Get in here. You're letting in the cold air." Her laugh warmed his soul.

"You're a regular riot, Alice." He dropped into the seat

with a squishy *slosh*. "Where's a hero's welcome when he deserves one?"

"You're right. Thank you. Very much. The stallion of Rosebud to my rescue." She shoved the heat slider to high and eased the Bug forward.

"Boy, you *do* remember everything. The stallions of Rosebud . . . I haven't thought of that nickname in a long time." He ran his hands though his drenched hair but there was no place to dry his cold, wet hands. "Sorry about this mess."

"When you don't have a life, you pay close attention to others." She chuckled softly. "I can still see you, Eric, Edward, and Kirk Vaughn strutting down the school halls, three abreast, patting your chests on football Fridays, rapping some stallions of Rosebud song."

Tom laughed. "Yep, 'We're the stallions . . . of Rosebud High . . . fear the name, we're what we claim, when you're not looking, we're gonna crush ya . . .'" He drummed the rhythm on the dash. "Ole Kirk, I miss him." Kirk had gone pro but died in a small aircraft crash while doing mission work during the off season.

At his funeral, Tom's heart first stirred toward full-time ministry. Something he swore he'd never do. He'd watched his father and wanted nothing of that life.

"Such a senseless death."

"I can still hear Eric's voice when he called to tell me . . . I couldn't believe it." Tom glanced at her. "But Kirk died doing something he believed in. At his funeral, I stood in the back of Brotherhood Community Center—there had to be a thousand people crammed in there—and bawled like a baby. That day changed me."

"How did that day change you?" The VW nosed down again. Ginger urged the car with a bit more gas, trying to move quickly through the rut.

"I just knew. No more fooling around with God. I had to get serious."

"Serious with God? Were you not serious? The preacher's kid?"

"I was the opposite of serious." The car hit another water patch and fishtailed sideways before listing to port, finding another rut and sinking. The engine gurgled and died with a tired sigh.

"No, no, no," Ginger rocked in her seat, trying to reignite the engine. But the rain, ruts, and mud had won. "Matilda, we were almost there." She pointed to a small light on the distant horizon before turning to Tom. "See if you can push."

"Ginger, face it. Elements one, VW Bug with humans, zero." Tom leaned out his door, looking under the car. "The back left is buried." He ducked back inside. "We're going to have to walk."

"Walk? In this?" Ginger angled over the wheel, peering at the rain. "Maybe we can wait it out."

As if the heavens heard, the clouds rumbled, lightning flickered, and the rain fell in double-time. The car sank a bit lower.

Tom offered her his hand. "I say we run for it. You with me? Do you have a flashlight?"

"Dear diary, Bridgett Maynard's wedding was a blast. I got to run in the rain and mud." Ginger popped open the glove box, producing a flashlight, then slipped the keys from the ignition and reached around behind the seat for her purse and small duffle bag. "I can't believe this."

"I was on a patrol like this one night in Afghanistan."

"In a VW?" Ginger clicked on the flashlight, shot open her door, and stepped out. "Oh, wow, it's cold. And muddy. Ew, I'm sinking."

"No, in a Humvee. And hold on." He sloshed his way around to her and without hesitating or pausing to see if she'd care, he slipped his hand into hers and pulled her past the car onto a piece of solid ground. "Better?"

"Better." She exhaled, glancing up at him, shining the flashlight between them. "Thanks for coming with me."

He curled his hand into a fist, resisting the urge to wipe the rain from her cheek. "Wouldn't have missed it." This was ten times better than sitting around with a bunch of guys, wondering if she was all right.

"Well . . ." She turned toward the small light beaming through the rain. "I say the last one there is a monkey's uncle." With a rebel yell, Ginger launched into a full-on sprint, the beam of the light bouncing about the darkness.

"What? Wait—" Dang, the girl had wheels. He caught her in a few strides and was about to swoop her into his arms when Ginger disappeared, face first, into a slop of mud, the flashlight sinking with her hand while her purse and duffle floated beside her like useless life preservers.

"Ginger?" He bent for her, swallowing his laugh. It really wasn't funny. No . . . it was hilarious. "Are you all right?" He looped her bags over his head, settling the straps on his shoulder. What was another ounce of mud or two sinking into his shirt? "Here, let me help you." He offered his hand but she refused.

"Mud. I hate mud." Ginger pushed to her feet, bringing up the flashlight, letting loose a blended laugh-cry. She shook her fist at the storm. "You can't beat me."

"Come on, Scarlett O'Hara, let's get to the house. We can argue with the storm from the other side of warm, dry walls." He took her left hand, striding forward. But a dozen steps in, Ginger went down again.

"That's it. Sorry, Ginger, but—" Tom swung her duffle bag to one side as he ducked down and hoisted her over his shoulder in one swift move.

"Whoa, wait a minute, what are you doing?" She hammered her fist against his back, kicking.

"Simmer down." He picked up his pace, his feet chomping through the water and thick, sucking mud. "I want to get to the house without you falling into the mud every five feet. Hey, can you pass me the flashlight?"

She was light, an easy load. One he wouldn't mind shouldering for, well, the rest of his life. But the history . . . Not between them, but their parents. Did she even know?

"Nothing doing. I hand you the light and you drop me, leaving me out here all night."

Tom jogged on, double-timing it. "I just picked you up. Do you seriously think I'd leave you out here?"

"Well, you do have a reputation for leaving a girl without so much as a by-your-leave or kiss-my-grits. Now, really, put me down." She kicked, pushing on his shoulders, trying to get free. "I don't need to be rescued."

"Really?" Without a by-your-leave, kiss-my-grits? So, she did remember the night they were supposed to eat pizza and watch a movie. Tom had wanted to call her that night but he'd spent the time battling with his dad, refusing to pack his suitcase until his baby sister came out of her room, hysterical with tears. *Stop it! Stop fighting.*

"Tom, put . . . me . . . down."

"Seems to me you were losing that battle with the mud." She struggled against him but he hung on. "If you keep squirming, I'm going to drop you."

"Good, do it. Better than being carted around like a sack of seed."

He should've let second-thoughts surface before releasing her but she seemed so intent on her demand. So . . . he let go, sending Ginger to the ground. She plopped into a soggy puddle and bobbled for balance while Tom continued on, plowing through the rain and muck.

"Hey!" Her call bounced through the raindrops. "What's the big idea?"

He turned, walking backward, seeing nothing but the white glow of her flashlight. "You said, 'Put me down.'"

"And you believed me?" Her sloshing and complaining trailed after him, the white light bobbing, until she finally caught up, whapping him on the back of his head.

He laughed, feigning a yelp, and caught her around the waist, spinning her around. "My mama taught me to respect women's wishes."

"You think she intended you to dump a girl to the cold, muddy ground?"

"Yes, if that's what she demanded." Slowly he set her down, her lean frame against him, shivering and soaked. Her breath mingled with his, their heartbeats in sync. Even with the flashing light aimed behind him, he could see every inch of her face. "Ginger—"

"Tom, I-I'm—" She gently freed herself from his embrace, from whatever his heart was about to confess. "Freezing. We'd better get to the house." Ginger aimed the light ahead, spotlighting the old ranch homestead.

"About another thirty meters." Tom took her hand and the flashlight, not caring if she protested, and led the way, holding her steady, instructing her around the ruts and puddles.

The yellow dot fifteen minutes ago was now a full-blown porch light. Tom jumped the veranda steps, the cold starting to sink in, bringing Ginger along with him.

She tried the door handle. "Locked," she said, shaking. "She sent me to a locked house? What happened to 'Daddy never locks the house'?"

"Hold on." Tom tried the windows by the door. Also locked.

"So, when were you a Marine?" Ginger said, following him.

"Between semesters." All of the front windows were bolted. "Stay here, let me scout out the place."

"Between semesters? Like on your school breaks? You ran down to Paris Island and said, 'Hey, I'm here.'"

He smiled back at her. "Something like that." Tom hurdled the veranda rail and jogged to the back of the house. He didn't care about Ginger's wagging finger; Bridgett was going to hear about this. It was one thing to be the caught-up bride but another to be so self-focused she disregarded her guest's well-being.

On the back deck, Tom tried the knob on the French doors, grateful when they gave way to his gentle push.

Stepping inside, he found a switch and with one click, a set of recessed lights over the fireplace beamed on. Excellent. The power was on. He started to step forward but the slosh of his shoes drew him back. With a sweeping glance Tom checked out the place. The work of Mr. Maynard was evident. He kicked off his shoes. Can't track mud across the hardwood.

Crossing the spacious room with its vaulted ceilings and crown molding, he flicked on the end-table lamps.

At the front door, he opened up and stood aside for Ginger to enter, dropping her bags from his shoulder to the floor. "Please, enter your humble abode."

"So, like, the power was on?" She huddled by the door, a muddy mess as she glanced around. "Wow. *This* is the *old* homestead?"

"Well, consider the source. Bridgett Maynard."

"It's beautiful." Ginger slipped from her shoes and wandered toward the kitchen, then back to the great room. "I think I got the better deal coming out here."

"But everyone else is at the house with food and maids. Does this place have anything to eat? Is the water on?" Tom stepped around to the kitchen, trying the faucet. Water flowed freely. "Looks like you're set then." Tom locked the French doors and picked up his shoes. "Keep the doors locked. There's homeless camps in those woods. Even in this cold."

"Thank you. For everything." She motioned to the doors unaware that the dark scarf she wore swung loose, exposing the neck she worked hard to hide.

He fought the urge to touch her, to tell her the wounds would be all right. She didn't have to hide. But that would definitely cross all of her boundaries. Real or imagined.

"Well, then, I guess I should get back." He made a face as he set down his shoes and slipped in his feet.

"Oh, Tom." She whirled toward him. "See, I knew you shouldn't have come. Now you have to go back in the rain. By yourself."

"Like I said, I've been in worse."

"It's freezing out there. You'll catch a cold or something. I don't think Bridgett and Eric will like you hacking and sneezing through their big society wedding tomorrow."

"Can't stay here, though, can I?" His gaze met hers and for a moment, he was back in high school, watching her in math class, wondering how he could work up the nerve to ask her out. She was so walled and guarded. Then and now.

"I guess not." She stepped toward him. "See you tomorrow then."

"See you tomorrow." In that moment, it felt like something passed between them. But he couldn't quite grab onto it.

"Hey, why don't you try Eric again? He did say he needed his best man tonight. He could come get you."

Tom slipped out his phone, none the worse for the muddy wear, and rang Eric. Again, no answer. He tried Edward to no avail.

He offered up his silent phone to Ginger. "Guess I'm trekking." Tom gestured to the fireplace. "I noticed firewood out back. Do you want—"

"No." She shook her head. "I'm an electric-heat-and-blankets girl all the way."

"Right, sorry." He reached for her hand, the one she didn't hide under the sleeve of her sweater, and gave it a gentle squeeze. "If I had to be out on a cold, rainy night, I'm glad it was with you." He stepped toward the door. "Good night."

"Tom?"

"Yeah?"

"Why didn't you call me? That night? To tell me you were leaving?"

With her questions, time peeled back, and he saw her waiting at her apartment for him to come. But he never did. "I didn't know I was moving until I went home. Dad announced he'd resigned from the church and we were going to Atlanta. No debate, no questions, no argument. I was seventeen years old and my father had just destroyed my world."

"Why didn't you stay with your Granddaddy? Or one of your friends?"

"Dad refused. Insisted we move as a family. The night we packed up to go, Dad and I argued so much we almost threw punches. Then my sister came out of her room, hysterical, begging us to stop." Ginger listened with her arms wrapped about her waist, the warm light of the homestead haloing her. "It scared me, humbled me, when I saw her pain. Then I saw the angst on my father's face and I gave up my fight. I didn't understand everything that was going on, or why we were heading out of town like bandits, but it had my dad, and mom, in knots. I'd never heard them so much as raise their voices to each other, but that night, they weren't even speaking. Nevertheless, I still managed to be a major pain-in-the-backside. I barely spoke to him for two months after we moved. Though he tried really hard to make things right between us." Tom winced at his confession. "Now I realize at the worst time in his life, his family was all he had and all he wanted."

"Trust me, if you have family, you have everything." She shivered but he wasn't sure it was because of the cold, muddy water clinging to her jeans.

"I'm sorry I never called you, Ginger. Or emailed. You were my friend and deserved better. I thought maybe we'd become more than friends. But when we moved, I put Rosebud and everything about it behind me."

"More than friends?" Her eyes glistened. "Even if you'd stayed in Rosebud, we'd never have been anything. We were barely friends. Your *friends* would've never allowed it."

"Allowed what? For us to be friends? Or more than? My

friends had no say in my relationships." He took a watery step toward her.

"Are you sure? Seemed to me they had everything to say about your relationships. Who you hung out with, when and where. Every time we had study hall together, they pestered you to skip out. They barely spoke to me when we were together, forget when we weren't."

"Ginger, I could make up my own mind. Even then. They had no say. I asked you to the movies, didn't I?"

She furrowed her brow, shrugging. "As a payback for math help." She smoothed her sandy colored hair over her shoulder, and shoved her scarf into place. "We would've never been anything more."

"If I wanted there to be more—"

A bold knock startled away the intimacy of their conversation and Tom opened to find Edward on the veranda, Scott and his four-wheel drive idling by the steps.

"We've come to rescue you." Edward barged inside. "Passed the VW on our way . . ." He gave Tom the once over. "Man, what happened to you?"

"We tried to push the car out." Tom followed Edward's glance across the room where Ginger stood on the other side of the reading chairs.

"Ginger," Edward said.

"Edward."

"You know our boy here is starting a church?" Edward clapped Tom on the shoulder.

"So he said."

"No offense, but considering all that happened with Tom's dad, we can't be too careful. Especially around you."

"Around me?" She fiddled with her scarf, smoothing it higher up on her neck. "What are you talking about?"

"Edward, let's go." Tom tugged on his arm, reaching for the door knob.

But Edward remained planted, his smile neither warm nor pleasant. "You know what I'm talking about, Ginger. I realize time has passed and with Tom not being married the rules are different, but nevertheless, there *are* expectations. We have to protect him from scandal and gossip all the same. He needs a good start in Rosebud if the church is going to make it."

"Edward, that's enough." Tom jerked him toward the door. "Ginger, I'm sorry."

"Sorry for what? Edward, what are you talking about? 'Protect him from scandal'?" Ginger gazed at Tom, her lips pressed in defiance. *See? Your friends won't let you.*

"She doesn't know?" Edward glanced at Tom, incredulous.

"Ginger, you're freezing and muddy. We'll get out of your hair," Tom said. Ed and his big mouth. He never did have any tact. "Say . . . I'll come get you in the morning. What time?"

"Don't dismiss me, Tom Wells. What don't I know?"

"Nothing, Edward is just talking. You know, how it's probably not good for Rosebud's newest, young, single pastor to be alone on a dark and rainy night with a beautiful woman."

She snapped back, her expression sober, the sheen in her

eyes a blend of confusion and what-did-you-just-say? But she stayed on task. "Edward, what are you talking about?"

"Don't you know, Ginger?" Edward stepped around the wingback chair toward her. His voice was smooth, his movements calculating.

"Edward, enough." Tom came around the other side, pressing his hand into the man's chest. "Let's just go."

"Your mom was the reason Tom's dad had to leave town. Or at least she was the final blow."

Tom dropped his head with a heavy exhale. Edward had been wanting to do this since Tom agreed to start the church. He thought Tom should, "Get it out in the open."

"We don't need any gossip or scandal cropping up."

Ginger glanced between them. "Excuse me? My mom? The woman who hates church? Who . . . wouldn't . . . even . . . take me?" Her words slowed as some sort of revelation dawned. But only for a moment. "No, no, not my mama. Preachers were definitely not her type."

"Say what you will, but Shana Winters was in love with Tom Wells Sr."

"Edward!" Tom shoved him out the door. *What was wrong with him?* "Ginger," Tom paused inside the threshold. "I'll come for you in the morning."

"What are you talking about? She never even knew Tom Sr., let alone fell in love with him. My mother and your father? It's laughable." She turned away from them, disbelief tainting her expression. "My mother? She's a lot of things, but not a home wrecker."

"You're right. She wasn't a home wrecker," Tom said. He could deck Edward. Seriously. "We can talk about this later."

"No. Edward brought it up, so let's talk about it now. My mother is responsible for your family leaving town, for your father losing his church? For you never calling me again?"

"Okay, here's the truth. My *father* is responsible for losing his church, for us leaving town, and *I'm* responsible for never calling you."

"So my mother wasn't involved? Edward is lying?"

"Not exactly lying. Your mother and my father were friends—"

"He said something about love."

"Ed," Tom said. "Can you give us a moment?"

He started to protest, then turned for the door. "Hurry, it's late. Eric's waiting for us."

As the door clicked closed, Tom reached for Ginger but she stepped away. "Edward doesn't know the whole story."

Ginger exhaled, the light in her golden eyes dimming as she closed the small window she'd opened to him.

"Then what is the whole story?"

From beyond the door, the truck horn sounded. Tom grumbled low. Wait until he was alone with Ed.

"Tell you what," he said. "I'll pick you up and we can talk about it in the morning." He smiled, coaxing her agreement. "Go, shower, get warm. I'll see you at . . ."

"Eight. But is there any truth to what he said?" she said after a moment.

"Some." He peered at her, gaze holding gaze.

She sighed, sinking down to the chair, then standing back up, remembering she was wet and muddy. "Even more reason now."

"Reason for what?"

"That we can't be more than friends. I told you your friends won't let you."

"And I told you, my friends have no say. See you in the morning, Ginger. And please, do not worry about this. Trust me." The door clicked closed behind him and he jogged toward the waiting truck. Climbing in, he thumped Edward in the head. "Nice going."

"She needed to know." The man showed no remorse. "But really, Tom, her? Of all the women in southern Alabama?"

Tom mulled over the challenge as Scott revved the truck toward the big house, the powerful beast undaunted by the muddy, rutted terrain.

Why not Ginger Winters? She was kind and considerate, more than the man next to him who claimed to be a Christian. Every time Tom saw her in the past few days, she caught a piece of his heart.

But could he be more than friends with the daughter of the woman who played a role in his father's demise?

Yeah, Tom had some praying to do. A conversation with God was about to go down. He'd be open, listening. But in the moment, the answer to Edward's question was a resounding, *Yeah, her. Really.*

Chapter 6

♡

SHE'D TOSSED AND TURNED HALF THE NIGHT, TRYING to piece together Edward and Tom's story as she listened to the rain. It peeled off around midnight as a strong wind swept over the grounds, batting the western corner of the homestead.

Mama and Reverend Wells? Ginger counted a half a dozen times she'd seen Mama talking to the senior pastor, but she never imagined there was anything more than a how-do between them.

Mrs. Wells, Tom's mama, was a beautiful, well-respected woman. And nice. Not cranky and twisted-up like her own mama, used and spit out from too many poor relationship choices.

Mama never listened to anyone when it came to men. She picked her man and that was it. The police could show her a rap sheet a mile long but if Mama believed in him, wanted him, she hung on like a dog with a bone.

Dressed and ready for the day, Ginger chose a scarf from her duffle—a dark forest green—and wound it around her neck. She wanted to get her stuff from the car and get to the main house before Tom showed up. She didn't need him to rescue her.

But his defense of her last night resonated with her. He'd stood up for her. The notion warmed her with some sort of hope.

With a glance in the mirror, she secured her scarf, then headed out, slipping on her jacket and looping her purse over her head. If she learned anything as Shana Winter's daughter, it was not to mistake kindness as affection. Or love. She'd end up like Mama if she didn't watch it—bitter and used up.

She already knew no man would ever want to hold her ugly, scarred body.

Dawn had not yet kissed the meadow, so if she hurried, she'd be at the house before Tom was out of bed. Plan for the day? Avoid him as much as possible.

But when she opened the door and stepped into the crisp morning, she was confronted with a white orb of a light and Tom Wells astride a ginormous horse.

"Good morning."

Ginger stumbled back, hand over her heart. "Good grief, you scared me. What are you doing here so early?" She pointed to the mocha-colored beast. "On that?"

"Waiting for you. Help you get your car out of the mud." He aimed the flashlight at her feet. "It's still a mess out there."

"Well then, let's go." She hammered down the steps with a manufactured bravado, shoving past him and his monstrous mount.

"Ginger, you don't have to walk." Tom chirruped to the

horse, bouncing the flashlight over the grassy, muddy path still shadowed in the remainder of night.

"I'm not getting on that thing." Ginger pointed back at the horse and plodded on, jumping over the muddiest parts, grateful for Tom's light since she'd clearly forgotten hers. "What happened to Scott's truck?"

"He got stuck himself doing some midnight mudding. The Maynards' stable horses are here, so I borrowed one to come help you."

"Seriously . . . with a horse?" Ginger's next step sank into a gloppy rut hidden by a clump of wild grass.

"Have you seen this brute? He could pull a barn off its foundation. He's a worker, Ginger." Tom landed the light on her, his sweet chuckle floating down around her. But she didn't dare look up. "We hitch your VW to his harness, he'll be like, 'What's this little thing chained to me?'" Tom's laugh traveled through the cold dawn.

Ginger stopped, glancing up at him. "You think this is funny? I have a job to do and you're making jokes."

"Then why are you being stubborn about help? Ginger, get on the horse." Tom extended his hand toward her. "You're sinking deeper as we speak."

"I've got this." The farther away she strode from the house, the softer the ground and the wetter the grass. Her feet plunged into the mud, loading down the hem of her jeans.

"You got this?" Tom dismounted and sloshed alongside her, guiding her with the flashlight's wide beam. "Mind telling me how you're going to get your car out of the mud?"

She stopped, turning around, causing him to pull up short just before she spun into his thick, sculpted chest. "I . . . have . . . no . . . idea. There, you happy?"

He stiffened, drawing back. "Wow, forgive me. I didn't know you wore bitter so well."

She stepped into him, releasing the scent of clean cotton and soapy skin. "I find out about your dad and my mama from Ed Frizz? Why didn't you tell me?"

He sighed, running his hand the length of the horse's reins, aiming the flashlight down at his feet. "I didn't know myself until a few months ago. At the time of the move, my parents told my sister and me they had marriage issues to work on but that everything would be all right. When I told Dad I was returning to Rosebud to start a church, he gave up the rest of the story. That Shana Winters was the reason he had to leave."

"What kind of *reason*? Edward seemed to know a whole sordid bunch."

"Yeah, Ed's a blowhard. He likes playing the role of big shot but he doesn't know any more than I do."

"But he thinks he does and he's using it to tell you what to do."

"No, he's not. It's just Ed being Ed." He sighed and clicked to the horse to walk on. "Let's just get your car out of the mud, then you can drive to the house."

Ginger stopped, wrestling with the sense she was the bad guy in this scenario. Tom was the hero, literally riding up on a dark horse to save her. How then was it her fault Tom's father and her mother had been somehow involved? Which made Ed cast shadows on her?

Ginger's emotions flowed into words. "Hey, I'm not the bad guy here." She chased after him, stumbling into yet another sloppy mudhole to coat the hem of her jeans. "No one said a word to me. Never heard one shred of Rosebud gossip. Come on, I'm the scarred, freak girl. Surely someone was dying to tell me how my mama toppled the county's most successful preacher."

Ginger's intensity shaved the ice from the air. The gelding raised his head, snorting, his breath billowing from his broad nose.

"I'm sorry I didn't tell you, Ginger. But between now and three days ago, when was I supposed to do that? 'Hey, I haven't seen you in a dozen years, and oh by the way, how about your mom falling in love with my dad? What a trip!'"

"Is that what happened?" Now that would be typical Mama. Always loving what she couldn't have, from cars to men to other people's daughters—the pretty, smoothed-skinned ones.

"Yes." He peered down at her. "For what it's worth, I'm sorry I left town without talking to you. And for never writing or calling. I was so mad for so long, then I didn't know what to say once I got over myself."

"T-thank you. Sorry for hating you ever since."

"Hating me?" He slapped his hand to his chest. "Really?"

"Okay, maybe not hate but really, really dislike. Strongly." She spied her poor, sinking Bug in the distance. Reaching for his arm, she raised the flashlight's beam. "There she blows."

"She looks so sad. I think she missed us."

"Do you hate her? My mom?" Ginger jumped a puddle, heading for her car. "For whatever she did?"

"There's no benefit in hating anyone. Takes too much energy and returns so little. In truth, though, my parents both say the whole situation worked for good."

"Worked for good? I find that hard to believe." Ginger glanced over at Tom, the pale light of dawn rising behind him, accenting his broad shoulders.

"It's a gift of God. Working all things for good." He muttered a low "whoa" as they approached the VW. "Easy, Clyde."

"So this is Clyde?" Ginger hesitated, reaching up to stroke his nose. Clyde shoved his head against her palm. She jumped back with a short laugh.

"He likes beautiful women," Tom said, walking the workhorse around to the front of the car.

He'd said it again. Called her beautiful. Twice in less than twelve hours. The notion warmed her down to her cold toes. But surely he didn't mean it. Not really. Perhaps in some metaphorical, symbolic way. But oh, she wanted to believe.

Kneeling by the car, Tom hooked a set of chains to the chassis, talking to Clyde in low, tender words. "Good boy . . . you can do this . . . hang with me gentle giant . . . then we'll get you home, cleaned up, with a bucket of oats for breakfast."

Emotion swelled in Ginger's chest. No one had ever spoken to her in such sweet tones except Grandpa.

Not even when she was pulled from the fire, when she lay in a hospital bed weeping from the pain, did anyone offer her kind encouragement.

"Ginger," Mama used to say. *"Stop all these tears. There's just no other way to heal but go through the treatments. Now, come on, do you want to watch* Gilmore Girls *reruns with me?"*

Tears pushed to the surface as Tom hopped up, claiming, "Ready." Ginger ducked behind the back of the car to hide her swimming eyes.

"Born ready."

"You all right?" His soft tone drifted over her shoulder and into her soul.

"Yeah, whatever, let's just do this." Ginger wiped her eyes clear and ducked behind the car, hands on the engine's hood, bracing to push, her feet sinking into the wet, cold ground.

"Ginger, you don't have to—"

"Tom, can we just get this done? I need to get cleaned up before Mrs. James comes down for her appointment."

"Okay. But you drive, I'll push." He bent over her, his nose inches from hers. She could see straight through his sea-blue eyes and into his guileless soul.

"D-drive?" She swallowed.

"Steer? Find the high ground . . ." Tom threaded Clyde's reins between the open door and the windshield.

"Yeah, right." She tugged her keys from her pocket, her heart firing. *No, you can't do this.* She squeezed her eyes shut, holding her breath, shutting down her heart's puttering. "I drive, you push."

He grinned. "Sounds like a plan. Ready?" Tom stepped back, but held a narrow gaze on Ginger. "You sure you're all right?" He angled forward. "I mean with the news and all. It's okay if you're not. We dumped a shocking truth on you last night. Did you call your mom?"

"No. And Tom, stop trying to be Mr. Fix It. Let's *goooo* already."

"Pardon me for caring." His sharp tone pierced her fragile facade. When he moved to the back of the car, Ginger sat behind the wheel.

Oh, Mama . . .

"Here we go," he called. "Clyde, chirrup. Go boy, go."

Ginger shifted into neutral and gripped the wheel as Clyde lowered his head and leaned into his harness, air clouds swelling from under his nose. Ginger turned the ignition but the wet engine sputtered and moaned. The tires spun and whirred, finding no traction.

"Push," she called.

"I'm pushing."

Tom chirruped to Clyde again and in one lunge, the grand beast freed the car from the mud. With a shout, Ginger fired up the engine by popping the clutch. The small motor sputtered to life.

Shifting into neutral, Ginger jumped out. "We did it."

But no one told Clyde his mission was complete. With an easy gait, he trotted on, the engine sputtering.

"Hey, horse, wait—" The back wheel-well grazed Ginger's leg, shoving her to the ground, face first into a very cold puddle.

"Ginger, are you all right?" Tom, trying not to laugh, extended his hand.

"Do I look all right?" She clasped her hand in his, rising from the mud, watching as Clyde picked up his pace, gaining the feel for old Matilda, and galloped toward the plantation house, the open car door swinging from side to side, Clyde's reins slapping the Bug's interior.

"Ginger, why didn't you grab the reins?"

"B-because . . . y-you didn't tell me to grab the reins. Why didn't you grab them?" She flipped her hand at him, ignoring the flutter in her middle inspired by Tom's sparkling grin. She scooped the mud from her shirt and jeans. "Look at me . . . I'm covered." With a grumble, she adjusted her scarf and started walking, cold, muddy water slinking over the top of her ankle boots.

"Want some company?" Tom skipped alongside her.

"Only if you can keep quiet." The breeze nipped at her, and the golden warmth of the sun peeking over the edge of dawn seemed galaxies away.

She needed to think, deal with the big issue, the dark hole in the pit of her stomach. A hole formed long before she learned that her mama had liaised with a pastor, before Tom Wells Jr. ever entered her life.

This particular hole existed despite her résumé of a big-city career, successful years with Tracie Blue, or ownership of Ginger Snips in the center of Main Street.

She, Ginger Lee Winters, was stuck. In life. In her heart. In what she believed about God, herself, and Tom. Cold tears threatening, Ginger quickened her pace, avoiding the heat of Tom's gaze.

"You okay?" The tenor of Tom's voice sweetened her mood. Ginger squinted up at him.

"Why are you being so nice to me?"

Tom evened his stride to match hers. "Maybe because I *like* you."

Ginger laughed, loud, plodding on through the long grass, combating the swirling, swooning sensation of Tom's confession. Like her? No man *liked* her. Not in the way his tone indicated.

After a moment she stopped. He was a man of God— maybe he knew the answer to her nagging question. "Does God care?"

"Yes." Sure. Without hesitation. Catching her off guard. She expected him to pause, ponder, hem-and-haw. Because how could a man really know if God cared?

"Yes? Just like that?" She snapped her fingers in the icy air.

"Yes, just like that." He didn't move his eyes from her face. And she flamed on the inside.

Ginger walked on. "Okay, yeah, I guess it's too early in the morning for a serious conversation."

"I am serious. Any time you want to talk, let me know."

She glanced over at him, saying nothing, feeling more conflicted and twisted up than before she asked the question.

If God cared, where was He when she was trapped in the fire? Where was He in the years following? She liked being mad at Him, thinking He owed her something.

But at the moment, what bothered her more than the news about Mama or that God left her in a fire, was the fact that Tom Wells Jr. looked every bit like she imagined Jesus might if she met Him in person. Warm, kind, without accusation, but with a blue-eyed intensity.

However, on this cold wedding morning, she was not ready to trust any overtures of kindness, of love. Not from Tom Wells. And especially not from God.

Chapter 7

♡

THE ATMOSPHERE IN THE THIRD-FLOOR ATRIUM WAS electric. Gone were the cold, embedded fragments of her morning in the mud with Tom and Clyde, who, by the way, nudged Ginger's shoulder after Tom unhitched him from the car as if to say, "You're welcome." She felt a rush of joy at the tenderness of the gentle giant.

However, digging out of the mud, communing with horses, cracking open her heart, even the tiniest bit, to Tom Wells, and musing over her past and the existence of God was completely out of Ginger's element.

But in a room full of women, doing hair? This was Ginger Winters's wheelhouse. And she intended to never leave. Gone were her insecurities and trepidations.

Once she and Tom arrived at the barn, where Clyde had taken the VW, Ginger accepted Tom's help to unload and haul in her crates and cases. They did so in a contemplative silence that was not quite comfortable but not at all awkward.

He bid her a quick good-bye when they were done, holding onto her gaze for a second longer than her beating heart could stand, then jogged down the hallway.

Ginger slapped her hand over her heart, willing every beating corpuscle to forget the handsome visage of one Tom Wells Jr.

Ducking into the bathroom, she'd rinsed off in a hot shower, soaping away the chill of the dawn, cleaning off the mud and sending any lingering thoughts of *him* down the drain.

Then she dug clean clothes from her bag and tugged on her spare boots, entering the atrium, her heels resounding on the tile.

By three-thirty, she'd coiffed, twisted, teased, and sprayed the hair of three grandmothers, two mothers, one great-aunt, seven bridesmaids, and two flower girls.

All the while the music was blasting everything from Michael Bublé to Jesus Culture to Beyoncé's "All the Single Ladies."

Laughter tinged along with the music, becoming a part of the melody and percussion.

Right now the bridesmaids were circling Bridgett, turning up the music, belting out the lyrics with their heads back, arms wide. *"You call me out beyond the shore into the waves . . . You make me brave . . ."*

Ginger closed her eyes, leaning against the makeshift beauty station, breathing in the lyrics. If there was a God who cared, could He make her brave? She liked the idea of it all.

A blip of laughter from the older women chatting on the matching sofas caught her attention.

They reclined in their wedding attire, the glitter in their dresses snapping up the light draining through the high arching windows, and sipping a fruity Ginger Ale punch.

"I sure could have used a song like this on my wedding day." One of the grandmas pointed to the singing circle. "I was so nervous I could barely stand let alone belt out a song with my bridesmaids. It took all of my gumption to make it down the aisle."

"That's nothing," said the great-aunt. "At my wedding, Daddy turned to me just as the pianist started the bridal march and said, 'Lovie, you don't have to do this if you don't want.' Lord a-mercy, I liked to have crowned him right then and there."

Ginger smiled and checked her watch, picking up her own punch glass. Three forty-five. An hour and forty-five minutes until the wedding. So as soon as Bridgett was done singing about bravery, Ginger would have her in the chair.

Hair and makeup was her world. Where she was in command, captain of her destiny. But out *there*, in the everyday world, she was the poor, pitied, scarred one. And now the daughter of the woman who took down a preacher.

Which was why she'd remain hidden in her shop behind long sleeves and peacock-colored scarves. And she'd glean a little of life from the women and men who entered her shop, sat in her chair, and told her their stories.

The song ended and the girls laughed and cheered, drawing Bridgett into a hug, forming a magical bloom of beauty.

Ginger would never fit in their garden. She'd be pruned for sure.

But in the field of helping others, ushering every woman, young and old, into a realm of beauty, she'd thrive.

"Oh, Ginger, look, my hair is coming undone." Miranda broke from the circle with panic in her voice, making her way to Ginger. "Look." She patted the loose weave Ginger had given her.

"Have a seat." Ginger patted the chair, squinting at Miranda's sandy-beach colored updo. It was perfect. And practically impossible to fall since she'd plastered it in place.

"How about some long strands . . . for curls?" Miranda said, trying to tug strands from the clips.

"Mandy, good grief, let Ginger do her job. She's the best. Your hair is perfect." Bridgett stood off to the right, beaming, wrapped in a white robe and drinking a sparkling water.

"I just like long curls over my shoulder."

"Because you always wear long curls over your shoulder. Be *brave*, do something new."

Ginger smiled at Miranda through the mirror. "Trust me, this twist works perfectly for your face. If you want curls, we'd have to start all over which means washing your hair."

Miranda made a face. "Fine, but I still think some long curls around my neck would look good." She pointed at

Bridgett. "Wait until you're in this chair. You'll be bossing Ginger around all right."

"Watch me. I'm going to face away from the mirror, that's how much I trust her."

"Then here you go." Miranda stood, shaking the folds from her long gown. "Your turn to be *brave*."

Without a word, Bridgett turned the chair away from the mirror and sat with a glare at her friend. "Ginger, do your thing." She glanced up. "We go back a long way, don't we?"

"We do." In these moments, high school became a mythical, fun place with treasured memories, where, for a brief second in time, Ginger was a part of the sorority.

"Remember when you pulled my backside from the fire the night I tried to—" A deep red blushed Bridgett's cheeks as she stumbled over her words. "I mean, the night I tried to . . ." She swallowed, ". . . color my hair, and . . . green. Everywhere . . . green."

"It was a class A emergency." Ginger let the reference to fire pass. When she commanded her *space*, not even her dark tragedy overshadowed her.

"It was my first date with Eric and my hair was all kinds of messed up. I ran, literally, to Ginger's house, crying the whole way."

"And look at you now," Ginger said.

"Marrying"—Bridgett's voice broke—"That same man."

"Who probably would've never noticed green hair."

"True, so very true." Bridgett's laugh sweetened the room, and the bridesmaids *ahhhed.*

Ginger combed through Bridgett's slightly curled hair, then divided it into sections, planning to fashion a light updo with tendrils drifting down the curve of her neck. Because the bride's hairstyle should tell her story, reflect her essence.

Bridgett's updo was intricate with twists and curls, but entirely and altogether elegant and rich.

Ginger teased the top of the hair, slipping into her space of contentment and peace. Because no matter how scarred or hideous she was to others, no one could take this away from her.

If she had any true courage, she might bless the tragedy that introduced her to her destiny, to her superpower.

As she twisted and pinned Bridgett's hair, the women continued talking, laughing, calming the distraught wedding planner who barged into the room announcing the flowers had not yet been delivered.

Ginger watched the drama through a covert gaze, all the while twisting, tucking, and smoothing. When Bridgett's hair was pinned and frozen in place with hair freeze, her mother called for the dress. The designer entered along with her assistant as Bridgett stood.

"Here we go." She glanced back at the mirror, then at Ginger, her eyes glistening. "Exactly how I imagined my hair. Thank you."

Suddenly the burn of the previous night's banishment dissipated and all was right with the world.

Slipping from her white robe, Bridgett stepped into the fur-trimmed gown, fitting it on her shoulders and setting it on her slim waist, the crystal beading catching the light.

Then, like bustling elves, they straightened and buttoned, helped Bridgett with her shoes, then last, handed her veil over to Ginger.

"Will you do the honors?" her mother said.

Standing on a stool, Ginger fitted the comb at the base of Bridgett's silken poof and draped the blusher over her face.

"Oh darling . . ." Mrs. Maynard cupped her hands over her mouth, not worried about her tears streaking her makeup. "You look beautiful, simply, elegantly beautiful."

"Eric's eyes are going to pop out of his head." Miranda said.

Bridgett glided across the room to the full-length mirror and sighed. "Just like I dreamed." She turned to Ginger. "I knew you'd make me beautiful."

"I think Mother Nature took care of that for you."

Bridgett was the perfect bride, the prettiest Ginger had ever seen. And now that her job was done, she felt herself slipping from her empowered zone into the wishing well of wanting to be a part of the bold and the beautiful.

But she'd never be a bride, let alone one like Bridgett. Ginger slipped out of the atrium onto the deck and leaned against the railing, breathing deep, swallowing the truth.

Ginger watched the reception from the doorway of the plantation's grand ballroom, away from the guests and the photographers ducking in and out of the shadows of the ornate plantation ballroom with a fresco ceiling and an imported tile floor.

The guests dined under the light of a handcrafted Waterford chandelier that disseminated light like golden scepters.

Candlelight flickered on linen-draped tables adorned with polished silver and custom-designed China. In the far corner of the room, a fire roared in the river-rock fireplace.

The aroma of prime rib and roasted duck lingered in the air as the best man and maid of honor toasted the bride and groom. While the guests cheered and silver tinkled against cut crystal glasses, Eric kissed Bridgett and the band started a Glenn Miller tune.

In less than a music measure, the dance floor was thick with folks juking and jiving.

Ginger sighed. Every hairdo she had sculpted today remained in perfect place. Of course . . .

Proud of a job well done, she debated now if she should just go on home. It was getting late and she was tired. And, despite her success with the grandmothers, mothers, aunts, and bridesmaids, she felt a little out of place and alone.

"Hey."

Ginger glanced around to find Tom approaching. "Hey."

"Having fun?"

"Sure."

Tom leaned against the other side of the doorway. "Word is Bridgett's stylist is nothing short of a wonderkid. You brought out the best in her. In all of them."

Ginger gestured to the beaming groom. "I think he's the one that really brings out the best in her."

Bridgett was a vision. She'd changed into a simple white satin gown for the reception, accented with a white, wintery shrug. Eric drank her in with such adoration and desire that

Ginger could only watch for a moment, feeling as if she were a voyeur into his intimate, private feelings.

With a sigh, she slipped her hand into her hip pocket. Just once, she'd like a man to look at her with such admiration. Such love. To take her in his arms and move across the dance floor.

She loved dancing. Or at least she thought she did. She'd never *been* on a dance floor.

"By the way, when I was giving Clyde his oats he said to tell you hi."

She snorted a laugh, covering her lips with her fingers. He got to her way too easily. "Tell Clyde hi back."

"He said he'd like to give you a ride sometime."

"How sweet. But I don't *do* horses."

"Yeah?" His tone smiled.

"Yeah." She tried to sound fun and sexy but her shallow breath made her voice thin and weak.

"Do you like dancing?"

"I used to watch dancing videos all the time. Mama would rent them for me from Blockbuster." Ginger stood straight, pinching her lips. *Hey, no giving up secrets.*

"But have you ever danced? On a dance floor? With a man?"

"Does it matter?" She faced Tom, hesitated, then gathered a wad of courage and pulled up the sleeve of her blouse, exposing the harsh terrain of her arm. She didn't dare expose her side or back. This would be enough to gross him out. "No one wants to dance with this."

"You seem to know what others think without asking them." He tried to snatch her hand but she was too quick.

"I don't need to know what they think." She shook her arm at him. "This is ugly, not fun to touch." She regretted her action, exposing herself to him. Really, she needed to get in her car and drive away. In a matter of mere days, Tom Wells had flashed his light over her heart and she was nearly ready to show him her deepest, darkest corners. "I'm a freak."

"Ginger, we're all freaks. We're all scarred. That's why Jesus came. Why He died and rose again for us."

"Yeah, that's what a girl loves when she makes herself vulnerable. A sermon. Save it for Sunday, Tom." She flashed her palm. "I'm not interested."

"Ginger, come on, your scars don't bother me." He gently took her hand in his, then, with his eyes on hers, traced the marks on her hand and wrist.

"Stop. Let go." She tried to wrench free but he held on. "Tom, don't . . ."

"Your scars don't bother me." He held her hand a bit tighter and slid his hand along the rugged texture of her arm.

"Stop . . . please." Her whole body trembled, shaking her to her core.

The music from the bandstand changed, slowing down to a soft, melodic "Moon River."

"How did it happen?" He turned her arm over, exposing its tender but damaged underside, and traced his fingers, moving so delicately along the puckered ridges. "I never asked. You never told me."

"T-the . . . rattletrap . . . trailer . . ." Each stroke of his hand stole her breath. She tried to pull free again, but lacked strength and will to really be without his touch.

A tingling sensation crept up her arm and rode over her shoulder, and down her back. A gulp of pleasure filled her chest.

Never had she been touched by a man. Never, ever had she experienced such a feeling.

"You lived in a trailer?"

"North of town, off Highway 29. The wiring was rotten, eaten by squirrels." She should pull her arm away before she puddled at his feet. Did he realize what he was doing to her?

She swallowed, drawing a deep breath. "The place caught fire . . . I was sleeping. Mama . . . had gone out . . . after I went to bed. I called and called her but she didn't answer. I thought she was dead. I had to find her but the only way to get out of my room was to run through the flames . . . my nightgown caught on fire."

"Ginger, that took a lot of courage." He held their hands palm-to-palm and linked his fingers with hers. "These scars don't make you a freak. They are not ugly."

"Because you don't live with them every day. You don't see the looks, hear the whispers. 'Oh, isn't it a shame?' 'Yes, yes it is.'"

"Maybe they're amazed how a girl with such obvious scars could be so beautiful." His low tone carried an intimacy that saturated her soul with the same intoxication as his touch.

"Stop, Tom." She broke free and shoved down her sleeve.

"You're a preacher. You shouldn't say things that aren't true." Guests were coming out of the ballroom, so Ginger fell in line with them, heading toward the foyer. Time to go.

"What's not true?" Tom followed, intense and determined.

"That I'm beautiful."

"But you *are*, Ginger." He slipped his hand around her arm. "Would you like to dance?"

"No. You don't have to pretend to be interested in me. To be kind." Because she'd rather have people exclaim, "Oh what a pity," than to discover Tom Wells was just being a *nice* guy.

"What if I'm not pretending?"

"To be kind?"

"To be interested."

Ginger fell against the wall, half in the light, half in the shadow and folded her arms. "After confessing to me that my mother played a part in your father's demise? How could you possibly be interested in me? What would Edward think?"

"Who cares? I don't. I like you. I think we could be *friends*." His breath clung to "friends" for a moment longer than necessary. "Ginger, it's a wedding. Come on, one dance."

She gestured toward his tuxedo, then the couples coming down the hall. "The attire is formal. I'm wearing jeans."

"You think anyone is going to care?"

"Yes, I do. Mrs. Maynard for one. There's a governor, two senators, and a newspaper publisher in there. And a boat load of photographers."

"So what?" He slipped his hand into hers again and the dying embers of his touch flared again.

"Tom, do you ever listen?" Her eyes welled up. He was going to make her confess it. "I'm not one of *them*. One of you." She'd pulled her hand from his. "I need to get going." Get back to her life and her world where everything was comfortable. Where her lines were clearly drawn.

"Why do you want to watch life from the shadows?"

"Did it ever occur to you I like the shadows?"

"Did it ever occur to you that you were made for so much more?"

She stared at him, her insides a hissing stick of dynamite. Once she thought she was made for more. She'd even tried for bigger things on the road with Tracie. But . . .

"Have a good evening, Tom. Good luck with your church." Ginger headed down the corridor. She needed to escape the house, escape all the love and happiness in the ballroom, escape *Tom*.

But he followed her down the hall, past the bustling kitchen, warm with the smells of roasted meat and baking bread, through the grand room toward the arching foyer with the sweeping staircase.

"Ginger, please one dance."

And risk her heart toppling over in love? She tugged open the foyer door, inhaling the sweet scent of her escape. "Good night, Tom."

Chapter 8
♡

BY WEDNESDAY THE WARMTH AND SUNSHINE HAD RE-
turned to southern Alabama and Ginger settled back into her
weekly routine of blue hair wash-and-blowouts, and the chatter
of Ruby-Jane, Michele, and Casey.

She could almost forget the weird snow day, the odd wedding
weekend, and Tom Wells Jr. with his probing powder-blue eyes
and intoxicating, tender touch.

Just the memory of his fingers running along her arm made
her shiver.

"You cold?" Ruby-Jane said, walking by with an armload of
clean towels.

"What? No. Loving these warm temps." Ginger put the finishing touches on Mrs. Darnell's short, teased hair.

Drat that Tom Wells. She was going to have to dump her
head in one of the sinks after closing and wash that man right
out of her hair.

"Well . . ." Ruby-Jane stood in the middle of the shop. "Hump day. What are y'all doing this evening? Want to try that new burger place by the shopping plaza?"

"Not me," Michele said, counting out her tips. "We've got basketball tonight."

"Church for me," Casey said.

"Ging? What about you?"

She gazed at Ruby-Jane through the mirror. "Got plans. If you're looking for something to do, you could finish painting the shop."

The place looked rather awkward with one long wall painted a smooth pinkish-beige while the other remained a putrid pea green.

"Ha, nothing doing. I'll help you if you want but I'm not staying here by myself."

"I would but I need to take care of something." Ginger took command of the conversation, going over Thursday's appointments and deciding with her stylists which supplies needed to be reordered.

Then she closed the shop and picked up Chinese takeout from Wong Chow and drove across town to Mountain Brook Apartments as the winter sun drifted beyond the edge of the earth's curve.

Pulling into a parking spot under Mama's second floor apartment, Ginger gathered the takeout bags and jogged up the steps.

"Hey, baby," Mama said, smiling, taking a long inhale of the food as Ginger entered. "I was surprised you called."

"Well, we haven't seen each other in awhile." Ginger slipped off her sweater, straightening the long bell sleeve of her top, glancing about the small, charming apartment, decorated with Mama's artistic flair.

"I heard the wedding was lovely." Mama set the fried rice on the dining table as Ginger searched the cupboards for the plates. "Just use paper. In the cabinet by the sink."

Ginger set the plates on the table. "Bridgett was a beautiful bride. But no one expected less."

"Did you have a nice time?"

She shrugged, taking the napkins and chopsticks from the bag. "It was a job."

"Put any yearnings into your head?" Mama wiggled her eyebrows and did a jig across the linoleum. "Maybe a wedding of your own?"

"Hardly."

"And why not? You're smart, successful . . . *p-pretty*."

That's how Mama always said it. *P-pretty.* Stumbling. Hesitating. As if she was trying to believe her own confession.

"Actually, I didn't come to talk about me." Ginger sat at the table, reaching for the beef and broccoli. "Did you know Tom Wells was in town? Starting a church?"

"What?" Mama's complexion paled, but she disguised it by jumping up. "I forgot the iced tea. I made some this afternoon."

"Tom junior, Mama. Not senior."

Her back stiffened and the pitcher of tea shimmied. "T-that boy who stood you up all those years ago?"

"Mama, I know."

"Know what?" She came to the table, chin up, gaze down. "Oh, shoot, I forgot ice. Give me your cup."

Ginger pressed her hand on Mama's. "About you and Mr. Wells. Tom Senior."

Mama snatched the cup, and her hand, from Ginger's grasp. "What in the world are you talking about?" She jammed the plastic cups under the ice dispenser. "This town is a gossip petri dish."

"Apparently not, Mama. I never heard word one about you and Pastor Wells before. Is it true? Are you the reason he left town?"

Mama pressed her forehead against the fridge, filling the cups to the brim with ice. "Certainly not. Who told you such a wild tale?" She came to the table and sat with a *harrumph*, tucking her bobbed copper hair behind her ears.

"Edward Frizz. Tom confirmed it."

"Just like that?" Mama scooped more rice than she'd ever eat onto her plate. "They walked up to you at Bridgett Maynard's wedding, of all places, and said, 'Hey, your mama ran Pastor Wells out of town?' Land sakes, that was twelve years ago. Some folks have to learn to let things go." Her hands trembled as she dumped almost all of the Moo Goo Gai Pan over her rice.

"You're seriously going to eat all the Moo Goo?"

"Oh, see what you made me do?" Mama shoveled some of it back into the container. "Ginger, I don't know what possessed—"

"Is it true? You and Pastor Wells?"

Mama set the container down, her eyes glistening, and stared toward the bright kitchen, sniffling, running her hands through her hair. "You were to never know."

"Why not?"

"How in the world did Edward Frizz find out?"

"I don't know about Edward. But Tom, of course, knows. His dad told him the whole story when he decided to return to Rosebud. Tom's starting this new church."

"I suppose . . . So, Tom's dad told him? Warned him?" Mama's eye sparked with a wild, rebellious glint. "Stay away from the Winters women?"

"Who knows? Probably." Ginger's stomach rumbled, asking for food, rejecting the forming rock of tension as any kind of nourishment. Tom certainly didn't heed his daddy's warning. "Did you have an affair?"

"No! No . . ." Mama broke open a set of chopsticks and swirled her chicken through a pile of fried rice but never took a bite. "Remember Parker Fox?"

"I think. Wasn't he the banker you dated?"

"I finally thought I'd found me a good one, you know? He adored you."

"If you say so." None of Mama's boyfriends ever adored Ginger.

"He wasn't a drinker or doper. He wanted a nice suburban life. Just like I wanted when I married your daddy."

"So what happened?" Ginger scooped a forkful of rice and beef into her mouth, exhaling, willing this conversation to be about truth. Maybe healing.

"He asked me about your scars."

Ginger set down her fork and wiped her mouth with her napkin. "He didn't want a stepdaughter with such ugly scars?"

"No, Ginger, why do you always assume the worst?"

"Because it's usually true."

"He wanted to know how it happened. So I told him. He was aghast. First that you were trapped in a trailer fire but mostly because I'd left you alone. I told him you were twelve and that I'd only gone down to the Wet Your Whistle for a beer and burger with a guy from work. That was too much for him and he wanted out." Mama snapped her fingers. "He didn't feel I'd be a fitting mother should we ever have kids."

Ginger shoved her food about her plate. "I'm sorry, Mama." But in a small way, she understood Mr. Fox.

"I was pretty messed up. Started having nightmares of you trapped in all sorts of fires. Only I couldn't rescue you. I'd wake up in a panic, trembling like a pup in a rainstorm."

"Where was I? How did I not know this?"

"You were sixteen, trying to figure out life for yourself. Wasn't fitting for me to dump my burden on you."

"But we were supposed to be the Gilmore Girls. Best friends and all." A bit of the sarcasm she loathed coated her response.

"Don't be impertinent, Ginger. Anyway, that's when we started attending church."

"And you hooked up with Pastor Wells?"

"I did not *hook up*. I started wondering if this God business was what I needed. *We* needed. I had a few questions and

A Brush with Love

Pastor Wells agreed to meet with me. We discovered we both liked nature and art. He lent me a book on John Audubon. I showed him a few of my sketches. I started attending the women's Bible Study on Tuesdays before work and I started stopping by his office before I left." Mama lifted her gaze. "He was so kind, you know? Actually listened to me. No man, not even Parker Fox, ever really listened to me before."

"So you had an affair? With a married man of God?" Ginger shuddered. Having experienced fire, she had a deathly fear of hell. And of the God, if He existed, who claimed He could send her there. Real or imagined, she tried to avoid ticking God off at all costs. So messing with His men was way off limits.

Another reason to avoid Tom Wells Jr.

"We didn't have an affair." Mama snatched up her glass of sweet tea, taking a big gulp. "But I was falling for him. Found myself thinking of him all the time." She pressed her hand over her heart. "He started living in here more than he should. I was falling in love . . . So I told someone."

"Who?"

"The leader of the women's Bible study, Janelle Holden."

Ginger had some experience with church women in the shop. Having a crush on the pastor was a big, fat no-no.

"Why would you tell *her*? Why not Aunt Carol or your buddy, Kathleen?"

"Because Janelle said she was there to help us, to guide us to Jesus. Ha, what a crock. She went from friend to foe before I even got to the end of my first sentence. Next thing I know

I'm sitting before an elder board, confessing the whole story without a moment to defend Tom or speak to him privately. He didn't really do anything, Ginger. He was just sweet and nice. Maybe too sweet and nice. I don't know why they made him leave, but boy howdy, I wasn't surprised when I found out Robert Holden was the new pastor." Mama sighed. "I was so stupid and naive. At thirty-seven to boot. I was thinking I'd like to be saved, give Jesus a chance to straighten me out. Maybe He'd be able to lend you a hand too."

"Well, falling in love with a married preacher isn't the way to get straightened out. Did he say he loved you?"

"No, never." Mama's eyes swam as she rolled her gaze toward the popcorn ceiling. "But he showed signs of being interested. I thought he might have feelings for me."

"Mama, he was *married*."

"Ginger, for crying out loud, I know." Mama slammed her glass down on the counter. "You think I wanted to fall in love with an unavailable man? Even if he became available, there'd be scandal and gossip, but I was . . ."

"Hoping?"

"Yes," she glared down at Ginger. "And what of it? Don't I have the right to a good man? One who cares, listens, understands?"

"Not when he's married to another woman. How did I not know about this? How was it not all over school? One of the most popular boys, a football star, upped and disappeared at the beginning of his senior year and no one came at me?"

"I agreed to keep quiet if they agreed to keep my name out of it for your sake. Everyone seemed more twisted up about Tom Senior and what was going on in his life than about me. I'm sure Janelle was all ready to blab if Tom didn't step down and leave. She didn't care about me. She cared about getting Tom out and her husband in."

"Then he must have had feelings for you. I mean, to leave the way he did."

"I don't know. We never spoke again. But I heard there were other issues with the church, with his wife, and I was the icing on the cake." Mama shrugged, swirling her tea, the ice clinking against the sides. "Who knows what's really true?"

"So that's why we never went to church again?"

"I figured they'd brand me with a scarlet *A* or something." She shook her head. "And I was pretty sure God didn't want to see the woman who caused His man to resign his church."

"Were you at least sorry?"

"Sorry? I was confused. And poor Tom. It seemed like such a brouhaha over something so one-sided."

"Why didn't you tell me? You knew how upset I was by Tom Junior disappearing without a word."

"Because I felt so foolish." She returned to the table, shoving her plate forward, cupping her tea in her hands. "I'd lost my friend Tom and my women's group. I didn't need you loathing me any more than you already did."

"I didn't loathe you."

"Yeah, whatever . . . So, now you know." Mama popped the table with her palm. "Aren't you proud? Oh, who am I kidding? It's just more of the same. Where was I the night of the fire? Where was I half your teen years?"

"Can we not rehash this?" Ginger spent most of her teen years and twenties forgetting the past. Trying to build a future with her handicaps.

"I suppose not. You don't need further proof I failed you."

"Mama." *Sigh.* "You didn't fail me." Ginger wanted her confession to at least sound true even if she didn't believe it. Not entirely.

"Look at you, all scarred on your arm and side, across your back and that sloppy skin graft on your neck. That's what government-funded medical care will get you. And you have a sexy figure. But can you show it off? Wear a nice bikini down to the lake? No—"

"Mama, stop. I don't need an inventory. I see myself every morning in the shower. Can we talk about something else? How's your Moo Goo?"

"Cold." Mama picked up her plate for the microwave. "What's going on with you and Tom Junior?"

"Nothing." A low warmth crept across Ginger's cheeks. At least she had the treasure and memory of his touch.

"Are you sure?" Mama's tone lightened, her words lilting and teasing. "He was mighty handsome as a young man."

"Mama, no, come on." The bit of rice Ginger scooped into her mouth went down sticky and dry. "I'm no more right for him than you were for his daddy. Even if Tom Senior wasn't married, Mama, you never cared about serving your own daughter let alone serving others or being a woman of faith."

"I thought you didn't want to talk about how I failed you."

"I didn't. I don't."

"Look, Ginger, just because I messed up with Tom Senior doesn't mean you can't like his son. If there's something between you, then—"

"Is it seven o'clock already?" Ginger scooted away from the table, downing the last of her tea. "I need to run. The shop's books await."

"Ginger, don't deny your heart."

She snatched up her purse, a Hermès Birkin clutch gifted to her by Tracie. Styling for celebrities had its perks. "I'm not denying my heart. Tom Wells is not for me."

If she said it enough, her heart would believe it.

"Listen to me." Mama grabbed her by the shoulders. The only touch Ginger allowed without flinching. "I ruined things with your daddy because I was young and stubborn."

"He left you, Mama."

"But he wanted to come back and I wouldn't let him. Thought I wanted something better. How did that work out for me? All these years later and I'm alone."

"No, Mama, you're not alone." Ginger drew her into a hug, resting her chin on her shoulder. "You have me."

"And that is a true gift." Mama stepped back, her eyes glistening. "Now go on, get your books done. How's that cute apartment of yours?"

"Good. I like living above the shop."

"Thanks for dinner," Mama said.

"Thanks for the truth."

Ginger made her way down the concrete steps to her car, tossing her bag into the passenger seat, glancing up to the pale light outside Mama's door.

Tonight she'd discovered a few things about her own heart. She appreciated Mama more than she realized.

And she learned to never make the same mistakes. Which meant loving the wrong man. Ginger marked an X on the image of Tom Wells drifting around her soul. He was officially off-limits, no matter how much she yearned for his tender touch.

On Thursday evening, Tom stepped out of the Rosebud *Gazette* office and inhaled the smooth fragrance of an Alabama winter, feeling rather pleased. His interview with Riley Conrad had gone well.

Her questions were thought-provoking and interesting. They laughed and reminisced about Rosebud traditions, recalled old names and faces. Including his father.

"Can you tell me? Did he leave town in disgrace? Did he have an affair?" Riley said.

"No, to both counts. He did have some issues to work out and along with my grandfather and mother's wisdom and support, he resigned his church, took a job in Atlanta, at which he became very successful, and fixed the things he needed to fix in his life. Look, being a pastor doesn't have to be a lifelong call. My father came to the end of that season in his life."

"But it took an outside situation to force him to make a change."

"*Doesn't it for almost everyone? You left Rosebud, Riley. Why'd you come back?*"

She gave him a wicked grin. "Outside situation."

Tom paused on the corner of Main and Alabaster, the glow of a street lamp on his shoulders. Riley's piece would be this Sunday morning's feature and hopefully inspire Rosebud's citizens to check out Encounter Church.

So, now what? Tom glanced left where Alabaster curved around into Park Avenue, ending at Mead Park. To his right was Main Street and downtown.

He'd parked his car in front of Sassy's Burgers, where he'd eaten every night this week. Most of the shops were open late on Thursday and their golden light fell across the sidewalk in large squares.

Including Ginger Snips. The main window glowed with a string of white lights. Was she there? It was after seven. Tom brushed his hand over his slightly gelled hair, wishing he needed a trim. Wishing he had an excuse to stop by the shop.

But did he need one? Couldn't he pop in to say hi? He'd told Ginger he wanted to be friends.

He stepped off the curb, ducking in front of a car turning left, and took long strides to Ginger Snips before he changed his mind.

He found the front door open, paint fumes scenting the breeze.

"Well, looky what the cat dragged in again." Ruby-Jane spotted him. Tom took a cautious step over the threshold. "What brings you here on a Thursday evening, *pastor*?"

"I was down—" He paused when Ginger emerged from the back room with a paint tray and a bucket swinging from her hand, "—at the *Gazette*."

She stopped when she saw him. "Tom, what are you doing here?"

"Just saying hi. So, y'all are painting tonight?"

Ruby-Jane huffed, folding her arms. "That's what she tells me. Of course the other two, Michele and Casey, get a pass."

"Leave it alone, RJ. You know why."

"Still doesn't seem fair. Just because they have families."

Ginger set her tray down without a word or a backward glance. "We can waste time talking about it or get to work and be done with it."

Tom slipped off his jacket and draped it over the nearest chair. "Can I help?"

"No," Ginger said. "We only have two roller brushes."

Ruby-Jane shot him a sly smile. "No worry. He can have mine."

"No, he can't." Ginger rose up, steel in her words, a hard glint in her eyes. "Stop yapping and start working." She peeked at Tom. "Word of advice. Don't hire your friends to work for you."

"Duly noted." He nodded, trying to hold her gaze. *You okay?* The recessed light dripping down from the ceiling haloed her chestnut hair and reflected in her hazel eyes.

She was breathtaking. But he couldn't see her for himself, could he? He had to see her as God's daughter. Pop's advice from before the wedding had been coming back to him all week, "If you love her, win her to Jesus," along with the whisper of the Lord, "Tell her she's beautiful."

"I meant it," he said. "I can help."

"It's okay, Tom." Ginger hoisted the big paint can, sloshing some over the side as she filled the tray. "We got it."

Tom stepped over, reaching for the handle as she tried to set it down without hitting the corner of the tray.

His fingers grazed hers. When he looked at her, she was looking at him. His pulse drummed in his ears. "Y-you can let go."

She hesitated. Then, "Ruby-Jane and I are perfectly capable of doing the job."

"I never said you weren't. But many hands make light work."

"Hey, Ging," Ruby-Jane said, walking over to Tom, offering him her roller. "I need to run. Daddy just called and Mama's made a big ole spread for the entire family." RJ held up her phone as if to prove her story. "Apparently my brother just drove into town . . . So, y'all two got this?"

"What brother? *All* your people live in town." Ginger rebuffed Ruby-Jane with a stiff lip and a firm jut of her chin. "RJ, you *can't* leave."

"Family first. Besides, I'm on salary, not an indentured servant. Tom, I hereby dub you my replacement." Tom reached for the long handle. "Do me proud." Ruby-Jane edged toward the back door. "See you in the morning, Ginger."

"RJ? RJ, wait." Ginger chased her to the back room but to no avail. When she returned, she took up her roller and slapped it against the wall, mumbling, ". . . brother who just drove into town, my eye."

"She seems to think we should spend some alone time together."

Ginger rolled, rolled, rolled on the paint. "I had enough of you last weekend, no offense."

"None taken. Now, where can I power up some tunes? Let's get this place painted and beautiful."

Chapter 9
♡

SHE WANTED TO BE INDIFFERENT. TAKE HIM OR LEAVE him. Forget Tom Wells was in her shop, singing along with the music from his iPhone piped into the shop through the sound system.

She just wanted to paint, get the job done, go up to her apartment and cleanse her senses of any reference to Tom's soapy scent.

"How's it looking?" Tom pointed to his cut-in work at the top of the wall, just under the ceiling.

"Great." She gave him a thumbs up, then went back to her portion of the wall.

Actually, he irritated her. Why was he here? What did he want with her? Why did he volunteer to do the neck-breaking cut-in work, even borrowing a ladder from Fred's Grocer across the street, to do the job?

And the music? Smooth and soothing, raining down peace in the shop, watering her soul.

"*. . . you're beautiful,*" Tom sang softly with the music, to himself.

Ginger pressed her roller against the wall, squeezing out the last of the beige-rose paint.

"*. . . I can tell you've been praying.*"

"Who is this? Singing?"

"Gospel artist, Mali Music."

"Never heard of him."

"Neither had I until a few years ago. He's the real deal. I like him."

Real deal? As opposed to a fake deal? Christians and their language . . . that irritated her most. Their two-faced kindness. Their faux helpfulness. Since her discovery of truth with Mama, Ginger had grown a pound of sympathy for her mother. Shana had tried to get it right, to be honest.

Tom's low, silky bass swirled through her, leaving her with the same sensation as his touch. Squirming, squeezing his vocal notes out of her soul, Ginger glanced up at him as he cut-in under the ceiling. A singing, kind, handsome pastor? Look out. He'd have women all over him.

Desperate ones like Mama who'd surrender their hearts if he'd ease a bit of their pain.

"So, Sunday," she said, shaking off a strange jealous wave. "You ready?"

"I think so. I've got my sermon in my head. Just need to write out my notes." The beam of his smile went to the bottom of her being and she trapped it there, not willing to let it go. She could create a trio of Tom Wells Jr. treasures—his touch, his voice, his smile.

She would never be with him, but she could remember the one man in her life who made her *feel* what it was like to be a woman.

"And just what do you hope people will encounter at Encounter Church?" She filled her roller brush in the paint tray, then pressed it against the wall, working around the blue tape protecting the trim and window frame.

"God, His emotions toward us. I hope they find love and friendship with each other." He laughed low. "Maybe a good potluck dinner now and then."

"God has emotions?"

"Absolutely. Love, peace, joy. God *is* love, First John tells us." He gazed down at her. "Love's an emotion, right? God created us with emotions. Why wouldn't He have them Himself?"

"Because emotions can be manipulated. Go bad . . ."

"Ah yes, if you're a human. But God has perfect emotions. Don't you think it's kind of cool God feels love or delight in you?"

"Me?" Ha, ha, now he talked crazy.

"Yes, you." Tom came down the ladder and toward her. "He loves you. He also likes you."

"You don't know any such thing." His gaze, the intensity of his words, set her heart on fire. "I prayed once. It didn't go well."

"Wimp."

"Excuse me?"

"You prayed once and gave up? Is that how you became the stylist to the stars? By giving up the first time 'it didn't go well'?" He took the roller from her hand and rested it against the paint tray. Then he moved over to his iPhone and started the song again. "Follow me." He led her to the center of the shop and took her in his arms, resting his hand against the small of her back.

As the music played, he turned her in a slow, swaying circle, singing softly in her ear.

. . . you're beautiful.

For a moment, she was enraptured, completely caught up in the swirl of being in his arms and the velvet texture of his voice slipping through her. But only for a moment.

"Tom, stop fooling around." She pushed away from his warmth and into the cold space of the shop. "Don't be singing about how I'm beautiful."

"But you are."

"Don't you understand?" She gritted her teeth and tightened her hands into fists about her ears. She jerked off her scarf and gathered her hair on top of her head, exposing the botched skin graft. "Beautiful, huh?"

"Yes." He stepped toward her, hand outstretched.

But she backed away. "And this?" She turned her back to him, raised the lower hem of her top, and exposed the crimped, rough skin of her back and right side. "It's disgusting. And not desirable. So don't come up in here singing, 'you're beautiful' when it's not true."

"Who told you it's not true?"

"Me. My bathroom mirror. The men Mama dated when I was a teenager. 'Too bad about all those scars, Shana, she might have been a real looker.'"

"Most people don't see your scars. You cover them up. Just because a few foolish, lustful men projected their idea of beauty on you, you accept it? Ever think those scars protected you? Kept you from predators?"

"Also from nice men like you who might have been my high school boyfriend or taken me to the prom."

"I like your scars."

She reached down for her roller. "Now you're just being mean."

"I like that they've made you a fighter. I like your face, your eyes, your smile, your heart. I love your ability to see beauty in others and bring it out for the rest of us to see. Those are the things that make you beautiful and extraordinary."

Eyes flooding, she rolled paint onto the wall, her back to Tom. "You'd better get back to work or we'll be here all night."

"But first . . ." He rested his hand against her shoulder and turned her to him. "Tell me you're beautiful."

She refused, eyes averted, unable to contain her tears. In her ears, her pulse roared.

"Ginger." He touched her chin, turned her attention to him. "Say it. It's the first road to healing. You are beautiful."

"I'm not your project, Tom."

"Agreed. But you are my friend. And I hate to see my friends believe lies about themselves."

"I believe what's true."

"Then say it. 'I'm beautiful.'"

She dropped her roller brush and crossed the room. "You're infuriating. Why do you care? I'm the daughter of the woman who helped ruin your father's ministry. I asked her about it, by the way, and she confessed. She loved your father but nothing happened between them."

"That doesn't disqualify you from God's love, from my friendship, or from admitting you're beautiful."

"Tell that to Edward. What would he say if he saw you in here, with me?"

"Edward isn't my God or my conscience. My father and family have moved on, Ginger. Seems your mama has moved on, too. But you're stuck as the trailer fire girl. So let's put a big bucket of water on that fire by confessing your beauty."

Stuck. Isn't that what she confessed Saturday morning, standing in the muddy meadow? But she'd never give Tom the satisfaction. Ginger gestured toward the door, willing him to go and leave her be. "You can go, Tom."

"Not unless you say it." He didn't respect her space at all. He came up to her and swept his fingers over the scar on her neck. Ginger nearly buckled at his touch.

"Why do you want me to say it?" Her voice wilted as she spoke.

"Because I want you to combat the lie in your heart with truth."

"If you get the burned girl to say she's pretty, do you earn a gold star from God?"

"Man, are you really so cynical? Ginger, I like you. I always have and I've always seen a beautiful woman—"

"Who allowed himself to be intimidated by his friends?" She used the courage he admired to push back.

"I was seventeen. Give me credit for maturing a little." He walked to the front door, flung it open. "You want me to defend you to Edward Frizz? To Rosebud?" He ran into the middle of Main Street. "Hey Rosebud, Alabama—"

Ginger dashed to the door. "Tom, no, what are you doing?"

Arms wide, head back, Tom shouted, "Ginger Winters is a beautiful woman. And I don't care about her scars! I don't care what her mama—"

"Oh my word, stop. Get in here." Ginger steamed into the middle of the street, hooked him by the arm, and dragged him to the shop. "You're making a fool of me."

"You? I was the one doing the shouting."

"You are so infuriating. I don't get this. Why does any of this matter to you?"

"Remember the end of the movie *The Proposal*? Drew says to Margaret, 'Marry me because I'd like to date you.'"

"Y-yes . . ."

"I'd like you to believe the truth about yourself, so then maybe, if you decide you can give Jesus a try, you'll let Him in, and see yourself as you really are from His perspective, incredibly beautiful."

"What does that have to do with the movie?"

"Because, then, if you'd have me, I'd like to date you."

Her tears spilled. "I can't risk my heart with you. With

God." What was she doing before he started all this beautiful nonsense? Oh yes, painting. Ginger picked up the paint tray. "I think you should go."

"Say it. 'I'm beautiful.'"

"I'm not playing, Tom. Go." She walked to the back room, trembling, with barely enough strength to hold herself upright.

"Will you come to church on Sunday? Please."

"I said, go, Tom, just go."

She hid in the dark corner until she heard his footsteps echoing across the shop, then fading away out the front door.

Slowly she sank to the floor, cradling her face against the top of her knees, running her hand over her scars.

Horrid. Ugly. The opposite of beautiful. She'd cried oceans of tears mourning that reality, and no one—not God or Tom Wells Jr.—could ever convince her otherwise.

Chapter 10

♡

ON SUNDAY MORNING, TOM SAT IN THE OLD PARSONAGE parlor, sunlight streaming through the window, praying through the swirl of excitement and peace in his soul.

First Sunday morning in his own church. He never, ever thought this would be his reality, his passion, but at the moment he knew he was in the right place at the right time.

For such a time as this.

His sermon was ready. His notes typed into his iPad. Alisha had the worship band prepped, arriving at nine for their pre-service rehearsal. Above all, his heart was ready.

If it was only Tom, the band, and the Holy Spirit who showed, Tom would consider the day a huge success.

If Ginger showed, he'd mark his first Sunday with a miracle.

He'd thought about her all weekend, prayed for her, for himself. Had he crossed lines, demanding she declare she was beautiful? Was it too intimate? Too romantic when he had no freedom to pursue her?

It was one thing for a believing man to have affection for a nonbelieving woman. It was another thing entirely to woo her heart, defraud her, then brush her aside.

He didn't want to be that man.

If he was going to pastor this church, he had to find a wife who believed. Who could run this race with him.

He didn't care if she played the piano, led a Bible study, or managed the women's ministry. But he cared for her to be surrendered in wholehearted love to Jesus. To kick Tom's butt when he needed it.

Lord, here's my heart. My thoughts of Ginger. Have it all.

The mantel clock that came with the house ticked eight-thirty. Tom rocked out of the chair, taking his iPad from the side table. Might as well walk over to the church, get things powered up and going.

He was about to exit out the kitchen door when a loud knock sounded from the front. When he opened it, Edward stood on the other side.

"Did you see this?" He held up the Sunday *Gazette* and barged into the parsonage.

"No, not yet. I was going to read it after church."

"What in the world did you tell her?" Edward crossed into the parlor, popping open the paper and holding up the front page for Tom to see.

The Tale of Two Pastors

How Will Rosebud Fare with a Third
Generation Wells Preacher?

By Riley Conrad

Tom snapped the paper from Edward. "How will Rosebud fare? What is she talking about? We discussed the church, how and why I came back to Rosebud, what I hoped to accomplish."

"Clearly she doesn't want another church in this town. Especially one headed by a Wells man. I ask again, what did you tell her?"

"Nothing."

"Doesn't read like nothing. She exposes the whole scandal." Edward walked toward the kitchen. "Got any coffee?"

"Yeah, sure, use the Keurig." Tom dropped to the rocker, iPad tucked under his arm, anxiety mounting.

Tom Wells Jr. is in Rosebud, seeking a flock of his own. With the American church becoming more of a consumer than a provider of spiritual insight, one has to wonder if he isn't one of the many up-and-coming young pastors with charm and good looks aiming to do nothing but build his own kingdom on the backs and with the pockets of the Rosebud faithful.

"This is an opinion piece."

Edward returned, mug in hand, blowing on his coffee. "Yep."

A bit of backstory. Wells is the grandson of well-known, popular evangelist Porter Wells, who traveled the country holding tent revivals for twenty years

before taking his message international. He eventually returned to the States to continue his ministry in large churches and on television.

The elder Wells retired back to Rosebud in the middle 2000s. His son, Tom Wells Sr., followed in his footsteps, planting a church in Rosebud and building the congregation to more than two thousand people before scandal routed him out twelve years ago.

What scandal? An affair. Not of the obvious kind but the emotional kind, which some declare more devastating than a physical affair. Pastor Wells spent too much time with a woman in need. Feeling defrauded, she confessed her feelings to a trusted friend who reported the misbehavior to the church elders and leaders.

The Wellses left town in a shroud of mystery, leaving nothing behind but questions and wounded hearts. My grandmother was one of the disappointed and questioning faithful. What happened to our beloved pastor?

Tom lowered the paper and sighed. "She's taken up her grandmother's offense."

"It's an opinion piece, bro. Of course she's got an agenda."

"I want a rebuttal."

Edward's countenance darkened. "My advice? Leave this be. The more you make of it, the more you fan the flames. Keep reading."

But he didn't want to keep reading. He wanted to toss the paper aside and go back to his place of contentment and contemplation. He wanted his heart to be soft for worship and the Word.

But he needed to know what preconceived notions would arrive with the congregants this morning.

The truth of the story was buried since the Wellses left town so quickly, literally in the cover of night, the congregation being told only that Wells had an extraordinary opportunity in Atlanta and felt "the Lord wanted him to take it."

So the lies compounded. Rosebud rumors suggested Wells had an affair, but with whom? When? Above all, why?

Maybe he took "love your neighbor as yourself" a bit too literally.

When I realized his son was back in town, I wanted to know the rest of the story. So I did some digging. Who was the woman in the center of the Wells scandal? Why hadn't the complete story ever been told?

I found a lead with a former church member, Janelle Holden.

"I was leading the women's ministry when one of the newer members, Shana Winters, confessed to me rather out of the blue that she was in love with Pastor Wells. That he'd been counseling her, helping her, befriending her."

According to Holden, Wells admitted to counseling Winters, whose daughter Ginger Winters owns Ginger Snips, a local salon, and was tragically scarred in a trailer fire at the age of twelve.

The senior Wells denied having an affair of any kind, but when the church board called an inquiry, he did admit to an emotional connection with Winters that went beyond propriety.

So, he abandoned his flock and fled town. Are you following my case here?

Twelve years Rosebud has rested, free from charlatans using the "Word of God" to dupe the weak and the willing.

Enough. Tom slapped the paper into Edward's open palm. "This will humiliate Ginger. She'll probably never darken the sanctuary doors now."

"Were you hoping she would?"

"Yes, Edward, I was because she needs Jesus. Frankly, I'm thinking you need a good dose of the Spirit yourself." Tom started for the door. "By the way, Ed, yeah, really, *her*. She's gorgeous, smart, caring and yeah, a bit physically flawed, but I'd take her over some . . . beauty queen any day." Tom slammed the door behind him.

"Tom!" Edward called after him. "Think of your career . . ."

But he kept on walking toward the church, the nine o'clock bells ringing for the first time in over two decades, waking up the community, waking up Tom's heart.

Come, take up your cross, and follow Me.

Ginger woke to the sound of church bells. But they didn't sound like they emanated from Bridge Street Baptist. These chimes were older, distant, coming from the west.

Climbing out of bed, she opened her front window, letting in the crisp, pristine breeze as she peered down onto Main.

You're beautiful.

Tom's voice had moved into her head and no amount of shop hustle and bustle, Tracie Blue music, or back-to-back movies on the Hallmark Channel could get him out.

You're beautiful.

Then Friday afternoon Mrs. Davenport caught her attention in the mirror as she styled her hair. "What's going on with you, Ginger? You look *different*. You're positively glowing."

You're beautiful. Then the melody of the song from Bridgett's wedding crashed over her. *"You make me brave!"*

Now she leaned against the screen, remembering, and inhaled the fragrance of the January morn as the bells chimed, seven, eight, nine.

Could she be brave? Go to church? She always said she'd go if someone invited her. Technically, Tom had invited her.

Ginger hesitated. She liked her Sunday morning routine—a latte and muffin while reading the Sunday *Gazette*. But if she hurried, she could have her breakfast, skim the paper, and still make it to the morning service.

She closed her eyes. *Do it. Don't think.* Dashing for the shower, she actually let herself meditate on the pleasure of seeing Tom Wells again.

You're beautiful.

Peeling off her nightshirt, Ginger examined her familiar wounds, trying to see them with new eyes. She stared at her reflection.

"Y-you're beau—" She choked. It wasn't true. "Ginger, say it." She heard Tom's truth in her own voice. "Y-you are . . . you are . . ." She leaned toward the mirror. "B-beautiful."

A quick wind swept through her apartment. Through her soul.

"Ginger, you are"—she raised her voice—"Beautiful."

The wind swirled around her again.

"Ginger!" She yelled, arms raised. "You are beautiful!"

Joy in the form of tears ran down her cheeks, somehow watering all the dry, barren places where truth had not flowered in a long time. If ever.

"Ginger Winters, you are beautiful!"

Chapter 11

♡

TOM DID HIS BEST TO FOCUS ON THE MUSIC, THE SONGS, and worshipping his Lord, but felt the pressure of his inaugural Sunday morning. Along with the humiliation of bad press.

Alisha, God love her, curled her lip at the article. "Who cares? Is it true? No. Let God defend you, Tom."

Her confidence stirred his.

Now, as Alisha brought worship to an end, Tom prepared to take the pulpit. He'd not looked over his shoulder for the entire worship set so he had no idea if one or a hundred people filled the old, wooden pews.

In truth, he wanted to see one face. Well, two. Pop's and Ginger's. Mostly Ginger's. He needed to know she was okay. That the article hadn't stirred up bad memories.

The last note rang out from the keyboard and Alisha nodded to Tom. Go time. Up the platform steps, he faced the sanctuary and his heart soared.

The place was full. To the brim. Standing room only.

"Good morning. Welcome to Encounter—"

"Is it true?" A woman in the second row rose to her feet. "Your father nearly had an affair?"

Tom recognized her from the old days. Shutting off his iPad, he came around the pulpit, his eyes drifting over the people. "Is that why you all are here?"

Heads bobbed. Voices assented.

The heat of confrontation beaded along his brow. "Then let's just get it all out on the table. Some of the article is true. Dad had an inappropriate amount of affection for Shana Winters." In the back, the sanctuary doors opened and Tom halted, a cold dread slipping down his back as Ginger eased inside.

No, no, not today. But it was too late to reverse rudder and preach his prepared message. To pretend the article never appeared.

He caught her gaze and she smiled, offering a small wave before accepting a seat in the last row from an older gentleman.

She looked . . . different. Radiant.

"Riley Conrad," he said, "gave us her opinion about me and my family. She also dragged out the names of fellow, private citizens. I won't speak for them but I can promise you my devotion to Jesus is greater than my devotion to any of you. Than to this ministry. If the Lord said, 'Shut it down tomorrow,' I'd do it. I've already been a rebel, the resentful, bitter son of a preacher and by the grace of God, I don't care to go back. Come to Encounter Church if you want to encounter God's love for you. If you want to love others. If you want to share life and the Gospel with the Rosebud community. Don't come here if you're looking to gain something for yourself. If you have any sort of agenda. Come here if you love or want to love Jesus."

Tom shot a glance toward Ginger, who was on her feet, moving forward. "Can I say something?" Her voice carrying through the crowded sanctuary. Heads turned. Voices murmured.

"Are you sure?" Tom said. He could see her trembling.

"Hey, some of you know me. But for those who don't, I'm Ginger Winters." She held up a copy of the Gazette. "My mama and Tom's dad had a friendship that went too far in my mama's heart. It caused some problems for Reverend Wells, and he chose to leave. He has his reasons, and if you want to know, ask him."

Tom watched, surprised, astounded. Something had happened to Ginger Winters.

"But don't hold what our parents did against Tom here. When we were in high school, and no one wanted to talk to the freaky burned girl, me, he did. This past weekend at a wedding, he treated me like I mattered when others didn't. He made me see that I expected them to treat me that way because that's how I see myself." She smiled up at him. "I guess I was listening."

"Amazing," he said, moving toward her. "Considering I talked way too much."

Ginger faced the congregation again. "He challenged me to believe the truth. That I was, am, beautiful. Scars and all.

He told me Jesus loved me and while I'm not sure what all that means, I'm starting to wonder if this Gospel business isn't exactly what I need. I've never trusted any man with my heart. Shoot, I barely trusted anyone. But I'd trust Tom Wells. With every part of my being." Her voice wavered and watered. "He challenged me to tell myself I was beautiful and this morning, for the first time, I looked into the mirror, saw my hated scars, and told myself I was beautiful. Out loud." Her smile rivaled the sun peeking through the windows. "And for the first time," a bubbly laugh overflowed from within her, "I believe it."

Epilogue

♡

Eight months later . . .

THAT JANUARY DAY IT HAD SNOWED IN ROSEBUD changed Ginger's life in ways she never imagined. Just goes to show, true love causes even the most closed heart to fling wide.

"Okay, the final touch." Ruby-Jane, in her maid of honor dress, a silk tea-length of royal plum, plopped an old, wooden chair next to Ginger and stepped up, holding the rhinestone clips of the Bandeau veil.

"Careful, RJ." Michele raised up on her tiptoes, pensive, wiping a bit of sweat from her brow. "That updo is two hours of work. Don't *undo* it in two seconds."

"As if. You put enough spray in her hair to withstand a hurricane." Ruby-Jane patted the top of Ginger's teased bouffant.

The air conditioner kicked on, humming as it swirled the room with cool air.

"Rubes, careful, please. It might not fall down but it could crack." Ginger cut a glance at Michele, laughing, reaching for her hand. "Thank you. I've not seen it yet but I know your work. I'm sure it's stunning."

"No," Michele smoothed down what must have been a flyaway strand, "*you* are stunning. Ginger, I can't believe how much you've changed. I guess I shouldn't say that but—"

"It's true." Twitters and electric pulses crisscrossed Ginger's middle. She inhaled, her legs trembling, buckling a little as Ruby-Jane settled on the veil.

She had changed. She'd listened to Tom and believed she was beautiful. But it took letting Jesus have her whole heart to truly *get* it. To let the truth settle in and change her identity. Tom walked her through it all. As a friend. Then five months ago, she woke up one morning to realize she was completely in love with him.

A month later, during a pizza and movie night in her apartment, he slipped to one knee, kissed her hand, and proposed. "Will you marry me? Please?"

When he slid the diamond ring on her finger, she let go of her last tear and her heart became aflame with love.

"Yes, Tom, yes. I would love to marry you."

And now on her wedding day, because of love, she was going to expose herself to all.

Though at the moment, she tried to remember what had possessed her to be *so* daring with her gown. A sleeveless, V-neck chiffon Donna Karan. A gift from Tracie Blue.

"There." Ruby-Jane jumped down, sweeping the chair aside. "Oh, Ginger . . ." Her eyes watered as she pressed her fingers over her lips.

"Be honest, please." Ginger swept her gaze from RJ to Michele. "Am I crazy? Do I look ghastly?" She offered up her bare, scarred arm, the gold glitter in the body makeup catching the late afternoon light floating through the window. "Is it too much? The glitter?"

"It's perfect. You are going to blow Tom away."

She touched the skin patch at the base of her neck. The sleeveless gown was a surprise for him. Her gift. "I can live with my arm and back being exposed, but what about this?" She motioned to her neck.

"You're fine, Ginger," Ruby-Jane said. "Don't second-guess yourself now."

She was right. If she was going to be brave, then be brave. Next month, Ginger had an appointment with a renowned plastic surgeon, a friend of her future father-in-law's, who had volunteered his time and skill to repair the botched graft.

But truth was, she'd already met a renowned surgeon. Jesus. Who'd healed the inner wounds no one could see. And all it took was love. His and Tom's.

A sweet laugh escaped her lips.

"What?" RJ said, smiling, leaning in, wanting to join Ginger's joy.

"Nothing." She shook her head, treasuring the moment.

"I'm just happy." Ruby-Jane still insisted God watched from a distance, so any talk of *Him* would spark debate.

"Ready to see what you look like?" Michele turned Ginger toward the full-length mirror.

"Ready." Ginger closed her eyes and followed Michele's leading—one, two, three steps to the right. She'd insisted they get her ready without a mirror. In case she panicked. Believing she was beautiful was still a battle some days.

"Open your eyes."

Ginger inhaled, then opened her eyes on the exhale. The glass was filled with her image, clothed in white, her ombre hair sculpted on top of her head in a retro '60s updo, and gold glitter filling the creases of her scars.

Tears bubbled up.

"Wait, here, for the final look." Ruby-Jane dashed for Ginger's small, wired bouquet of roses and gypsophila. "Perfect, so per—" RJ's voice broke so she finished her thought with a sweet, weepy smile and a nod.

A tender knock echoed from the door. "Ready?" Maggie Boyd peeked inside. She'd returned home from Ireland two months ago, demanding to be Ginger's wedding director.

So much favor came when she accepted love. When she accepted God. And her destiny.

"Ginger, oh, Ginger," Maggie drew a deep breath, wiping her eyes. "We're going to have to pick Tom up off the floor."

"Let's hope so." Ginger grinned, winking. She had a bit of confidence because he'd seen her scars. He'd asked two days ago to see her side and back, so tonight, when they became one, she'd not fear him seeing that part of her for the first time.

He traced his fingers along every jagged, rugged crevasse of her disfigurement, whispering prayers of healing, peace, and joy.

Not only for her body but for her heart.

His tenderness and care, as he ran his hand over the damaged flesh that would become his on their wedding night, along with his weepy, whispered prayers created an emotional exchange between them that nearly overwhelmed Ginger.

She could never doubt God's love for her. She saw it manifested every day in Tom.

Tucked deep in her heart, that odd January day it snowed in Rosebud and Tom had reappeared in her life would always be one of her sweetest treasures.

"Baby, it's four-thirty." Mama popped into the room. "The sanctuary is filled to the brim." She pressed her hands to her cheeks. "I think my heart is about to burst. Ginger, sugar, you are so beautiful." She said it plainly, without stuttering.

Mama was changing too.

Ginger took one last glance in the mirror. She'd chosen a sleeveless gown because she loved it. Because it fit like a glove. Because if she didn't have wounds on her arm and back, this would be her dream dress.

Go for it . . . Tom. Always Tom. The voice of truth and courage.

"Ah, I hear the orchestra, the music is starting." Mama had worked double shifts at a diner after her city day job to earn money for a fifteen-piece orchestra. It was her way of, as she put it, "doing my part."

"RJ, maid of honor, get going." Maggie shoved Ruby-Jane toward the door. "Don't forget this." She snatched a bouquet from the nearby table.

Ruby-Jane's heels thunked against the wide hardwood. "Shifting gears from helping the bride to being maid of honor." She grinned at Ginger. "See you down there."

Michele also slipped out the door, blowing Ginger a kiss. "Going to find Alex and the kids. Go get 'em, Ginger."

"I'm proud of you." A corner tear glistened in Mama's eyes. "And I'm sorry for everything I've done to hurt you."

"Mama, no, no," Ginger soothed away Mama's tears. "Today is my wedding day. A fresh, new start. And you know what, we're going to bury all the junk of the past in the past. You're forgiven. It's all forgotten. From this day forth, we're going to create so many good, *new* memories, Mama." Her own speech made her cry. "Now, are you walking me down the aisle or not?"

"I am, yes, ma'am, I am." Mama snatched a tissue from the box by the mirror, the folds of her chocolate trumpet chiffon skirt with the lace bodice and ruffle beading flowing about her legs. "I'm sorry your daddy didn't see his way clear to make it."

"Last apology, Mama. That's on him. I still love him. It's just, well, life doesn't always turn out like we hoped but—"

Mama traced Ginger's arm. "We find ways to make it our own kind of beautiful."

"All right, I hate to break up the love fest but the orchestra is a minute into 'Unchained Melody' and we've only got another minute and a half so if you want to walk down the aisle I suggest you get a move on." Maggie gestured toward the door.

Mama offered Ginger her arm and together, they made their way to the sanctuary doors, Ginger's heart palpitating with electric excitement.

The ushers pulled the doors wide at Maggie's command. Ginger rounded to the entrance, catching her breath to see her handsome groom at the altar, waiting for her.

Mama trembled slightly as she escorted Ginger down the aisle. All eyes were on her now. Seeing her scars. What were they thinking? That she was hideous? Crazy for exposing herself? The thought shot a bolt of panic through her.

Then she saw Bridgett and Eric, their faces like beacons among the sea of guests. Smiling, Bridgett clasped her hands together in a "victory" pose. Eric gave her a vigorous thumbs-up.

Maybe, just maybe, she could join the bold and the beautiful.

Ginger continued down the aisle, shifting her gaze from the people to her groom. The man she loved so deeply and desperately. What did it matter what the guests thought? His opinion was the only one that mattered.

She met Tom's glistening gaze. He approved, she could tell by his expression and his trembling chin.

By the time she arrived at the end of the aisle and the

music faded, the sanctuary echoed with feminine sniffles and masculine throat-clearing.

Tom's cheeks glistened. "Hey, babe . . ."

"Hey . . ."

Then Pop, who was officiating, stepped up and asked, "Who gives this woman to be married?"

"Yours truly," Mama said, placing Ginger's hand in Tom's. "I mean it now . . . I said it once, I'll say it again, you take care of my girl."

"Always, Shana. Always."

Taking Ginger's right arm, she expected Tom to lead her up the altar steps but instead he faced the guests.

"I didn't plan this but my heart is about to burst. I'm so proud of my beautiful bride . . . the bravest person I know. A year ago, she hid her scars beneath long sleeves and scarves. Even on the hottest summer days. But today, she—" His voice faltered. "I told you, babe, you are so beautiful."

Then the guests, one by one, rose up, applauding.

Tom's glistening blue eyes locked onto hers. "Ginger, I am so honored to be your husband."

"Husband?" She made a face, grinning. "Not yet. You better walk me up those steps to your Pop and get this thing going. Because I want to kiss you."

Tom laughed low. "Then by all means."

He walked her up the altar steps to Pop and she peered sideways at him. "You know I love you, Tom Wells."

"You know I love you, Ginger Winters."

Pop led them through their vows and when he'd pronounced them man and wife, Tom drew Ginger to him, his right hand about her waist, his left hand on her scarred arm, and he kissed her with passion, sealing their vows with the sweet brush of love.

Love in the Details
♡

BECKY WADE

For the One who makes all things
possible, even novellas.
Thank you for entrusting me with this ministry and
for equipping me to write each and every page.

Prologue

♡

Josh,

Since I broke up with you, I can't stop crying. Can you please forgive me? I love you. I'm certain I'll always love you.

Today would have been our eight-month anniversary. When you left for MIT a month and a half ago, I never imagined that we wouldn't keep dating or that I wouldn't see you again at Thanksgiving. The long-distance thing has been miserable but our marathon phone calls and our back-and-forth emails throughout the days were getting me by.

Now I've lost all of it, and I'm heartbroken without you.

Here's what you don't know and what I can't tell you. Your mom came to see me. She drove to UT San Antonio, met me in my freshman dorm room, and took me to lunch. She cried, Josh. She cried because she's so upset over the fact that you're unhappy at MIT. She said you told her that you wanted to leave and come back to Texas to be near me.

She's a single mom and you're her only son and she loves you. My heart went out to her.

You've worked so hard. You're a genius and you've earned the financial aid scholarship that MIT offered you. Please understand I don't want anything to get in the way of that, especially me. You deserve to go there and you have to make the most of this opportunity because your mom can't afford to pay for you to go to college anywhere else.

She held my hands and, with tears streaming down her face, asked me if I'd break up with you. She said that so long as we were dating, you wouldn't be able to pour your whole focus and determination into your education. She said you'd always be torn between two places.

Maybe I should have stood up to her and refused to break up with you. Maybe I should have told you about my meeting with her, even though she begged me not to.

Your mom has always been wonderful to me, Josh. I respect her and I care about her and I couldn't turn her down. So I called you and ended our relationship without giving you any good reason other than that my feelings had changed and that I wanted to be free to date here at UTSA.

My feelings haven't changed, Josh. I don't want to date anyone but you. And I can't stand the fact that I let you think otherwise. Since our breakup, I haven't taken your phone calls and I haven't returned your emails and I won't mail this letter. But it's not because I don't love you. And that's why I can't stop crying.

You might not know it yet but you're going to do great things.

I know it. I love you. And I'm very, very, very sorry for hurting you. Can you ever forgive me?

> With all my heart,
>
> Holly

Chapter 1

♡

THE MOMENT HOLLY HAD IMAGINED, DREADED, AND obsessed over had arrived. Josh Bowen—oh, my goodness it really was him, *Josh*, um, holy smoke!—was walking toward her down Martinsburg's Main Street sidewalk. Josh had returned to town temporarily, and thus, she was about to come face-to-face with her high school boyfriend for the first time in eight years.

Holly came to a halt, sensing the coffee inside the three to-go cups in the cardboard tray she held sloshing at the suddenness of her movement. Her heartbeat sped into nervous panic mode.

He hadn't spotted her yet. She could dash into the candy shop and hide. Or maybe the children's boutique . . . Only, she'd known for some time that Josh planned to visit Martinsburg, Texas, for Ben and Amanda's wedding. She'd been giving herself pep talks about this very moment, steeling herself to confront him again, practicing, even, what she would say. She shouldn't hide. She should deal with this, with him.

Thank God, she'd actually taken a bit of time on her appearance this morning. While her jeans, white top, and well-worn-in brown leather jacket weren't what she'd have picked for this reunion, they were decent enough.

Josh.

He looked much like he had at eighteen, except taller, his facial features less soft, his whole bearing more international. He no longer dressed like a graduating senior from a small-town Texas high school. In a navy pea coat open down the front, gray sweater, and flat-front charcoal pants, he gave off a hip and urban vibe. He *was* hip and urban now. Since she'd seen him last, Josh had leveraged his brilliance into a ridiculously successful tech company and moved overseas.

A piquant mixture of sweet memories and bitter heartache rose within her.

He glanced at something in a store window, giving her a view of his clean-lined profile. Then he turned his face forward and his attention intersected with her squarely. His expression went blank. His stride faltered.

Oh, boy. Holly attempted a pleasant smile. God had been merciful to her by allowing her to see him first, at least.

Josh seemed to recover himself and continued toward her at a slower pace.

A good number of people, mostly tourists, strolled the sidewalk. At a quarter past ten in the morning on this third day of November, many of the shops on Main had just opened for the day.

Holly stepped to the side, close to a section of brick in

between two storefronts. Here, they could say hello to one another without blocking traffic like a boulder in the middle of a stream.

Josh came to a stop facing her.

She could hyperventilate, say something, or run. She chose the second option. "Welcome back."

"Thank you."

"It's good to see you again." The intimacy they'd once shared had been as enormous as China. In the face of that, her paltry sentence felt as small as Luxembourg.

His brown eyes assessed her with a tiger-like intensity that caused all the things she'd planned to say to slide out of her brain. There was something in those eyes that hadn't been there before. A shadow. A shadow of guardedness and hostility.

What had she expected? They'd loved each other once. Then, without warning or explanation, she'd shut him out of her life.

"Ben told me that you were planning to come to Martinsburg early for his wedding," Holly said.

"Yes."

Josh and Ben had met in the ninth grade, become best friends, and remained close. Ben's dad had never been a part of his life, and Ben's mom had always been overstressed and cash-strapped. Holly couldn't imagine her handling any mother-of-the-groom responsibilities for Ben's wedding. None.

So Josh had relocated to Texas from now until Ben's Thanksgiving weekend wedding so that he could give his friend the kind of support that counted. Ben had told Holly that Josh had taken over the planning and the funding for both the rehearsal dinner and the bachelor party weekend. Based on the Josh she'd known, his show of generosity and loyalty did not surprise her. "It's nice of you to make the effort to be here for Ben."

No affirmative reply.

"I'm Trinity Church's volunteer wedding coordinator. Since Amanda and Ben have decided to get married at Trinity, I'll be working with Amanda's professional wedding coordinator behind the scenes, representing the church . . . Anyway, I'll be helping out on Ben and Amanda's big day."

His tiger eyes continued to assess her with such absorbed concentration that her mouth went dry. Wrongly, her heart seemed to be gaining speed instead of steadying.

She bit the inside of her lip to keep herself from babbling about the wedding or—at all costs—from blurting out that she was sorry. These many years later, that's what she most wanted to say to him. It was a sentiment that had often filled the letters she'd written him and never sent, how horribly sorry she was for ruining what they'd had, when what they'd had, she'd realized more and more clearly over time, had been rare and beyond price. "How have you been, Josh? I've heard you've done very well."

"I've been okay," he said carefully.

"I'm glad."

"How about you?" He asked it seriously, like he actually cared about the answer.

"Great." She gave him a bright smile. He was super smart. He could probably see through it. It was a smile overly, falsely bright. "I write young adult novels."

"I know."

"You do?"

"Yes."

"I. . . ." How did he know about her novels? "I . . . really love writing. When I'm not on a deadline, or banging my head against my keyboard, or out of ideas. Which is most of the time."

In answer, his lips indented upward on one side. Josh had a face perhaps a bit too angular and a nose perhaps a quarter of an inch too long to be considered classically handsome. His was an arresting face, grave and interesting, appealing to Holly in ways hard to define. His straight dark brown hair had fallen across his forehead when they'd been dating. Now it looked as though he warmed an expensive men's hair product in his palms, parted his hair on the side, then combed it back with his fingers to keep it in place.

Holly held onto her cup tray like a kickboard in a choppy sea. She really hoped her mascara hadn't smudged or that the sip of coffee she'd taken before she'd seen him hadn't left whipped cream on her lip.

"How's your family?" he asked.

"They're all fine. None of them live in Martinsburg anymore. My dad sold his construction business so now he and my mom only stay in their house here a few months of the year. The rest of the time they're at the lake house or their apartment in Austin cuddling Mark's baby—did you know that my brother got married and had a little boy?"

"I did know."

Was Ben filling Josh in about her the way that Ben filled her in about him? "And Jessica's in law school."

He nodded.

"So I'm the only one left in town." She gave a little shrug as if to say, *I'm still living in Martinsburg, despite that my parents, older brother, and younger sister have all moved on. But I really don't mind because I like it here and I'm very content and secure. Very!* "How's your mom?" Josh's father had died when Josh was twelve.

Warmth slightly softened the austerity of his expression. "She lives in Colorado now, near her sister."

"Is she retired?"

"She can retire whenever she wants." Which Holly translated to mean that Josh had set her up in such luxurious style that she'd never have another financial care in her life.

"But she doesn't like to sit still," he continued. "She's working at a charity that helps unemployed women find work."

"That's good to hear." Before Josh's mom had moved, Holly had run into her around town from time to time. Each meeting had filled her with complicated emotions of affection and pain. She didn't blame his mom for asking her to break up with Josh all those years ago. How could you blame a person for advising you to do the right thing, the thing that had become the springboard for all the success Josh had achieved afterward? On the other hand, Josh's mom couldn't have known how very much Holly had loved Josh or how much losing him had devastated her. So, deep in her heart, she couldn't bring herself to hold his mom completely blameless, either. She inhaled, seeking calm, rooting around for another topic of conversation—

"Well." He flicked a few fingers in the direction he'd been walking. "I'd better be going."

"Sure." She didn't allow her disappointment to show as she edged closer to the wall to let him pass. "I'll see you around."

"Bye."

"Bye."

He moved off.

Somewhat dazed, she watched him go.

His steps paused.

She jerked her face toward her tray and made a show of straightening the cups.

"Holly?"

"Hm?" She pretended to be surprised to discover that he hadn't left.

"I'm planning Ben's rehearsal dinner and I need to find a venue. I'm not familiar with Martinsburg anymore. Would you be willing to help me look for a place?"

He was asking *her* for assistance? "Sure."

He produced his phone. "May I have your number?"

She gave it to him.

"Thanks. I'll contact you." He nodded curtly, then strode down the street.

She was going to search for rehearsal dinner venues with Josh?

Because of the wedding and the smallness of Martinsburg, she'd known that she'd cross paths with Josh during his time here. But she'd envisioned their interactions as short and formal. She hadn't expected to spend real time with him. Or share real conversations.

She made her way along the sidewalk in the opposite direction, passing an art gallery, a wine shop, and a women's clothing store before coming to the home furnishings store she lived above. A narrow alley between buildings took her to an exterior staircase. From there, a hallway led to her building's three second-story units. She left Rob's coffee outside his doorway. He worked late every night as a sous chef and typically woke around this time. She knocked quietly on Mrs. Chapel's door. Her elderly neighbor opened the door the width of the inner chain she always kept latched.

"Here you are, Mrs. Chapel." Holly squeezed a cup through.

"Thank you, dear. Did you remember to put in one and a half packets of sugar?"

"I did."

"The cup feels cold."

"Sorry about that. I ran into an old friend on the street. Just zap it in the microwave for thirty seconds."

Mrs. Chapel patted the cup accusingly with arthritic hands. "If you're going out again later, I could use a new pack of Depends."

Holly laughed. "Now Mrs. Chapel, you know I'm just your friendly next door neighbor and coffee delivery girl."

"Fine." The old lady winked sagely at Holly. "I'll guilt one of my daughters into picking up the Depends for me."

"Good plan." Holly dashed around the corner to her door before Mrs. Chapel could ask her to buy Ensure or Vitamin K.

She'd scored the best apartment of the bunch. It overlooked Main and boasted lots of windows and spacious everything: living room, kitchen, bedroom, bathroom. The moment she set aside her tray, she dug her phone from her purse and texted her girlfriend, Sam Sullivan. Lunch today, 12, Taqueria.

Josh continued along Main Street until he was sure he'd left Holly far behind him, then ducked blindly into a store. One sweeping view of the place told him that the shop sold Texas nuts.

The middle-aged woman behind the counter caught his eye. "Welcome. May I help you?"

"I'll take whatever's most popular." He hadn't come in for pecans. He just needed a few minutes of privacy.

"Certainly. Our hickory smoked trail mix is our most popular item."

"Fine."

She held up an empty sack. "Two-pound bag all right?"

"Yes."

Josh took up a position near the front window, his back toward the shop, his shoulder set heavily against the side wall.

There was a reason he'd avoided returning to Martinsburg.

And his reason had the most infuriatingly beautiful gray-blue eyes.

He'd spent his college summers taking courses and working close to the MIT campus. For the most part, his mom had come to visit him in Massachusetts. The few times he'd stayed in Martinsburg for Christmas, he'd gone to great lengths to make sure he never saw Holly.

Seven months ago, Ben and Amanda had gotten engaged and announced that they'd be marrying in their hometown of Martinsburg, Texas, population 10,000. Shortly afterward, Josh had made plans to return to Martinsburg for the four weeks prior to Ben's wedding. So long as he had his technology with him, he could work away from his home base in Paris for up to a month.

He'd told himself it would be fine. He'd told himself that the thing with Holly had happened in another lifetime. He'd had seven months to get his head straight, to prepare himself.

Seven months hadn't been long enough.

Eight years hadn't been long enough, either.

"Here you are!" The store employee displayed the trail mix like a fine wine. "Our best seller."

"Thanks."

"Would you like to come to the counter for a nut tasting?"

"No. I . . . just need a minute to myself." He gave her a level stare.

"Ah. Okay. I'll have this at the register for you when you're ready."

He scowled back out the front windows.

Holly Morgan. The Holly who'd once been his.

Josh had never done anything halfway. It wasn't in his

makeup. He hadn't done academics halfway in high school or college. He hadn't done his business halfway. He'd always worked like a machine and still did. In fact, part of what had initially fueled him in his career had been his desire to prove to Holly that he was worth something, that she'd made a mistake when she'd cut him loose.

No, he didn't do anything halfway.

Unfortunately for him, he hadn't fallen in love with Holly halfway, either. Theirs had not been a lighthearted romance. They'd kept it pure, but it had also been intense.

Holly had been smart and kind, creative and genuine. She hadn't had the sort of in-your-face, commercial prettiness that had characterized the popular girls in their high school. But to him, she'd been more gorgeous than any woman he'd ever laid eyes on before or since.

When he'd known her, she'd worn her light brown hair straight down her back. Now it fell a few inches longer than her shoulders, layered slightly, wavy, with some shiny dark blonde strands in it. Her thoughtful, heart-shaped face held a sweetness that couldn't be faked. She had great cheekbones and little brackets that formed at the corners of her lips when she smiled.

He'd continued to gain height in college. She hadn't. She stood about six inches shorter than he did now, her build slender but not skinny.

When he'd caught sight of her on the sidewalk just now it had knocked the air from him. He turned his hands palms up and watched the tremor in them. Fisting his fingers, he buried his hands in his coat pockets.

He'd lost two people in his life that he'd never recovered from. His dad and Holly. There hadn't been a day that had gone by that he hadn't thought about them both.

The last time he'd seen Holly, they'd hugged each other in an airport terminal like they never wanted to let go. The departure time for his flight had drawn closer and closer. His mom, who'd already gone through security and was waiting for him at the gate, had started calling his cell phone. He'd held onto Holly for as long he could. When their time had run out and they'd kissed for the final time, his heart had felt like it was breaking clean in two.

He'd looked back at her from the security checkpoint line. At first, she'd given him wobbly smiles and brave waves. The final time he'd looked back, tears had been running down her face.

He'd worked hard to earn his scholarship to MIT, but once he'd arrived there, he'd wanted, desperately, to give it up and return to Holly. Without her, school seemed pointless, his loneliness endless. He'd been certain he'd be able to make a success of himself regardless of which institution issued his degree. He'd wanted to make a success of himself with Holly. But before he could follow through on his desire to leave MIT, she'd broken up with him.

People drifted by on the far side of the shop's window.

Martinsburg had been founded in the Hill Country of central Texas in 1848 by Germans who'd come for economic and religious freedoms. These days, tourists were drawn here by the town's old-fashioned charm, surrounding wineries, hunting, wildflower fields, B&Bs, and underground caverns.

Upon arriving two days ago, his strategy had been to limit his interaction with Holly as much as politely possible. But, a few minutes ago, when he'd had the chance to walk away and leave her behind, just as he had in that airport terminal all those years ago, he'd failed. In that instant, he'd wanted some tie to her, some small link. So without thinking it through, all instinct and no logic, he'd asked for her help searching out a rehearsal dinner location.

He shouldn't have done that. She'd shattered him when she'd ended things between them. The memory caused his pride to twist and burn.

It had been unbelievably painful to talk with her this morning, and their conversation had only lasted for a few minutes. Why had he signed himself up for more?

He could cancel. Or go on one outing with her and call it good. Pulling free his phone, he brought her name and number up on his screen.

Holly Morgan.

It shamed him that he still hadn't gotten ahold of himself. He needed more time to recover, standing here in a nut shop.

Seven months. He'd had seven months to prepare himself for his reunion with her.

And it hadn't been long enough.

Chapter 2

♡

"HOLA!" SAM SLID INTO THE BOOTH AT THE TAQUERIA opposite Holly, bringing a light waft of Chloe Eau de Parfum with her. "What's something we can say to one another in honor of this fine Mexican food establishment?"

"Uh, chimichanga?" Holly offered. "La Bamba? I should have taken Spanish in high school, seeing as how I live in a state that borders Mexico. Instead, I took French." Holly scooted the chip bowl toward Sam. "I've never once visited France."

Sam scooped salsa onto a tortilla chip.

Sam and Holly had made it their New Year's resolution to eat at every restaurant in Martinsburg over the course of twelve months. Their town offered a total of one hundred and three restaurants. So far, they'd made it through eighty-seven.

"So?" Sam asked. "Why the urgent summons? It's Tuesday and we weren't supposed to have lunch here 'til Thursday."

"I saw Josh today."

Sam's manicured eyebrows lifted. "As in your high school love Josh?"

"The same."

"High school love turned billionaire Josh?"

"Yes."

"Already arrived in Martinsburg to ride to the rescue of his loyal pal Ben."

Holly nodded.

"Tell me all."

Holly recounted her meeting with Josh, starting with his appearance and ending with his request for her help searching out rehearsal dinner locations.

Sam had the sleek dark hair, oval face, and beautifully pampered skin of a woman born and bred on the East Coast, which, in fact, she had been. She'd married a man Holly affectionately referred to as Mr. Perfect two years ago and moved to Martinsburg when Mr. Perfect's engineering expertise had scored him a job with Martinsburg's largest employer, a clean energy company. Sam worked as a CPA and had chosen a navy pin-striped suit for today's work ensemble.

"He must have it bad for you," Sam said. "Otherwise why ask for your help?"

"He isn't familiar with Martinsburg anymore. Maybe he just needs a local to offer up ideas."

"A man that rich can hire someone to scout locations. Also, how come he hasn't already booked a place for the rehearsal dinner? Amanda and Ben's wedding is what, three and a half weeks away?"

Ben's fiancée, Amanda, was the beloved daughter of Martinsburg's wealthiest family. Her upcoming wedding had become one of the town's favorite topics of conversation. Not above football, of course. But it had edged past the ongoing dispute about whether Billy's barbeque rub was better than Johnny Earl's.

"Maybe he's been busy?" Holly suggested.

Sam snorted. "Busy dreaming of a reunion with his high school girlfriend. Did you set a date to scout rehearsal sites?"

"No, I gave him my number."

"Holly, Holly, Holly." Sam shook her head pityingly. "Now you've handed him all the control. You're going to have to sit around on pins and needles waiting to hear from him."

"Does the sitting around have to involve pins and needles?" Holly took hold of a lock of her hair and wound it around her index finger. The truth was that seeing Josh had already turned her brain to mush and made her stomach so jumpy she doubted whether she'd be able to consume even a single cheese enchilada. More's the pity. She liked Mexican.

"You should have asked for his number," Sam informed her. "Or you should have said that you'd be free on, say, Saturday from two to five."

"This is why you're married to Mr. Perfect and I'm dating no one."

Sam pointed a tortilla chip at Holly. "My husband is indeed perfect."

"Yes. I realize." Mr. Perfect made good money, dressed like someone who knew how to sail, cooked, shopped for groceries, cleaned their house, and frequently showered Sam with gifts.

"He made chicken piccata last night," Sam said, "and told me to rest while he cleaned it up."

"Boo! I ate cereal for dinner."

"I'm now going to leverage the man IQ I used to land my husband to help you land your high school love turned billionaire—"

"No! No, no, no."

Sam waited for her to explain her reluctance while mariachi music played softly and the scent of cilantro sifted over them with the air conditioning. A few banners of colorful cut-out tissue paper rectangles swagged above them.

"I can't fall for him again, Sam."

"Why not?"

"He lives in Paris, you realize. He'll be leaving town right after the wedding."

"Not all long-distance relationships are doomed to crash and burn."

"Okay, setting aside the long-distance part, if I let myself care about him again, then I risk putting myself through all the heartache I went through the last time we broke up. I can't do it again."

Sam's face softened. Not usually given to physical displays of affection, she reached across the table and wrapped her hand around Holly's forearm. "My first man IQ lesson? Nothing ventured, nothing gained. Do you want Josh?"

"No."

"Yes you do. And this is your chance! You have proximity." She squeezed Holly's arm to underscore the urgency in her words before sitting back in her booth seat. "I counsel you to mount a full-scale assault on his heart."

"I typically only mount full-scale assaults on my To Be Read pile of books."

"Man IQ lesson number two: you have to start thinking of yourself as superior to him."

Holly laughed. "What?"

"I'm just telling it like it is. In order to catch this guy, you're going to have to believe that *he's* the one who will come to care about you so much that *he'll* be heartbroken when your time together runs out. Are you following me?"

"Um . . ."

"What's the problem? You *are* superior to him. You're wonderful in every way."

"Not in every way. I have allergies and go to work in my pajamas and still haven't earned the affection of Rob's lab. Aren't labs supposed to love everyone?"

"You're a bestselling author."

She gave Sam an unconvinced look. A few of her dystopian YA novels had snuck onto the very bottom of the *USA Today* list. She'd written two books a year since college. Not all of them had done as well.

"Your novels star a fearless eighteen-year-old girl," Sam said, "who never hesitates to take names and kick bootie. *You* are your heroine."

Holly wrinkled her forehead. "She's like the superhero

cartoon version of me. She's amazing with a rapier, for pity's sake."

"Well, you're going to need to channel more of her in order to convince your billionaire to put a ring on it."

"He's not my billionaire and I don't want to convince him to—"

"Also, you might want to think about wearing tighter clothing, more makeup, and getting a gel manicure every two weeks. Just sayin'." Sam shot her a big grin.

"Now I know you've lost your mind."

She was supposed to be writing.

Holly had returned to her apartment hours ago after lunch at the Tacqueria. She'd stationed herself at her desk, which faced a glorious old window overlooking Main. She had her computer document open in front of her. Her environment cocooned her appropriately with quiet. Her pumpkin-spice candle was flickering and she'd answered her email. She should be writing. But all she'd been actively doing was waiting for a text or call from Josh.

Sam would not approve.

Beyond the window panes, the sun melted toward the horizon, casting amber light over Martinsburg—

Her phone rang. Holly lunged for it like a woman in sugar withdrawal lunging for the final truffle at a chocolate shop.

The screen announced the incoming caller as Amanda's mom. Spirits sagging, Holly set the phone down and let it go to voice mail. Because of her volunteer position as Trinity Church's wedding coordinator, either Amanda or Amanda's mom called her almost daily. Holly found it more efficient to compile all their questions and address them at one time.

The cursor on her computer screen blinked, awaiting excellence. She tucked her feet underneath her crisscross style and swiveled her chair to face the interior of her home. It had taken her a good deal of time to exchange out all the old furniture her parents had loaned her for these new pieces she'd purchased for herself. Nowadays, her little place looked like the residence of an actual grown-up. Area rugs over the hardwood floors. Quality furniture she'd scored in back-of-the store bargain rooms. The sofa and padded ottomans were pale gray, brightened by one fabulous yellow raw silk chair, and several navy and white trellis-patterned throw pillows.

She'd built a home for herself in Martinsburg totally independent of her family and Josh. The home she'd made included her writing career, this community, her church, friends, relatives.

It hadn't been easy to get herself to this place. It had been hardest of all during the months following her breakup with Josh. She could remember praying daily back then, hourly even, asking God what she should do, whether she should contact Josh.

Every time she'd prayed about it, she'd sensed God steering her to leave things as they were. Not to contact him.

The tremendous success Josh had enjoyed since then proved that God had been working out His plan for Josh's life through the guidance He'd given her.

So how come she'd felt their old chemistry when she'd

seen Josh today? She'd been faithful to God's leadership way back when. So why hadn't God done her the favor of taking away her feelings for Josh?

She planted an elbow on her chair's armrest and leaned the side of her head into her hand. She'd been on plenty of dates with good guys, guys who were genuine and sweet and sometimes even very cute. Why hadn't any of her adult relationships moved from interest/attraction to that thing much harder to attain: love?

The Sunday school answer was, of course, that God had been busy teaching her to be totally content in Him alone. Which was well and good, except that the pesky, romantic bent of her soul refused to quit hoping for a husband and one day, children. She was forever striving to balance peace with her singleness against her ongoing prayer asking God to prepare her for someone and someone for her.

Experience had taught her that heart-tugging, love-inducing men were scarce. She'd had one. Maybe she'd used up her quota.

Her phone chimed. She swung her chair back around and scanned the new text message. Are you free on Thursday afternoon to visit rehearsal dinner locations? If not, we can go whenever it's convenient for you. Thanks, Josh.

Oh, bother. Here came all those unwelcome feelings again-giddiness, fear, excitement. She pushed one finger at a time into her palm, stopping just short of cracking her knuckles, while she pondered the gracious tone of his message. Appropriately grateful.

She channeled Sam and decided to wait an hour to reply. He didn't need to know that she'd pounced on his text. She'd certainly reply in the affirmative even though a Thursday afternoon appointment would mean missing her favorite Zumba class.

Zumba would be available forever. Thursday's outing with Josh presented her with a rare opportunity to achieve something with Josh she'd long wanted.

Closure.

If, when Josh left town in a few weeks, she could part with him on amiable terms, then perhaps she'd be able to close the chapter of her past with his name on it and move on to the *someone* God intended.

Chapter 3

♡

SHE SPOTTED JOSH FROM HALF A BLOCK AWAY. CASUAL and still, he leaned against the side of a black Range Rover, waiting for her. Even in jeans and a black crew-neck shirt, he gave off the impression of power, competence, and leashed intensity. He'd pushed his hands into his pockets.

Had he—this sophisticated man—really loved her once? It seemed a distant, fuzzy impossibility. *You're here for closure*, she reminded herself. And to lend assistance to an old friend.

She'd contemplated taking him out in her car, since she was the one who knew the area. But she hadn't been sure what twenty-six-year-old tech gurus were driving around in these days. She'd feared her aging Mazda Miata convertible too dated for him, its quarters too cramped.

She'd instead suggested he drive and that they meet here, at Smith's Smokehouse. Parking around Main could be tricky for nonresidents without assigned parking spots. Smith's had a big lot and a location near her apartment.

She stopped a few feet from him. "Hi."

"Hi." Josh studied her. "Thanks for helping me with this. I appreciate it."

"I'm happy to. It's a nice day for a drive." The temperature had stretched all the way up to a crystal bright seventy-five. "You've given me a good reason to get out from behind my desk." He opened the passenger side door for her. Buttery tan leather upholstery immediately embraced her.

He started the car and pulled onto the road. "Should we go see one of my picks first or one of yours?" he asked.

Via text they'd agreed that they'd each come up with two potential rehearsal dinner venues for today's outing. "Either one."

"Ladies first."

"In that case, turn right at the light." Holly took her wedding coordinator's notebook from her purse and settled it on her lap. "Let's start with the Texas Olive Oil Company's farm. It's just ten minutes outside town and they have a wonderful barn."

A few moments of quiet. "The Texas Olive Oil Company you said?"

"Yes. I heard a rumor that they've started renting out their barn for functions. So I called them and asked if we could stop by for a tour." She'd spent an hour or two brainstorming and researching fresh new rehearsal dinner ideas before deciding on her top choices. No one wanted to eat at the country club for the thousandth time.

"Would I need to rent tables and chairs and have the food catered if I hold it there?"

"Yes. Approximately how many guests are we talking about for the rehearsal dinner?"

He glanced across his shoulder at her. "Seventy."

"I suppose that's about right, considering the ten bridesmaids, ten groomsmen, the house party, the ring bearer, and seven flower girls."

"Plus out-of-town family. Do you think this barn of yours will be big enough?"

"This barn of mine, I do believe, will be big enough."

He rolled down his window and rested a bent arm on the door. Sunlight shimmered against his TAG Heuer watch and made clear the details of his beautifully masculine forearm, wrist, hand. His firm, aristocratic profile could have belonged to an Italian prince.

Try to think of him in a kindly fashion, Holly. Not so much prince-like as pleasant-old-friend-like. "So, you live in Paris now."

"I do."

"What brought you to Paris?"

"I lived in New York after college, when my company was a start-up. But I knew I didn't want to live there long term. I can headquarter just about anywhere."

"Your company specializes in apps for smartphones and tablets?"

"You know about my company?"

"You knew about my books."

"True."

Holly's knowledge about Josh's company derived from two

sources: Ben and her own thorough study. Over the years, she'd read every article on Josh and his business—both in print and online—that she could get her hands on. He'd been on the cover of *Forbes* once. Numerous times, he'd been given awards or asked to deliver speeches.

Josh's mind had always fascinated her. Most of the kids in high school had been far more impressed by athletes who'd excelled at football or basketball. They'd viewed Josh—their very own version of Matt Damon's character in *Good Will Hunting*—as somewhat of a mystery. Josh had been so off-the-charts brilliant that even his AP math teachers hadn't been able to teach him anything he didn't know. He'd crushed the SAT and ACT, and his GPA had been far enough above a 4.0 that no one, not even very-brainy Jim Wong, had come close to challenging Josh's status as valedictorian.

Holly had been a relatively smart high school girl in her own right, just open-minded and quirky and mature enough to appreciate intelligence over how a guy's bottom looked in football pants. Her strengths, however, had centered around subjects like English and history. Like most writers, she was anti-math. Nor was she terribly technological. She couldn't comprehend the things that went on in Josh's brain and yet his brain awed her just the same. "Since you can headquarter anywhere, why did you pick Paris?"

He scratched the side of his upper lip with his thumb.

"Because of the crepes?" she asked.

His dark gaze flicked to hers, glinting with humor. "The crepes aren't bad."

"No. I imagine the croissants and soufflés and macaroons aren't terrible either."

"Have you been to Paris?"

"Never. But I might have to go one day. For the crepes."

He drove quietly.

"You decided to live in Paris because?" she prompted. He still hadn't explained why he'd chosen it.

"It interests me. It's historic and busy and full of art and beauty."

"You love it there."

"I like it there but I'm not tied to it. I may move somewhere else in a year or two. Berlin or London or Zurich."

"But not back to the United States?"

They'd come to a light. He assessed her, his eyes saying a lot of things, all of which were shielded so carefully that she couldn't decipher a single one. "Not anytime soon."

For some reason, his answer saddened her. She issued more directions on how to get to the farm.

The outskirts of town ebbed away, replaced by the famous scenery of the Texas Hill Country. Rugged land, populated with cedar and live oaks, punctuated with outcroppings of granite and limestone rolled against a cerulean sky.

"Where are you staying while you're in town?" Holly asked.

"My assistant rented a house for me in the Hollow."

The nicest neighborhood in Martinsburg had been nicknamed the Hollow so long ago that no one remembered why. The home Holly had been raised in, which her parents still lived in part of every year, was located there. "What about this car? Also arranged by your assistant?"

"Yes."

"It must be nice to have an assistant. Do you think I could find one who'd work for me for five dollars a day?"

"No."

"Which explains my lack of one."

"If you were willing to pay an assistant more you wouldn't have to get your own coffee."

He was referencing the coffee tray she'd been carrying the other morning. She refrained from mentioning that if she didn't go out for coffee, she'd lose her mid-morning reason to change out of pajamas. "I'm willing to pay more; it's my puny bank account that isn't."

They pulled into the olive farm. Bushy, thin-leaved trees that looked like something straight out of Galilee spread away from the barn and outbuildings in neat rows.

Josh and Holly climbed from the car and made their way toward the barn. Across the property, a middle-aged farmer lifted his head from a piece of machinery he'd been working on. "Hello there! I'll be right with you."

"No hurry," Holly called back.

She and Josh waited by the two huge metal door panels that slid on tracks to open the front-facing side of the barn. A large flagstone patio extended from where they stood, overlooking a view that sloped gently down to Lake Cypress Bend.

Holly peeked up at Josh. He wasn't admiring the view. Instead, he was watching her.

Warm, discomfiting attraction tugged within her. "What do you think?" She extended an arm to encompass the scenery. "Beautiful, isn't it?"

He gave it an obligatory scan. "It is."

"If the weather's nice, you could serve drinks or appetizers or dessert out here." The nearby trees formed canopies over the open ground between rows, like charming tunnels of nature.

He returned to looking at her. "Tell me about your writing."

She remembered that he'd always been quick to change subjects. He'd never had the patience to chitchat about things that didn't interest him when he could jump the tracks to things that did. "What would you like to know?"

He asked educated questions about the business of publishing and about her writing process. It touched her that he cared to know about her whimsical and cherished profession.

She relaxed by degrees as they talked, just the two of them surrounded by air that smelled like fresh soil and the lavender growing around the base of the barn. It was a unique spell, this. A hawk rode the faraway wind—

"Hi there, y'all."

She'd been so engrossed in their conversation that the arrival of the farmer came as a small surprise. A friendly man with a John Deere hat and a sun-worn face, he pushed open one of the sliding metal doors and ushered them inside the barn.

Unlike many of the leaning, ramshackle barns dotting the Texas countryside, this structure had likely been built in the last five years. It had plenty of windows, exposed wood walls, and wonderful cross-timbered beams spanning the peaked ceiling.

"A while back the boss had the idea of renting this place out for parties and such." The farmer nodded toward the olive pressing machinery. "We put all the equipment on these here rolling platforms so we can move it out when needed."

"Is it available Friday, November twenty-seventh?" Josh asked.

"Let me go get the book." He bustled out.

"You like this barn of mine," Holly stated, because she could see that he did. "You can see its potential."

"Definitely."

The farmer returned, holding a big and dog-eared calendar. Computerized calendars had not, it seemed, made their way to the Texas Olive Oil Company. "What date did y'all say?"

"The twenty-seventh."

"Shoot. It looks as though the barn's already booked that night."

"*It is?*" She was a Martinsburg insider. As far as she knew, this site had only been used for a few high-end events in the past several months, mostly corporate. She hadn't once doubted its availability.

"It sure is. I'm real sorry about that."

Josh appeared unperturbed as he shook the man's hand. They both thanked him and set off for Josh's car.

Holly took one last, heavily disappointed look back at the barn. Such an ideal setting! Drat, drat, drat. "I apologize, Josh. I should have asked over the phone whether this place was booked that night and saved us the trip. They just began to hold events here and hardly anyone knows about it. I thought this place was still a secret."

"Don't worry about it."

They drove next to Holly's second choice, a historic dance hall outside of town still used for the occasional visiting singer or county-western dance night.

Then on to Josh's very unoriginal first choice, the country club. Thank goodness, the Ladies Golf Association already had it reserved the night in question. Lastly, they visited Josh's second choice, a luxurious restaurant on the outskirts of town called the Lodge.

At each stop, Josh treated everyone with excellent good manners. He also took very little time to survey his options. Both the dance hall and the Lodge were available on the twenty-seventh, but he remained noncommittal.

"You don't seem to be feeling the same urgency that I am about booking one of these places," Holly commented as he steered the Range Rover toward downtown Martinsburg.

"I haven't found what I want yet. I don't like to settle."

"Um, do you realize how particular Amanda can be?" Amanda would have wanted engraved rehearsal dinner invitations in the mail a week ago, minimum.

"I realize." He smiled slightly, looking ahead at the road.

Holly considered that smile. Self-assured, unintimidated.

"Very well then." She refused to angst over the rehearsal dinner. She had her hands more than full already with wedding details.

It was enough that she'd started to accomplish today what she'd hoped for with Josh: a more upbeat ending to an important relationship that had ended on a huge downbeat the last time.

Their conversation had flowed easily enough and she'd come to feel mostly comfortable in his presence—which was above and beyond what she'd hoped for before he'd arrived in town. If their light interaction this afternoon felt shallow somehow, that was to be expected. Of course it felt shallow: it didn't come close to addressing the magnetism, tension, and pain that lay between them.

During their last phone call before the breakup, they'd whispered words of love to each other. Now they were two independent adults in the latter half of their twenties, discussing things like whether a room had enough space for ten round-tops.

They drew near the north side of the Hollow. "Would you mind stopping by my parents' house?"

"Not at all."

"Do you remember Shadow?"

"The cat?"

"She still lives at the house. She's the only resident when my parents are out of town."

He quirked a brow at her.

"I know, it's weird. When my parents bought the place in

Austin we decided that Shadow would move in with me. But she ran away twice—" She had to catch herself from telling Josh where to turn. He turned in the right place without assistance. He remembered the way. "Both times Shadow ran away, I found her back at my parents' house. So I installed a cat door. I stop by every day to feed her."

"It seems like you could leave more than a day's worth of food. Then you wouldn't have to come by as often."

"But then, you see, Shadow wouldn't get enough social interaction."

He parked in the driveway of her family's stately 1930s two-story. If Holly did say so herself, the house had been kept up well, its shingles painted a pretty beige, its rock chimney standing proudly straight.

"How come you don't live here with Shadow?" he asked.

"Because I'm not eighteen anymore. It would seem sort of . . . I don't know. Sorry? To live here alone at this point. I like my apartment." She gave him a questioning look. "Would you like to come in? It'll just take a minute."

"I'll stay here. I have some business I need to check." He motioned toward his phone, sitting in the middle console.

Holly nodded and let herself inside the house.

Josh had no doubt that text messages and business emails awaited his attention, but he hadn't asked to stay outside because of them. For a man who didn't lie—he preferred blunt, straight-up communication—he'd become quite the liar where Holly was concerned.

Just sitting in the driveway of this house brought up a

storm of old memories. He had no intention of going indoors and seeing the places where he'd held hands with Holly, talked with her parents and siblings, picked her up for prom.

In case Holly caught sight of him through a window, he set his phone on his leg and looked down at it.

He was pretty sure he was losing it because he wanted more time with her. She made his mind, body, and senses rush to life in ways they hadn't in too many months to count. Whenever he met her eyes, attraction snapped like electricity between them. Her smile left him wordless.

He could buy many things in this world, but he couldn't buy the way she made him feel.

He dealt in math and science and computers. If someone had asked him last week whether magic existed, he would have said emphatically that it didn't. But Holly was like magic to him. Somehow, she was. She made his cynical heart want the one thing he'd be an idiot to pursue. Her.

When she'd broken up with him, she'd done it over the phone, without warning, in under ten minutes. Kindly cool on her side. Heatedly upset on his side. She'd said the sort of clichés that people always say at breakups. She hadn't given him any reason that made sense to him, that he could accept. Then, afterward, she'd refused to speak to him or return his emails. She'd betrayed his faith in her, and the last thing he wanted was to make the mistake of caring about her or placing his trust in her again.

He turned his phone in slow half-circles on his thigh, frowning, his forehead grooved.

Did anyone in this town have any idea how talented she was? He'd read every one of her novels. He always pre-ordered them, then read them obsessively, not working or sleeping until he'd finished the final page. They were beautifully written, wise, hopeful, filled with adventure and courage. He had no idea how she did it, how she dreamed up worlds and people and plots out of thin air.

He'd been to Martinsburg's one bookstore. There'd been no big display about their famous local author. They'd had only one copy of her latest release, on the shelf spine out in the YA section. From what he could tell, the people of Martinsburg had overlooked her entirely.

Holly returned, sliding into her seat. "Thanks for bringing me by. You saved me from having to make a trip back later today."

"How was Shadow?"

"As entitled as usual." The afternoon rays pouring into the car from behind Holly turned a section of her hair to glowing honey. She was so achingly pretty that his chest squeezed.

"Since we didn't find a site today"—the level tone of his voice hid his steely determination—"I'm thinking we'll need to try again soon, if you have the time." He was not a good person.

"Okay. I . . . have the time."

The bond between them pulled and the moment grew heavy. He longed to tell her things he had no business telling her. Namely, the truth about how much she'd hurt him and his frustration with himself regarding the resentment he still harbored toward her because of it.

He backed down the driveway, silently calling himself *stupid*, *fool*, *self-destructive*, and much, much worse.

Chapter 4

♡

RIGHT ABOUT NOW, THE SATURDAY-AT-ELEVEN ZUMBA class Holly sometimes attended was probably merengue marching and shimmying to their heart's delight. There wouldn't be any shimmying for her this morning, thanks to a wedding meeting with Amanda, Amanda's mom, and their professional wedding coordinator.

Holly crossed her arms and rested her hip against a pew while watching the bride and mother of the bride trail their coordinator around the sanctuary of Trinity Church.

Mitzi, the woman they'd hired to orchestrate the big day, looked every inch as serious as her name was not. In a sleek gray suit, with earrings as big as doorknobs and an auburn hairstyle a First Lady would have envied, she gave off a chic and able impression. Somewhere in her mid-fifties, Mitzi's body bore the ruthlessly thin, muscled stamp of someone who pounded the asphalt every morning in a pair of Nike Airs.

Mitzi had never before toured the church. Since arriving thirty minutes ago, she'd spent a good deal of time whisking her tape measure in and out and looking vaguely displeased. Which had Holly, here on Trinity's behalf, fighting back a case of defensiveness.

Trinity Church possessed a tremendous amount of charm, but there was no hiding the fact that the building was *old*. It had been constructed out of stone in 1890 by Germans who'd brought with them their motherland's excellent taste in church architecture. The building boasted a soaring steeple and arched front doors crafted of heavy oak. Inside, rectangular stained-glass windows marked the side walls and an understated altar stood on a dais three steps above the level of the pews.

Holly experienced a rush of fondness and respect every time she entered the place. She'd grown up here. God spoke to her here. Even though the median age of the membership at Trinity probably hovered at ninety, it had never occurred to Holly to switch congregations. Where would she go? That big new box of a church with the thumping music and a bustling marriage mart otherwise known as a singles ministry? Oh my, no. Jumping ship at this point would feel like high treason.

A year ago, sweet Violetta Mae Gaskins had retired as Trinity's longtime wedding coordinator and personally asked Holly to take over her duties. Holly had immediately assured her that she would. The truth? She enjoyed her role. It satisfied something within her, to help arrange other people's happy endings. It made no difference whether those people were real, here at Trinity, or fictional within the pages of her novels.

So far, Holly had presided over six weddings as the church's representative in all things nuptial. A few of the brides (those on tighter budgets or planning more intimate weddings) hadn't brought in professional coordinators. In those cases, the bride, Holly, and sometimes the mother of the bride had managed the big day themselves.

None of the prior weddings had been nearly as ambitious as Amanda's would be, however. This wedding, scheduled to take place in just twenty-one days, was destined to test Holly's skills. It had already begun to test her patience.

Mitzi launched into an animated monologue about floral arrangements.

If Mattel ever decided to roll out a Yellow Rose of Texas Barbie, Amanda could serve as a blueprint. Her long and highlighted blonde hair always looked shampoo-commercial worthy. She wore leather boots and a print dress beneath a fitted jean jacket.

Amanda Warren had been born with extraordinarily good taste. At one week of age, she'd probably begun selecting her own smocked onesies and coordinating baby caps. Goodness knows, Amanda had sailed through adolescence without an awkward stage. She'd been named Fraternity Sweetheart and Homecoming Queen at SMU before returning to Martinsburg to start her own interior design business.

In a life of excellent decisions, Amanda's best by far was her choice of groom. Tall, strapping, ginger-haired Ben Hunt was outgoing, warm, quick to laugh, and genuinely interested in everyone he met.

Holly picked a tuft of lint off her ivory cable knit sweater. She and Amanda were the same age and their parents had been members here at Trinity in the same era. She and Amanda had been pushed together since toddlerhood with the expectation that they'd play together in a mannerly fashion and become bosom friends.

They'd certainly played together in a mannerly fashion. In fact, there'd never been a cross word between them. Yet, they'd never become bosom friends. They lacked that mysterious link that leads to confidences and transparent affection. To wit, Amanda had selected ten bridesmaids and a house party of six for her wedding. Holly had not been invited into either camp.

"Sorry for the long wait, Holly." Amanda approached, the older women in tow.

"No problem. Take as long as you like."

"I think we're ready to talk through a few things with you."

"Sure. We can sit down here," Holly indicated the pews, "or we can use one of the meeting rooms."

Mitzi opted for a meeting room, so Holly brought them to the nearest one. A table dominated the plain space. Holly sat on one side with her pen and notebook in front of her, and the other ladies took chairs opposite her. Amanda lowered an accordion file as large as a carry-on onto the table. Mitzi propped up an iPad attached to a small keyboard and began typing furiously. Amanda's mom, Christine, met Holly's eye.

Christine resembled her daughter, except thirty years older

with a chin-length bob. She presided over the Ladies Golf Association at the country club in Lilly Pulitzer clothing and small-heeled sandals with gems on them. The bulk of her communication consisted of "Mm" and a well-bred smile that could as easily mean *I'm thoroughly charmed by you* as *I hope you rot in your grave.* Holly could never tell. She was a little bit afraid of Christine.

"We're concerned about how many people the sanctuary can accommodate," Mitzi stated, glancing at Holly without fully lifting the angle of her face.

"Mm," Christine concurred.

"The sanctuary seats three hundred," Holly said.

"We're expecting at least that many."

"You're welcome to use the choir loft." It functioned much like a small balcony in a theater.

Mitzi and the others theorized over how many bodies they could squeeze into the choir loft.

"Do you have any other suggestions?" Mitzi asked.

"I'm sorry, I don't." Holly understood their concern. Amanda and Christine were going to have a tricky time fitting Martinsburg's ten thousand residents into Trinity Church. Apart from asking guests to sit on each other's laps or straddle each other's shoulders, Holly had no solutions.

"Do you think the pews could accommodate three hundred and fifty?" Mitzi squinted one eye.

"Only three hundred," Holly answered.

"I'd like to give the ushers some specialized training the night of the rehearsal," Mitzi informed Christine and Amanda.

"Sounds good," Amanda answered, still wrestling with the accordion file.

"What does the church have in the way of tables?" Mitzi asked Holly, her earrings clunking the sides of her neck.

"What kind of tables?"

"We'll need a table in the foyer for the guest book and another for the wedding programs and a flower arrangement. We're going to want tables that are suitably special."

"Mm," from Christine, paired with what might have been an I'm-thoroughly-charmed-by-you smile.

"I'd be happy to show you what we have," Holly said.

"If we can't find what we're after here," Mitzi said, "we'll import our own."

"You're welcome to."

"And I do believe we've decided to bring in our own musicians and organist as well."

Holly's loyalty pricked. "Our organist, Doreen, is great." Doreen would hate to miss the opportunity to brag to her friends about playing the organ at Amanda's wedding.

"I think Doreen's great too," Amanda said. "But my dad's second cousin's wife plays the organ professionally in Vienna, so she's going to play for the wedding, if that's okay."

"Of course." *Doreen,* Holly wrote in her notebook, to remind herself to bring Doreen a bucket of caramel corn (Doreen's favorite) when she broke the bad news.

"We're going to want," Mitzi declared, "to take down all the tacky papers and posters and announcements and such that are currently featured in the public areas of the church."

Holly chewed the inside of her lip and wondered if she was too young to start drinking Alka-Seltzer. Thank goodness she had a rehearsal dinner scouting session scheduled for this afternoon with Josh. Otherwise, today might've turned into a real pothole.

Josh. A mental image of him, standing beside her and turning his face to watch her, took shape. That dark hair. The sleekly muscled body. His height and strength. Those unwavering eyes, focused solely on her . . . *You can't let yourself care about him!*

"Holly?" Mitzi asked.

"Ah . . ." *What was the question? Oh, yes.* "You can take down the announcements in the public areas at ten on the day of the wedding. We'd just ask that you put them back up after the ceremony."

Mitzi's fingers paused on the mini-keyboard. "We have a large staff coming. A floral designer and her team, a lighting designer, a group of ribbon specialists, a garland expert, a videographer, the photographer, not to mention the musicians."

What about a flock of cherubs? No cherubs?

"It would be extraordinarily helpful," Mitzi continued, "to have access to the premises at least twenty-four hours prior."

Amanda and Ben's wedding would take place at five o'clock on the Saturday following Thanksgiving. After which, guests would make their way to the reception at a local winery. "I'm sorry, but we have a prayer meeting every Friday night and a lady's Bible Study every Saturday morning. The church will be available at ten."

"Mm." Christine's smile took on a I-hope-you-rot-in-your-grave tinge.

Holly stuck her pen behind her ear and inhaled deeply. This was going to be a long meeting.

Holly and Josh went location shopping that afternoon, and every other afternoon for the week that followed. With each passing day, the weather turned cooler and crisper. Amber leaves began their downward dance from Martinsburg's trees. The scent of wood smoke tipped the air. Holly brought out throw blankets from her linen closet. The bakery started carrying their eagerly awaited autumn walnut cake with apricot preserves. And Josh *still* hadn't booked a rehearsal dinner venue.

Twelve days before Amanda and Ben's wedding, on her way back from her morning coffee run, Holly set Rob's black coffee at his door, then knocked on Mrs. Chapel's. "Good morning!" She edged the cup through the gap between the door and the jamb.

"Thank you, dear. Did you remember to put in one and a half packets of sugar?"

"Yes, indeed."

"Will you be going out again later?"

"I expect to."

"I'm in need of some Efferdent Plus for my dentures."

"I see. Is it an urgent type of thing?"

"Very urgent."

"In that case, I'll see what I can do." Holly waved and moved toward her door.

"Remember to get the Plus. The Efferdent Power Clean Crystals aren't worth the packaging they're sold in."

"Got it," Holly assured her. "Efferdent Plus."

Inside her apartment, she settled herself and her caramel nutmeg latte at her desk. Between fielding calls from Christine and Amanda, the time she'd spent with Josh in person, and the much larger amount of time she'd spent thinking about Josh, she hadn't accomplished much work of late. Her deadline had made an appearance on the horizon. She'd need to make steady progress toward it in order to avoid becoming a basket case the month before the manuscript was due. She pushed up the sleeves of her cotton shirt, determined to pound out some genius.

One minute dragged into five, then ten, while she squinted at the document open on her computer screen.

Well, it didn't look like genius would be forthcoming today. She'd settle for mediocre hogwash. Then, at least, she'd have something to work with. Hard to edit and revise blank pages.

Work, Holly. Focus.

She ended up sipping her latte instead, her attention sliding toward Main Street while she thought some more about Josh.

They hadn't made headway with a rehearsal location, but their friendship had progressed. Whenever they were together, they spent the whole time talking, slowly catching one another up on the events of the past eight years, accustoming themselves to the people they'd become.

More and more powerfully with every meeting, Holly had grown attuned to Josh's movements, the timbre of his voice, his expressions, his clothing.

There were moments, very fleeting, when she suspected her awareness of Josh might not be one-sided. In those moments, her breath would still and her hopes would tangle with her weighty sense of caution. Then the moment would break.

Afterward, she'd tell herself that he most likely didn't like her in *that way* anymore. If by some miracle he did feel the same magnetism toward her that she did for him, she was pretty positive that he'd never act on it. Josh was a very controlled person, private and complex, with a fair amount of pride.

They never spoke about their dating relationship or how it had ended. She'd begun to wish that she could tell him the truth about why she'd broken up with him. She wanted to explain.

But did she want to explain for his sake or for her own selfish reasons? It would be cathartic to unburden herself, yes. But would dredging up the past be of any benefit at all to Josh at this point? She couldn't very well throw his mom under the bus. And how exactly was she supposed to bust out old confessions, anyway?

"*This restaurant has an excellent wait staff, Holly.*"

"*I feel badly about breaking up with you when we were teenagers, Josh! Let me tell you why I did it!*"

No. They were friendly with each other and she was helping him find a rehearsal dinner site. That was it. Josh had moved on. He wasn't her eighteen-year-old first love anymore, he wasn't someone she confided in anymore. He was flourishing.

She was the one she should be concerned about. Her heart needed every possible layer of protection against him—

No. It was all right. She'd been doing a good job at keeping things straight in her head. So long as she didn't let herself go all gooey over him on the inside, it was safe enough to help him with dinner venues. Their outings together were too uncommon and wonderful in their poignant way to pass up.

She could afford to spend a little bit more time with him while he was in town. Just a little bit more.

Chapter 5

♡

HOLLY ENTERED DAS LOKAL, RESTAURANT NUMBER ninety-one in their Year of Restaurants. Sam followed her inside, as did Holly's neighbor Rob. A rush of warm air greeted her as she unwound her scarf and hung her coat on the rack.

Das Lokal enjoyed its status as a town favorite. People, the clink of silverware, and the mouth-watering dinnertime smells of steak, frites, and apple strudel packed the small pub-like interior. Holly scanned the space, looking for an empty booth on the far side—

Her gaze collided with Josh, who'd already caught sight of her. "Oh." He and Ben sat at the bar, a plate of buffalo wings between them. Josh's vision remained steadily leveled on her. Solemn and glittering. Her heart thumped, then skittered into a fast rhythm.

"'Oh' what?" Sam asked.

Holly didn't want Rob to hear, so she leaned near Sam's ear. "Josh is here."

"Your high school love turned billionaire?"

"The very same."

"What? I'll be subtle, but I demand that you take me to him immediately. Immediately! Make haste."

Holly threaded through the crowd toward Ben and Josh's position. Running into Josh around town unexpectedly, outside their scheduled meetings? Fine. She was cool with it. She could handle it. No problem.

He had on a simple white business shirt with the collar open one button at the neck. He always looked at ease in his clothes, even though his garments had likely come straight from an expensive French clothier. The Texas sun had lightly tanned his strong, masculine features. As usual, his hair looked sexily finger-combed.

She'd really like to finger-comb that dark hair with *her* fingers—

"Holly!" Ben hugged her. "Good to see you."

"You too." Holly stepped aside to include her friends in their circle. "Do you both know Sam and Rob?"

"Sure, sure." Ben smiled and shook hands. He knew everyone in town. If he ever decided to run for mayor, he'd win.

"This is Josh," Holly said to Sam and Rob, hoping the he's-an-extremely-cute-math-genius-and-my-first-love part didn't show in her expression.

"Nice to meet you," Sam said, then, bless her, adeptly steered the conversation toward Ben and Amanda's wedding. She gave no indication that she knew or cared anything about the intimate details of Josh's history.

Rob gently bumped Holly's shoulder with his. "I see a booth opening up. I'll go grab it for us."

"Okay, thanks."

The rest of them watched Rob's progress as he commandeered the table. He took a seat, then gave them a salute.

"Does he work at Donovan's?" Ben asked.

"Yes," Holly answered. "He's a sous chef." Holly and Rob had become friends when he'd moved into her building. He was twenty-four, rarely missed a workout, wore his shoulder-length blond hair in a ponytail, and could panfry a mean salmon. Rob had yet to ask Holly out, despite Sam's predictions that he would, and soon.

"Rob's more than a sous chef." Mischief lit Sam's smile. "He's a *handsome* sous chef. And luckily for Holly and me, he's off tonight."

Josh frowned.

Ben chuckled. "You're married, Sam Sullivan."

"I'm not the one Rob's interested in, Ben Hunt." Sam gave Holly a pointed stare. "Like every other man in this town, he's into Holly."

Holly burst out laughing at the absurdity of Sam's statement.

"Why are you laughing, Holly?" Ben grinned. "It's true."

Bantering about Rob in front of Josh. If she ignored all the internal clanging and panic then this situation was still no problem. None at all. "Yes, goodness knows I've always had to beat men off with a stick. Such is my lot in life. At least this one can cook."

"A man who can cook is never to be underrated." Sam headed toward their booth. "I'll go keep the handsome sous chef company until you arrive."

Sam's departure opened a pocket of quiet between them.

"How was your day?" Josh asked.

She moved her full attention to him. Those dark brown eyes! They were so sharply intelligent and at the same time, burned with emotion.

"I had a good day. I was able to get some work done. Plus, I saved Mrs. Chapel from a lack of denture cleaner and spoke with Amanda for thirty minutes about the parking attendants for the ceremony. You'll be pleased to know, Ben, that the attendants will be receiving a tutorial directly from Mitzi the day before the wedding."

"Thank my lucky stars! Now I'll be able to sleep at night." The reddish freckles that matched his hair made Ben's cheerful face even more endearing. He gestured to the buffalo wings. "You want one?"

"No thanks."

"So." Ben glanced back and forth between Josh and Holly. "This clearly isn't the first time you two have seen each other since Josh came back to town."

Josh seemed to stiffen. "No."

Josh hadn't mentioned to Ben, his best friend, the groom, that they'd been scouting venues for the past several days?

"Should we go ahead and order dinner—" Josh said at the exact moment that Holly said, "We've been driving around town looking for rehearsal dinner sites together—"

Ben regarded Holly with confusion, then placed his palm on his chest. "What? For my rehearsal dinner?"

"Yes," Holly answered slowly.

"Amanda's excited about having it out at the Texas Olive Oil Company," Ben said. "It's going to be awesome. Can't wait."

"The Texas Olive Oil Company?"

"It's up north of town. They have a barn." Ben pushed to his feet. "Excuse me for minute. A buddy of mine from work just came in."

He left, leaving Holly alone with Josh. The two young women sitting on Josh's far side cut disgruntled looks in her direction, letting her know they weren't pleased with her for hogging the attention of Martinsburg's most eligible visitor.

"I booked the Olive Oil Company," he said calmly.

"But someone else already had it reserved."

"It was reserved by a group who were planning to hold a charity fund-raising meeting there. Turns out they were willing to move their meeting back a week in exchange for a sizeable donation to their charity. Look, I . . . . I'm sorry you found out about it this way. I should have let you know sooner that I'd booked a location."

"No, it's okay." She refused to feel hurt. She wasn't the event's cohost. She was just the person who'd offered up some venue suggestions. "When did this happen?"

"Recently."

"All expertly arranged by your assistant, I'm guessing."

A lazy smile started on one side of his mouth and grew.

The sight of it warmed Holly in ways that had nothing to do with the room's temperature. "Exactly," he said.

"That's wonderful." It *was* wonderful. The Olive Oil Company barn couldn't have been a more perfect location. But this development also meant that she and Josh had lost the one pursuit that connected them. She swallowed against a foolish sense of disappointment. "If you recall, the Olive Oil Company was my very first choice."

"I recall."

"So what this means is that you went with *my* choice." She smiled.

"You're obviously very gifted with both weddings and rehearsal dinners."

"Obviously."

"How are you with caterers?"

She paused. Was he asking her for more help? "How am I with choosing a caterer? Inexperienced."

"My assistant has already chosen a caterer."

"Of course."

"I'm wondering how you are with choosing a caterer's menu?"

"You mean to tell me that your assistant didn't already select the rehearsal dinner menu?"

"She lives in Paris and is unavailable to sample dishes."

"I'm relatively experienced at sampling dishes. Sam and I have been to more than ninety of Martinsburg's restaurants since January."

"Then you're more than qualified."

"*You're* more than qualified, Josh. You've probably eaten at the finest restaurants on every continent. You don't need my help."

"No," he said bluntly, "I do."

He had a tiny scar on his jaw from a bike riding accident when he was a kid. She could remember kissing the spot.

She *could not* go gooey over him! If only he wasn't so distractingly handsome. If only he'd quit looking at her so intently. It made her feel . . . lovely, when she wasn't. "You don't need my help." Her voice came out confidently, loyally covering her internal weakening. "You didn't need my help with the rehearsal dinner location either, it seems."

"I might not need your help, but I want it."

She was playing with fire! She should turn him down. More contact between them was not wise.

"Please," he said.

She caved. "All right. I don't really have the willpower to turn down"—*more time with you*—"a trip to a caterer's shop to sample delicious food."

"Good. Now that I think about it, we'll probably have to go twice. Once to select appetizers and salads and once to select entrees and desserts."

Ben returned to his bar stool, breaking the bubble for two she and Josh had created. All the sounds and colors of the bar rushed back. "I'll be in touch," Josh said.

"See you guys soon." She made her way to the booth and slid in next to Sam.

"What's something we can say to each other in honor of the German heritage of this restaurant?" Sam asked.

Rob slid down slightly in his booth seat and gave them a mock scowl. "For the record, I think it's goofy when y'all do that." He'd been to several of their Year of Restaurants meals.

"It's so much more fun when we have someone here to find us goofy," Sam insisted. "My husband is home mopping the kitchen floor—"

"—being perfect—" Holly noted.

"—so you're all we have, Rob."

"*Guten* appetite?" Holly ventured, holding up her water glass.

"*Danke schön.*" Sam murdered the pronunciation with her thick East Coast accent. "Wiener schnitzel! Dachshund!"

They all laughed and even Rob reluctantly clicked his glass to theirs.

"Dude," Ben murmured. "You're going to have to stop staring at her. She'll notice."

Josh twisted on his stool to face the dinner one of the servers had slid onto the bar. He and Ben both had burgers and shoestring fries in front of them. Josh didn't even remember ordering. He'd lost his appetite.

"I knew you'd fall for Holly again once you saw her," Ben said. He dipped a few of his fries in ketchup. "I remember how crazy you were about her."

"Yeah." His lungs felt hollow. Who was Rob? Holly couldn't actually like that guy, right? With the ponytail? His thoughts shifted in pessimistic patterns, turning his mood sooty and dark. Of course she could like him. Rob was more handsome than he was. Rob kept smiling at Holly like she'd hung the moon. Plus, he lived here.

Not everyone in Martinsburg had overlooked Holly. Rob hadn't.

"Holly's even prettier than she was in high school," Ben said. "She's made a success of her career and she's nice to everyone in this town. She's sort of like our glue. You know?"

Josh took in an uneven breath. "I know."

Ben's face communicated sympathy. "Why don't you tell her how you feel about her?"

"Because I don't want to get involved with her."

Ben whistled. "You could've fooled me. You've been watching her ever since she came in."

Josh pushed the heel of his hand against his forehead. "I'm an idiot."

"Tell her that you're an idiot for her. Women like that kind of stuff."

"I'm leaving soon."

"Relocate here."

"I don't want to live here, Ben." Everything in this town reminded him of the kid he'd been.

After his dad had been killed by a drunk driver, his mom had moved them to Martinsburg so that she could take a secretarial position a friend had offered her. Josh had arrived in Martinsburg grief-stricken and mad at the world. A loner. Desperate inside. He'd been terrified and ashamed of his terror because he'd been fourteen years old and his mom had needed him to be strong. He'd been all she had left.

His mom had insisted he play on the JV soccer team, and looking back, he was glad she'd insisted because that's how he'd met Ben. Ben was the child of a single mom, too, but unlike Josh, Ben had a naturally outgoing and optimistic personality. He'd befriended Josh when Josh hadn't had anything likable to offer. He'd been Josh's closest friend ever since.

All through high school, Josh and his mom had lived paycheck to paycheck and barely had enough to cover rent and groceries. To help out, Josh had worked loading and unloading inventory at a warehouse after school and in the summers. The money he'd made had never gone far enough. He'd realized early that if he wanted a better life for his mom and himself he only had one option: to ace his academics and earn his ticket out of Martinsburg, a town that had become, for him, a symbol of hardship and shame.

The second semester of his sophomore year of high school, he'd sat two chairs behind Holly Morgan in AP English. She'd entered his gray life like a bolt of sunshine. And almost from the first day of that semester, he'd loved her.

It had been as simple and as fast and as inexplicable as that.

He'd loved her.

Holly's manner had been easy and the kindheartedness she'd extended to him sincere. The fatherless and sullen kid, who had plenty of smarts but just one friend, had fallen helplessly for her. She'd been his point of hope, the one aspect of life in Martinsburg he treasured. She'd treated him as a friend for the next two years but his feelings for her had never wavered.

Then one night in the winter of their senior year, when he'd been helping her study for a math test, he'd sensed that things between them had shifted. He'd gathered his courage and taken hold of her hand. She'd squeezed his hand in response. He could still remember the way his heart had pounded and his thoughts had blown out of the water, sitting there next to her at that table with a math textbook open between them, her hand in his.

He'd been introduced to faith as a kid, but Holly was the closest thing to a miracle his teenage self had ever experienced. During the months they'd dated, he'd looked into her eyes and seen God's love for him looking back. She'd taken him to church and talked through spiritual things with him.

Then the girl who'd strengthened his belief had also become the one who'd most tested it when she'd broken his heart. It had taken him a few years to find God again after that. But eventually, he had. His relationship with God had been his life's anchor ever since.

Josh sliced a glance across the restaurant and saw Rob lean toward Holly to say something. Holly tilted her head to listen.

Pain and wanting washed through Josh so powerfully that he had to brace against it.

"Look away," Ben said.

Josh did.

"How come you didn't tell me you'd seen her?" Ben set down his burger and wiped his hands on a napkin.

"Because I haven't been able to decide in my own head if seeing her is a good idea or not."

"What was she saying about looking for rehearsal dinner locations? You've had that Olive Oil place booked for six months."

"I lied to her. I ran into her on the street and I asked her if she'd help me look for a location. I wanted to see her again and that was the only reason I could come up with on the spot."

Ben's forehead creased. "Let me get this straight. You've been driving around town searching for a place to hold the rehearsal dinner when you already have a place? Because you want to spend time with Holly?"

"Yes."

Ben clapped a hand on his shoulder. "Tell her the truth. About all of it."

"I can't. I don't want to get involved with her."

Ben's expression turned pitying. "You've got it bad, dude. Seriously bad."

Chapter 6
♡

"THIS IS DELICIOUS." HOLLY POINTED HER FORK AT A plate containing melt-in-your-mouth spare ribs. Oh, how she adored spare ribs. Maybe today hadn't been the best day to wear a snug belt with her jeans.

Josh finished chewing. "I agree."

Five days had passed since their discussion at Das Lokal, two since their first visit to the caterer.

Josh had picked her up in his Range Rover an hour ago (She'd blown off Zumba class again, but really, who could think about exercise at a time like this?) and driven them thirty minutes to his caterer's shop in the nearby town of Hollis. Compared to a big city, Hollis was a pipsqueak. Compared to Martinsburg, a flashy metropolis. Just like at their first visit, the caterer had seated them at her one table, which was framed by a deep bow window. On the far side of the square-paned glass, the afternoon crouched gray and chilly. Inside, the shop brimmed with bright and cheery warmth. It didn't hurt that the dear lady who owned the place kept bringing them plate after sampling plate of wonderful food.

Josh leaned back in the white iron filigree chair he'd been given, a chair so girly that it made him look extra-manly in comparison. He wore a chocolate-colored sweater that had a very slight V at the neck. The sweater's austerity, and the way it fit close to his body, suited him. "I'm not much of a party planner," he said.

"I imagine you're pretty busy, what with being a technology mogul and all."

"True." The wry humor in his eyes made her mouth go dry. "I'm very important."

"Very. And armed, lest we forget, with an assistant who seems skillful at everything, including party planning." *Holy smoke, these ribs should come with a warning label.*

"I have a party planning question."

"You could speed-dial your assistant."

"I'd rather ask you."

Her lips quirked. "All right."

"Amanda told me she's having a sit-down dinner at her reception. Should I avoid having a sit-down dinner at the rehearsal dinner?"

Holly considered his question while setting aside her fork. "Your rehearsal dinner is going to be *very* nice, Josh. I'd counsel you to avoid doing anything similar to what Amanda's doing at the reception. It'd be a shame to show up the bride."

"Point taken." He speared a bite of buttermilk fried chicken. "How would you recommend I serve the meal?"

"Food stations? They're classier than a buffet, and in keeping with the rustic, Texas feel of the evening."

"I'm listening."

"I'm guessing you'll want to begin with appetizers and drinks on the patio at sunset. Weather permitting, of course. It's Texas. It could be freezing or it might be perfect."

"Did you try this chicken?"

"Yes. It's amazing."

He indicated the brisket. "What about this?"

"Outstanding," she said.

"You were saying? About the appetizers . . ."

"Right. I'd serve them on the patio. Then, you can have food stations set up inside the barn with the main course dishes, salads, cheeses, fruit, bread. I'm guessing Amanda and Ben will want to say a few words to their guests at some point during the evening?"

"Yes."

"So maybe dessert could be served to everyone individually, at their tables, during that portion of the evening."

The caterer, a woman in her early forties wearing a floral apron, bustled in. The kitchen heat had flushed her face but done nothing to stifle her proud smile. "What do you think?" She placed her hands on her hips.

"I think you should apply for Master Chef," Holly said. "You'd win."

She beamed. "Have you decided which dishes you like best?" She directed the question to Josh, knowing full well he was the one in possession of a Visa Black Card.

"Whatever the lady decides."

"What?" Holly held up her hands. "I'm just a writer and a volunteer wedding coordinator and the girl who feeds my family's cat."

"She also brings her neighbors coffee and denture cleaner," he told the caterer.

The caterer nodded, amused.

Josh angled toward Holly. Unhurried, he hooked a hand around the top of her iron filigree chair. "What do you like best? Whatever it is, that's what I'm ordering."

She wasn't used to anyone putting so much stock in her opinion. She could probably get used to it, if forced. She looked over the assembled main dishes. During their last visit, they'd decided on appetizers and salads that had a Southern flair, so she'd continue in that theme. "I love them all, but if it were up to me—"

"It is," Josh said.

"I'd choose the spare ribs, the fried chicken, and the . . ." she wrinkled her nose and closed one eye. Saying good-bye to any of these dishes felt criminal. "Turkey pot pie."

"Excellent." The caterer began stacking the plates on a tray.

"Are you sure you're okay with those?" Holly asked Josh, under her breath. "Because—"

"I want what you want," he assured her.

He hadn't moved his hand from her chair. Having his hand there, such a simple thing, really, caused a crippling longing to break open within her.

The caterer propped her tray on her hip and paused to speak to Josh about rehearsal dinner logistics.

Holly and Josh had shared an uncommon intimacy once.

Holly had never again been able to attain that sort of intimacy with a boyfriend. On the contrary, she'd hardly had a boyfriend serious enough to want to go to the movies with.

She ached to have someone that was hers to share her feelings with, to hug, to laugh with. She'd been hoping and waiting and praying for that person, the person God had in mind for her.

Just—just not him, Lord. I can't feel this longing for Josh.

She looked down at her hands, clasped in her lap. She'd been a fool to come here. Up until today she'd been managing her feelings for him. But just now, those feelings had leapt over the line. She was falling for him. Again.

Josh straightened in his seat, removing his hand from her chair. She was in serious trouble, because she was sorry, not glad like she should have been, to lose the sweetness of that small connection.

The caterer swept from the room and returned moments later with five plates of dessert. Josh smiled at Holly, anticipating her delight.

"Oh. My. Goodness," Holly breathed. Red velvet cake, sheet cake, apple pie, two different cobblers.

They made steady progress, taking time to savor each bite and debate the merits of one dessert against the others. She definitely shouldn't have opted for a belt today.

When it came time to make the decision, Josh once again

asked Holly for her choice. She picked apple pie à la mode. Flaky, cinnamon-y, and perfect for fall.

The caterer thanked them and disappeared into the kitchen with the plates and silverware.

"I'm going to be gone this weekend," Josh said, "for Ben's bachelor party weekend."

"Where are you headed?"

"I'm taking the guys to Lost Pines Resort outside Austin to golf."

"It's beautiful there. Should be fun." It said a lot about Josh that he hadn't just thrown money at Ben's wedding events then blown in on a private jet for forty-eight hours. He'd come to Martinsburg to spend real time with his friend and to handle the details himself.

"I'm expecting two straight days of humiliation," he said. "I'm a terrible golfer."

"Not many golf courses in downtown Paris?"

"Not many. Any chance that you have time to meet me up at the Olive Oil Company when I get back? To discuss how we should arrange the tables and food stations?"

She wanted to say yes more than she wanted an appearance on the *New York Times* bestseller list. But she had to say no. "I'd like to, but I can't. I'm booked solid next week."

Josh searched her face, then nodded. "No problem." He set aside his napkin, rose to his feet, paused. As if second-guessing himself, he returned to his seat, facing his body toward hers. "Can I ask you something?" Consternation stitched through his brow.

"Of course."

Seriousness, the sort of seriousness that hadn't entered any of their prior conversations, fell between them. Her pulse began to quicken.

"Have you been helping me because you're friendly and took pity on me?" Ruefulness curled one corner of his mouth and caused a dimple to flash briefly in his cheek. "Or has any of it been because you wanted to spend time . . . with me?"

Was he asking because he'd guessed that she'd developed feelings for him and wanted to gently disabuse her of any crazy notion of a romance between them? Or maybe he was asking because *he* wanted to spend time with *her*?

No, no, no. He hadn't given her any indication of that.

She smiled breezily and adjusted her position to put more space between them. "I've been helping you because I'm friendly and also because I wanted to spend time with you." Through dint of will, she kept her voice sunny. "It's been nice to catch up with you. I always hoped you were doing well, Josh. Ben told me you were but it's been really nice to have the chance to see that for myself." She'd used the word *nice* two times and in so doing, damned their current relationship with faint praise.

He concealed his thoughts expertly. She could see no change in him outwardly. None. He was an astute business-man, after all. The owner of a company. He hadn't gotten to where he was in the world by having the transparent feelings of a girl scout.

And yet . . . she could sense the shadow of sadness that

lived in him deepening. Which made her regret her smoke-screen approach. She should have replied to his honest question with an honest answer. He'd given her an opening and hadn't she been half-hoping, maybe three-quarters-hoping, for just this kind of an opportunity to talk to him about the past?

She should be brave—right now at this very moment—and tell him the things she'd been yearning to tell him for eight years. She spoke before she could lose her nerve. "Josh, I . . ."

"Yes?"

She had a hard time getting the rest out. "I want you to know that I'm sorry for any hurt I may have caused you when we broke up."

He gazed at her, his features guarded and grave.

Why wasn't he replying? Doubt assailed her. "It could be, of course, that I didn't cause you any hurt. In which case, you can ignore what I just said."

"You did hurt me, Holly."

His bluntness came as a relief. It bolstered her courage. "Okay. I thought so. Are you still angry with me?"

She could hear a distant dog barking and the quiet conversation of the caterer and her employee, cleaning up together in the kitchen.

"There's a part of me that is," he admitted.

Her stomach dropped. She didn't want him to be angry with her, and yet, if she put herself in his shoes she could understand why he was. She fought to order her spiraling thoughts into words. "Here's the thing. I didn't tell you the truth back then about my reason for breaking up with you."

Several taut seconds dragged past. "You told me something about how your feelings had changed and that you wanted to be free to date other people," he said.

"Yes, that's exactly what I told you, but neither of those things were true."

He frowned, his eyebrows drawing down in the center.

"Should . . ." The concerns that had kept her silent on this topic until now rose to the fore of her mind. "Should we just let bygones be bygones? Or do you think there's value in revisiting what happened at this point?"

"There's value in it for me, Holly. Even now."

She slowly inhaled. "Do you remember, back when you first started MIT, that there was a time when you considered returning to Texas?"

"Yes."

"Your mom . . ." She swallowed. Was this really a good idea? Maybe the bygones thing was better.

"What about my mom?"

"She was upset about the possibility of your leaving MIT. She couldn't afford to send you anywhere else. But more than that, I mean, *MIT*, Josh. It was the best possible school for you and she and I both knew it. You were brilliant. You deserved a chance there."

"And?" he asked grimly.

"Your mom came to see me at UTSA and asked me to break up with you. I—"

"What?" He spoke the word quietly, almost whispering it. Nonetheless, it vibrated with menace.

"She asked me to break up with you so that you'd stay at MIT and focus on your studies."

His brown eyes blazed as he struggled to process what she'd said, to reframe their breakup through a different lens.

"I still remember her tears," Holly said. "She cried when she came to see me. Your mom liked me, I think. I definitely liked and trusted and respected her. It wasn't easy for her to ask me to end things, but she did, and she made a very strong case."

Josh bent his head and stared at the table as if trying to decipher a code in its surface. "You should have told me that she came to see you." He lifted his chin again to meet her eyes.

"Maybe. I didn't because I promised her I wouldn't."

"If you had told me, we could have talked it out."

"Yes, but would you have stayed in school?"

"I don't know."

"See? By breaking up with you, at least I could be fairly certain that you'd excel in school and in your career. Those were the things that your mom and I wanted for you."

"What about what I wanted?" His frank question caused her whole body to still. "Did you or my mom ever stop to consider that?"

"We . . . I mean, we thought that you wanted to leave MIT and come home to Texas."

"Would that have been so terrible?"

"Yes!"

He cocked his head to the side an inch, waiting.

"Look at you," Holly said. "You're a tremendous success."

"Business success isn't everything in life."

She parted her lips to defend—defend what? Defend his own outstanding accomplishments? Business success *wasn't* everything in life. She couldn't take the position that it was, especially since she didn't know how fulfilled or unfulfilled his own success had left him. "I broke up with you because I wanted what I thought was best for you more than anything else. Do you believe me?"

"Yes."

"Can you forgive me?"

She nearly had cardiac arrest while she waited for him to answer. He was a thoughtful man. A man who could not be slowed when his mind had been made up or rushed when he needed time to think.

He gave her a small, sad smile and placed his hand on his knee, palm up. An invitation.

She placed her hand in his and his fingers tightened around it. She was holding his hand! Sensory details rushed through Holly's nerves, buzzing and spinning, wondrously sweet. He'd offered her his hand in a gesture of camaraderie, a nostalgic acknowledgment of all they'd shared when they'd been young and bound together by first love.

"It's forgiven," Josh said. "I just need time to . . . process."

"Sure." Hot moisture pushed against the backs of her eyes.

All this time, she'd wanted to tell him that she was sorry. What she hadn't realized until now? How crucial it would be to hear him say he'd forgiven her. "Thank you."

"How's anyone supposed to stay mad at you? Is there a mean bone in your body?"

"There are a few. I can be downright cruel to fictional bad guys."

He did not appear impressed.

"I have uncharitable thoughts about Mitzi, Amanda and Ben's wedding coordinator."

"Huh."

She got lost in his beautiful eyes, in the texture of his strong, warm fingers around hers. "It took me a really long time to get over you," she murmured before she'd thought through the comment or given herself full permission to speak it.

"But you eventually did?"

"Eventually." Maybe that answer was close enough to true not to be a lie? Or maybe that lie would become true next month or next year?

He stood, breaking the link between them, then helped her scoot out her chair. They chatted about the weather while they collected their outerwear. He shrugged into his navy pea coat.

That dratted coat. It made him resemble a hero in a romantic movie. Six-plus feet of intelligent, unattainable handsomeness. She had an overpowering urge to grab the lapels of that coat and rise onto her tiptoes to kiss him. She wanted to ruffle his hair and his mastery of himself, and she really wanted to shatter the careful good manners between them.

That wayward thought, coupled with her uninvited affection for him, sent a stab of fear through her.

What was that famous groundhog's name? Punxsutawney Phil? Every time he saw his shadow and returned to his hole, folks could expect six more weeks of winter. She did not want Josh to become her Punxsutawney Phil. She refused to face eight more years of heartache every time she saw him. She'd done one bout of heartache courtesy of Josh. She could not do another eight years. No thank you.

They drove back to Martinsburg, the car filled with subdued conversation about her next book release and his favorite brands of coffee. Inwardly, though, Holly was already beginning to wonder whether she'd done the right thing when she'd told him her schedule was booked. She'd done what she'd had to do for the sake of self-preservation. Still, their outings had been wonderful. Talking with him, teasing him, seeing him smile. Those things had been a joy, the sort of deep joy that didn't often cross her path. The days ahead, days empty of him, already looked like a desert.

Holly, he must have fabulous women with names like Babette or Amelie available to him in Paris. He might even have a Parisian girlfriend at this very moment. She did not expressly know that he didn't. He probably did. She was simply a high school girlfriend from long ago.

She'd longed for closure and the talk they'd just had had

given her exactly that. Everything she'd hoped to say to him, she'd said. He'd told her he'd forgiven her.

It was enough.

It had to be enough.

Chapter 7

♡

ON SATURDAY, HOLLY SAT CROSS-LEGGED ON THE floor of her parents' kitchen, Shadow in her lap. Nothing but the sun easing through the windows illuminated the chilly interior, which they warmed to sixty-five for Shadow's comfort in the fall and winter months.

The cat lifted her head and purred while Holly scratched under her chin. "Nice home you got here, Shadow."

The feline gave her a haughty look that said, *It's no less than I deserve.*

"Quite right." More chin scratching.

She hadn't heard from Josh since their outing to the caterer. She hadn't expected to. Yesterday, he would have left town for Ben's bachelor party.

He didn't live in Martinsburg. In fact, Josh had only returned to Martinsburg eighteen days ago. So it infuriated her that she was so strongly aware of his absence this weekend. Everywhere she went felt devoid of excitement. The colors muted. More lonely. Why? Because she knew that *he* wasn't here anymore.

"This is why I can't get any more twisted up over him than I have already," she told Shadow, whose eyelids were drooping closed. "The time I spent with him has messed with my head enough."

Meow, Shadow said. Which Holly translated to mean, *Get a grip, girl.*

"Get a grip is precisely what I need to do. I'm going to leave here and go home and write like the wind. I'm really . . . I'm just going to pour out some great, great pages that will keep readers up late into the night. I left my heroine in a den of cutthroats with nothing but her rapier for defense in order to come here, you realize. Now I need to go home and rescue her."

Shadow cracked one dubious eye.

"Have I given you enough socialization?"

The cat gave a terrific stretch, which meant she wanted more petting. "Fine." Holly stroked her family's cat and reminded herself that this was how she spent her weekends. This was her destiny.

Was this really his destiny?

Josh sat in the driver's seat of a golf cart, watching one of Ben's college fraternity buddies hit a drive. The twenty guys on the trip hadn't been content with eighteen holes. They'd played eighteen this morning, stopped for lunch, and were out on the course again for another eighteen. To be honest, he'd far rather be discussing asynchronous JavaScript and XML with one of his programmers. "Nice shot."

Another of Ben's friends moved toward the tee box.

In the distance, Josh could see Ben putting on the green. It had been satisfying to watch Ben and the others enjoying the weekend, despite that he felt like a spectator to their fun rather than a participant.

He'd been in an irritable mood since the day he and Holly had last gone to the caterer's. After their conversation, he'd made himself wait a day so that he could organize his thoughts and emotions before calling his mom. She'd confirmed everything Holly had told him and reiterated all the reasons Holly had voiced. She'd even gone so far as to tell him that she'd always felt guilty about the grief she'd caused him and Holly.

She'd expected both him and Holly to rebound and start dating again after their breakup, she'd said. They'd been eighteen years old. She'd thought that they'd recover faster than they had. She'd apologized to him and asked him to pass along her regret and heartfelt best wishes to Holly.

He tightened his grip on the steering wheel, rubbing the side of his thumb against it.

Despite his mother's good intentions when she'd asked Holly to end things with him, there was no possible way that she could ever fully know what it was she'd screwed up. She'd viewed his relationship with Holly the way most parents probably viewed the relationships of their teenage children, as light and passing and juvenile.

He and Holly were the only two people who knew how

much they'd loved each other. And only he knew the scars Holly's loss had left on him.

None of them were completely without fault. He'd been shortsighted to want to leave MIT. His mom had been wrong to take matters into her own hands. And Holly should have told him about his mom's visit the day it had happened.

Did he fault Holly the most, though?

No. Back then, his mom had been a forty-five-year-old woman armed with a mother's fierce protectiveness of her only child. Holly had been a college freshman living apart from her family for the first time. He understood why she'd been swayed, and he believed her when she told him she'd done what she thought best for him.

It was going to take practice to think of Holly without the bitterness that had accompanied his thoughts of her for so long. But it also felt right to try. She'd explained and apologized. He'd forgiven her.

Who's to say, anyway? The way things had happened might actually have been the best thing for him. He'd built his company into the stuff his dreams had been made of.

Josh adjusted his Nike ball cap, slanting it lower.

He hadn't needed Holly to shop for rehearsal dinner locations with him, nor to visit his caterer once, much less twice. She'd been humoring him. He'd made up something about visiting the Olive Oil company next week, solely so that he'd have another reason to see her. She'd turned him down. Even so, when she'd whispered that it had taken her a long time to get over him, stupid hope had gripped his heart.

He hadn't planned to say anything to her, that day or any day, that would make him vulnerable to her again. But he'd asked her if she'd gotten over him eventually.

She'd looked at him with that painfully beautiful face, her dusky blue eyes kind, her skin clear, faint pink on her cheekbones, a long strand of glossy, light brown hair falling in front of her shoulder. Instead of saying *not yet* or any other answer he could have worked with, she'd said that she had. Gotten over him.

He wished he could say the same for himself.

Her words, spoken in the sweetest possible way, had hit him like a slap because they'd shown him just how different her emotions were from his own.

Josh's passenger pushed his driver into one of the bags strapped to the back of the cart and took his seat. Josh drove them toward where he'd hooked his ball.

He was here for Ben. In Texas during the month of November, and also on this weekend trip. It frustrated him that he couldn't seem to think about anything except Holly, the woman he'd been trying not to love for eight years. He was weary of trying not to love her.

He wasn't someone who gave his trust and affection easily. He had a cautious personality, a tendency toward solitude, and just a few close friends and family members. He was powerfully self-controlled.

Was. Because none of that held true around Holly. When he was around her, he wanted to buy her things, and take her places, and hold her in his arms. He'd cared about her more than she'd cared for him all those years ago. And he cared about her more again now. What was his problem?

His problem was that she was his weakness.

He'd succeeded at a lot in this life. How could it be that he'd failed, and was continuing to fail, at not loving her?

For weeks, Sam had been telling Holly that Rob liked her and that it was only a matter of time before he made his move. Late on Sunday afternoon, he finally did.

When she heard the knock on her door, Holly immediately thought, *Josh?* Even though Josh had never knocked on her door and wouldn't even know where to find her apartment. She answered the door in a state of breathlessness.

She found Rob standing in the hallway. He had a Thor vibe going, what with the muscles and the long blond hair. He'd paired a white T-shirt with a pair of those baggy pants that chefs favored. His white coat lay folded over his shoulder.

"Hey," Holly said. Of course it wasn't Josh. She had no reason to feel let down. "On the way to work?"

"Yeah. Since it's Sunday it'll probably be slow. I'm thinking I'll be done around nine-thirty."

"Cool."

"Would you like to meet me afterward at Vinnie's for dessert?"

Whenever she and Rob had gone places in the past, they'd gone in a group that included Sam. Sometimes Mr. Perfect or one of Rob's buddies joined them. "Sam and Mr. Perfect are shopping at Pottery Barn in San Antonio today." Which is pretty much how Holly imagined young married couples without kids spent the bulk of their time.

"I know." He gave her a cute I-was-hoping-to-get-dessert-with-you-alone smile.

"Oh. Well." Her thoughts darted in five nervous directions. "Sure. You know me. I never pass up a chance to eat Vinnie's chocolate pie."

"Good." He turned on his heel. "I'll text you."

"'Kay."

Holly spent the next hour pacing her apartment. Josh had asked her to go with him to the Olive Oil Company and Rob had asked her out for dessert. Two men had issued invitations in the space of a week. Single, handsome men! Instead of elated, however, the invitations—one she'd turned down, one she'd accepted—had left her feeling troubled.

She grabbed her coat, scarf, hat, and reversed her Miata from its parking space. Twenty minutes passed before she realized she'd driven by many of the places where she and Josh had spent time together during their romance. She'd taken herself on a Josh Memory Tour without meaning to.

At the Brenners' house, she and Josh had sat inside Bryan Brenner's Jacuzzi during Bryan's graduation party. Green light had illuminated the still, hot water surrounding them. She could remember how Josh had looked, staring at her through the steam.

A bank and a 7-Eleven now occupied the plot where Josh's apartment building had once stood. She could taste the microwave popcorn, seasoned with paprika and parsley, that had been his mom's specialty. They'd eaten it while watching X-Men DVDs in the small living room.

Their high school hadn't changed in any way, except for the new sign out front. Josh had first said *I love you* to her on one otherwise normal day during the spring semester of their senior year. They'd been in the hallway together. The bell had already rung and kids had been hurrying past them. She and Josh had been about to part and go in opposite directions when he'd pulled her back to him.

"I love you," he'd said. And he'd said it with the most solemn seriousness, as if he'd been unable to wait another minute to tell her, as if he was about to be shipped overseas to fight a battle, as if he was dying. And Holly had felt like she was dying, too, except from bliss and lack of oxygen because he'd stolen all her breath.

Then he'd smiled a crooked smile at her. She'd known she loved him before he'd said the words. But it was that crooked smile there in that school hallway that had settled the matter in her heart.

Sam would definitely *not* approve of her Josh Memory Tour.

Sighing, Holly turned onto the road that wound past a park and picnic area at the edge of Lake Cypress Bend. The sun had just set but full darkness hadn't yet descended. She parked and went to sit on top of a vacant picnic table.

The bulbs on the light posts glowed through the hazy evening, making their illumination appear soft, round, enchanted. Several families dotted the area, some at the playground, some at the lakeshore or on the dock, fishing. Everyone had bundled up to ward off the chill. The children's voices carried on the same breeze that spun leaves from their branches.

She and Josh had sat here, on this exact table, numerous times. This had been their spot. Sometimes they'd come here to eat. Sometimes, just to hang out and talk. She'd sat here with him, her head resting on his shoulder, contentment weaving circles around and around her. She could recall how he'd kissed her, and how her body had rushed in response with the joy and awe of it.

A twig cracked behind her and she swung to face the direction with a gasp. *Josh?*

The twig had been broken by two kids, kicking up leaves.

Rob just asked you out. Your neighbor and friend, Rob, who is a very decent person and good-looking to boot. Think about Rob, Holly. Think about Rob.

Holly came to understand, in very clear detail, why Sam scorned the idea of waiting by the phone for a man to call. Sam scorned it because living that way stunk.

Even though Holly knew Josh wouldn't call, she took her phone with her everywhere. It was ridiculous. Josh had no reason to call her. He no longer needed help planning the rehearsal dinner.

Nonetheless, when she slipped into bed at night, she rested her cell phone within arm's reach on her bedside table. She double-checked it frequently throughout the day to ensure that it was charged and prepared to receive a text message or a call from Josh.

Neither came.

She looked for him when she drove around town and each time she entered a shop or restaurant, without success.

Her rational mind knew that remaining separate from him was the best possible thing for the preservation of her well-being. Her irrational heart, however, couldn't get over the fact that she'd never again have this sort of proximity with him. Josh's time in Martinsburg was vanishing.

The days leading up to Thanksgiving, beautiful days gilded with autumn, should have been too full to dwell on Josh. Her wedding coordinator duties had kicked into fourth gear thanks to Mitzi's astonishing doggedness. Her work on her book had intensified too. Like a round stone that had topped a rise and begun to roll downhill, her plot was picking up speed. She had blog posts to write for her website and marketing to catch up on.

In pursuit of their Year of Restaurants quest, Holly and Sam hit Martinsburg's only Indian food joint and then the most girly sandwich/salad/soup restaurant the town had to offer.

Holly and Rob's dessert date had gone smoothly. In fact, it had been much like their group outings, minus other humans. There'd been chocolate pie, but no romantic feelings on Holly's part. Rob had asked her out again afterward, but since she didn't know how she felt about more one-on-one dates with him yet, she'd declined.

The day before Thanksgiving, Holly's immediate family (and her sister's fabulous new boyfriend) poured into Martinsburg. In tandem with their arrival, great, low-lying banks of clouds rolled over central Texas and coated the town with a steady drizzle. The precipitation escalated on Thursday to rain that alternated from light to downpour.

As was their tradition, the Morgans sat down together in their family home for a formal Thanksgiving meal of turkey and all the fixings, served on Holly's mother's Lennox wedding china.

Afterward, they gathered in the living room in front of the fireplace. Holly's dad coddled the fire into snapping peaks of flame. The smell of pumpkin pie hung in the air and football played on TV. Drowsy from the tryptophan she'd just consumed, Holly daydreamed about where Josh might be spending the day while the rest of the family engaged in their two most popular pastimes: cooing over Holly's older brother's gorgeously chubby toddler and revering Holly's younger sister for her pursuit of a law degree.

The only member of the family not present? Shadow. The cat had hidden under Holly's parents' bed in mute protest of the invaders who'd overtaken her residence.

Late that night, Josh was fighting insomnia and thinking of Holly, when a sudden suspicion slid into his mind. He sat up in bed, paused for a few seconds to think, then dashed aside the covers.

He hoped he was wrong. He really hoped he hadn't overlooked something so important. Surely, he hadn't.

In his plaid pajama pants, he padded down the stairs of his rented house into the kitchen. His laptop waited on the granite counter. Scowling, he pulled up his assistant's final guest list document for the rehearsal dinner.

He scrolled down the list of alphabetized names. The tile floor chilled the soles of his feet and cold air blew across his bare back.

Holly wasn't listed. She'd spent hours driving over the Hill Country with him to look at locations. She'd shared advice and ideas with him. All for a rehearsal dinner he'd forgotten to invite her to. She hadn't mentioned his oversight to him the two times they'd gone to the caterer. She'd remained quiet and polite about it while helping him pick out the menu, for pity's sake.

Josh blew out a breath, disgusted with himself.

It had occurred to him, after that night at Das Lokal when he'd told her he'd booked the Olive Oil Company, that he needed to ask his staff to double check the guest list, and if she wasn't on it, to mail Holly an invitation. He'd made a mental note of it. Planned to do it. But the list in front of him proved that he hadn't followed through.

He'd been distracted and forgetful lately. He'd been distracted and forgetful because his mind was so occupied with Holly.

The rehearsal dinner would take place tomorrow night. He straightened, pushing both hands into his hair as he stared down at the glowing screen.

He was a jerk. A jerk who needed to make things right.

Chapter 8

♡

"THANK YOU, DEAR," MRS. CHAPEL SAID TO HOLLY THE next morning, as she accepted her coffee through the door. "Did you remember to put in one and a half packets of sugar?"

"I did."

"I'm in need of some Bengay for my poor back. Would you be able to pick some up for me later, do you think? If you wouldn't mind?"

"I wish I could help you, but I'm not going to make it to the store today. My family's in town so I'm spending the day with them before the wedding rehearsal up at the church."

"Speaking of the big wedding, Doreen told me that someone else is playing the organ." Mrs. Chapel pinched her lips and shook her head disapprovingly.

"That's true."

"She said that you brought her caramel corn to help her recover from the slight."

"Also true."

"Good girl." She gave a decisive nod, her rheumy eyes regaining their twinkle. "And don't you worry about the Bengay. I'll shame my younger sister into buying it for me."

"No one's more of an expert at shaming than you are, Mrs. Chapel."

"Why, thank you!"

Holly moved toward her apartment.

"Some things were delivered for you while you were getting coffee," Mrs. Chapel called after her.

"Oh?"

"By a *handsome man*."

Holly shot her a questioning look.

"I think he's still there," the old lady whispered, loudly enough for passersby on Main Street to hear.

Holly walked around the hallway corner and found Josh— *Josh!*—leaning against the wall next to her door, an array of items covering her doormat. He pushed to standing at the sight of her.

He wore a shirt and tie beneath a sweater vest. With his tall frame and lean physique, he could pass for an Armani model. A sheepishly smiling one. One that moonlighted as a professor of Unfathomable Math.

"Hi," he said.

He'd either become more gorgeous since she'd seen him last or she'd forgotten how gorgeous he'd been to begin with. Her heart, her poor heart, was melting at the sight of him. "Hi."

He lifted a hand and flipped an envelope face up as he

extended it to her. "I brought you this." He'd written her name on it in handwriting that hadn't changed much since high school.

"Thank you." She took it from him.

"Here." He lifted the coffee carrier with her lone drink from her hand. She'd forgotten she'd been holding it.

She began to pull open the flap on the heavy stationery. "Is this when you inform me that you've secretly been buying up all the real estate in Martinsburg?" A smile played across her lips. She'd thought to herself once that he'd have no way of knowing where she lived. She'd been wrong. "Are these my eviction papers?"

"I typically save my evil real estate plotting for towns large enough to merit a Walmart."

"Ah." She uncovered an engraved invitation to the rehearsal dinner.

"It didn't occur to me until last night that I hadn't made sure that you were invited," he said. "I'm sorry."

She moved her attention from the lovely invitation to him. "There's no reason to be sorry. I'm just Trinity's wedding coordinator. I'm not actually in Ben and Amanda's wedding."

"I'd like for you to come."

"I—"

"I'm the one paying for the rehearsal dinner and you're the one who helped me with the planning. You're coming. All right?"

She bit the side of her lip. "If you like."

"I would."

"Then I'll be there." She examined the collection of things sitting in front of her door. "What's all this?" A huge vase of flowers. Three flavors of ground coffee. A sheet cake from the caterer. (It had been her favorite, despite that apple pie had been a better fit for the rehearsal dinner.) Five packages of denture cleaner for Mrs. Chapel. And a twenty-four-pound bag of Meow Mix.

"A few thank-you gifts. And a few gifts to apologize for the fact that your invitation was delivered so late."

Delighted laughter broke from her lips. "You didn't have to do this."

"Do you like any of it?"

"I like all of it." She was so touched and surprised by his thoughtfulness that she almost wanted to cry over it. "Thank you." Her voice emerged wobbly with emotion. "How did you know that Shadow eats Meow Mix?"

He lifted one masculine shoulder. "I remembered from eight years ago. I'll help you carry it in, then I'll get out of your way. I know your family's in town." He must have heard, of course, every syllable of her exchange with Mrs. Chapel.

She opened her door and dazedly tried to lend a hand, while he, in actuality, did all the work.

She stood in her small kitchen, the counters covered with his gifts, the invitation in her hand, quiet resting over them as they smiled at each other. Thank God she hadn't left wadded up panties or something on her floor.

"I'll see you tonight at the rehearsal," he said.

"See you then."

He held eye contact with her for a drawn-out second, then let himself out.

Holly blinked at the items. Did Josh like her? Hope, worry, and confusion battled for control of her mind. Hope, because she dearly wanted him to like her. Worry, because giving him power to hurt her terrified her. Confusion, because she didn't know which was stronger.

The hope. Or the worry.

Where was Holly?

Ben and Amanda's family and friends had arrived at the Texas Olive Oil Company and gathered on the patio for drinks and appetizers thirty minutes ago. Josh hadn't joined them. He stood alone inside the barn, wearing a suit and watching the side door that had been left open for arriving guests.

He glanced at his watch, frowning. Concern tightened around his chest and lungs.

Earlier, at the rehearsal at the church, Holly had welcomed everyone to Trinity and offered a prayer. The minute she'd finished praying, Mitzi had taken over. Mitzi had made them run through the routine they'd follow during the ceremony three times.

Holly had stood off to the side the whole time, close enough that Mitzi or Amanda or Amanda's mom could ask her questions. She'd been wearing business clothing instead of party clothing and holding a pen and the notebook she'd brought with her when they'd looked at venues together. Each time Josh had glanced at her during the rehearsal, she'd either been looking carefully elsewhere or down at her notebook.

Josh turned, taking in the view beyond the open sliding doors of the guests and the scenery. The stormy skies had disappeared around noon. They'd left behind clear, still weather ideal for everything Holly had imagined this night could be. He couldn't accept that she wasn't here to see it.

"Josh," one of the bridesmaids called to him. "Come on out. I have some people to introduce you to."

"Be there in a minute."

He returned his gaze to the side door. Holly had told him she'd come tonight. But maybe she'd chosen to skip it at the last minute. She might be tired. Or maybe she'd made plans with Rob.

Should he call her to make sure she was coming?

He was an idiot. A ridiculous—

Holly appeared in the doorway.

He froze at the sight of her. She wore a dress of burgundy lace on a flesh-colored background fabric. She'd pulled her hair into some kind of loose bun at the back of her neck. High heels.

She looked like a princess.

Need, sharp and painful, broke open inside him. At eighteen, he'd been fatherless, poor, without influence, and sure of just one thing. His love for Holly. Years had passed, but that truth had not changed. The man who didn't do anything halfway still loved her.

He made his way toward her. She approached him with a smile.

"I was worried you weren't going to come," he said.

"I took time to change and redo my hair after the rehearsal."

"You look beautiful."

"Thank you. Is everything going well so far?"

"Yes." He offered the crook of his elbow and she set her hand in it. He guided her through the barn.

"It's like magic," she said. "I can't believe the transformation."

The equipment had been moved out and round tables brought in. Linens, votive candles, and large flower arrangements decorated each table. The caterer had suggested they hang lanterns staggered at different heights from the overhead beams, and he'd agreed. "Do you like how it turned out?" It mattered to him that she did.

"I absolutely love how it turned out. Everything's even better than I expected."

If only she'd let him, he'd throw her parties like this, or buy her jewelry, or take her on trips, or hire someone to socialize Shadow, or whatever else made her happy. "Anything you'd change?" he asked. "If so, I might still be able to make it happen."

"I wouldn't change anything about this rehearsal dinner. Nothing at all."

I wouldn't change you, he thought.

They made their way through the guests to the far edge of the flagstones. When they came to a stop, she stepped gently away from him. Conversations and laughter surrounded them with a friendly hum. Rows of string lights extended from the roof of the barn over the patio, like a canopy.

"Can I get you something to drink or eat?" he asked.

"Maybe in a minute. Wow, look at the view."

In the distance, the lake reflected the glow of sunset like a bronze coin. The fading light made her earrings sparkle and her skin glow.

"I thought the rehearsal went well at the church," he said, making an effort to steer his thoughts toward safer ground.

"Yeah. I thought so too." She glanced up at him out of the corners of her eyes. As usual, the gray-blue depths shone with wry humor. "You did a good job charming the flower girls."

"I try."

"You kept them calm when they started to get rambunctious."

"It was the least I could do."

"Heroic. What're you going to do next?" She angled her chin toward the edge of the patio. "Take a running leap off this thing so we can all watch your cape unfurl as you soar off to charm more five-year-olds?"

"No." One side of his lips rounded upward. "I don't like capes."

She chuckled, then took a moment to let her attention sweep slowly over the guests. "How does this party compare to the ones you attend in Paris?"

"Favorably."

"Really? But there aren't any French women here."

"No."

"French women are famously chic and beautiful."

"Are they? I hadn't noticed."

"You mean to tell me you don't have a French girlfriend?" She arched an eyebrow.

"No."

"Are you sure? Does the name Genevieve ring a bell?"

"No."

"Margaux?"

He shook his head. "Would you be happier if there were French men here?"

"I prefer Texan men."

"Texan men who can cook?" The question showed too much of his hand. He sounded like a jealous boyfriend, except that he was only one of those things. Just the jealous part.

She sized him up, looking highly entertained. "Cooking skills are optional."

Two of Ben's groomsmen joined them. The guys clapped him on the back and introduced themselves to Holly. He watched her shake hands with them, then nod and listen to the story one of them was telling about how badly Josh had played on their golf trip.

Josh had almost made it through his time in Texas. He was leaving day after tomorrow. One more day. He only needed to survive one more day without doing or saying something stupid to Holly and making a royal fool of himself.

She'd been kind to him, but there was a big jump between feeling kindly toward someone and loving them.

One more day. Could he manage to hold back the words inside of him for one more day?

The first rule of mingling on a flagstone patio: avoid accidentally wedging a high heel into a crack between stones. Holly focused on exactly that while chatting with Ben and

Amanda's guests. She knew many of them because such a large number lived in Martinsburg.

Even Mitzi had come, something of a surprise. Holly would have expected Mitzi to spend the evening before Amanda's wedding running twenty miles, drinking organic green tea, and working feverishly on her iPad.

The sun vanished below the horizon line, putting on a great show of artistry and color before the light ebbed away and the temperature dropped.

When they moved inside, Josh showed her to a table at the front. The name cards revealed that he'd assigned her the seat beside his.

"I don't have to sit right here next to all the action," she murmured. "Really. You could have put me at a table in the back corner. I wouldn't have minded."

"I'd have minded. I like talking to you more than I like talking to anyone else here. Sit and let's eat some buttermilk fried chicken."

She gave him a bemused look.

"What?"

"I've been waiting all my life for a good-looking man to order me to eat fried chicken. I guess I can cross that off my wish list."

The dinner commenced in a blur of happiness, delicious southern food, and rustic Texas charm. It had been ages since Holly had had a reason to don her Spanx or shoes more formal than TOMS wedges. She'd been browsing through a boutique months ago when she'd found the burgundy lace sheath she had on. At the time, she'd had nowhere to wear it. She'd bought it anyway, because her intense dress-crush had outweighed practicality. She was very, very glad she had.

During the meal, Josh frequently left Holly's side to attend to his duties as host. Whenever they were apart, she could sense his whereabouts. She'd spot him across the room only to have him look over as if her gaze had called his attention to her. Each time that happened, she returned to the table's conversation with a warm glow spreading through her.

When the last bite of apple pie had been eaten and the final toast given, everyone rose to exchange subdued chitchat and good-byes. The euphoria that had hovered over Holly all evening began to dissipate. She didn't want the night to end. But it was ending, with or without her go-ahead.

When just ten or so guests remained, Holly found herself alone with Josh. She picked up her purse. "I'd best be going."

"I'll walk you out."

They headed toward the patio. "I had a wonderful time," Holly said.

"I'm glad. Thank you for all that you did to help me plan the dinner."

"You're welcome." Such dismaying formality! Next, she'd be curtsying and he'd be bowing crisply like a soldier.

The outdoors greeted them with a very faint fog of rain. Holly glanced upward toward the moon, glowing dimly through clouds.

"Let me see if I can find an umbrella for you," Josh said.

"No, that's all right." The water hadn't formed into droplets.

Instead it seemed to hover in the air, misty and magical. "I like it." She smiled up at him.

Laugh lines fanned out from his eyes as he returned her smile.

Thunk. One of her high heels wedged between two flagstones. She swayed a little and Josh immediately caught her forearm and helped right her balance. "You okay?"

"Fine." She blew a strand of hair out of her eyes, got both shoes on a level stone, and laughed. He still held her arm protectively. "I was just thinking earlier that I needed to avoid doing that very thing." *But then you smiled at me, and I couldn't tear my eyes away from you, and so I lost my concentration.* "I was kind of hoping to make it through the entire night without falling on my face."

"You did."

He was standing so close that she could feel his body heat. "D–did what?"

"Make it through the night without falling."

Literally, perhaps. But not figuratively. She'd fallen, all right.

His expression turned utterly serious and for the first time since Josh had returned to Martinsburg, Holly could see past his defenses. She saw tenderness in his eyes. Tenderness for *her.*

Warm goose bumps spread over her body. He *did* still like her. More, he was going to kiss her. He stepped closer.

He was going to kiss her! She wanted him, physically and in every other way. He was her Josh. The one she'd never gotten over. Anticipation coursed through her. Her breath went shallow with desire—

Wait.

What was she doing? Instinctive worry clashed with confusion. And, abruptly, she stepped away.

His hand dropped from her arm. He looked down and to the side. As if irritated with himself, he gave a slight shake of his head before returning his attention to her. Awkward silence solidified between them. "Holly. I was—"

"Excuse me," the caterer said as she approached, wearing her floral apron. "Sorry to interrupt. I have a quick question for you, Josh."

He inclined his head to listen to the caterer, keeping his vision on Holly.

She could practically feel her heart shriveling. He'd been about to kiss her and she'd stepped back. She'd rejected him even though they'd had the most perfect dinner in the history of perfection. Even though she'd been married to her cell phone for days on the off chance that he'd call. He liked her and goodness knows she liked him. He'd told her himself earlier that he didn't have a girlfriend.

So why had she stepped back?

Two of the women in Amanda's house party walked from the barn onto the patio. "Want to walk out with us?" They looked from her to Josh.

Um. She wanted to stay and let Josh finish his sentence.

"Go ahead," Josh said to the women. "Holly and I will follow in a second." He exchanged a few more words with the caterer, then he and Holly fell in step several paces behind the women, who were in the midst of a discussion about the benefits of Brazilian blowouts.

"I'll look for you tomorrow at the wedding," he said.

Gamely, Holly tried to act as if she hadn't just ruined her one chance at kissing him. "I'll be the one at the wedding impersonating Mitzi's lap dog."

"Someone has to."

"That someone is me."

"I'll be the one in the tuxedo."

"I'll do my best to recognize you, seeing as how men in tuxedos all look alike."

His lips bowed into an imitation of humor. He wasn't actually amused, she knew. His eyes remained troubled.

Remorse twisted hard within her.

Josh slowed his progress. "Good night," he said, loud enough for the ladies in front to hear.

The other women fell over themselves thanking him, flirting with him, and wishing him goodnight.

He responded with his trademark politeness. His suit jacket spread open as he thrust his hands in his pants pockets. He nodded to Holly right before she was bustled toward her car by the women's excitement and chatter.

She drove home with a lump in her throat and tears stinging her eyes, trying to understand what had just happened.

She'd been working so hard to battle back the love for Josh she'd always harbored. Nonetheless, her time with him had softened her heart toward him. It had. When he'd dropped his guard just now, she'd seen that her feelings weren't one-sided. He cared about her too. She'd felt the attraction behind his intentions and experienced the leap of her own response.

So what had gone wrong inside of her? What had sabotaged her?

Fear. That's what had derailed her. She'd been afraid. Not of Josh. Of what, then?

She reached her building, climbed the exterior staircase, and let herself into the hallway. Rob, gone. Mrs. Chapel, long asleep. Loneliness waited for her within her dark and solitary apartment. Beyond her apartment's windows: people coming and going. Inside, emptiness.

She didn't bother turning on lights. The depressing mood of the place suited her. Slipping out of her heels, she walked to her cold fireplace and stood before it, her arms crossed tightly.

Ruthlessly, she raked through her thought patterns, trying to get underneath her fear. Why was she afraid?

She was afraid because she didn't think a romance between Josh and her could possibly end well. She wanted to blame that certainty on the fact that he lived overseas, or on the fact that they'd run out of time in which to cultivate a relationship, or their past history.

But none of those things were the real, hard truth. The real truth was that she didn't think it could end well for them because she didn't believe she was . . . enough for him.

How humiliating! Maddening. She had good self-esteem. She liked herself and she liked her life. But somewhere along the line, a small voice had started whispering to her that Josh was too good for her. Maybe the voice had been there long ago, when they'd been dating, which would partly explain why she'd followed through on his mom's request that she break up with him. In her heart of hearts, perhaps, she hadn't thought herself worthy of him.

Or maybe the voice had begun in those dark days after they'd broken up, when she'd told herself their romance never would have worked anyway, in an effort to make herself feel better. Or maybe all the years of disappointing dates, of watching her family members move on to bigger and better things, of humble middle child syndrome, had given the voice credence. Unlike what they said about a lot of people of her generation, Holly was not filled with a sense of entitlement. No. Quite the opposite.

Somewhere along the line she'd become like Shadow the cat, content to remain alone in the place where she'd always lived, because this was where she felt she belonged and what she deserved. Martinsburg was safe and familiar. She'd closed herself off to opportunities for change. For adventure.

For love. Tears brimmed on her lower lashes before seeping over.

"Holy smoke, Holly. Enough already. Quit it." She swiped the tears from her cheeks.

That sly voice that had been whispering to her wasn't God's voice. She saw that very clearly, standing before her fireplace in her bare feet and her beautiful dress. Josh might be intelligent and successful and rich. But God valued her every bit as much as He valued Josh. Her worth, just like Josh's worth, was found in Him alone. Without consciously knowing it, she'd let doubts creep in and distort her vision.

If she cleared her mind, she could see how Josh's return to Martinsburg might even be considered somewhat . . . ordained. Amanda and Ben could have married in any number of fabulous destinations. Instead, they'd decided to marry here, which had brought Josh back into her life.

It was as if God was saying, *Do you trust me, Holly? Do you believe my timing is best? You've been asking me to prepare you for someone and someone for you, and I've been busy doing exactly that. You and Josh were too young the first time. You both had a lot of maturing and growing to do. But now I've brought him back because he's ready and you're ready and he's the one. I've brought him back to you, Holly. I am, after all, a God of grace and second chances.*

She dearly wanted a do-over of that moment on the patio when fog had encircled them like a blessing and Josh had been on the verge of kissing her. She might not get a do-over. But if she did, she'd draw on God's strength and use it to kick her fears to the curb.

Then she'd risk all.

Chapter 9

♡

"CHAO BAN," SAM GREETED HOLLY THE NEXT DAY.

It was lunchtime and they'd decided to meet at restaurant number ninety-five in their Year of Restaurants. Martinsburg's only Vietnamese food place centered mostly around the take-out side of their business. They offered a mere two tables, both pushed up against a wall.

"Can you repeat that?" Holly took the seat opposite Sam. The restaurant's interior had been painted in clean, bright shades of orange and pale green and white. The smells were promising.

"Chao ban. It's Vietnamese for hello, friend." Sam held up her phone. "I googled it."

"In that case, *chao ban.*"

"Your appearance here leads me to believe that you were able to sneak away from the preparations for the wedding of the century."

"Yes, but I have to hurry back. There are dozens of people at

Trinity right now doing all sorts of decorating. It's taking every bit of my energy to defend the church's dignity."

"Has Amanda's professional wedding coordinator gone on a rampage?"

"On the contrary. Mitzi's remained firmly in control of herself and everyone else. Especially me. I think she views me as her handy and inexpensive personal assistant."

Sam sipped her ice water. "If I were you, I'd tell her to stick that assumption where the sun don't shine."

"But you see, unlike you, I'm a nice person." Holly winked.

"Niceness isn't all it's cracked up to be."

"No. Mitzi's already informed me that she needs me to wrangle the seven flower girls and one ring bearer from the time they arrive up until the start of the ceremony."

"Dare I ask the ages of these children?"

"Two through six."

Sam rolled her eyes. "I recommend giving them all Benadryl. I've heard a rumor that it calms kids down."

"Sam!"

"You disapprove? Fine, then give yourself some Benadryl. I have nieces and nephews that age. Trust me when I say you're going to need an emergency stash of non-messy candy to pacify the kids. I suggest gummi bears."

A server arrived and patiently explained the menu choices to the two Vietnamese food rookies.

"So?" Sam asked, after the server moved off. Her expression communicated expectancy.

"So?"

"Tell me about the rehearsal dinner."

A memory of how Josh had looked last night, sitting beside her at dinner, turning his head to watch her with affection, filled her mind. She relayed all the critical information to Sam. Everything but the almost-kiss.

"Holly, are you totally in love with your high school love turned billionaire? Or are you merely halfway in love?"

"I've never admitted to any degree of love for my high school love turned billionaire."

"You didn't have to. It's written on your face. Now fess up. If you asked me a pointed question about my husband, you know I'd give you a straight answer."

"I don't want to ask you a pointed question about Mr. Perfect. The answer would just depress me."

Sam's smile glinted with self-satisfaction as she flicked her long sable hair over her shoulder. "After he finished vacuuming this morning, he encouraged me to get a pedicure and do some shopping. He's going to be busy all day building me a backyard water feature and planning next week's menu."

"See? Depressing."

"Rob's into you, Holly, lest you've forgotten."

"I haven't forgotten. I like him. He just doesn't make my knees go weak."

"And the billionaire makes your knees go weak. I understand why. I saw him at Das Lokal with my own eyes, remember. He has this really sexy, brainy, intense thing working for him. It's not possible for mortal women to resist that kind of thing for long."

"No," Holly agreed. "It isn't."

Sam considered her, lips pushed to the side. "Have you been taking my advice? Remember the first part? Nothing ventured nothing gained?"

"I'm working on it."

"What about the second part? Have you been viewing yourself as superior to him?"

"Funny you should mention that. I spent a lot of time thinking on that topic last night."

"And?"

"I'm working on that part too."

Sam released a long-suffering sigh. "Your time with him is almost done, Holly. I'll be honest with you. At this point, there may only be one hope left for you and Josh."

"Which is?"

"Divine intervention."

Four forty-five p.m. Fifteen minutes until the wedding ceremony.

Fifteen minutes had never before seemed like such an impossibly long stretch of time. Holly had been corralling the flower girls and the ring bearer for an hour already. At first, she'd trailed the photographer around as the intrepid woman attempted to capture pictures of the little tykes. That hadn't been too terrible, because most of their moms had been in the mix. But then the moms had deposited the kids in this boring anteroom that was beginning to resemble a prison and deserted Holly to go find seats in the jam-packed sanctuary.

The church was *so* jam-packed for Amanda and Ben's wedding, in fact, that Holly had said a prayer asking God to keep the choir loft from buckling under the extraordinary weight. *Here's hoping the ceremony doesn't include architectural collapse and death-by-crushing.*

"I'm hungry," one little flower girl stated.

"I'm thirsty."

"I need to use the potty."

The ring bearer! He'd climbed on top of the bureau with the help of a chair. Holly dashed over, scooped him up, and deposited him safely on the floor.

Each of the children were gorgeously dressed. The ring bearer in a mini-tux. The seven flower girls in dove gray gowns with satin bodices and full tulle skirts. Every hair had been combed into place by the moms. Every black ballet slipper tugged into position. Their angelic appearance had so far proved deceiving.

One of the flower girls screeched and pushed her sister, also a flower girl.

"Girls." Holly placed herself in between the fighting siblings. "Let's be sweet to each other."

They both released a string of tattling aimed at the other.

Oh, no. The ring bearer and the tiniest flower girl were on their way back up the bureau. Determinedly, Holly intercepted the climbers. "Would anyone like some gummi bears?"

"Me!" they all chorused.

She went to her purse for the big package of gummi bears

she'd purchased on her way back to the church after lunch. The itty-bitty set followed her as if she were the Pied Piper. God bless Sam.

"Sit down nicely in a circle, everyone, and I'll come around and give you each gummi bears." With child number two, she learned the importance of making sure she gave them each the same number of gummi bears in the exact same variety of colors.

After she'd dropped gummi bears into the final child's hands, the door creaked open and Josh leaned in.

Joy suffused Holly at the sight of him, as if it had been months since she'd seen him instead of hours.

Josh's face seemed to ease at the sight of her. He stepped fully into the room. He was wearing—*Have mercy on me, Lord*—a tuxedo that looked as if it had been made for him. Which it probably had been. It fit him the way James Bond's tuxedos fit.

The children peered up at Josh while chewing loudly.

Holly skirted the circle of kids and approached him, slightly mortified at the thought of what she must look like. She'd dressed in jeans and a long-sleeved mint green cotton shirt this morning because she'd planned not only to oversee the wedding setup, but also to offer a helping hand if needed. She'd intended to return home before the wedding to change and fix herself up. The second part of her plan hadn't materialized. Mitzi had kept her flat-out busy. A while ago, she'd gathered her hair into a low side ponytail, but even that felt bumpy and askew at this point.

"Hi." She stopped near him, wishing she could blurt out how sorry she was about her kiss-fail.

"So this is where you've been," he said, his voice pitched low.

"Yep. I've been hanging out here with the flower girls—"

"—and the ring bear," the lone boy added. "Grr. I'm a bear."

That set off a round of giggling and loud talking. The sisters began to fight again, so Holly plopped a curly red-headed flower girl in between them.

"Can we have more gummi bears?" one of them asked.

"I still need to go to the bathroom!"

"Keeping care of this group seems like a fun job," Josh remarked.

"Oh, it is. My heart is full of thankfulness."

Just then, one of the girls made an awful choking sound. The best behaved of all the flower girls, a dark-haired five-year-old girl with her hair in two side buns, was half-coughing, half gagging.

Holly knelt beside her. "Are you okay, Olivia?"

Olivia couldn't answer. She was hunched over, wheezing too much to speak. Fear spiked deeply into Holly. *What should she do?*

Josh lowered onto his knee on Olivia's other side, his hand on her back.

Should they give Olivia the Heimlich? she wondered, panicking. *Get water? Thump her back?* Holly wasn't a mom and didn't know—

Olivia hacked and threw up a wad of chewed-up gummi

bears right into the lap of her tulle skirt. After a few deep breaths, she straightened and looked up at Holly, eyes round.

"Are you all right?" Holly asked.

She nodded.

Thank God! Holly smiled tremulously and patted her shoulder. Thank God she was fine.

What wasn't fine?

Olivia's dress.

"New rule, everyone." Holly went to the cupboard and found napkins inside. "You may only eat one gummi bear at a time. Chew it very, very carefully before swallowing. All right?"

They chorused assent.

Josh calmed Olivia and the other kids by asking them questions like *Are any of you married yet?* and *Who did you have to pay to get the gig of flower girl in this wedding?*

With Olivia's attention diverted, Holly did her best to keep her bile down while using the napkins to scoop the . . . *mass* from Olivia's lap. Though she wiped the area as best she could, a stubborn round stain the color of red gummi bears remained.

Holly caught Josh's eye and gestured toward Olivia's skirt, asking him with a somewhat wild-eyed expression, *What in the world should I do about this?*

Mitzi would have her head. She'd been the one pumping the kids full of hard-to-chew gummi bears.

"Any scissors around?" Josh asked.

"I'll check." Was he thinking to cut the stain out? How?

Inside a bureau drawer, she found a pair of scissors that looked like they were circa 1952. She handed them to him.

"How many layers of fabric do your dresses have, girls?" he asked the group. "A hundred?"

"Mine has forty thirty."

"I think mine has a million!"

"I'm two," the youngest flower girl offered.

"I think whoever said a million is probably right," Josh said. "Your dress has so many layers, Olivia, that I don't think it'll miss the top few. What do you think?"

She just blinked.

He escorted her to an empty patch of floor and went to work cutting off the top-most layers of tulle.

When Olivia shot her an uncertain expression, Holly responded with a big smile and a thumbs-up. That dress had probably cost a bundle. If Holly had been the one with the scissors, she'd have hesitated and debated with herself. Josh didn't.

When he finished, Olivia's dress looked slightly less puffy and slightly more sheer, but otherwise as good as new. Olivia scampered to one of her friends. Josh hooked the ring bearer (who'd ascended halfway up the face of the bureau again) under his arm and walked over to Holly.

"I suspected that you were a superhero yesterday," Holly said. "Now your secret identity is definitely busted."

"And here I'd worked so hard to protect it."

Mitzi tossed open the door. "Josh! The wedding is starting in two minutes. I need you to take your position at point

D." Mitzi's method of assigning letters to ceremony positions would have baffled a field general.

"I'm on it." He met Holly's gaze, ruffled the ring bearer's hair, and disappeared.

Mitzi's huge earrings pulled at her lobes as she aimed her laser-beam focus on Holly. "It's time for the children to assemble at point B."

Holly passed the flower girls their petal-filled baskets. She handed the ring bearer his pillow, which didn't actually cushion any rings since Mitzi would never have trusted a child with something so critical.

Out in the hallway, Holly worked to keep peace among the squabbling sisters. She pulled a gummi bear from where it had been hiding, stuck near the hem of the redhead's dress. And she kept reminding the girls to keep the petals *inside* the baskets until the right moment.

Amanda's mom passed by Holly's group with an I'm-thoroughly-charmed-by-you "Mmm." High praise.

Mitzi arranged everyone in the order of the procession, then the enormous group slowly made their way into the church's foyer. The first piece of music gusted through the organ's pipes, all but causing the church to vibrate with majesty.

The flower girls and ring bearer gradually edged closer to the front of the queue.

A dash of white caught Holly's eye and she turned in time to see Amanda and her father enter the foyer. *Oh*, Holly thought, awe settling over her at the sight of Amanda as a bride. Amanda had always been stunning. But today, in her beaded ivory gown, so full of delight and excitement, she looked prettier than Holly had ever seen her look. The kind of pretty that could put a single girl in a mint green V-neck shirt into a trance of fascination.

Amanda had parted her blonde hair on the side and swept it into an intricate style at the base of her neck. Her veil had been positioned at the top of her updo. Its sheer fabric cascaded downward into a train. Her bouquet burst with fall colors of russet, apple green, pale orange, and trailing vines of autumn berries.

Holly earnestly wished Amanda and Ben the very, very best. She caught Amanda's eye. "You look beautiful," she whispered.

Amanda beamed. "Thank you," she mouthed back.

When the flower girls and the ring bearer reached point A, Mitzi sent them down the aisle. The guests responded with a collective "Aww." Then the grand notes of the wedding march began and Amanda and her father swept into the sanctuary.

Holly found a spot in the far corner of the foyer where she could listen and watch the ceremony unobtrusively through a window. If the choir loft came crashing down she'd be squashed like a bug.

Ah, weddings. She loved them. She really loved them. Weddings were magnificent declarations of all that was good in this life. Loyalty. Honor. Love. Esteeming another above yourself. Weddings never failed to stir her or arouse in her a bittersweet wistfulness born of her own hope of marrying one day.

When Amanda and Ben exchanged vows, Holly sighed

and went a little teary-eyed. Or maybe she was going teary-eyed over Josh, standing so solidly next to Ben. The best man. Indeed.

One of the candles in the unity candle set was slow to light. And the maid of honor almost bobbled Amanda's bouquet at one point. But those were the little things that made weddings charming and real. Everything else went perfectly.

When the ceremony concluded, Holly dashed around like a runner on a steeplechase course, making sure that the flower girls and ring bearer were all returned to their rightful owners. Then Mitzi trapped her and fired a dozen staccato questions at her regarding parking issues and when the decor could be taken down.

After Mitzi departed, Holly looked around and saw that the entire church had emptied faster than a glass bottle of Dr Pepper. She hadn't caught even a glimpse of Josh since he'd walked down the aisle during the recessional with the maid of honor on his arm.

She let herself into the sanctuary and trailed her fingers along the long swags of ribbon, the glass hurricanes confining candles that had already been blown out, the sprays of flowers mounted on the inside ends of the pews. She took a seat on the very first row.

She needed to rally herself, go home, get cleaned up, then make an appearance at the reception. She'd sent in a response card saying she'd attend. Far more critically, the reception would be her last chance to see Josh.

She'd rally. She would. But the day had drained her

physically and emotionally, and she needed a minute to sit and take in the hushed calm of her surroundings.

One of the decorators had brought in a towering wrought iron arch that stood on the dais in front of the altar. A garland of large waxy leaves, twigs, and the same flowers that had graced Amanda's bouquet covered the entire arch and even rippled a few feet onto the dais on either side. Lovely.

During the ceremony, the arch had served as a picturesque frame for Ben and Amanda. But it hadn't framed only them. On its far side, it also framed the altar. As Holly studied the altar, light gleamed and slid along one plane of the cross.

When she'd parted from Josh eight years ago, God had remained. He'd been at her side through her hardest moments, her saddest moments, her loneliest.

Whatever comes, I trust you, God. If your plans for me don't include Josh or don't include marriage, then I'll keep on trusting you. The silence of her aloneness settled over her like pixie dust. She couldn't stop herself from adding a short p.s. to her prayer. *If Josh does happen to . . . perhaps, maybe, please . . . be the one for me, then I pray that you'll give me just one more opportunity with him.*

The side exit door whooshed open and Holly snapped her head to the side to see Josh standing in the opening, backlit by a late November sky. His dark gaze cut across the space and locked onto her.

Her pulse leapt then began to pound. What could he be doing here? He was the best man. He was needed at the reception.

He walked toward her. "I was looking for you. Out in the parking lot, and then on the road to the winery. I couldn't find you."

"I'm not," she motioned to her clothing as she pressed to her feet, "dressed for the reception yet."

His brows drew down. He appeared both determined and unsettled, standing there, sleek in his gorgeous tuxedo. "I've been looking for you a lot lately, Holly. All day today. Last night at the rehearsal dinner. Just now. I . . ." His hair was slightly mussed. His eyes bright with fervency. "I realized that I've been looking for you for years. I've been looking for you ever since I left Martinsburg."

Hope rose within her painfully. What? Had he . . . had he really just said that?

He continued, recklessly honest. "I don't want to spend the rest of my life looking for you."

"You don't?" Her voice emerged as fragile as a skein of silk.

"No. I don't want to make a fool of myself in front of you, either." He raked a hand through his hair. "I've been telling myself to keep my mouth shut around you until I leave Texas. But I'm not going to make it." His lips settled into a hard, reso-lute line. "I'd rather make a fool of myself than remain silent."

She gaped at him in patent astonishment.

"I can't not tell you that I love you," he said. "I . . . I des-perately love you."

Holly inhaled a jagged gasp. His words were almost too marvelous to process. He'd handed her dearest dream to her without warning. He loved her? Joy began to unfurl inside her.

She walked to him, stopping so close that she was able to rest her palms on his chest. She hadn't touched him in a girlfriend-like manner in ages. To do so now felt like pure, heady bliss. She smoothed his lapels, feeling the tremor in her hands.

He stared down at her as if he was afraid to believe that the news might be good.

The news was very good. For them both. She was still a little afraid, but God was faithful. He countered her fears by filling her with an undeniable sense of rightness. She looked directly into Josh's eyes. "I love you too."

He gave her the exact same crooked smile he'd given her the day he'd first told her that he loved her. "You love me?"

"I do. I love you."

"I've loved you since high school," he said. His arms came up to support her back. "I tried to stop but I couldn't. Seeing you again has only made me positively sure that you're the one for me."

"I've loved you since high school too." She interlaced her hands around his neck. Laughing breathlessly, she quoted his words back to him. "I tried to stop but I couldn't. Seeing you again has only made me positively sure that you're the one for me."

He kissed her. And she kissed him back. And he kissed her more for good measure. There, with the altar's cross watching over them and the day's last sun rays pouring through the stained glass like a benediction.

Holly's heart soared with amazement and gratitude and love. Josh! Josh loved her.

He pulled back a few inches. "I lied about needing your help to find a rehearsal dinner location. My assistant booked the olive oil farm months ago. I misled you because it was the only way I could think of to spend time with you."

"Your assistant booked the olive oil farm?" she asked, like one of those parrots that repeats things. It was hard to think straight at this particular moment. He'd just incinerated her with his kisses and sent her whole world spinning with the declaration that *he loved her*.

"Yes."

"Months ago? Your assistant had the very same idea that I had and booked the farm months ago?"

He nodded and swept a section of her hair away from her cheek. "I'm sorry for deceiving you."

"You're forgiven. And also, by the way, you have a *very* good assistant. Has she considered turning her attention to brokering peace in the Middle East?"

His expression warmed with amusement. "I love you."

"I love you."

"I'll stay in Martinsburg," he said. "I can work from anywhere."

"So can I, Josh. I'm a writer." Her hands were still intertwined behind his neck. Oh, the happiness of this! "Relocating to Paris for a while doesn't actually sound too shabby to me."

"It doesn't?"

"If this is Paris, France, home of the Eiffel Tower and the Louvre and croissants that we're talking about, then no. It doesn't."

"You'd move to France?"

"Yes," she answered, growing more sure of it. "I would." He'd given her an irresistible motivation to grab hold of her very own real-life adventure.

"I love you, Holly."

"I love you, Josh. Now kiss me some more." She was grinning and crying at the same time. "But be quick about it. You're the best man and we have a wedding reception to attend."

Miracle of miracles, God had brought Josh back to her. And this time, she wouldn't let him go. This time, Josh wouldn't leave her behind.

This time, the timing was perfect.

Epilogue
♡

Holly,

Today is our wedding day. In just a few hours I'll get to see you in your wedding dress, you'll walk down the aisle to me, and before God we'll promise ourselves to each other for the rest of our lives.

Thank you for agreeing to be my wife. For loving me. For showing me what matters in this life.

Neither the years we spent apart nor the distance between us had the power to change my love for you. My heart was, and is, and always will be yours.

Je t'aime, Holly. I love you. Till death do us part, my love.

—Josh

An October Bride

♡

KATIE GANSHERT

For my dad—the best father
and Papa Bear around.
I love you more.

Chapter 1

♡

THE SUDDENNESS WITH WHICH LIFE CAN UPEND IT-self is alarming. One second you're two months away from matrimony—unable to find that perfect dress but confident it's out there in the wide abyss of bridal boutiques—and then *wham*. An MRI reveals a tumor in the brain of the man you love more than life.

Only that man isn't your fiancé.

This singular diagnosis turns your entire world on its head. Instead of the bride-to-be, you are the woman who has canceled the cake order and returned the ring, all while apologizing pro-fusely to your wounded ex-fiancé who was nothing but kind and patient.

It's a hard thing to recover from—these sharp, unexpected upheavals.

And just when my life started to normalize, everything went

flip all over again. Three weeks fresh and I'm trying to accli-
mate. After all, if Dad can do it—if he can go from the picture
of health, to the trenches of cancer-battle, to the cruel tease
that was four months of remission, to the shockingly cold
waters of a two-month time clock, then what's my excuse? In
my weakness, I have forced my father to be the strong one, to
comfort *me*, yet *he's* the dying man.

This has to stop.

I take a deep breath, inhaling the aroma that is Mayfair,
Wisconsin, in the beginning of autumn—a paradoxical com-
bination of fresh air, burning leaves, and the scent of Eloise's
famous pumpkin bars wafting from the front windows of her
bakery. A flock of geese honk overhead. I look up at the clear
blue sky—the dark bodies in V-formation—wondering if I
couldn't join them somehow. Grow a pair of wings and take
flight to someplace where time and death do not exist.

Instead, I let out my breath, remove the two-day accumu-
lation of mail from the mailbox, and head up the walkway,
taking in the modest home of my childhood—buttercream
siding with country-blue shutters, flower boxes outside the
windows, and a pair of burning bushes that bookend the front,
their leaves a vibrant bloodred. It's a house that carried my
brother and me from infancy to adulthood and has since
treated a pair of empty nesters with kindness these past nine
years. At least until the diagnosis.

Will Mom put it on the market after he's gone?

Shaking away the question, I unlock the door, step inside,
and blink at the mess before me. Saying yes to cat-sitting while

my parents drove up to Door County for the weekend was my first attempt at climbing aboard the be-strong-for-Dad train. If Mom and my brother can hop on so quickly, going about life with smiles and unshakable faith, then surely I can at least feed the cats and empty the litter box. Animals are, after all, my forte. What I failed to remember, as I eagerly agreed to the favor, was that my parents' cats are not normal cats.

Case in point?

The mess of kitty litter and down feathers scattered across the hardwood floor. A groan escapes from my mouth like a slow leak. Off to the side, Oscar lounges beside the emptied-out carcass of a throw pillow.

"Seriously?"

His furry tail twitches lazily.

I head down the hall toward the room with the closet where Mom keeps the cleaning supplies. Floorboards creak beneath my cross trainers as I smooch the air and whistle for the other beastly feline to come out from hiding. The tabby is a no-show, which can only mean she's responsible for the mangled pillow.

I cross the small office that was once my brother's bedroom to set the stack of mail on Dad's desk. Something catches my eye. A familiar leather-bound journal sits precariously close to the desk's edge—a birthday present I gave Dad three years ago, before cancer cast its ugly shadow over our lives. My father isn't much of a writer, but I knew the collection of quirky quotes on the top of each page would make him chuckle.

Trailing my finger down the spine, I find myself wishing I could go back to the time when tragedy was something that happened to other people, or better yet, wishing I could fix what is wrong now. My inability to do anything but cat-sit leaves me with a helplessness I'm unaccustomed to feeling. As I turn away from the desk, the journal falls to the floor with a *whap*, and a piece of paper slips out from its pages.

I bend over, but the words—written in neat, straight script at the top—stop me mid-reach.

Bucket List.

I pick up the paper carefully, delicately—like it is a find as rare as the Dead Sea Scrolls. These are my father's dreams. His dying wishes. The things he wants to accomplish before the end. Carefully written on the sheet of paper I now hold in my hand. I sit on the edge of Dad's swivel chair, knowing this is private but unable to resist the temptation. If there is something on this page I can give him or help him accomplish, how can I look away?

Take Marie to Ireland.

He did. Two years ago, after his surgery. Before his first round of chemo. Dad got himself a passport and booked the tickets, and they flew across the Atlantic. They spent a whole week visiting pubs, riding bikes through ancient ruins, looking into Mom's genealogy.

Let Liam teach me to ride a motorcycle.

He did that too. I'll never forget watching the pair of them in matching Harley Davidson bandannas, driving around Mayfair's town square while Mom clutched my arm, convinced her two boys would become one with the cement.

Run a half marathon with Emma.

I smile at the extrabold line crossing this one off, as if showcasing my father's triumph. Dad is not a runner. I was a bit perplexed when he asked if he could train with me, but I welcomed the extra time together.

Fix the boat with Liam.

Just how much time did those two spend in the garage, resurrecting that hunk of junk? All four of us took it out on the lake for the first time this past Fourth of July. I'd strapped on a life preserver and brought rations, sure we'd either sink or be stranded. Turned out, I didn't need either. The day had been a success.

Go on a hot air balloon ride.
Swim with dolphins.

Emotions well in my throat—a hot, sticky mixture of joy and sadness. As much as I don't want my father to go, I'm so proud of the way he's going. Moisture builds in my eyes as I reach the items that are not yet crossed off. *Yet* being the key word, because I know my dad.

Spend a weekend in Door County.

(He'll get to cross that off as soon as he comes home and relieves me of crazy cat duty.)

Take dancing lessons with Marie.

(Mom will love that.)

Walk Emma down the aisle.

The words are like a sucker punch to the gut. I deflate in the chair. Unable to swallow. Unable to breathe. Unable to do anything but press a palm against the pit forming in my stomach.

Chapter 2

♡

MY BRAIN HAS SWITCHED TO AUTOPILOT. I'M NOT SURE how I arrived at my small bungalow on the edge of town. At some point, I must have put the page back in Dad's journal, cleaned the mess in the living room, fed the cats, and driven home. But it's all a fog. I keep picturing myself as a little girl, donning my mother's veil and her oversized white high heels, walking down a pretend aisle on my daddy's arm toward Scooby, our very first family dog. A great stand-in groom, may he rest in peace. The memories wrap around my heart and squeeze tight while my mind worries those five words raw.

Walk Emma down the aisle.

The pit in my stomach grows—deepening and widening while I walk haphazardly through the yard. As sick as the discovery has made me, at least I saw it now instead of after, when it would have been too late. At least I have a chance to do something. My thoughts scramble this way and that, grappling for a solution, until one comes—wild and half-baked. What if I called up Chase and told him I changed my mind? Never mind the fact that I ripped his heart out two years ago; we should get married after all. Would he hear me out, or would he hang up the second I announced myself on the other end of the line?

I step onto my porch, over two loose floorboards, and stop. The front door is ajar. My brow furrows at the thin strip of space that leads into my home. Forgetting to lock up is one thing—a common side effect of growing up in a tiny northern Wisconsin town. But forgetting to shut the door all the way?

No, I wouldn't do that.

Which means the latch must be broken—one of many broken things in my well-loved home. It's a perfectly logical explanation, and yet I find myself clutching my purse tighter as I quietly open the screen door. This is the moment in scary movies when viewers scream, "You fool, don't go inside!" I step over the threshold anyway. This is Mayfair. There are no serial killers. There probably aren't even any burglars. Even so, the lack of greeting from Samson has me on edge. A vision of my beloved pooch drugged and dragged into the bathroom while some drug dealer strips my home for cash flashes through my mind. It is the epitome of far-fetched. Knowing this, however, does not stop me from exchanging my purse for the vase on the sofa table.

Muffled sounds come from the kitchen.

I raise the vase over my shoulder, prepared to hurl it at the perpetrator's head. I am creeping toward the noise when, out of nowhere, Jake Sawyer steps into view. I yelp. He jumps. And the vase falls to the floor with a heavy clunk.

"You scared me half to death!" I say, clutching my chest.

"Who did you think I was—Ted Bundy?"

"I had no idea. You didn't announce yourself."

"My truck's in your driveway."

"It is?" I look over my shoulder, as if I might see through the walls of my house. How did I not notice Jake's truck on my way in? Then I remember those five words on my dad's bucket list, the ones that had me on autopilot. "Where's Samson?"

"Out back chasing squirrels." He cocks his head in that way he does whenever he's concerned. "You okay?"

I wave my hand, then bend over and retrieve the vase. Not even a chip. The thing is made of thick, sturdy glass—the kind of material that probably wouldn't have knocked out a burglar so much as killed him. I'm very thankful I didn't chuck it at Jake's head. "What are you doing here?"

He holds up a wrench. "You said your kitchen sink faucet was leaking."

"Oh, right." I return the vase to the sofa table and cup my forehead, trying to gain my bearings. "You didn't have to come over on your day off."

Jake runs his father's hardware store. Arthritis makes it hard for Mr. Sawyer to do much besides chat with the customers, so Jake does all the real work. And whenever he's not working there, he spends time in his gigantic man-shed, making and restoring furniture. He calls it a hobby, but I know better. Jake is a craftsman. If it wasn't for loyalty to his dad, I have every bit of confidence he could turn his "hobby" into a lucrative, full-time profession.

"I figured I needed to fix the leak before Mayor Altman issued you a citation."

I smile, but only just. Our mayor has recently gone on a crusade to make Mayfair a "green" town. His enthusiasm over the cause has failed to spread to the rest of us.

Jake scratches the dark stubble on his chin, studying me like I studied the vase a moment ago. I wonder if he sees any cracks. "I was on my way out to get my toolbox."

"Oh, okay." My conversational skills are riveting today.

He heads outside, the screen door whapping shut behind him. The shock of finding that list, followed by the onslaught of adrenaline, has me out of sorts. I need to go upstairs and get cleaned up for the Fall Harvest Festival committee meeting. My best friend is the committee coordinator and has finagled me into joining in the planning, which means I should march up the stairs, wash up, change into something nice, and forget I ever saw Dad's bucket list. But chirping birds and late morning sunlight woo me outside. I sit on sun-warmed floorboards and rest my elbows on my knees.

Walk Emma down the aisle.

He never would have written those words if he would have known I'd see them, but I did see them and it can't be undone. Those five words are seared into my conscious, worse than the most stubborn of stains.

Jake pulls his toolbox from the bed of his rusted-out Chevy.

I squint at him as he walks toward me—broad shoulders clad in a flannel shirt, unbuttoned over a simple gray tee, backward Milwaukee Brewers ball cap, with his perpetual five o'clock shadow and eyes the color of the sky overhead. I wait for him to walk past. Instead, he sets his toolbox on the porch and sits beside me, bringing with him the unmistakable scents of cedar and pine. It's a fragrance that will forever and always be Jake. "Something on your mind, Emma?"

Should I tell him what I saw? Should I tell him about my crazy, half-cocked idea? This is Jake, after all. Buddies with my ex-fiancé, sure, but also my brother's best and oldest friend—which would make him like a brother to me, if not for the giant crush I hid over the course of my growing-up years. He's a guy who has the whole *quick to listen, slow to speak* thing perfected. I rub my eyes with the heels of my palms, thankful I'm not one for mascara. "I found my dad's bucket list."

"Bucket list?"

"Everything he wants to accomplish before he . . . you know."

Jake gives a slow, comprehending nod.

"Almost everything is crossed off."

"I'm sorry."

"Three are left. One he'll be able to cross off as soon as he returns from Door County. Another I'm sure is in the works. And then the last one is completely outside of his control." I grip my elbows. "But not mine."

Jake raises his eyebrows. "What is it?"

"Walk Emma down the aisle." And there it is, gathering quicker than I can blink—moisture in my eyes. I swipe at a lone tear and look away. "On my way home, I was contemplating calling Chase."

"Chase?" Jake says the name with disgust, like he can't believe my nerve.

"I know, but it's my dad. And this is finally something I can give him. You know how much I've been looking for a way to help. Well, here it is." Selfishly, I want it for myself too. What girl wants the sole memory of her father walking her down an aisle to be of her six-year-old self saying *I do* to an overweight, crooked-eyed Boston terrier?

Jake scratches his jaw. "Do you still love Chase?"

I shake my head, hating the answer even as I give it. I'm not sure if I ever really loved Chase, at least not in the way brides are supposed to love their grooms. He was a safe bet. I knew exactly what our life would be together. Until Dad got cancer and all bets were off, even the safe ones. "But he's a great guy. We get along. People get married for a lot less."

Jake takes off his cap and runs his hand over his dark hair as he looks out at my overgrown lawn and the leaves rustling on the branches of my maple tree. I can guess what he's thinking. Chase and Jake were friends, and I broke Chase's heart. Surely there's some sort of guy code that requires Jake to watch his buddy's back. Keep the ex far, far away. He slides his baseball hat back onto his head. "If you're looking for a groom, I can do it."

"What?"

"I'll be your groom."

I laugh. "Be serious . . ."

"I *am* being serious."

"You can't be my groom."

"Why not?"

"Because you're not . . . I'm not . . ." I fumble my words, trying to grasp one of a thousand different reasons. "You have a girlfriend."

He pulls his chin back. "A girlfriend?"

"That mystery woman the bunco ladies are always gabbing about."

He cocks his head, like he's disappointed I would believe anything that comes from the mouth of a sixty-year-old woman wearing a pink T-shirt with the words *Bunco Babe* on it.

"What—there's no mystery woman?"

He shakes his head, a hint of amusement in his eyes.

"But why?"

"The bunco ladies kept trying to set me up. I kept saying no. So they made an assumption I didn't bother to correct."

"No, I don't mean why isn't there a mystery woman. I mean why would you offer to be my groom? That's . . . that's . . . a little different than fixing my faucet."

Jake's cheeks turn pink, and Jake *never* blushes. He scuffs his work boot against the cement. Drags his broad palm down his face. My ravenous curiosity eats up more and more of my shock the longer he makes me wait. What could possibly motivate him to make such an offer?

"Ben." The name escapes on an exhale—shockingly un-expected.

"You're offering to be my groom because of your brother?"

"Remember when Ben made it to the Lumberjack World Championships in Hayward?"

"He was the town celebrity." I smile a sad smile. Despite graduating in the same class, Ben and I were never close. Our link was always Jake. Whenever we ran into each other, like people do in small towns, that's who we'd talk about—Jake, and how he was liking life in Milwaukee. But now Jake is back in Mayfair, and Ben . . .

"He begged me to come watch him compete. It was a big deal."

"You didn't know what would happen." Nobody did. Not a single person on this earth could have predicted that two days into the tournament, Ben would die in a freak accident. Everyone had high hopes that Hayward would be the first of many world championships for the youngest Sawyer boy.

"Doesn't change the fact that I didn't go."

I pull at the sleeves of my sweatshirt, wishing I could change the subject, wishing I could take away the sadness clouding Jake's eyes. Seems that's all I do these days—wish, wish, wish. Only there isn't a genie in sight and the stars aren't out yet.

"It was the only time Ben ever asked me for anything. And I didn't give it to him."

"Jake . . ."

"Trust me, Emma, you don't want to live with regret." He lets out his breath, then sets his hands on the floorboards behind us, leans back into his arms, and nudges me with his shoulder. "Besides, it'd get the Bunco Babes off my back. You can be my mystery woman."

The words unleash a flutter in my chest. I tell myself it's a silly, leftover reaction from days long gone. "Okay, but what happens after? I mean, you'd be . . . we'd be . . ." The rising heat in my cheeks makes me want to pull my hood over my head.

He clears his throat. "It wouldn't be a real wedding. I mean, we wouldn't sign the marriage certificate."

"Oh, right."

The crease between his eyebrows deepens. "Unless . . ."

I wave my hand, shooing away whatever his *unless* might be. I mistook his friendship once before. I promised myself a long time ago I would never make that assumption again. "No, of course that's what we'd do. But Jake, you don't have to do this. I mean, it would be . . ."

"Crazy?"

I laugh. "Beyond."

"Crazy's not all bad. I've actually heard that crazy can be fun." He smiles at me then—the kind of smile that is bracketed between a pair of parenthetical dimples. "So what do you say, Emma? You want to be crazy with me?"

It's nothing like my first proposal. There is no ring or

flower bouquet or man on one knee professing his undying devotion. There is no hesitation either. Without letting myself think about the consequences or implications, I say yes to Jake Sawyer. For my dad.

Chapter 3

♡

A COTTON CANDY SUNSET FRAMES MY PARENTS' HOUSE as Jake turns the key to his truck. The grumbling engine goes quiet. "You ready?"

I wipe my clammy palms against my jeans. "My stomach's been doing nonstop pirouettes since you picked me up." Up until this point, our less-than-twenty-four-hour-old engagement has been nothing but an enticing idea—one Jake and I talked through at length over an entire pot of pumpkin spice coffee yesterday, after he finished fixing my faucet and I had returned from the Fall Harvest Festival committee meeting. We sat at my too-tiny, can-never-have-more-than-one-guest-over-for-dinner kitchen table and hashed out a plan.

"Are you afraid they'll be upset?" Jake asks.

"Are you kidding? My mom will be thrilled."

"She will?"

"Come on. She's dreamed about us getting married since we were teenagers."

His eyes crinkle in the corners. "No she hasn't."

"Trust me, she has."

He leans back in his seat, the evening's shadows darkening his features. "Huh."

I take a deep breath, annoyed with my pesky conscience. According to doctors, my dad has one month, maybe two, and as far as I'm concerned, there will be no items left uncrossed on his bucket list. Not if I can help it. Whatever confessions I need to make can be made after he's gone. Surely God will understand. Surely, after twenty-seven years of playing by his rules, he will allow me this one indiscretion, if something so gray can even be considered an indiscretion.

"Emma?"

I blink.

Jake's staring at me. No baseball hat. No five o'clock shadow. Not even one of his flannels. His transformation from rugged to dashing does little to improve my focus.

"Sorry, what did you say?"

"I have something for you." This time, he's the one who wipes his hands on his jeans. The show of nerves is comforting somehow, a reminder that we're in this together. He shifts his hips forward, reaches into his back pocket, and brings out his fist. "I thought, since we're engaged . . ."

"Please tell me you didn't buy a ring."

He opens his hand.

My fingers move to my lips.

"It was my maternal grandmother's. I inherited it from my mother. I know it's not a diamond, but it seemed like something you would wear."

"Jake, I can't wear this."

"Sure you can."

I shake my head. Jake should save this for the woman he loves. For the woman he's going to spend the rest of his life with. That woman isn't me. I can't wear his grandmother's ring. But before I'm able to voice any of this, he slips the piece of jewelry onto my finger—a gold band set with an oval-cut pearl surrounded by tiny red gemstones. "Now they'll believe us."

I look at him, this man I've known since I was three. I grew up tagging along with him and my brother, at first wanting to be one of the guys, then wanting to date one of those guys, and here that guy is, putting his grandmother's ring on my finger. I stare down at my hand, reminding myself this isn't real. Jake is only doing me a favor. Besides, I laid my schoolgirl crush to rest a long time ago. Chase had been proof. "It's beautiful."

He winks, climbs out of his truck, and opens my door, letting in the chill. I swing my legs around and take his offered arm. Together, we crunch through the leaves in the same lawn we used to play in as kids—ghost in the graveyard, kick the can, capture the flag, and every other neighborhood game—when two things happen simultaneously: I notice my brother's motorcycle behind Dad's Lincoln Navigator, and the front door flies open.

Mom stands inside the door frame, beaming from ear to ear, her gray-blonde curls tucked behind her ears, a novel's worth of questions sparkling in her hazel eyes. Nix the gray and the wrinkles and twenty extra pounds, and I am basically her doppelgänger. "If it isn't Jake Sawyer!" She steps forward and gives Jake a tight squeeze, making eyes at me over his shoulder, mouthing his name as if I don't already know it. "What a wonderful surprise!"

"Good evening, Mrs. Tate."

"If I've told you once, I've told you a hundred times." Mom gives his chest a friendly prod with her finger. "It's Marie to you."

The pirouettes in my stomach pick up speed. We might be able to fool my parents, but my brother is a whole different ball game. To say his presence complicates our plans is the understatement of the year. "Liam's here?"

"He got back from his trip this afternoon. I invited him to join us."

Jake and I exchange a nervous glance.

"How was Door County?" he asks Mom.

"Oh, just wonderful. Gorgeous in the fall. Have you ever been?"

"A couple times as a kid."

"It's breathtaking, isn't it?"

He nods earnestly.

Mom looks from him, to me, to him, to me, her eyes dancing. "Should we go inside?"

I want to shake my head. Nope, no thank you. I would

much rather stand out here, away from Liam and his prying, astute eyes. Judging by the way Jake's feet do not move, I think he's in agreement with my plan.

"Come in, you two. Come in. Martin, Liam, look who's here!" Mom motions for Jake to go ahead, then takes my arm before I can follow, a question written all over her delighted face. *What does this mean?* As much as I'd like to stand out here where it's safe and attempt to explain my unexpected guest to her, I cannot leave Jake on his own. He's already doing enough.

"Mom."

She lets it go for now, and we join the men, who are busy shaking hands in the middle of the living room. Jake stands with a stiffness in his shoulders while a slightly sunburned, mostly tan Liam looks on with an unmistakable gleam in his eye, as if he's tucked a smirk into one corner of his mouth. We haven't even explained ourselves yet and already he doesn't believe us. I can tell. Trying to ignore him, I smile at Dad. Except for the scar on his bald head and the sharp edges of his shoulders, there is no trace of the cancer spreading throughout his brain. He's even gained back some weight since finishing his last round of chemo several months ago. His warm brown eyes sparkle as he steps forward and wraps me in a tight hug. I don't want him to let go. I want to stay right here, in this moment forever.

"Fun trip?" I manage to squeak out.

"The best." His voice rumbles against my ear, an ocean of calm. It makes the tightness in my throat tighter. My father has always been my hero, but these past two years, especially these past several days, has him superseding hero status. "How were the cats?" he asks.

"Don't get me started."

He chuckles, then lets me go and addresses Jake. "It's a nice surprise to see you here."

"Definitely unexpected," Liam adds.

Jake sticks his hands in his back pockets. "I thought you were sailing around the San Juan Islands or something like that."

"Finished a day early." My brother has an insane job. He actually gets paid—and good money too—to take rich people on outdoor adventures, all in the name of leadership training. He's climbed Kilimanjaro, hiked the Na Pali Coast in Kauai, and almost everything else in between. Technically, he lives in Mayfair. But he's gone more often than he's around. "So what's this?" He flicks his finger between Jake and me. "Are you two together?"

I look at my partner in crime, then back at my brother. "I guess you could say that."

Liam's eyes widen.

I give him my best pleading look.

It only makes the smirk in the corner of his mouth bigger. He gives Jake a friendly slap on the shoulder. "It's about time, man! Emma only had a crush on you all through high school."

Jake cocks his head.

My entire face catches on fire. "No I didn't."

"Then what was up with all those little hearts you drew everywhere?" He traces an invisible heart with his finger. "JS plus ET equals true love."

I am going to murder him.

"I think it's wonderful," Mom says.

"Me too. I've always thought you two would make a great couple." Dad claps his hands, then rubs them together. "Now Jake, I hope you're hungry. When Emma said she was bringing a guest to dinner, I think Marie thought the Packers' entire defensive line would be coming."

Jake pats his flat abs. "Starved."

"Anything else happen while we were away?" Mom asks.

I swallow, my throat suddenly parched. This is the perfect opportunity to make the announcement, only I find myself waffling. Liam was not part of tonight's plan. We were going to tell him after we eased into the charade by first telling my parents. I had come prepared for something akin to a warm-up speech, given in front of the safety of a mirror, only to find out there would be no practicing. "Well . . ."

Jake runs his finger under his collar. "Emma and I . . ."

"We're engaged!" I blurt.

"What?" Mom and Dad say the word in unison.

I hold up my left hand, grateful for Jake's forethought. It would have looked extra suspicious if I didn't have a ring.

"Engaged?" Dad asks.

"To be married?" Mom adds, as if there is another kind of engaged Jake and I might be.

Liam coughs, or maybe it's a laugh. I can't tell.

I stare at my parents, trying to gauge their reaction, wondering if we shouldn't have somehow led up to the announcement. Told them we were serious over salads, in love over the main course, engaged by dessert. "We know it's fast."

"More like warp speed," Liam says.

The fire in my cheeks spreads into my ears. My brother is many things—a charmer, an adrenaline junkie, the life of the party—but he's also shrewd and skeptical. And right now his shrewd, skeptical stare bores into the side of my face. I cannot look at him.

"Mystery woman," Mom mumbles.

"What's that?" Dad says.

Her face brightens, a tangible lightbulb moment. "*You* are Jake's mystery woman?" She laughs—fairy dust sprinkling the air, dissolving some of the tension.

Dad furrows his brow. "What mystery woman?"

"Jake's been dating someone for the past several months. All the ladies of Mayfair have been trying to guess who. Turns out, that woman is our daughter." Mom takes my hand and examines the ring. "This is gorgeous."

"It was Jake's grandmother's."

"Wait a minute," Dad says, apparently trying to keep up with Mom. "If you and Jake have been dating, why did you keep it a secret?"

"They probably didn't want to put pressure on the relationship, Martin. You know how nosy this town can be. I understand wanting to keep things private." Mom looks up from the ring. "What I don't understand is keeping it private from us."

"We're sorry. We, um, didn't want anything to be awkward. In case things didn't work out."

Mom shoos away my apology and examines the ring more closely. "Jake, are those rubies?"

"Garnets," he says.

I take my hand back and peek at Dad, watching the wrinkles gather on his forehead. Time is a funny thing when the end of a person's life draws near. Days that once flew by like discarded seconds turn into twenty-four-hour lifetimes. The definition of fast changes. This engagement came out of nowhere, but my dad's face softens. I wonder if he's picturing me in a white dress, my arm wrapped around his as he walks me down the aisle. I wonder if he's thinking about his bucket list.

This is for you, I want to say.

"This is really what you want?" he asks me.

"Yes."

That's all it takes—one simple *yes*. His face splits into a smile that transforms him into a happy, healthier, younger man. Then he grabs Jake's hand and pulls him in for a hearty thump on the back. "Congratulations!"

Jake thumps him in return. "Thanks."

"Now you'll officially be a part of the family," Mom says.

"Does that mean we get the family discount at the hardware store?" Dad gives Jake a wink. "I want to replace the floor in Emma's old room."

My fake fiancé jumps into this new conversation wholeheartedly and, much to my relief, avoids Liam as diligently as I do. He and Dad chat about the benefits and drawbacks of real hardwood versus laminate as they walk down the hall, toward the room in question. I want to go after them, pretend to contribute to their conversation. Instead, I'm left alone with Liam and my mother—the wolf and the over-excited puppy.

"Emma!" Mom swats my arm.

"What?"

"*What?* You are engaged to Jake Sawyer."

"Will you stop using his last name?"

"I'm sorry, it's all just happening so quickly. My head is spinning."

"Mom, you and Dad only knew each other for five months before you got married. I've known Jake my entire life." I peek sideways at my brother as I say it.

He stands with his hands folded behind his back, eyes slightly narrowed, as if measuring every single one of my words. I want to cup my hand over his eyes and tell him to stop staring.

"Oh honey, don't get me wrong. You know I'm thrilled, it's just . . ." I wonder if she's going to bring up Chase and the fiasco that was my first engagement. We dated on and off for six years before I said yes, and look how well that turned out. "Do you love him?"

"Mom."

Her expression turns serious. "It's an important question, Emma."

"It's Jake. Of course I love him."

"All right then." She smiles. "Have you picked a date?"

"October twenty-fifth."

Her eyes go buggy. "Of this year?"

"I know all of this must be overwhelming, but October's my favorite month. And if we wait until next year . . ." I don't have to finish the thought. The smirk tucked into the corner of Liam's mouth dissolves. All three of us are thinking the same thing.

If we wait until next year, Dad will be gone.

Chapter 4
♡

TOSSING A WAVE OVER MY SHOULDER AT A COUPLE OF men in yellow hard hats conferring in the middle of town square, I hurry across the street. The early morning sun is at my back, and caffeine is the last thing I need with this much adrenaline coursing through my veins. But Monday morning coffee at Patty's House of Pancakes is a ritual, something Lily Emerick and I have been doing since we were old enough to drive. According to Lily, rituals aren't meant to be broken. Besides, I have to tell her the news before she hears it from somebody else.

The upcoming announcement pulls my chest muscles tight.

My parents had no problem believing Jake and I were getting married in a little over a month. Sure, they were shocked, but that quickly gave way to delight, because we are quick to believe what our hearts want to be true. My dad wants to walk me down the aisle. My mom has always wanted me to be with Jake. And they'd much rather focus on a wedding than an impending funeral. Liam, I'm sure, didn't buy it, but at least my parents' presence kept him from verbalizing his doubts. He remained suspiciously quiet throughout last night's dinner, and neither Jake nor I attempted to rouse him.

My best friend, however—straight shooter, no-nonsense, can't-get-anything-past-her Lily—will not be so accepting. Her senses are unclouded by grief, and not only do I need to tell her the news, I also need to convince her to help me. With Dad officially retired as of three weeks ago, I am now the only veterinarian in Mayfair, which means I'm too swamped at the clinic to pull off an entire wedding in such a short amount of time. This is what Lily does for a living—she plans parties and events. So surely she will help me.

I open the door and step inside Patty's, inhaling the salty-sweet aroma of fried sausage and syrup. The place is all wainscoting and wallpaper and wood-framed pictures, with a counter spanning the length of one wall and booths lining the other, a space in between too narrow to fit any tables. I give the place a quick scan, but Lily is MIA.

Patty, on the other hand, lights up like the sky on the Fourth of July the second she notices me in the doorway. Almost as wide as she is tall, she waddles out from behind the counter wearing her pale pink Bunco Babes T-shirt, puts her umber hands on my cheeks in a gesture befitting grandmothers everywhere, and pulls my head down so it's level with hers.

"Um, hi, Patty." This is not her typical greeting.

"Child, how on God's green earth did you keep it a secret?"

Oh no.

"You and Jake Sawyer getting married?" She lets go of my face and shakes her head. "You, the mystery woman?"

A wave of panic rolls through my limbs. Patty is not a soft-spoken woman, and Lily will be here any second. "Where did you hear that?"

"Please. *Where did I hear that?* Your mother stopped in for a to-go coffee after that 5:00 a.m. Zumba class she's always going on about." Patty turns toward two men who sit across from each other in one of the booths, a game of gin rummy between them. The one on the left is Jake's great-uncle, Al, and across from him is Al's best buddy, Rupert—Mayfair's oldest residents. "Did you hear the news?"

Al looks up from the cards splayed in his hand. Somehow, his sagging jowls, stretched earlobes, and bulbous nose mesh together in just the right way, giving meaning to the phrase "He's so ugly he's cute." This morning he wears his cowboy hat tipped back as opposed to pulled low—a sign to the world that he woke up in a good mood. "What news?"

Rupert—not so decidedly cute in his old age—looks up too, squinting at Patty as though keener eyesight might make up for his pitiful hearing.

"Our very own Emma Tate and Jake Sawyer are engaged."

"What's that?" Rupert asks.

I shake my head. Wave my hands. Consider cupping one over Patty's mouth, but I am not quick enough.

"Emma and Jake are engaged!"

The diner goes quiet.

"Jake Sawyer, my great-nephew?" Al says.

"What other Jake Sawyer do we have in this town, Al? Of course your great-nephew!" Patty turns back to me. "Now let me see that ring. Your mama said it was something."

Eager to dispel her excitement as quickly as possible, I stick out my hand.

"Oh!" Patty brings her hands to her ample chest and leans closer. "But it's an unusual engagement ring, isn't it? Not a single diamond anywhere."

"An engagement ring?"

I shut my eyes. The disbelieving question belongs to Lily. Sure enough, when I look, she stands just inside the doorway, her expression every bit as disbelieving as her voice.

"You mean *you* didn't even know?" Patty's dark eyes widen. "Emma, you kept the news from your best friend?"

"What news?" Lily asks.

"Emma and Jake are getting married."

For a couple of seconds, Lily does not react. She stares, almost bored, back at Patty, until the corner of her mouth curls up, as if trying to meet the downward turn of her scrunched eye. It's a classic Lily face, code for *yeah, right*.

"Speak of the devil!" Patty points toward the window, where my fake fiancé is walking past—his baseball hat in place, carrying what appears to be a heavy load of lumber. "Nobody move. Coffee's on the house!"

If Patty hears my groan, it doesn't stop her. She bustles outside. I watch through the window in horror as she grabs Jake's arm and pulls him inside, lumber and all. When his attention lands on me, he raises his eyebrows.

I shrug apologetically.

Patty grabs a full coffeepot and hurries around the diner like a whirling dervish, topping everyone's mugs. She forces a mug into Lily's hand, fills it up, then scoots me over so I'm standing next to a bewildered Jake. His shock is this palpable thing beside me. We both stand there like a pair of open-mouthed idiots, and I cannot—will not—look at Lily.

"To Emma and Jake." Patty raises her own mug high into the air and waits for everyone else to follow suit. "I've known you both since you were in diapers, and now look at you—the town sweethearts. May your life together be filled with health and happiness!"

"And a passel of Sawyer babies!" Al adds.

My body flushes as mugs clink together and customers take delicate sips.

"What are you waiting for?" Rupert calls. "Kiss your woman!"

Someone whistles in agreement.

My heart jumps into my throat. I have never kissed Jake. Not once. Not even during our spin-the-bottle phase in junior high. And now we're supposed to kiss here, in Patty's restaurant? A nervous laugh flutters past my lips. This was not a detail we discussed when we made our game plan on Saturday.

"Yeah, Jake, kiss her," Lily says.

I dare a glimpse, just one. Enough to catch Lily's quirked eyebrow, her expression so dry I could douse it with all the coffee Patty just poured and it wouldn't make a difference.

Patty nudges me closer. My back bumps against Jake's bundle of two-by-fours. I look over my shoulder, up into Jake's face, which registers the same panic I'm feeling. He hesitates for a moment, then dips his head and does what everyone urges him to do. He kisses me. Jake is kissing me. Oh my goodness. He smells really, really good. And he's kissing me.

Before I can register anything else, the kiss ends. The onlookers cheer. And I force myself to breathe. In all my schoolgirl fantasies—wherein Jake realized that he was madly in love with me—I never imagined our first kiss would be in front of his great-uncle Al.

Jake clears his throat. "I, um . . . have to get back."

I nod like an overeager bobblehead doll and bite my lip, tasting cinnamon—Big Red. Only I'm not chewing Big Red gum. I taste it because Jake chews Big Red and his lips were just on mine.

He looks at me one last time before turning around and walking out the door.

Our captive audience returns to what they were doing before Patty caused a scene, like nothing crazy had just transpired in the house of pancakes. I slide into an empty booth, attempting to feign casualness. Setting her mug on the table, Lily sits across from me, tucks a strand of her chin-length strawberry-blonde hair behind her ear, and crosses her arms.

I want to push her eyebrows down her forehead. Instead, I give her some halfhearted jazz hands. "Surprise."

"There is no way you and Jake are engaged."

"Why not?"

"Because as of Saturday, you weren't even dating. I'm pretty sure you would have told me."

Little did she know, we were already "engaged" by the time I attended the Fall Harvest Festival committee meeting. "You know what they say about whirlwind romances."

She gives me an exasperated look. "You spent an entire week agonizing over paint samples when it came to updating your bathroom."

"So?"

She plops her elbows on the table and curls her long fingers around the mug. "So you expect me to believe that Jake proposed to you on Saturday, out of nowhere, and you said yes?"

Patty approaches, humming "Here Comes the Bride." She sets a mug in front of me, fills it up, gives my arm an excited squeeze, then waddles away. I wilt beneath Lily's deadpan stare. Who am I kidding? I can't keep this from her. I look around to make sure the coast is clear of eaves-droppers, then lean over the table and tell her the story—starting with the bucket list discovery and ending with the fiasco just now in Patty's House of Pancakes, as well as everything in between. By the time I finish the last word, I feel as though I've shed three layers of body armor.

Ribbons of steam curl up from the dark liquid in our cups, clouding the space between us, but not so much that I can't see Lily gaping.

"Would you please say something?"

She dips her chin. "Have you gone insane?"

The question puts me on the defensive. I didn't realize until now how much I was counting on her support. "My dad is dying."

"I know, but—"

"This is my chance to give him something before he's gone."

"A fake wedding?"

"The experience of walking his only daughter down the aisle."

"But Emma, it's not real. You're giving him an illusion."

Her words cut. I don't let myself examine the wound. I can't afford to. This is my chance to do something for Dad, and we've already told my parents. Jake phoned last night to say he'd told his father as well, and he was just as happy as my parents are. As we sit here and speak, the news is spreading all over Mayfair. I've set this train in motion, and now I must ride it to its foregone conclusion—my father walking me down that aisle, which is exactly what I want. I can't let Lily's disapproval distract me from that.

I look down at my mug until the steam disappears. Patty makes the best coffee in town, and I can't bring myself to take a sip. "I should get going. The Montgomerys' new puppy is scheduled for vaccinations at nine."

"Emma . . ."

"What?"

"I'm worried about you, okay? We never really talk about your dad or how you're doing. I'm afraid you're using this as an excuse to avoid reality."

"I'm not avoiding anything."

"The last thing you need added to the mix is a broken heart."

My exasperation grows. "A broken heart? Lily, it's Jake. My heart is safe."

She stares at me in that way she does—cutting straight through the nonsense, getting right to the bone.

"This is for my dad."

"Does Jake know that? Because it seems like a pretty drastic favor to offer a person."

"Jake knows what it's like to live with regret. He doesn't want that burden on my shoulders." If only my best friend could feel the same. "That's all this is."

She couldn't look any more skeptical if she tried. "I think it's a disaster waiting to happen."

"No, a disaster would be finding Dad's bucket list after it was too late to do anything." I shake my head and move to stand. "I was hoping for your support, but I guess that's too much to ask."

She reaches across the table to stop me. "I needed you to hear me say it. But now that we're clear, okay."

"Okay?"

Lily shrugs. "We're best friends. If you really think this is something you have to do, then I'm here for you. Disaster and all."

I melt into the booth. "Good, because I need help planning the wedding."

Chapter 5

♡

AFTER COFFEE WITH LILY, I SPEND THE REST OF THE day with animals, doing well-checks, diagnosing various ailments, prescribing medicine, and administering vaccinations. Edna Pearl, owner of the local dance studio, brings in her parrot, Polly, right before I close, under the pretense of sickly behavior. Really, I think she wants an excuse to pepper me with questions about the engagement announcement. I end up staying fifteen minutes past five, poking and prodding a perfectly healthy parrot to the backdrop of, "*Squawk!* Can't believe it. *Squawk!* Jake and Emma."

As soon as Edna and Polly leave, I head over to my parents', hitch Dad's minitrailer to the back of my Honda, and drive out to Sawyer Farm—passed down from Al Sawyer to his son, Wayne, who now runs it with his son, Steve. They stock the town with Christmas trees in the winter, strawberries and raspberries in the summer, and every imaginable size and shape of gourd and pumpkin in the fall. Since Lily grudgingly agreed to help me with the wedding, the least I can do is help her with the decorations for Mayfair's Fall Harvest Festival, and the best place to get decorations is Sawyer Farm.

As I drive the backcountry roads, the crisp air whips strands of hair from my ponytail. I crank up Miranda Lambert and try to lose myself in the colors—green leaves surrendering to red and orange and gold, their foliage made brighter against a bruised sky. It's best if I don't think—not about Jake or that kiss or the ring on my finger or Lily's disapproval or my pesky doubts or Dad's waning life. Instead, I belt along with Miranda until I turn down the road that winds toward the farm. Gravel crunches beneath my tires as I catch sight of a familiar Chevy parked amid a smattering of pumpkins in front of the Sawyers' big barn. I turn down the music and squint at the plates, but of course it's Jake's truck. The rust is in all the right places.

What's he doing here?

I pull up beside his truck and step outside, twisting the ring around my finger. Pumpkins, gourds, hay bales. Decorations for the town square. That's what I've come for.

The screen door to the farmhouse squeals open and out steps Wayne, then Jake, then Wayne's wife, Sandy, who spots me first. As soon as she does, her storklike legs take her down the porch steps and eat up the short distance between us. She wraps her long arms around me and nearly lifts me off the ground. "I knew you two would get married someday!"

Apparently, they've heard the news.

"If Papa Al hadn't told us, I'm not sure Jake would have made a peep. I've been trying to get him to share the details ever since he brought over my new rocking chair, but you know Jake. Never one to blather."

I glance toward the men.

Wayne gives me a friendly wave, skirts around the new rocking chair—polished walnut, beautifully designed—and steps off the porch. "Congratulations, Emma."

"Thanks."

"Jake tells us the big day isn't too far away."

"October twenty-fifth," I say, silently scolding my erratic heartbeat. It's Jake. I have no reason for the sudden bout of nerves. Except for the whole kissing thing.

Jake steps off the porch, too, and stands by my side.

"We insisted you have the wedding here at the farm, but Jake said he'd have to speak with you about it first." Sandy looks at me eagerly, as if waiting for me to make the decision here and now. "It'd be a free venue. And with the date approaching so quickly, it might be the only one available."

Wayne wraps his arm around Sandy's waist, highlighting their height difference. While she is tall and lanky, he is short and stocky. On any other couple, the disparity might look awkward, but not on them. "Give the girl time to breathe, Sandy. She just got here."

"I can't help it. I'm just so excited."

Wayne pulls Sandy closer, kisses her cheek, then nods toward a tractor hitched to a hayrack near the barn. "You ready to load up?"

I nod. Next week the farm will open to the public. Not only pumpkins and hayrack rides, but a petting zoo and a corn maze bigger than any other in northern Wisconsin. Sawyer Farm puts our tiny town on the map. "Thanks for giving us first pick. Lily will be thrilled."

"Not a problem. Now, how about I give you two a ride out to the patch before the rain starts up? Jake, you can help your fiancée load up for the festival and discuss the location of your wedding along the way."

"Oh . . . um . . ." I peek at Jake, who wears an inscrutable expression. "You probably have to get back to the hardware store."

"I have time for a hayrack ride."

"Good. Let me just pull the tractor around." Wayne heads off while Sandy begins explaining the many benefits that come with having the wedding at the farm. She doesn't quit until Wayne pulls up on his tractor and Jake and I climb into the hayrack. We settle onto the bench in the back and wave at Sandy while we slowly ride away.

When she's out of earshot, Jake clears his throat. "About that kiss . . ."

I let out a nervous laugh. "Yeah."

"I'm really sorry."

"Me too." We ride over some rough terrain. I set my hands on the bench and curl my fingers beneath the wood so as not to jostle up against Jake. I don't want to set off any more alarms in his head. Between Liam's comment about my childhood crush last night and Jake being forced to kiss me this morning, he no doubt has plenty going off already. Poor Jake is probably worried I'm getting false ideas, reading too much into his offer.

He wipes his hands down his jeans. "We should probably come up with a plan."

"So it doesn't happen again."

He gives me a self-deprecating, sideways smile. "I was thinking more about how we're going to play this out."

"Oh." The hayrack ride brings us closer to a field dotted with rows and rows of orange.

"I mean, the Bunco Babes will probably expect a certain level of . . ."

"Affection?"

His dimples flash. "Only if you can stand it."

And just like that, the tension seeps from my muscles. I loosen my grip on the bench. Jake is such a good sport. "So what exactly do you have in mind?"

He looks down at my hand, then takes it in his. "This seems easy enough."

Swallowing, I stare at our interlaced fingers—his large and tan, mine small and a bit paler. "Not too horrible," I tease.

"Almost natural."

"We'll get there."

He relaxes back against the bench.

I smile. "You didn't know what you were signing up for, did you?"

"I knew."

Smiling, I look around at the rolling hills, dotted with maples and oaks. "So we're getting married at Sawyer Farm?"

"Only if you want."

A pinch of giddiness wiggles in my chest. I can imagine

it—the crisp weather, an azure sky, the melody of Canon in D or maybe even "Ave Maria" as the guests stand and I slip my arm around Dad's. "I think it's perfect."

"Good."

We ride the rest of the way in comfortable silence—the kind carved from years of knowing one another. When Wayne pulls to a stop, Jake helps me off the hayrack and we wander up and down the rows of pumpkins—large, small, circular, oval, lumpy, and smooth. It's a wonderfully diverse crop this year.

"Emma?" Jake asks.

I straighten from examining some gourds.

Jake nudges a pumpkin with his shoe. "Why did you break your engagement to Chase?"

The question escapes into the cool air and floats between us. This is a topic we haven't talked about. When it first happened, Jake was living in Milwaukee. He kept in contact with Liam but not me. When he came back to Mayfair a year and a half ago, he was a wounded man, picking up the pieces of his grieving family after Ben's death. My broken engagement didn't seem important. Since then we have always managed to skirt around the issue. Chase and Jake were friends, and I hurt Chase badly when I called things off. I never, ever intended to, but intentions don't mean much when someone's hurting. I got the feeling Jake wanted to stay out of it. Yet now he asks. I stuff my hands into the pockets of my corduroy jacket. "I'd just found out my dad had cancer."

He cocks his head.

"Something like that has a way of making you think, you know? Make a good, hard assessment of your life."

His eyes contain an ocean's worth of understanding, because Jake knows.

"The diagnosis changed him."

"Chase?"

"No, my dad. He started living with so much courage. I realized that when I said yes to Chase, it wasn't because I loved him. It was because I didn't want to lose him." I gather several gourds into my arms, Jake grabs two pumpkins by their stems, and we make our way back to the hayrack to drop off our first load. "It's ironic."

"What is?"

"I called off my wedding because of my dad's cancer. Now I'm having another one because of the same thing."

A hint of pain flickers across Jake's face, only I don't know what it's for. Or who it's for. "Do you wish you never would have called off the first one? I mean, if you hadn't, you wouldn't be in this mess now, pretending to be engaged to me."

I grab some smaller pumpkins nearby and place them beside the two big ones. "No regrets."

Chapter 6

♡

THEY'RE WHAT?" I STOP IN FRONT OF TO HAVE AND TO
Hold, the only bridal boutique in the county, so fast that Lily
bumps into me from behind.

"Golfing, honey," Mom says again.

"Liam, Dad, and Jake?"

Mom scrunches her forehead as if I am being purposefully
obtuse, then bustles Lily and me through the front doors. Dresses
of every fabric and design spill off racks. Chiffon, organza, satin,
and lace. Ball gowns with exorbitantly long trains, short gowns
with no train at all, and everything in between. Along with veils
and shoes and jewelry galore. The place is like an overstuffed wedding turkey. I turn around, ready to continue my line of questioning with Mom, but I've already lost her. The sudden onslaught of
white has mesmerized her, drawing her in like an insect to the
light. This is her happy place.

Me? I can't seem to find one.

We are five days from October, a full week into my engagement, and only four weeks from the wedding day. Two emergencies at the clinic—one of which resulted in euthanizing an eight-year-old Lab—on top of all my regularly scheduled appointments hurled me into a put-out-the-fire mentality. All this week, I've managed to avoid Lily completely and Liam for the most part. Dad has been his usual rocklike self. And Mom has turned into a spaz. According to her, "We have no time!" Which is exactly what I don't want to hear, because on the other side of that aisle is a reality I'm not ready to face.

"Emma, you have to try this on." Mom glides to the nearest display, her hand outstretched like she can't resist touching the poufed skirt.

I take in the layers of bustled organza and wrinkle my nose. I did enough of this two years ago to know what looks good on my body and what doesn't. Bustled organza might work for stick-thin, tall models. For a five-foot-four gal with some muscle on her bones? Not so much. "Mom."

She turns. "What?"

"Why are Dad, Liam, and Jake golfing?" Jake doesn't even like putt-putt.

Mom arches her eyebrow. "Why are you so fixated on the golf?"

"I just . . . Jake . . . doesn't golf." Never mind that this means Jake will be spending the entire morning with Liam, when both of us have gone out of our way to avoid him. I ran into him once this past week over at Mom and Dad's, and the entire time he grinned at me like I was free entertainment. Now Jake is partaking in the one sport that drags on into an eternity with my smirky-faced brother, who will no doubt use that eternity to razz my poor fiancé.

Mom slides a few dresses along one of the racks. "Your father loves golf, and now that Jake is officially a part of the family, he invited him to go along."

I worry my lip. This is no good.

Mom pulls a mermaid-style dress with one too many sequins off its hanger and holds it up to my body. "What do you think, Lily?"

Lily rubs her chin, beholding all the sparkles, then scrunches her nose and shakes her head. "How's Liam doing?" she asks. "I haven't seen him in a while."

"He's fine." I avoid looking her in the eyes when I answer. I can tell by the tone of her question that she's inquiring about more than Liam's general well-being. She wants to know what he thinks about the engagement.

A young woman with bangles on each wrist offers to start us a room. Mom hands over the two dresses that have caught her attention.

"We should all get together tonight," Lily says. "Hang out."

"That's a wonderful idea!" Mom runs her fingers along the train of another dress. "We could make use of the fire pit. We haven't done that in a long time."

I eye my best friend. She's had a thing for my brother ever since we realized cooties were a plot devised by parents to keep boys and girls apart for as long as possible. What I can't figure out is whether her suggestion is an excuse to hang out with Liam or if it's her attempt to find out if Liam knows the truth.

"It could be our reward for a day of hard work." Lily holds up her iPhone. "I've got a whole list of things we need to accomplish today if we're going to pull off a wedding by the twenty-fifth."

"The first backyard fire of the season. Your dad will love it." Mom squeezes my elbow and gives me a reassuring smile. "Now, let's find you a dress."

So that's what I do. Or try, at least. It's hard to muster up the enthusiasm when my mind keeps playing out golf course scenarios, wherein Jake crumbles beneath the weight of Liam's questions and spills the truth to not only him, but also my dad. I imagine the disappointment and hurt on Dad's face. And that uncrossed item on his bucket list. It would taunt me for the rest of my life. To add even more angst to the situation, sporadic flickers of giddiness at the memory of Jake's kiss and our hand-holding at Sawyer Farm bubble to the surface.

I need to get a grip.

Doing my best to attend to the task at hand, I nod or shake my head at the dresses Lily and Mom select, until I grow tired of all the white and head over to the bridesmaid section. I hold up a periwinkle monstrosity with an impossibly short skirt and puffy sleeves. "Hey, Lily! How about this for the maid of honor?"

She steps away from a rack and joins me.

I hang the dress up and pull out another—calf-length and seafoam green. "This would bring out your eyes."

"Are you asking me to be your maid of honor?"

"Isn't that assumed?"

"Wow. I've never been a maid of honor at a fake wedding before."

"Shhh!" I dart a look over my shoulder.

"Don't worry, she can't hear." There's an undercurrent to Lily's words. I can tell she wants to say something more, but she presses her lips together.

I should be grateful that she's keeping her opinions to herself. After all, I asked Lily for her support. But her silent disapproval rankles. "You should be thrilled about this, you know. I'm giving you an excuse to dance with Liam."

"That is one way to look at things." She peeks at Mom, then dips her chin and leans closer. "Does your brother know?"

I shake my head, then wander toward Mom, eager to escape Lily's questions. She follows. Halfway there I stop. Directly in front of me is the dress I've always envisioned wearing on my wedding day, all the way back when I was a little girl obsessed with Cinderella. It's the dress I scoured every boutique across the upper Midwest for two years ago but could never find. Yet here it is, in this bridal shop not more than twenty minutes from my home. A strapless ball gown with a sweetheart neckline, a chapel train, intricate beadwork, and an accompanying jacket.

"It's beautiful," Lily says.

"It's perfect." I run my fingers along the lace sleeve of the jacket, then check the tag. "And it's my size."

Lily and I smile at each other. Fake wedding or not, we can't help ourselves. I take the dress off the rack and hurry toward the changing room. The woman with the bangles assists, zipping and buttoning and adjusting, while Lily and Mom wait impatiently outside, telling us to hurry up already.

When I step out of the changing room, Mom's eyes fill with tears.

I take in my reflection, and that giddy feeling swells. I twirl, relishing the rustling sound the skirt makes, and smooth my hand over my waist.

Mom dabs her eyes with a wadded-up tissue. "I have to buy it for you."

"No way." The words come too quickly, but there's no way I'm letting her spend a dime on this wedding. Even if it weren't fake, even if Jake and I were planning on actually being married, my parents have a mountain of medical bills to climb. "I have money saved up."

"And it's half off," the woman with the bangles adds.

The front doors of To Have and To Hold swing open, letting in a gust of chilly autumn air. Jake strides inside, so out of the blue I don't have time to react. When he spots me in front of the mirror, he stops, his dark hair ruffled from the wind. His attention travels up the length of the dress, then lands on my face, but before I can decode his expression Mom jumps out of her seat and throws herself in front of me like a shield. "Jake, you can't see her!"

"Mom—"

"It's tradition, Emma. He can't see you in your dress. It's bad luck!" She holds up her hands. "Jake, close your eyes!"

Jake covers his eyes with his palms.

"Mom, this is silly." Not to mention confusing. Jake isn't

supposed to be here. He's supposed to be out on the golf course with Liam and Dad. I look around my mother. "Jake, you don't have to cover your eyes."

"Yes, he does!" She shoves me toward the changing room.

I go willingly and hurry out of the dress as fast as one can hurry out of a wedding gown. By the time I'm back in my jeans, hoodie, and cross trainers, I've had plenty of time to replay the look on Jake's face—panicked before he saw me, stunned after. I'm not sure which one has me hurrying more. As soon as I step out of the dressing room, Jake takes my elbow. "Can I speak with you for a second?"

"Sure, of course." I glance at Lily, then follow him outside. "What's wrong?"

"Liam knows."

"What?"

"Your brother. He knows."

"How?"

"You know Liam. He was asking so many questions, and he wouldn't let me get away with half answers. Finally, I had to pull him aside and tell him what was going on."

The warmth drains from my face. "What did he say?"

"He laughed."

"He laughed?"

Jake rubs the back of his neck and nods.

"Is he going to say anything?"

"I don't think so."

"You didn't ask him?"

"We didn't have much time."

A groan slips past my lips. I do not want to talk to Liam about any of this. I especially don't want to hear him express the same doubts Lily did.

"I'm sorry, Emma."

"You have no reason to apologize. I'm the one who's put you in such an awkward position."

"Actually, I asked you, remember?"

I look down at the ground and cross my arms to ward off the chill in the air.

"That was a really pretty dress."

When I look up, Jake stands closer than before. "Thanks."

Mom pokes her head outside. "Hey you two, Lily had the most fabulous idea!"

Jake and I turn our heads toward her at the same time.

"I was telling her how your father and I are taking dance lessons tomorrow night. She thought you two should join us. Practice up for your first dance as a married couple."

Another groan pushes up my throat, but I swallow it down.

"So . . ." Mom beams at us. "What do you say?"

I squint against the sun and start to shake my head, because I am not going to make Jake suffer through dance lessons. But he shifts behind me. "Sounds like fun."

If only his voice didn't drip with uncertainty.

Chapter 7

♡

THE FIRE CRACKLES AND POPS AND BREATHES SMOKE into the star-strewn sky, the gentlest of breezes carrying it slightly north, where the woods line the edge of my parents' backyard. The smell of burning wood mingles with the crisp air as I pull my stocking cap more snuggly over my ears and lean forward in my chair, closer to the heat. Across the fire, Lily lets out a burst of laughter that echoes into the night. She stands beside Liam, who stabs marshmallow upon marshmallow onto a roasting fork.

Somehow I managed to thwart his attempt to accost me when I arrived fifteen minutes ago. Liam rarely listens to me, but my "Not now" came out so sharp and ominous, he actually backed off. I'm positive the reprieve will not last, but I'll take it for now.

I look up the length of the long backyard. So far, no Jake. Dad pokes the pile of burning wood with a fire iron. Sparks of glowing embers jump from the flames, then slowly extinguish into black. He sets the iron stick aside, slides his hands inside the pockets of his Green Bay Packers fleece jacket, and sits down beside me with a groan. "Your old man's getting old."

The words hit me the wrong way, rupturing a pocket of fear I try to leave alone. Fifty-seven is not old. It is much, much too young. I gaze into the fire, praying that this fake wedding can be something we all laugh about together in ten years. Something crazy Emma did for Dad, who was miraculously healed.

"How's your heart, Emma-girl?" Dad asks.

I look down at my shoes and smile a little. Cancer has zapped his patience for small talk. He has replaced the standard and largely accepted *How are you doing?* with this bad boy. And he will not let anyone get away with *fine.* He will poke and prod until something more substantial than smoke arises. "My heart is hoping God will heal you."

Dad sets his hand on the armrest of his chair and seems to contemplate my answer.

I bite my lip, trying to keep it together, but I don't deal well with unknowns. Not when I was a child and not as an adult either. I attempt to loosen the growing tightness in my throat. I attempt to be strong. But the words swell until I can't hold them back any longer. "You can't die."

"We all die, Emma."

"You know what I mean." I shake my head, unable to fathom a world without my father. "I don't think I can handle it."

"God's not asking you to handle it right now. Right now,

I'm here." He pats my knee, as if I need the extra reassurance. "And when the day comes and I'm no longer here, God will equip you with what you need to handle it then."

This is another thing cancer has done—taught my father the art of living in each moment. He doesn't look ahead. He doesn't let himself spiral into a storm of what-ifs. He relies on God's strength for today and trusts him with tomorrow. For me, it's a constant struggle. I let out a puff of breath. "You make it sound so simple."

"Trust *is* simple." He holds up his pointer finger. "Not easy, but simple."

The sound of a car door slamming and more of Lily's laughter cuts our conversation short. I look toward the house and spot Mom, closing the distance between us. She skirts around the fire and offers us a bowl of candy corn—my long-standing favorite. Dad's too. I take a few pieces and pop one into my mouth.

"I do believe your fiancé just pulled up in his truck," Mom says.

"Speaking of your fiancé . . ." Dad takes a handful for himself.

Something about the serious set of his brow makes me stop chewing. "Yeah?"

"My heart is heavy, Emma."

My muscles tense. Does Dad suspect something? And if he does, would he run with it anyway? Like the surprise party on my twenty-first birthday. I knew about the party, and I'm almost positive my parents knew I knew, but when I walked into the restaurant, I did my best rendition of shocked and neither called my bluff.

"As your father, I feel it's my responsibility to tell you"—he sets his hand over his chest and shakes his head—"That he is truly an awful golfer."

I roll my eyes, trying not to give away my relief. "Har, har."

"But I guess there are worse things." He finishes off the rest of his candy corn as Jake appears around the corner of the house. He strides toward us, something strapped around his chest. Dad pats my knee again and stands, because the lawn chairs are doubled up—three sets of two around the fire pit—and apparently, the chair closest to mine belongs to my fiancé. When Jake approaches, Dad slaps him on the arm. "I was just telling my daughter about your golfing skills."

Jake chuckles, the glow from the fire flickering along his jawline.

"You brought your guitar," I say, sitting up straighter.

He runs his thumb beneath the strap. "Figured some music might be fun."

"Of course it will." Mom gives Jake a hug, then she and Dad sit in the pair of chairs to our left.

"Sorry I'm late." Jake pulls the strap of his guitar case over his head and sits beside me. "I was working in my shed and lost track of time."

I stick my hands beneath my knees. "What were you working on?"

"A gift."

"Care to be less vague, Mr. Nonspecific?" I ask, raising my eyebrow.

He raises one of his eyebrows back at me, leaving it at that, then leans forward and bumps his knee against mine. "Hanging in there, kiddo?"

The nickname and the gesture trigger a major bout of déjà vu. All of a sudden, I am eighteen again, sitting next to this same fire pit and this same boy, only it's the night of my graduation party. I had been warming my hands by the fire, the temperature much lower than it should have been for late May, when Jake sat beside me and bumped his knee against mine. "Doing all right there, kiddo?"

I wasn't going to let him get away with it. "You aren't allowed to call me that."

"No?"

"I am officially a high school graduate. I'm not a kid anymore, Jake."

"So I've noticed." I'm not sure what warmed my skin more—the fire or the words or the long look we shared after them. All day, there had been a palpable chemistry between us. I was sure he could feel it too. There had even been flirting.

He popped a few knuckles, a nervous habit. "So . . . there's something I've been wanting to tell you."

My heart rate picked up speed, growing faster and faster the longer Jake delayed saying whatever he wanted to say. Maybe if I helped him along, encouraged him a little. I leaned forward. "Jake, I—"

"Chase."

The name drew me back. "Chase?"

Jake wiped his hands along the thighs of his jeans and nodded.

I glanced past the fire, where Chase stood chatting with my brother. "What about him?"

"He likes you."

"Oh." My hopes plummeted so hard and fast I could do nothing but blink. Jake wasn't going to profess his feelings for me, because Jake didn't have any feelings for me. He was checking to see how I felt about his friend. I felt like an idiot.

"Nothing to say?" he asked.

Trying my best to hide my disappointment, I smiled too brightly. "I think Chase is really great."

"So you like him too?"

"Let's just say that if Chase asked me out, I wouldn't say no."

Jake leaned back in his seat, his expression hidden by the night. "Okay, then."

I narrowed my eyes at him. "Why didn't Chase just tell me himself?"

"Because he's a chicken."

The fire lets out a pop, pulling me back into the present, away from the memory. But not the lesson I learned from it. Jake has only ever had platonic feelings toward me. I am the queen at misreading him. Still, the feelings I put to death back then are doing their best to resurrect themselves now, and I'm not sure I have the strength to fight them.

"Anybody want one?" Liam holds up his roasting fork,

which bows toward the ground with the weight of what appears to be an entire bag of jumbo marshmallows.

We all laugh.

The fire crackles as we enjoy our s'mores, and conversation gives way to reminiscing, and reminiscing gives way to Jake and his guitar. As he strums the chords, I close my eyes and relish this moment, right now. With a fire and music and all the people I love most.

Chapter 8

♡

MY LOFTY GOAL FOR THE EVENING? DO NOT LOOK LIKE an idiot in front of Jake. Which may sound simple enough, unless you've seen me dance. I had a few words with Lily over her idea on Saturday. She laughed, until I suggested that the maid of honor and best man should join us. I wish I hadn't, because now the maid of honor sits shotgun in my Honda and the best man sits in the middle of the backseat, grinning as I recite the complete story of my engagement with as much matter-of-factness as possible.

When I finish, Liam lets out a whistle. "Wow."

I grip the steering wheel tighter and turn onto the gravel road leading toward our destination.

"That's a pretty big offer for Jake to make."

"That's what I said," Lily mumbles.

I ignore her. "You know what happened with Ben. He doesn't want me to feel the same regret that he feels."

Liam doesn't look convinced.

"Please, Liam. I know you probably think this is the dumbest idea in the world, but can you please not say anything to anyone?"

"I never said it was a dumb idea."

Lily whips her head around. "What?"

My grip loosens on the wheel. "Really?"

"It'll be like one last hurrah for Dad. Family will be there. Friends too." He leans forward between my seat and Lily's and props his elbows on our armrests. "Mom and Dad are both thrilled about it."

"But it's not real," Lily says.

"Neither is Santa, but you don't hear kids complaining."

Lily makes a face. "What does that have to do with anything?"

"I'm just saying that, sometimes, reality is overrated."

Sitting up straighter, I make eye contact with Liam in the rearview mirror. "So does that mean you'll behave?"

"Don't I always?"

It'll have to be good enough, because we have arrived. I pull up behind Jake's Chevy and park. Edna Pearl gives dance lessons in her husband's old barn, everything from your basic box step to the Viennese Waltz, all beneath the watchful eye and occasional commentary of her parrot, Polly. Edna and her husband never had any children of their own, but they did inherit her grandfather's bird after he passed twenty years ago.

The waning daylight fades in the west as we climb out of my car. Jake's truck door slams shut. Gravel crunches beneath his feet as he walks over, making our threesome into a familiar foursome. All of us seem to inhale at the same time, creating an awkward pause that has my insides doing some impressive acrobatics.

Liam chuckles, then offers his hand with a bow to Lily. "May I have this dance?"

With a rosy hue blossoming in her cheeks, she slips her hand into his and the two disappear inside the barn, leaving Jake and me alone, at dusk, surrounded by plowed fields and milk cows lowing in the distance.

I fiddle with the hem of my shirt. "Jake, thanks for doing this." It seems that's all I can say to him these days—thank you.

"You know, I'm not too bad of a dancer."

"Liar." I smile up at him. "I've danced with you before, Sawyer." Back in high school gym class, when I was the quiet, artsy sophomore and Jake was the cute, athletic senior. When the dreaded four-square unit came up, he offered to be my partner. Even then, he cared about my feelings. Didn't want me to be partnerless. Or maybe he wasn't willing to make a fool out of himself in front of any of the other girls. He couldn't have known, as we laughed and fumbled, that I lived for those ridiculous four-square lessons.

"Gym class was a long time ago, Tate." There's a teasing twinkle in his eye, one that makes them look extra blue. "A lot's changed since then."

So much, and yet nothing at all. "I'll believe it when I see it."

The familiar melody and crooning of Elvis Presley's "Can't Help Falling in Love" emanates from the barn. The lyrics have my insides resuming their circus act.

"Looks like they're starting without us." Jake holds out

his arm, motioning for me to go ahead. As soon as we step inside, I spot Dad waltzing Mom around the floor while Liam engages Lily in a spastic polka, hopping her across the barn in complete disregard of the music's beat. They swoop past Polly, who squawks from her bird stand.

The music stops.

Liam does too. "Hey, I was just getting the hang of it."

Lily looks flushed. I can see the grin itching to take full shape.

"We were doing the box step, dear." Edna lets out a long-suffering sigh, then spots Jake and me standing in the barn door. "The bride and groom are here!"

Dad turns around and smiles at me. There's a glow to his cheeks. "Hey, sweetheart."

"Hi, Dad."

Edna claps her hands, gathering our attention. "You, my lovelies, are late."

"Sorry," Jake says.

I nod toward the parrot, who shuffles along her perch. "How's Polly?"

"As fit as a fiddle. Now, Mr. Sawyer, do you know the basic box step, or would you like me to lead you through it?"

"I think I'm good."

"Okay, then! Let's start again. Remember your carriage, men. And ladies, you follow their lead." Edna flips on the stereo. "Take your women, gentlemen."

Jake presses his warm palm against the small of my back and takes my hand, his grip firm and confident as he moves us in perfect synchronization to Elvis's crooning and Edna's counting above the music.

I narrow my eyes up at him. "Jacob Elliott Sawyer."

His cheeks dimple. "I'm just getting warmed up."

Elvis turns into Vince Gill who turns into Harry Connick Jr. And just like that, my worry dissolves. It's impossible to look like an idiot with Jake leading me around the dance floor. Edna focuses most of her attention on Dad, because Liam is hopeless and Jake doesn't need instruction. Jake has the box step mastered. We laugh and we tease and we dance until Edna turns off the music and teaches us the basic step for swing dancing. Jake wasn't kidding about getting warmed up. He already knows the basics, and then some, delighting Edna so much that she steals my partner, calling out instructions to Liam and Dad while Jake twirls and flings her around. He keeps catching my eye as he does so, smiling smugly. I smile back, arms crossed, shaking my head, because this is most definitely not the same Jake who stepped on my toes during four-square.

When Edna finally lets him go, he helps me figure out the steps to Sammy Davis Jr.'s "Love Me or Leave Me," and then "Jump, Jive an' Wail" comes on, and we're off. I don't even have to think. Not about my steps, or Dad's cancer, or even what will happen after the wedding.

"Where in the world did you learn how to dance?"

"In college." He twirls me around. "I had to take some sort of fitness elective, and my roommate convinced me dance would be fun."

I let him fling me out and pull me in. "Remind me to thank your roommate someday."

"Will do."

I look over at Dad, flirting with Mom, his rhythm nowhere near as good as Jake's but much better than Liam's, and I decide that my brother is right. Reality is overrated. This wedding has made my parents happy. And honestly? It's made me happy too. Maybe swapping out my present reality for this shinier, happier version—where Jake is my fiancé and Dad is healthy—wouldn't be the worst thing in the world. Like the make-believe games Liam and I used to play when we were little kids. They were only really fun when we fully committed.

The music fades. Jake twirls me around one last time, then dips me toward the floor. And as we smile at one another, trying to catch our breath, I find myself thinking, for the first time in a long time, that God might give us a miracle yet. He can do it. God can heal my father. At some point, I stopped really believing that. But with Jake looking down at me and Mom's and Lily's laughter mingling with Edna's coaching and Polly's squawks, I can imagine that maybe, just maybe, there's a happy ending in this after all.

Chapter 9

♡

I HAD A DREAM ONCE WHERE I KNEW I WAS DREAMING. It was right after Dad was diagnosed with cancer, but in the dream, he wasn't sick. In fact, my dad could fly. Not only that, he could take me with him. Even though I knew I was asleep in my bed, I didn't want to wake up. I wanted to exist in that dream forever—with me and my healthy dad and his invisible wings.

I find myself in that same place now, except this time, I'm not asleep.

Between my duties at the clinic, planning a wedding, and helping with the Fall Harvest Festival, avoiding reality has not been as hard as one might think. People around town congratulate me about my engagement and, somehow, I smile and say thank you with a genuineness that borders on alarming. The only thing threatening my happy delusion right now is time. Sighing, I pull two bottles of Baumeister root beer from my fridge, remove the caps with the souvenir bottle opener Lily gave me last Christmas, and scan the calendar magnetized to my freezer.

Despite the hustle and bustle October has ushered into my life, I've done my best to protect each day, draw it out. Resist the rush. I've set new hours at the clinic, closing every Friday at noon so I can enjoy the afternoons and evenings with my parents and Jake. Last weekend we picked pumpkins at Sawyer Farm and had fun carving them while Mom baked the seeds. We've even gone to a couple of high school football games, rooting on our alma mater with Styrofoam cups of hot chocolate. But a day will only stretch so far. Time keeps marching onward, and somehow, here I am, the Fall Harvest Festival today and the wedding next weekend. Like that dreaded alarm clock, it's only a matter of ticktocks before life wrenches me awake.

As far as the wedding goes, Lily and I have managed to finalize most of the details. The ceremony will take place outside at Sawyer Farm. The reception will immediately follow, with barbecue pork sandwiches and a makeshift dance floor in the large barn. We've wrapped burnt peanuts in bright orange plastic wrap for wedding favors. Sent rustic gold invitations with bold red print to family and friends, most of them Dad's. We met with the florist to put together bouquets of red roses, orange calla lilies, burgundy Oriental lilies, and soft green hydrangeas. And we met with Eloise at her bakery, deciding on a caramel cake with ribbons of dark chocolate and buttercream frosting. If Lily rightly suspects I'm catering more to my father's preferences than my own, she keeps it to herself.

The sound of a pounding hammer filters through my opened kitchen window, and a flash of what my dreamworld future could be fills the contours of my imagination—Jake fixing the front porch, a dark-haired, blue-eyed little boy crouching nearby with a toy hammer clutched in his pudgy fist, a girl with blonde curls playing hopscotch on the sidewalk, and my parents stopping by for a Saturday morning visit, enjoying every moment of grandparenthood. My yellow Lab, Samson, nudges his wet nose against my hand, and the vision pops, leaving an empty, sad space in its wake.

Not wanting to be alone with it, I pick up the two bottles of root beer and head out to the porch, Samson on my heels. The screen door creaks open, then whaps shut behind us. I inhale the autumn air deep into my lungs, relishing its freshness. Fall is never long enough, not in northern Wisconsin. Here, the world is all too eager to rush into the cold days of winter. But this year has been a treat. Along with the perfect temperature for sweatshirts and jeans and stocking caps, the leaves have stayed on the trees longer than usual, turning into vibrant shades of gold, yellow, and red. Fall is a season of waiting. A long, drawn-out pause before the world falls asleep, and I find myself cherishing every moment.

Jake finishes wrenching up a loose floorboard, then slides his hammer into his tool belt. I offer him a root beer and he sits down beside me on the step. Samson licks Jake's arm, receives a scratch behind his ear, then trots off to sniff around the bushes.

"To a better porch," I say, raising my bottle.

He clinks his against mine and we drink in comfortable quiet, savoring the frothy sweetness that is old-fashioned

Baumeister root beer—nostalgia in a bottle. Finally, when our drinks are half gone, he nudges me with his shoulder. "What are you thinking about so intently over there, Tate?"

I smile down at the step. It's not the first time he's asked the question, one I'm dying to reciprocate, because I never know what he's thinking. Not when it comes to Jake Sawyer. I misread his cues back then, and I still do now. He'll press his hand against the small of my back or whisper something in my ear, and I never know why. To play the part? Or is there something more to it? "I'm thinking that I'm glad the festival is tonight."

"It's kept you and Lily busy."

"Next year when she asks me to be on the committee, I think I'll say no." Next year is something I don't want to think about.

He takes a sip of his root beer. "We should go."

"To the festival?"

He nods.

"We go every year."

"I mean together."

"Oh—yeah." For some reason, my ears turn warm.

"I'll stop by around seven. We can walk over."

"Sure."

"Good." He tips the bottle up to his lips to finish off what remains of his root beer, showing off those ridiculously cute dimples in the process. "It's a date."

Chapter 10

♡

MY DOORBELL RINGS AT SEVEN O'CLOCK SHARP. SAMSON barks, and my heart flutters. All day I've replayed Jake's words and the way he looked when he said them. *Good. It's a date.* They are easily spoken, innocuous words, yet I can't help but assign them meaning. I check my reflection one last time in my downstairs bathroom mirror, grab two cans of green beans off my kitchen counter, wrap a scarf around my neck, give Samson a good-bye kiss between his eyes, and step outside onto the porch.

"Hi," I say, a little too breathlessly.

"You look nice."

"Thanks. So do you." He wears what he normally wears—flannel shirt showing beneath an unzipped Carhartt and well-worn jeans. Only he's clean-shaven and sans his usual baseball hat. I'm probably reading too much into that too.

Jake holds up a plastic bag that already contains one can of pumpkin pie filling and another of cranberry sauce. I place my green beans inside.

"Shall we?" he asks.

Nodding, I pull my hair out from beneath my scarf and zip my coat all the way up. My breaths escape in puffs of iridescent white before disappearing into the night as we stroll through my front yard, down the street, toward the center of town.

I can't tell if the electricity I feel between us is a real thing or self-fabricated. All I know is that I'm hyperaware of all things Jake—the way he shortens his stride to match mine, the way his slightly-longer-than-usual hair curls up a bit over his ear, the closeness of our knuckles. All of it has me more nervous than I should be. "So how's your dad doing?" I ask.

"Pretty good. His arthritis has been flaring up with the colder weather, but he's never been much of a complainer."

"Like father, like son."

Jake smiles.

As we walk and talk about everything but the wedding, I try not to feel guilty about Lily, who called earlier and asked if I wanted to grab a bite to eat at Patty's before heading to the festival. Every year we've gone together, even when I was with Chase, since he always had to work. I felt awkward telling her that I was going with Jake and tried to make up for it by inviting her to join us, then immediately regretted it because I wasn't sure of Jake's intentions. What if his words—*Good. It's a date.*—weren't innocuous at all? What if Jake really did want this to be a date? It didn't matter, though, because Lily declined. We could find each other there. I'm pretty sure her glum tone had less to do with me and more to do with

Liam—who is away on another one of his trips and hasn't returned Lily's phone calls.

"You're kind of quiet," Jake says. "Something on your mind?"

"My brother's just being my brother."

"What does that mean?"

"I'm pretty sure he's giving Lily mixed signals. She's starting to fall for him again, and now he's backing off." Our arms swing in rhythm with our footsteps. I can't tell if he wants to take my hand or not, so I leave it out of my pocket, despite the cold and no gloves.

"N-C-L."

"Huh?"

Jake chuckles. "No Commitment Liam."

"Oh, yeah." That had been his nickname in high school. Unfortunately for Lily, the nickname still applies today.

"For what it's worth, I think your brother has always had a thing for Lily. He just doesn't have any clue what to do about it."

"Well, he better figure it out soon. She won't wait forever."

Jake scratches his jaw, his brow furrowing as the growing hum of activity catches my attention. We've officially reached the town square, where children jump in the bounce house, costume-clad teenagers solicit townsfolk to play carnival games, and the animals in the petting zoo oink and squawk and bleat. Several people meander around the baking booths, sampling various pumpkin-inspired recipes, voting for their favorite. Now is when Jake takes my hand, which makes me think the gesture really is for show.

We find Patty first, halfway hidden by a friendly-faced scarecrow. She works in front of a table stacked high with canned food.

"Evening, Patty," Jake says.

She stops sorting the cans into boxes and beams at our joined hands, the whites of her eyes looking even whiter against the night and her dark skin. "Well, if it isn't our town lovebirds."

She has taken to calling us this so often, it's caught on. I can't go in for my Monday morning coffee without hearing the phrase from Jake's great-uncle Al and his buddy Rupert, at least twice. "Seems like a great turnout this year."

"You're telling me. Lily really outdid herself."

Jake sets the plastic bag with our cans on the table. "Here's some more to add to the pantry. Happy fall harvest."

Patty wishes us the same. We wave good-bye and walk through the display of antique tractors—on loan from a few of Mayfair's local farmers—then head straight for the candied apples, which weigh more than any food item should ever be allowed to weigh. We take sticky bites while checking out the jack-o'-lanterns, which range from impressively elaborate to crudely simple, all submitted by Mayfair residents. Jake finds one with an uncanny resemblance to our old history teacher, Mr. DeVree, who had a giant forehead and the world's largest comb-over. I put a tally mark on the sheet in front of it. At the end of the festival, the person with the most tallies takes home a pumpkin-carving trophy. Phil Nixon has seven proudly displayed on the front counter of his convenience store.

"Mr. DeVree gets your vote, huh?"

"For the sake of nostalgia."

Jake slowly tilts his head at the pumpkin. "I'm not sure it's really supposed to be him though."

"Too late. Penciled tally marks cannot be revoked." I toss the remains of my apple into a nearby garbage can and lick the stickiness from my fingers. When I finish, Jake is staring at me. "What?"

"You have some caramel . . ." He touches his lip.

"Oh." Embarrassed, I try to rub the caramel away. "Did I get it?"

"No." Jake steps closer and touches his lip again. "It's right here."

I try more toward the left.

Jake's mouth pulls up into a half smile.

"It's still there?"

"Here, let me." He gently wipes the corner of my upper lip with the pad of his thumb, our bodies so close they are almost touching, the scent of cedar emanating from his skin.

I look up at him through my eyelashes. As our eyes lock, there's something in his expression—an intensity that has my heartbeat picking up speed. For one crazy second, I'm positive he's going to kiss me. But then his eyelids flutter and he steps away.

"Hey, Lily," Jake says, rubbing the back of his neck.

I spin around and find Lily standing not too far behind us, a sharpness in her green eyes that leaves me feeling flustered, as if I've been caught breaking the rules. "Hey, when'd you get here?"

"A while ago." Her attention flicks from Jake to me. "Was I interrupting something?"

I laugh—a nervous, too-loud laugh that is followed by a silence so painful I'm dying to fill it. Lily might be keeping her thoughts to herself when it comes to this engagement, but her opinion has been clear from the start, and right now I don't want to deal with it. I stick my hands into my coat pockets. "Did you vote for your favorite pumpkin?"

"Not yet."

"Jake and I haven't tasted any of the recipes. We were going to go try some if you want to come along." As much as I don't want to extend the invitation, this is Lily. I can't leave her behind while I trounce off with Jake.

She shrugs.

As we make our way past the gazebo, where Wayne and his son shuck corn like it's the race of their lives, it's obvious that Lily is making a concerted effort to avoid Jake. I can tell he notices it too by the furrow in his brow. It leaves me feeling stuck in the middle—like the two are fighting and it's up to me to get them to make up. "We're getting our dresses altered tomorrow at two," I remind her. The tailor had kindly agreed to come in on a Sunday afternoon to accommodate my hectic schedule.

"I know."

"Have you been fitted for your tux yet?" I ask Jake.

He glances at Lily, whose rotten mood has tossed an invisible blanket of tension over what was shaping up to be a very enjoyable evening. I try to remind myself that she's upset about Liam, but it doesn't help as much as it should. "I went yesterday. Liam's going this Tuesday when he gets back."

We reach the booths with all the baked goods. I try to enjoy the yummy smell of brown sugar, cinnamon, and pumpkin spice, but the awkwardness between my two best friends is beyond distracting. So much so that I barely taste my bite of Clara O'Malley's famous chocolate pumpkin bread.

"So how does this work?" Lily finally asks. "Am I supposed to throw you a bachelorette party? I'm not sure I understand the etiquette for this type of situation."

I shoot Lily a look.

She ignores me. "Is Liam throwing you a bachelor party?"

Jake's furrow deepens. "I'm not really a bachelor party kind of guy."

I hurry over to the next booth, where Eloise stands beside a glorious-looking pumpkin cake with ivory whipped cream frosting, tiny pieces to sample tucked inside Dixie cups. "This looks delicious, Eloise," I say, handing one to Jake, another to Lily.

"If you like it, it's not too late to change your wedding cake order to pumpkin!" She smiles serenely—the perfect picture of a grandmotherly baker. "So, have you two decided where you're going for your honeymoon?"

I swallow my bite of cake, hating Lily's hot stare on the side of my face. "Oh, we're, uh . . . not taking one."

Eloise's serene smile crumples. "No honeymoon? Oh, but you have to take a honeymoon. It's the most romantic part."

Lily's stare does not relent. It is an annoying, unwelcome

reminder that this story I'm living isn't real. That it's only a matter of time before the alarm clock goes off and forces me awake. Resentment stirs in my chest. "We didn't have time to plan one."

"Well, maybe you can take a late one, in the wintertime." Her face brightens. "You could take your wife skiing," she says to Jake. "A nice lodge with a fireplace so you can enjoy a crackling fire at night. Sounds romantic, don't you think?"

Jake agrees, and we thank Eloise for the taste of cake and move on to a whole table filled with pumpkin pie. I don't have an appetite for any of it.

"You'll want to be careful on those ski lifts," Lily says. "Emma's afraid of heights."

"I know," Jake says.

"So, am I supposed to get you a wedding gift?"

I narrow my eyes at my friend.

"Or am I allowed to skip the pretense?"

"Lily," I say sharply.

"It's an honest question."

Maybe so, but I don't want to hear it. "Look, I know you're upset about Liam."

"This has nothing to do with Liam."

Jake pulls at his collar.

I can't stand his discomfort. I can't even stand my own. My frustration mounts. I don't want to deal with this right now. Not tonight. "I'll be back."

"Where are you going?" Jake asks.

"To get some cider." Without giving either a chance to object or follow, I pivot on my heels and weave through the crowd, reality threatening to descend. I do my best to fight it. What is Lily's deal anyway? It's not like my choices are harming anyone, and it's not like she's never made a questionably moral decision before either. Jake understands. Liam understands. I know my mom will understand. So why can't Lily?

As I cross my arms and continue walking, the *clop, clop, clop* of horse hooves and the sound of my name break through my internal venting. I look up from my shoes and spot my parents sitting in a horse-drawn carriage, illuminated by the streetlight, finishing the loop around the square. Mom sits on the edge of the bench and waves in my direction as the driver brings the horse to a stop. I walk up beside them.

"What are you doing here all by yourself?" Mom says. "I thought you were coming with Jake."

"I did. I was just trying to find us some cider." I look over my shoulder, toward the baking booths. "He's back there with Lily."

Her mother radar must be on full alert, because her eyes flicker in that way they do whenever she senses I'm in turmoil. "Why don't you take a ride with your dad and I'll go find us some cider."

"Are you sure?"

"Of course. Enjoy a carriage ride with your dad. I'll find Jake and Lily and let them know where you are." The driver helps Mom down from the carriage, then helps me up. I sit on the bench, wrap my arm around Dad's, and rest my head on his shoulder, savoring the rise and fall of his breathing. We ride without speaking for a while, taking in the sounds of the festival, the clopping of the horse hooves, the crisp evening air, and the moonlight spilling its light onto the tops of the trees. It's not until we round the second corner that I remove my head from his shoulder and look at him. "You've been looking healthy, Dad."

"I've been feeling healthy."

The statement has my hope growing into something desperate and unwieldy, something that refuses to be contained.

"The meds are doing a great job at managing the headaches and nausea."

"Maybe it's not the meds," I offer.

"Maybe."

But he doesn't believe it. I can tell. "You don't think it's possible? All the people who are praying for you to be healed—our whole church, this town—you don't think God can answer?"

"I know he can, honey." He pats my hand. "I'm just not sure he will."

And just like that, the dream I've been living in pops. As if it were nothing more substantial than a soap bubble.

Chapter 11

♡

IT'S HARD TO FALL ASLEEP AFTER YOU WAKE UP FROM a dream as long as mine. I toss and turn in bed, wondering how a night that started with so much promise could turn out like this. I keep thinking about Jake's confusion as I claimed a headache and he walked me home early. I could tell he wasn't sure what went wrong. At what point did the night derail so horribly?

In the morning, I wake up bright and early with swollen eyes and a foggy brain—a crying jag hangover. I don't want to go to church. I want to stay in bed. But if I'm not there, my parents will want to know why. So I take a shower and get dressed and try to cover up the aftereffects of a horrible night's sleep with makeup, then head to Patty's as soon as she opens the doors at seven, hoping a giant cup of hot coffee will do the trick. Not only do I have to make it through church at ten, but I also have to meet up with Lily at two o'clock to have our dresses altered.

I step inside Patty's to the usual early Sunday morning patrons—Randy Crandall, our town selectman, eating a hardy breakfast with his wife; Mick Horowitz, who bears an uncanny resemblance to his schnauzer; and Kathleen Baudin, the town cat lady, who makes a habit of dropping by the clinic to give me pamphlets on the dangers of declawing, as if vet school didn't educate me properly on the subject. Occasionally, she'll even sneak one under the windshield wipers of my car.

Patty appears from the kitchen and sets a plate of eggs and bacon in front of Mick. I join them both at the counter.

"Well, look who it is all bright-eyed and bushy-tailed," Patty says with a playful wink.

"Not feeling the best this morning." I set my purse on the counter. "Hi, Mick."

"Morning, Emma."

"How's Marty's leg doing?" Marty is his schnauzer. I often get their names mixed up.

He cuts apart his eggs with his fork, steam and yolk oozing from the wound. "His limp's mostly gone."

"That's good." I cover a yawn. "Make sure to bring him in if it comes back."

"Will do."

I look at Patty through bleary eyes. "I need coffee, stat. In the biggest cup you have."

"Decaf?"

I give her my best are-you-crazy face. It's a weird suggestion in the morning. Especially since I never do decaf. Not even when I stop by in the afternoon. "Decaf is not my friend, Patty."

She sets her pudgy arms on the counter and leans toward me. "Don't you think you ought to make it your friend?"

All right, now I'm officially confused. I mirror Patty's posture. "Why would I do that?"

"I'm no doctor, but I always thought caffeine wasn't good for the baby."

It takes me a second to fully comprehend what she's implying. When I do, my eyes go buggy. "The baby?" I glance at Mick, who pretends not to listen, then back at the woman behind the counter. "You think I'm pregnant?"

Patty frowns. "Aren't you?"

"No. Why would you think that?"

"Stacy Green told all the gals at bunco on Thursday." I must look pale, because Patty grabs a nearby coffeepot, sets a tall mug in front of me, and fills it to the rim. "She said it was the reason you were getting married so fast."

What an assumption to make! "And you believed her?"

"It's nothing to be ashamed of. A baby is wonderful news."

"Patty, I'm not marrying Jake because I'm pregnant." Anger coalesces with my shock, waking me up before I have a trace of caffeine in my bloodstream. "I'm marrying Jake because I'm in love with him."

The instant the words are out, I realize two things. They are true. And I am a fool.

♡ ♡ ♡

I pound on Lily's front door, then pace like a caged lion. I feel feral, like I can't exist in my own skin. My mounting anger—at Stacy Green for the rumor, at Patty for believing it, at myself for the position I've put myself in—has me wishing I could crawl out of it. As unfair as it may be, I need a scapegoat. I stop and knock on her door again.

A lock clicks from the other side and the door opens. Lily appears, still in her flannel pajamas. Her brows knit in confusion then worry as she takes in what can no doubt be my frazzled appearance. "Emma? What is wrong with you?"

"What was your deal last night?"

She gives me her deadpan stare, then opens the door wider. "Do you want to come in?"

No, I don't want to come in. I want to rewind to last night, make Lily behave, make my father take back his words, make the rumor go away, and continue on in happy oblivion. "Did you have to make those comments you made? What happened to giving me your support?"

"I've supported you for the past month."

"No, you haven't. You've been silently judging me."

"I haven't been judging you, Emma. I've been worried about you." Lily's shoulders sag. "At some point, you're going to have to face the fact that your father is dying, and a fake wedding isn't going to fix it."

I can feel myself slowly deflating, right there on Lily's front porch. Because her words are true. As much as I don't want them to be, they are. My father has terminal cancer. All the pretending in the world won't make it go away. And now, to add insult to injury, I have gone and given my heart to a man who never asked for it. "The town thinks I'm pregnant."

Lily bites her lip. "I may have heard that rumor."

"When?"

"Last night, before I met up with you and Jake. I heard a couple of the Bunco Babes talking about it."

I shake my head, tears welling up in my eyes. "Lily, my dad is dying."

"I know."

"And I'm in love with Jake." I shrug helplessly, because what else is there to do?

She pulls me inside and wraps me in a hug. "Would it help if I made cinnamon rolls?"

Chapter 12

♡

IT'S ONLY NINE O'CLOCK WHEN I PULL UP BEHIND Jake's Chevy and shift into park, idling in his gravel drive. But it feels as though I've lived an entire lifetime since crawling out of bed this morning. After a long heart-to-heart with Lily over cinnamon rolls and coffee, my voice is nearly hoarse and my eyes require Visine. But I know what I have to do. I can't keep pretending. As well-intentioned as Jake and I might have been, it's time to be honest. If only my heart hadn't fallen so hard in the midst of our make-believe, then maybe what I need to do wouldn't feel so impossibly hard.

My future stretches ahead of me—no Dad, no Jake—a landscape too bleak for contemplation. Twisting the now-familiar ring around my finger, I look out the windshield, taking in the expanse of Jake's property. Pine trees dot the periphery of a well-kept yard. A cabin-style ranch home sits on one side of the drive and a two-story man-shed sits on the other, only it's set farther away from the road. Jake has all the benefits of country living—the privacy, the property, the quiet—and none of the hassle or hard work that comes with a farm. Over the past several weeks, people have asked whether we'd live in my bungalow or Jake's cabin. Even though it was not a decision we really had to make, I'd find myself weighing the pros and cons. Usually, Jake's place would win.

Letting out a long breath, I swing open the car door, step outside, and head toward Jake's house, each step heavier than the one before. When I finally muster up the strength to knock, Jake doesn't answer. I turn around and head toward the shed, hoping he's at the hardware store. The place is closed on Sundays, but that doesn't mean Jake's not there, taking inventory or cleaning before church. If he's not here, that will give me more time. To think about what I will say. To rehearse the right words. To drum up the determination.

But a sound comes from the shed as I walk around the corner and stand in the large doorway. The sun shines at my back, illuminating the space inside—filled with beautiful handmade furniture in various stages of completion. Jake stands with his back to me, already dressed in his Sunday church khakis, sanding the top of a gorgeous oak table.

A bit of sawdust tickles my nose and I sneeze.

Jake spins around and broadens his posture, as if attempting to block the lovely table behind him. "Hey." He sets his palm on the edge of it and pulls at his earlobe, strangely flustered. "What are you doing here?"

I step inside and close the distance between us, my heart thudding so slowly, it could be a funeral dirge. The closer I get, the more Jake expands his shoulders and the more charged the air between us seems to grow. By the time I'm all the way there, I reach past him and touch the table, halfway expecting an electrical zap. "Jake, this is really exquisite."

His posture relaxes. "You like it?"

"Like it?" My fingers linger on the wood surface. "I love it."

"Good. Because it's yours."

I look up. "What?"

He smiles. "Patty kept heckling me about a wedding present. And you're always complaining about that small table in your kitchen." He scratches the nape of his neck, making his baseball hat tip up a little. "So I decided to make you a bigger one."

Jake made me a table—one that could comfortably seat a family of six. Does it mean anything to him? Or is this just another one of his kind gestures?

"Hey, Emma." He dips his head to catch my attention. "Is everything okay?"

The concern on his face undoes me. How could I have let myself get into this mess? Why didn't I just say no to Jake's proposition that day on my porch? Laugh it off like any sane, normal person would do? I know why. Because I had been in denial then—and a little bit in shock too. I shake my head. "I can't do this."

"Can't do what?"

I close my eyes. "The wedding."

Jake says nothing.

I take a deep breath and force my voice to come out steady.

"I'm so incredibly grateful that you were willing to do this for me and my dad. But it's not real. And I can't keep pretending that it is." I look up at him, hoping and praying he will argue. Hoping and praying he will tell me it was real for him.

He looks down at me, his face etched with desperation, like he wants nothing more than to reach out and sand away my hurt, patch up the broken bits. A hope I don't want to feel bubbles in my heart. It's a hope I've felt once before, after my high school graduation. "Emma, I'm sorry. I thought . . ." He shakes his head and drags his hand down his face. "I thought this would make you happy."

"It did for a while."

"That's all I want, you know. For you to be happy."

Happy.

Like a flower left too long in the sun without any water, my heart wilts. It's not enough. It's not even close. I slip the ring from my finger, place it in Jake's broad palm, and curl his fingers over the gift. He looks bewildered, dumbfounded. Like this is all happening too fast. I want to tell him that *he* makes me happy. I want to tell him that *us* makes me happy. But my throat is too tight to get the words out and I won't put Jake in that position. I won't jeopardize our friendship. So I squeeze his hand, then turn around and walk away.

I hate that he lets me go.

Chapter 13

♡

I SIT INSIDE MY PARENTS' HOUSE, WAITING FOR THEM
to come home from their usual post-church date, unmoving except for my hand, which strokes Oscar, who purrs on my lap. The
front door doesn't open until almost one o'clock.

Mom laughs as she steps inside, and I wonder if they are in
a dream of their own, if she is in denial and if Dad is letting her
live there. But then I remember our carriage ride and our time in
front of the fire and I think no. There is a big difference between
avoiding reality by pretending and enjoying reality for as long as
it's possible.

Mom hangs her purse on the hook by the door—the one
Dad installed just for her since she has a habit of misplacing it
around the house—and stops when she turns and sees me on
their sofa. "Emma, what are you doing here in the dark?"

Oscar jumps off my lap, away from his free massage, and lies
down in his favorite spot—where the sunlight usually shines in

from the large picture window and warms a patch of carpet. But clouds have rolled in and the sun is nowhere to be seen.

"We never saw you at church," she adds. "We didn't see Jake either."

I try to answer, but I can't seem to find my voice.

Dad slips off his shoes, a bag of goodies from Eloise's bakery in hand. He and Mom exchange a concerned look.

"Emma?"

My voice refuses to cooperate. It's like my body has decided that stillness is good, stillness is tolerable, so it will never move again.

Mom takes the bag from Dad, then comes over to me and pulls me off the couch. "Come on. Whatever is bothering you can't be so bad that we can't discuss it over cookies. We got a few extra, in case you and Jake stopped by."

I ignore Dad's inquiring eyes and follow Mom into the kitchen, where she removes three plates and three glasses from a cupboard. Dad walks in behind us and opens the cupboard over the stove, where we've always kept our medicine. He uncaps a pill bottle and shakes a large white capsule into his palm. Mom fills one of the glasses with milk, hands it over, and Dad swallows the pill. His face has a pallor to it that wasn't there yesterday. Or maybe it was and I just wasn't willing to see it. Either way, it's a subtle reminder that I can't go back to dreamworld, even if I wanted to.

"I have to tell you guys something."

Dad looks at me, and Mom waits to respond while she fills

the other two glasses with milk and puts the gallon container back in the refrigerator. "We know it's not true, Emma."

The words pull my chin back. "You know?"

"Of course, sweetheart."

"Then why did you . . . ?" I'm so confused. Why did they let me go on then, if they knew Jake and I weren't really engaged? That isn't like them at all.

"We heard the rumor last night and didn't believe it for one second."

I look from Mom to Dad, trying to make sense of her words.

"You and Jake would have told us if you were pregnant. Your father and I know that. This is a small town, and one of the drawbacks of a small town is that rumors fly. Let people think what they will think. They will figure out the truth soon enough."

"We're not getting married," I blurt.

Mom and Dad stare at me, blinking but silent. I wait for my words to sink in. I wait for them to register.

Instead, Mom rattles her head, as if shaking her thoughts into place. "I don't understand. You and Jake aren't getting married at all because of a rumor?"

"No, it's not because of a rumor." I look down at my shoes, unable to face their disappointment. "I'm sorry. For all of it. I'm sorry for lying. I'm sorry for getting your hopes up. But most of all, Dad, I'm sorry that I can't give you that last item on your bucket list."

"My bucket list?"

"I saw it. When you were in Door County. I didn't mean to. I wasn't snooping. I was putting mail on your desk and your journal fell and your bucket list fell with it . . ." I fidget with the zipper of my jacket. "I wish you could walk me down the aisle. More than anything. But I can't keep pretending."

Mom sinks into the closest chair, as if my confession has buckled her knees. "You mean you and Jake were never really engaged?"

Shame sets my cheeks on fire. Now that my feet are firmly planted in reality, it all seems so foolish. What were Jake and I going to do—wait it out until my dad was gone and then come out with the truth? "I don't know what I was thinking. It was the only thing you couldn't cross off your list. So I went home and Jake was there, like Jake always is and . . . I don't know. I'd been feeling so helpless and it was something I could do."

Dad walks across the kitchen and stands next to Mom at the table. "Emma."

A braver woman would look up, but right now, I am not brave. I'm the exact opposite of brave.

"I wrote that list two years ago, when you were engaged to Chase."

I bite my lip. Mom has forgotten all about the stack of plates, the glasses of milk on the counter, the cookies in the bag. I think I might have permanently stolen her appetite.

"Sit down," Dad says as he drops into a chair next to Mom. I obey without question.

Dad lets out a long sigh. "Please look at me."

I pull my attention away from my jacket zipper and force myself to give my father the attention he deserves.

"Do I want to give you away? Yes. It is something I have imagined from the moment you wrapped those tiny fingers around mine. But Emma, walking you down the aisle was never about me. It was about you."

My eyes blur out of focus. I blink furiously, determinedly.

"For your joy." Dad reaches across the table and sets his hand over mine. "Giving you away would only be special if the man I was giving you away to was prepared to love and cherish you the way I've always loved and cherished you."

My chin trembles. "I wish that guy could be Jake."

Mom and Dad don't look shocked. I think they've always known. I think that's why they believed us when we made the announcement. They never questioned my side of the equation.

"Maybe it will be," Dad says.

I shake my head. "I gave him the opportunity and he didn't take it." I picture Jake, unmoving as I handed him back his grandmother's ring. "He didn't even reach."

"Sometimes we men are slow to figure things out." Dad smiles. "Give him some time. He might come around."

As much as I would love for Dad to be right, I can't help but think that if Jake hasn't figured it out by now, he's never going to figure it out.

Chapter 14

♡

RAINDROPS SPIT FROM A BLOATED SKY AND SPLATTER against my windshield. The sunny morning has given way to a dreary afternoon, appropriate weather for cancellations. I do not hem and haw or drag my heels or dip my toe into the water. I don't even let Lily help me. I created the mess. The least I can do is clean it up. So as soon as I leave my parents' house, I dive in, trying not to imagine the news spreading across Mayfair faster than kennel cough. I have already called and canceled the barbecue, the flowers, the alterations—leaving voice mail messages wherever live people were taking the Sabbath off. All I have left is the cake. Jake can take care of the venue, since it's his aunt and uncle's place.

My heart hurts, but I refuse to indulge in any wallowing. I'm not going to spend whatever time remains with my dad pining after Jake. I pull up to the curb and park my car as thunder rumbles in the distance, the black horizon hinting at the wrath to come. I climb out of my car, hurry across the street through the cold drizzle, and step inside the warmth of Eloise's bakery. I am glad she opens her shop on Sunday afternoons.

She smiles behind the counter, her face wrinkled with age and laugh lines. "Emma! What can I get for you this afternoon—some muffins?"

"Four of your chocolate cupcakes." Because it's my vet technician's birthday tomorrow and I'd like to take him a treat for all the extra hours he's been working. "And I need to cancel the wedding cake."

Her eyes widen. "Cancel the cake? But you have to have cake at the wedding."

"There isn't going to be a wedding." The tone of my voice does not invite further questions. I can answer them later, when my emotions aren't so raw.

Eloise's face falls. "Oh, well, I'm sure sorry to hear about that."

"Me too."

She processes my payment and hands me a container of cupcakes as the pitter-patter of raindrops turns into a downpour that pounds against the roof of the bakery. I turn around and look out the window. Normally, I'd wait inside and enjoy a muffin and some hot tea until the downpour passes, but I can feel Eloise studying the back of my head. Staying would only invite questions. I'd rather get wet. Clutching the cupcakes under one arm, I pull up the hood of my jacket, toss a wave over my shoulder, and make a mad dash outside, over the curb, out into the street.

"Emma!"

I stop in the middle of the road. Turn slowly. And my breath catches. Because it's Jake. Standing several paces away, his hat and the shoulders of his jacket soaked through, his chest heaving as though he sprinted all the way from his house.

"Jake?" I shield my eyes. "What are you doing?"

"I'm a liar," he shouts over at me.

"What?" I squint through the rain, positive the din from the storm warped Jake's words.

He steps closer, joining me in the middle of the street, and the storm around us is nothing compared to the one raging in his eyes. "Earlier today I lied. When I told you that your happiness is all I care about." Rain wets his lips. "It should be, but it's not."

I shake my head, unwilling to believe. Unwilling to hope.

"I left because of you."

"What?"

"All those years ago. The reason I left town is because I couldn't watch you get married to Chase. What I should have told you this morning, what I should have told you that day I offered to marry you on the porch, what I should have told you that night after you graduated high school"—he wipes his hand down his face—"Is that I love you."

I can't breathe. I can't even move.

"I feel like I've loved you forever, but I've never been able to say it. The timing was never right. You were my best friend's kid sister. I was going to college and then you were with Chase and then Ben died and your dad was diagnosed with cancer.

And I never could tell if you felt the same way. But no regrets, remember?" Before I fully process what he's saying, Jake gets down on his knee, in the middle of the street, in the middle of the rain, and takes out a small velvet box from the pocket of his coat.

My hand moves to my chest.

He opens the box and inside is the same ring I've worn every day since we sat in Jake's idling truck outside my parents' home. Only he's offering it to me now, not to make our story more believable but because this is real. Jake is down on one knee in the middle of the street in the pouring rain, and there's only one reason I know of for a man to get on one knee . . .

"Marry me."

Emotion climbs up my throat. I cup my hand over my mouth to trap the sob inside.

"I don't want a wedding, Emma. I want a marriage. To you. Because nothing—and I mean *nothing*—would make me happier than spending the rest of my life trying to make you happy." Jake looks up at me through the rain, waiting as his breath escapes in clouds of white.

Unable to remove my hand from my mouth, unable to show Jake the smile forming beneath my palm, I nod, my heart swelling with so much joy I think it might explode.

"Yes?"

I nod again, faster, and remove my hand. "Yes!"

And just like that, Jake has me in his arms. He twirls me in a circle, then kisses me—a rain-soaked, wonderful kiss with my feet off the ground, a kiss a thousand times better and more passionate than our first kiss in Patty's. And then we are both laughing, like we can't believe this moment. Like we can't believe ourselves.

"Do you really mean yes—not because of your dad's bucket list, but because this is what you want?"

"Jake, this is what I've wanted since the second grade."

He sets me down and presses his wet forehead against mine. "I am an idiot."

"Hey, that's my fiancé you're talking about. My real-life, not-fake fiancé." I stand up on my tiptoes and press my lips against his. It's a wonderful, giddy, heart-pattering feeling kissing Jake. I'm not sure I'll ever get over the wonder of it. "Now, if you don't mind, I'd really like that ring back."

Jake doesn't hesitate. As soon as it's back on my finger, he turns my hand up and kisses my palm. "Don't take it off again, okay?"

I shake my head. "Never."

Chapter 15

♡

LILY FIXES MY VEIL IN THE KITCHEN OF THE SAWYERS'
farmhouse, her eyes alight with all the excitement and happiness a maid of honor should feel for the bride. "Are you ready?"

I breathe in the beauty of this moment and the messy path
that led to it. Our lives are such a muddled pot of heartache and
blessing, loss and triumph, sorrow and joy. I nod and wring my
hands, a lump already in my throat. "I think so."

Lily opens the door and we step out onto the porch, into the
late October air. My father turns around, so handsome in his
tuxedo, and a breath of forever passes between us. One I will
carry with me for the rest of my life. I dab my knuckle beneath
my lashes, a vain attempt to save my makeup.

I don't know how much time we have. His tumor is growing every day and his headaches are worsening. We could have
two whole months—sixty lifetimes, each encompassed within a
single day. Or he could be gone in two weeks. I don't know how
this story will end. But I do know that I can enjoy right now. My

father has taught me this. Today, he is here. So I will praise God for today, and trust in his provision for tomorrow.

He cups my cheek with his palm. "You, my daughter, are too stunning for words."

A tear gathers and spills.

Dad catches it on his thumb, then holds out his arm, and the three of us walk through the yard, beneath a canopy of trees that have not yet lost all their color, toward the rows of white chairs filled with family and friends, and the soothing melody of Lily's sister playing "Clair de Lune" on her violin. We stop in front of a pair of trees that hide us from view of our guests. Lily gives me a hug, hands me my bouquet of flowers, then joins Liam ahead. He winks at me with a proud smile on his face. Lily takes his arm and they make their way down the aisle. There is a brief pause of anticipation as the violin stops, then starts up again with Canon in D. Everyone stands. The sunlight dapples through the leaves.

I look up at my dad—the man who has loved and cherished and protected me from the moment I entered this world. "Are you ready?"

"Emma, I've been ready for twenty-seven years."

Wrapping my arm tighter around his, I let my father lead me down the aisle. Toward Jake, my groom. The man who will love and cherish and protect me for as long as we both shall live.

Acknowledgments
♡

A Brush with Love

I heard the name Ginger and I knew she didn't believe she was beautiful. Then I thought of the hero, Tom, and knew his job was to make Ginger see her true beauty.

I cannot begin to expound God's faithfulness to me in the winter of 2014. Dropping this idea in the midst of crying out for help and ideas for another book is only one example.

I turned in the novel and went to a writers' retreat where I helped mentor eighteen aspiring authors. When the week was over, Susan May Warren, Beth Vogt, and Alena Tauriainen brainstormed *A Brush with Love* with me, beginning, middle, and end. I actually had enough story for a big novel! Their help and friendship was a blessing to the core of my soul. Another example of God's faithfulness.

To my editor, Becky Philpott, you are a dream. A friend. A

champion and cheerleader. Thank you for your partnership with not only this novella, but my writing journey. You're a treasure.

To Daisy Hutton, publisher extraordinaire, I love the honest conversations we've had and how you champion your authors. Thank you for giving me opportunities to do what I love!

Katie Bond, Elizabeth Hutton, and Karli Jackson, for being a fabulous marketing and editorial team. It's such a feeling of contentment to know I can email any of you, any time, and get a response. Katie, we've been together a lot of years now and it's more an honor day by day.

To the rest of the HarperCollins Christian Publishing team, let's keep writing and publishing for Him. You all are the best.

To my husband who lives with a writer. He is my hero. God knew what He was doing when He paired us together. I love you, babe!

To my canine writing partner, Lola, thanks for making me get up out of my chair from time to time. Ha!

To my writing partner, Susan May Warren, ten years we've been doing this biz together. Sometimes face-to-face but mostly phone call to phone call. I shake my head in wonder at how blessed I am to have you in my life. XO.

To my hairdresser, Michele Lacy, who's kept me looking beautiful and young for over twenty-three years. Thanks for your help on this one.

To my line editor, Jean Bloom, thank you for your time, insight, and help.

To all of the readers who take the time to curl up with a book I've written, thank you! It means more than you'll ever know. Be blessed!

Love in the Details

I'm grateful to Becky Philpott, my editor at Zondervan, for inviting me to participate in this wonderful collection of wedding-themed novellas. Thank you, Becky! You're kind, outgoing, and a pleasure to work with. I truly appreciate the opportunity you extended to me.

Many, many thanks to my agent and *Love in the Details'* very first reader, Linda Kruger. Your feedback on this novella was extraordinarily helpful, Linda. Oh, how I value your insight and friendship.

My husband has staunchly believed in my writing since the very first time I ever mentioned to him that I might like to attempt a novel of my own. His hands—on help (making dinners, watching the kids, doing the dishes, and giving me pep talks) made this novella possible. I love you!

And lastly, to my kids, who (almost) never complain about the hours I spend working. I'm so glad that I get to be your mom. Thank you very, very much for supporting my writing.

Acknowledgments

An October Bride

I'm a wordy person, so when Becky Philpott contacted me about writing a novella for their Year of Weddings series, I was honored but also a little frightened. Novels I could do. Novellas? Not so sure.

I had no idea that I would have so much fun writing this story! I fell in love with Jake and Emma and the small, quirky town of Mayfair, Wisconsin. I hope readers fall in love too!

A few shout-outs are most definitely in order . . .

A hearty thanks to all the people who have made this novella better than I could ever manage on my own—Becky Philpott, Jean Bloom, and Karli Cajka. It was a pleasure working with you!

Thank you to the entire team at Zondervan for inviting me to take part in such a fun project, Elizabeth Hudson for your passion and enthusiasm, and an especially loud shout-out to my fellow "bridesmaids." It's been an honor and a joy celebrating these novellas together!

Thank you to Marie Bates for giving me a sneak peek inside the life of a veterinarian, and to Joel Malm for helping me figure out the perfect occupation for adventure-seeking Liam. Any inaccuracies in the portrayal are all mine!

Carrie Pendergrass for sharing your husband's words to you at a time I really needed to hear them. They became the words Emma's dad shared with Emma in the horse carriage ride when she really needed to hear them. I pray they encourage readers as much as they did me!

Thanks, of course, to my agent, Rachelle Gardner, for all you do to get my work out there.

To my amazingly supportive husband and my wonderful family for all you do so that I can write.

To a lavishly good God for allowing me to do something that brings me such joy and for providing the words when I'm feeling wrung dry.

And to my fabulous readers—the ones who take that joy and multiply it exponentially with your support, your presence, and your encouragement. It's an honor to write stories for you, and I will continue as the Lord allows!

Discussion Questions
♡

A Brush with Love

1. Ginger suffered a tragedy that marked her inside and out. Everyone reacts differently to life events. Was there an event in your life that marked you in some way? Do you relate to how Ginger feels?

2. Tom's family, while Christians, are flawed. He wants to make amends for his father's mistake. But it's not always possible to undo what's been done. What's the best way to show forgiveness for a wrong? Or to seek redemption?

3. Bridgett seems all about herself, doesn't she? But in the end of the book, she's at the wedding cheering Ginger on. How do you see this? Did Ginger misunderstand her friendship with Bridgett?

4. We often see ourselves through our own wounds. We think that's how others see us. Does Ginger do this

when she's around the bold and the beautiful people? Around Bridgett?

5. Tom is influenced by Edward, a man responsible for bringing him back to town to start a church. Does he allow Edward too much influence? How do we walk in love with one another when we disagree?

6. Ginger's mama, Shana, was looking for help in the church. But her trust was misplaced. How can we love people who confess secrets to us? How can we bring them to truth without making them feel condemned?

7. I loved when Ginger was bold enough to walk down the aisle in her dream dress even though it exposed her scars. I actually cried writing that scene. What happened to her that she could brave such a thing?

8. Be honest, do you really believe God can change your negative emotions? Because He can. We don't have to be locked in darkness, despair, depression, and fears. How can you change your thinking to believe you are who He says you are? Ginger did it by confessing she was beautiful.

9. What aspects of Christ does Tom demonstrate to Ginger? How can you do the same toward your friends and family?

10. If you have scars, inside or out, list one thing you can do to overcome.

Love in the Details

1. Holly and Josh were one another's first love. Did anyone here marry their first love? Name one thing that you still remember clearly about your first love.

2. At its heart, *Love in the Details* is about the perfect nature of God's timing. When in your life did you face a disappointment, only to later realize that God's timing was ultimately best?

3. Near the end of the story, Holly realizes that her almost subconscious belief that she's not enough for Josh is holding her back. We all struggle from time to time with deceptive self-talk that assures us that we're "not good enough" or "not worthy enough." When has this most been a stumbling block for you? Share a story of how God has helped you have victory in this area.

4. How would you characterize Becky Wade's writing style? How was it different and/or similar to the style of other writers included in this collection of wedding novellas?

5. How is Holly and Josh's love story a picture of God's love for us?

An October Bride

1. In the beginning of the story, Emma finds her dad's bucket list. What are some things you would write on your own bucket list?

2. Jake knows what it's like to live with regret. Do you have any regrets in your life? Have you ever done something out of your comfort zone in order to avoid having regrets?

3. Emma saw her and Jake's "engagement" as a morally gray area. Do you agree? If you were in Emma's position, would you have done what she did? Of all the characters in *An October Bride*, who's reaction to the fake engagement did you relate to the most?

4. Halfway through the novel, Emma decides to enter completely into the fantasy world she is currently living in. Have you ever lived in denial about something in your life? What happened to finally make you face reality?

5. Emma has a lot of special relationships in this novel—her relationship with Jake, her relationship with Lily, and her relationship with her dad and her mom. Which relationship did you enjoy the most? What are some relationships you have in your own life?

6. There are a lot of quirky secondary characters in this story. Which one was your favorite?

Happily ever after begins today.

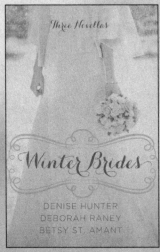

Winter Brides

Three Novellas

DENISE HUNTER
DEBORAH RANEY
BETSY ST. AMANT

Spring Brides

Three Novellas

RACHEL HAUCK
LENORA WORTH
MEG MOSELEY

Summer Brides

Three Novellas

BETH WISEMAN
DEBRA CLOPTON
MARYBETH WHALEN

Autumn Brides

Three Novellas

KATHRYN SPRINGER
KATIE GANSHERT
BETH K. VOGT

Available in print, e-book, and audio

They've helped orchestrate the perfect day for countless couples. Now twelve new couples will find themselves in the wedding spotlight.

Available in print, e-book, and audio

About the Authors

♡

Rachel Hauck

Photo by Emilie of E. A. Hendryx Creative

RACHEL HAUCK IS THE *NEW YORK TIMES*, *WALL STREET Journal*, and *USA TODAY* bestselling author of *The Wedding Dress*, which was also named Inspirational Novel of the Year by *Romantic Times* and was a RITA finalist. Rachel lives in central Florida with her husband and pet and writes from her ivory tower.

Visit her online at RachelHauck.com

Facebook: @RachelHauck

Twitter: @RachelHauck

Instagram: @rachelhauck

Becky Wade

Photo by Emilie Haney of EAH Creative

Becky Wade makes her home in Dallas, Texas, with her husband, three children, and two spaniels. She's the Christy and Carol award winning author of *My Stubborn Heart*, the Porter Family series, the Bradford Sisters series, and the Misty River Romance series.

Visit Becky online at www.beckywade.com
Facebook @authorbeckywade
Twitter: @beckywadewriter
Instagram: @beckywadewriter

Katie Ganshert

Photo by Iron and Lace Photography

Katie Ganshert is the author of nine novels and several works of short fiction. She has won both the Christy and Carol Awards for her writing and was awarded the RT Reviews Reviewers Choice for her novels, *The Art of Losing Yourself* and *Life After*. Katie makes her home in eastern Iowa with her family.

Visit Katie online at katieganshert.com
Facebook: @AuthorKatieGanshert
Twitter: @KatieGanshert